TAYLOR CROOK &
RYAN KIRK

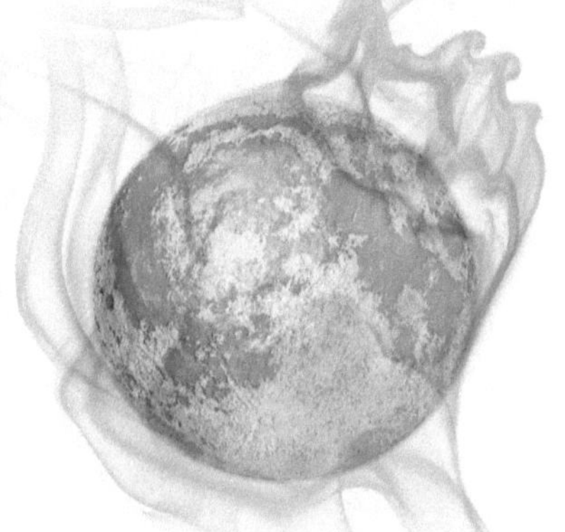

A PATH DIVIDED

THE SENTINELS SAGA
BOOK II

For Aunt Tina. All your support in all my endeavors helped lead to this success. A vodka cranberry, a chair on the deck, and a copy of my book in your hand. Enjoy.

PROLOGUE

Olivia followed Oscar along the deer run that led through the woods north of Hankala. Above them, the sky darkened as the sun continued to move towards the horizon. As a cold breeze cut through her clothes, she regretted agreeing to join her brother in a game of hide-and-seek.

"Come on, Oscar! We need to go back," she said, glancing at the deepening shadows to her left and right. "We shouldn't be so far from home after the sun goes down. You know the stories."

Oscar dismissed her concerns with a wave. "The woods are only dangerous when there's a full moon. It's a new moon tonight, so we'll be fine."

Olivia wished she possessed her brother's courage, but fear nagged at her. She kept looking back in the direction of their home, now far out of sight. Despite her misgivings, she pressed on. Oscar didn't play with her that much anymore, now that he was old enough to sip ale from a small cup at the table. He thought it made him a man, with no time for younger sisters. She didn't want to waste this chance, and she wanted him to have enough fun that he would invite her out again.

"We could play hide and seek in the yard like we usually do," Olivia suggested, hoping Oscar might compromise.

"It's not the same. I found the perfect spot, not far from here." Oscar stopped short and turned to face Olivia. "You're always saying you want to play with me more, right? Well, here's your chance. Stop being such a baby."

"I'm not a baby! I'm almost six," Olivia said, angry that she sounded like a baby as she said it.

Oscar continued on, leaving Olivia no choice. She looked towards the setting sun. He was right, of course. The nights everyone knew to stay inside were the nights around the full moon. She scampered after her brother. He turned off the deer run and led them into a small clearing with a large rock in the center.

Oscar walked up to the rock and patted it. "This is home. When you're It, you have to find the person hiding and then tag them before they make it back to the rock. Sound good?"

It didn't sound good to Olivia. She hated hide-and-seek tag with her brother. He was bigger and faster, so even if she found him, he was still going to win.

But they were playing together, and for now, that was enough.

"Fine." An idea occurred to her. "Can I hide first?" If she hid well enough, she could sneak back to the rock without being noticed and still win at least one round.

Oscar appeared to put some serious thought into the question. "Well, I'm the oldest, so I get to choose." He thought some more, making a show of his deep thought. "I choose to hide first."

Olivia did her best to hide her disappointment. Maybe it was for the best. While searching for him, she could also find good places to hide. She laid her head on her arms against the rock and started counting.

"One, two, three..."

"Count to a hundred!" Oscar called as he dashed into the woods.

Olivia kept counting. The longer she forced herself to focus on counting, the more her fear of playing in the woods dissipated. Though the sun was setting, there was still plenty of light.

"...one hundred. Ready or not, here I come!" Olivia shouted. She was startled by how still the forest was after her tiny voice echoed through it.

Olivia sprinted for a moment, but the exposed roots, gnarled branches, and uneven terrain slowed her to a walk as soon as she left the clearing. As she looked under logs and inside dense bushes, she kicked herself for not making Oscar explain the boundaries. He was always "forgetting" to tell her things like that. Details that would help him win.

She didn't hear him running for the rock, though, so he hadn't won yet.

After a few minutes, Olivia noticed the forest was growing darker.

A shiver ran up her spine. Oscar might make fun of her, but she really didn't want to be out here.

She searched for another few minutes, then decided she was done with hide-and-seek. This wasn't worth it. If their parents found out what the two of them were up to, they'd be furious. She walked back to the home rock.

"Oscar!" she yelled. "I don't want to play anymore. It's too dark! Let's meet at the rock!"

The words echoed through the woods.

Olivia felt as though she was disturbing a silence that was better left alone.

She waited and called again, and again there was no answer. Stupid Oscar. He knew she would get scared. He was probably hiding up in a tree snickering at her right now.

She forced herself to walk slow, to pretend like she wasn't scared. She faked a yawn as if she were bored.

Her heart beat faster and she wiped her hands on her pants. Stupid Oscar. If he wasn't careful, she was going to tell their parents everything. She almost yelled out the threat, but held back. Her voice wasn't welcome here.

She walked another dozen feet at a steady pace, and then she could pretend no longer. She ran toward the rock, her feet hitting the ground faster than her heart was beating.

Branches caught and pulled at her dress. She stumbled to the ground and heard the fabric tear. Her mother would be furious, but right now, Olivia would welcome her mother's fury. Anything was better than this perfect silence.

In the pit of her stomach a sickening feeling grew.

Bushes to her right rustled, breaking the silence, but she saw nothing move. No doubt, something was seconds away from grabbing her by the ankles and dragging her deeper into the shadows.

Olivia ran as fast as she could, always glancing behind her, certain a nightmare approached.

Finally she reached the clearing.

She fell to her knees and cried. Now all she needed was to find Oscar and get out of here.

A ghoul stepped from the trees surrounding the clearing. Olivia was about to scream, but then she saw it was Oscar.

Just like that, her heart slowed. She wiped the tears from her eyes, suddenly embarrassed. As much as he sometimes drove her mad, when she was near him, she knew everything would be fine. He would always protect her, and he was big and strong for his age. Father always said so. And maybe she had been acting like a baby, a little. "Oscar, can we go, please? I don't like this place."

He didn't answer.

The thin light of the new moon that penetrated the forest cast shadows across Oscar that made his limbs look longer and skinnier than they should have been.

"Oscar?" she asked.

Her brother was smiling at her, but his mouth was too large. His teeth were too big and too numerous. He reminded her, in a way, of a wolf.

Olivia cried again as a realization struck her.

The shadows weren't making her brother look all wrong.

He *was* all wrong.

She felt a warm wetness down her leg and started to turn, but Oscar was faster. She heard him chasing her down, and her heart felt like it would explode in her chest.

But she had no chance.

He had always been faster.

1

―――――

Shin stared at the dried-up husk of a Maraman sitting in the corner of the small room. Yuki hadn't bothered with any bindings, and for good reason. He could barely hold his head up. His rheumy eyes never stopped gazing around the room, though. There was an intelligence there that hadn't disappeared like the man's vitality. He was trying to take in everything he could, like he was the one studying them.

"You know what we're capable of," Yuki said, her voice sharp and commanding, "so it would serve you best to simply answer my questions."

The aged head swung to look at Yuki, but he said nothing.

Yuki had little patience. "I know you understand me. Your emperor would not have sent you here without the ability to speak our language."

The Maraman remained silent, but a smile crept across his face. Yuki sighed heavily and gestured to the sin standing behind her. The woman, Sia, closed her eyes and a dull red glow crept out from beneath her eyelids. After a moment, she opened them, revealing two balls of crimson light. They were mirrored in the head of the Maraman.

"They voyaged across the ocean in a...floating city." Sia spoke as if her voice was coming from a great distance. "They call it a juggernaut. It houses dozens of other ships. They sailed for many days. Seven or eight moon cycles, at least."

"When do the others come?" Yuki asked.

A heavy silence settled over the room as Sia worked. When she spoke again, Shin startled. "This one doesn't know. The trip can only be made at certain times. The storms rage often. If they were sending more, they would have left already."

"How many Maramans can this juggernaut carry?"

Another pause. Sia frowned. "Enough to colonize Samas. Hundreds per juggernaut, and they have several. This one was to come and open a portal to bring all of their military through."

"And the demons?"

"They can control some, but not all. The ones that push through the rifts into Samas are feral. The ones that they chained up are something else."

"Meaning?"

Again there was a prolonged silence. Shin fought the urge to join Sia's efforts, to lend her strength. "I don't know. Something is fighting me." Sia grimaced. "It's already in his head, and it's strong."

Yuki's eyes widened, the closest that Shin had ever seen to panic on her serene face.

"Cut the connection," Yuki commanded.

A few tense moments passed. Sia's teeth ground together, and every few heartbeats, her head twitched violently to the side, as though someone were jerking it.

Shin watched, wondering if there was anything she could do to help. Yuki held up a hand to stall her. The older woman missed nothing.

"I can't." Sia's confession came out as a whimper. Sweat beaded on her forehead.

Yuki's arm snapped out and the long stake attached to her chained weapon stabbed into the head of the aged Maraman. Blood splattered against the wall of the chamber and the Maraman's corpse toppled forward.

But his eyes still glowed red.

"You have to break the connection, Sia," Yuki said.

"I can't! Someone's holding me here."

"I can't help you, child. You have to do this." Yuki left the rest of the ultimatum unspoken, but Sia nodded.

Shin closed her eyes and followed the threads of sacrifice blooming from Sia and the dead Maraman. She'd been brought by Yuki as an observer, and she'd been eager to see new techniques firsthand, but she couldn't stand by and let one of the sin suffer.

Something plundered information from Sia's brain in the same way she had just been interrogating the Maraman. Shin cast about, hoping to find the same inspiration from the shadow realm that she'd found when she'd enchanted Harmony, but it eluded her.

She felt Sia losing the battle and decided on a different approach. She sensed how Sia fought off the invisible force, so she mimicked those techniques and willed her support into existence. She felt that terrible other realm open up and take something from her. A fleeting memory passed through her mind. The smell of the morning air in the spring.

She agreed to the terms of the sacrifice.

The memory disappeared. She wasn't sure what it had been, but once it was gone, she lent her strength to Sia.

Her defense bolstered, Sia sawed at the connections with the Maraman. One strand at a time, she severed their link. But it wasn't fast enough. Even with Shin's support, Sia's defenses crumbled. Shin readied another sacrifice to enforce the defenses again.

Then the connection snapped.

Shin sighed in relief. She opened her mouth to congratulate Sia.

The words died on her lips once she opened her eyes.

The blade of Yuki's weapon was embedded in Sia's heart.

"We were fighting it," Shin said. The words were barely a whisper.

Yuki growled. "I felt you readying another sacrifice. You can't give too much too fast. Your training has barely begun."

"You killed her!"

"She knew the risks."

Shin's anger flared at Yuki's callousness. Did she care so little? "She didn't have to die here! I could have sacrificed a little more."

Shin was sure it would have been a little thing. The realm liked the taste of her memories, and they certainly weren't worth a whole life.

"Your potential is too important to take risks with. Sia would have understood this."

"Then why didn't you help! With your strength, it would have been easy."

Yuki sighed again and sat down. She finally looked her age, weathered and worn by countless years. "I've already sacrificed so much, Shin. You are the future. Unfortunately, we are terribly exposed at present. Had that connection remained active much longer, I fear our enemies would have learned just how exposed."

Shin heard Yuki's concern, but her mind seized on the other statement.

"There's a limit to your power?" Shin couldn't believe that.

Yuki didn't answer at first, as though she wasn't sure how much she wanted to say. Then she answered. "At the highest levels of our power, we have the ability to get creative with what we sacrifice. How we sacrifice. I made arrangements that would allow me to wield power for a long time. Unfortunately, after the power I expended in the fields of Dahl, that bill has come due. None of us can sacrifice forever."

"What did you sacrifice?"

"More than you'll ever understand, girl." There was an edge to Yuki's voice that let Shin know she'd get no more from that line of inquiry.

"So, if the Maramans return, can you stop them?"

"If they return soon, no. So we must prevent that from happening. And while we do, we need to train you, so that when they do come, we'll be ready. Your power, hopefully, will be the difference in the battle against the emperor of the Maramans."

Shin's heart beat faster at the proclamation. Yuki wasn't one to make empty statements.

She thought of her parents, and the luan who had spent so much of their young lives hiding from those with power. For years, she'd dreamed of being stronger, and now the opportunity was before her.

She would save them all.

Perhaps, one day, she might even be stronger than Yuki.

The older woman seemed to think it was a possibility, at least.

Shin looked down at Sia's body. She hadn't been able to save the other sin, but she'd do everything she could to save others like her.

"Then let's get started," Shin said.

2

———————

"I already secured the food! I sent the mugo...the singun to redirect a supply train into Dahl," Beast snapped at the city official that pestered him.

"Yes, and that food is gone." The official spoke slowly, as though Beast was an imbecile.

"Gone! What happened to it?" Beast wondered if the sentinels had anything to do with the loss of food. Leave it to the greedy bastards to fill their stomachs while Dahl starved.

"It was eaten." Each word crawled out of the official's mouth.

"Already?"

"Yes. Most citizens need to eat every day."

Beast stepped closer. His shadow fell over the puny official. The man's forced, innocent expression suggested that he understood how close he was coming to crossing a line with Beast.

When the man didn't flinch, Beast growled. "Fine, we'll find more food. Right after I find more iron and wood to replace the gate and more bandages and poultices for the wounded!" By the end of the sentence, Beast was roaring.

By the sun, he wanted something to punch. Where was a sentinel when you needed one?

The official stood like a lighthouse bearing the brunt of a violent storm. He waited for a more specific answer, despite the risk to his well-being.

Beast waved his arms around in frustration. "I'll send out another group. There's plenty of food on the island; we just need to get it inside the city."

The official took a deep breath. "When, sir?"

Beast made a fist. The gesture wasn't missed by the sharp-eyed official. The smaller man gulped and took a step back, his composure finally cracking.

"Soon," Beast answered.

They both knew it wasn't good enough. While he dallied and debated, innocent lives might end, even though Beast knew there was plenty of food for now. It just wasn't *here*. But it was still the best answer he could give. The official, too, knew the battle was pointless. He'd made his point, and was still alive. It was the best he could hope for.

"Yes, sir. I'll leave you to it, then," the man replied.

Beast shook his head as the tiny bureaucrat scampered off. The man had never levelled a single accusation at Beast, but the thoughts were plain to read on his expression. Beast and the sin had saved Dahl from the Maramans, but Beast's attempts at rebuilding the city might just be what destroyed it.

Damn but he wanted something to hit. He hadn't had a good fight since the Maramans, and these battles for daily supplies weren't for him. He could face the world's strongest fighters and bring them to their knees, but he couldn't figure out how to get damned food into a damned city. This kind of logistical hornet's nest was exactly what he'd relied on Benji for.

He growled again as he thought about his friend. His throat tightened and he quickly stepped inside one of the fire-damaged buildings within the city. They had crews working all day and night to repair homes and businesses, but it seemed no progress was being made.

"Fuck," Beast cursed and punched a wall.

The whole building shook above him, and Beast considered a new target for his anger. Dahl's buildings were too weak a foe.

Benji.

The man who had made Beast's dreams possible. Strong as Beast was, he was only one man, who needed others to follow him. Warriors who needed food and weapons. It didn't matter how good you were with a sword when you were starving, drenched by rain, and against a company of archers armed with hundreds of arrows.

Benji had made sure none of Beast's warriors were ever hungry, and that they were always prepared.

Then he had to go and sacrifice himself to save this good-for-nothing city. He'd left Beast alone, to fight this battle he had no skill for.

He'd rather fight an army of sentinels than a ledger of supplies. But all the armies of sentinels had already retreated.

"Fuck," Beast said again. This time, he didn't even have the energy to raise his fist. Besides, the building couldn't take any more punishment.

He smiled at the thought.

Beast, dead because he punched a building to the ground while he was still in it.

Not quite the conclusion to his legacy that he was looking for.

"Beast?" In the streets beyond, someone called for him. "Beast?" Louder this time, getting closer.

He took a final moment to gather himself before leaving the building.

"I know, I know. We need to find some food." Beast said to the singun that had been calling him. "Get me our swiftest rider."

"No need for that, sir. Jurian just arrived with supplies. He asked for you."

Beast bristled at the news but kept his tone even. "Perfect. I'll go find him."

The singun nodded and continued on, looking to deliver his next message. Had Yuki sent Jurian because she thought he couldn't handle this? His first task after he pledged fealty to her, and she sent someone to babysit him?

Maybe pledging himself had been a mistake. It had seemed right, after the madness of the Maraman siege of the city. Now, in the cold light of day, he wasn't so sure.

He stormed toward the front gates, sure Jurian was only here to belittle him. When Beast saw the giant at the gate, his usual easy smile on his face, he made a fist yet again.

"Hi, Beast," Jurian said, ignoring Beast's frustration.

"What are you doing here?" Beast snapped.

Jurian gestured at the caravan behind him. "I brought food."

"Did Yuki tell you to help me?"

"Of course."

"I told her I would take care of it!"

Jurian's smile faltered. Beast recognized an incoming lecture from the weapons master. He'd been through plenty before, usually after getting pummeled by the man's fists. "Would you turn down aid, solely because of your pride?"

Beast considered hitting the man, just on principle, but he was certain Jurian was prepared. Besides, the sin had a point. "No," he grumbled.

"You aren't alone in this, you know. You're one of us now. We share our strengths with one another so that no weaknesses remain. Hanz will be returning shortly with tools and materials for the gates."

"I could have done that, too!"

Jurian didn't flinch from Beast's anger. Although, Beast supposed, he was one of the few people in the world capable of physically dealing with it. "How? No one ever showed you where we keep our supplies on the island, or who's in charge of storing them. What would you have done? You are only one man, Beast. Big, yes. Ugly, very. But still just one man."

"That was enough when I was leading the mugon!"

"You had Benji to help then."

Beast's rage broke through the last remnants of the dam. He shot forward and grabbed Jurian by his shirt with both fists.

"Don't tell me what I had with Benji. You don't think I know his worth?"

Jurian looked at Beast calmly. "Of course not. I'm sorry."

His apology only fanned the flames of Beast's anger. Though a part of him knew it wasn't true, he felt as though he was being placated. He needed an outlet. Some action. He needed pain and effort.

Beast cocked his arm back with every intention of breaking Jurian's nose. At the very least, a fight with the giant would wear him out.

Then he heard a crash, followed by screaming. He and

Jurian shared a look before Beast let go and they both took off running. They rounded a corner to see that one of the damaged buildings the workers were trying to repair had collapsed.

"Is anyone inside?" Beast asked.

"Two people," one of the stunned workers said.

The roof had collapsed onto the second floor, which had fallen partially into the first. There was a support beam blocking the door. Beast didn't hesitate. He moved to the beam, found a grip, and began to lift. Slowly, the beam rose.

"Help!" a cry came from inside.

"Working on it," Beast said through gritted teeth.

The beam inched higher until Beast saw an arm shoot out from underneath. Then another. Beast redoubled his efforts and the head and shoulders of a teenage boy appeared. Jurian grabbed his hands and pulled him out.

"Hurry, Dad!" the boy said once he was free.

"I can't fit," a terrified voice said from within.

Beast tried to find some hidden well of strength to draw on, but his reserves were tapped. Then the beam started to lift again. Beast looked at Jurian, still smiling, as he lent his strength to the effort. The beam shifted some more before jamming up against the wreckage that was the second floor of the building. It wouldn't go any higher.

"Hurry. The. Fuck. Up," Beast growled.

As before, arms led the way, followed by a balding head and thick shoulders. This time, a few citizens from the crowd came forward and pulled the man out. The second he was clear, Beast and Jurian dropped the beam. Dust filled the air as the building settled deeper into its ruin.

"Thank you!" The teenage boy ran up and bowed to Beast.

"Fine, fine. You're welcome. Off you get," Beast said.

Beast shouldered his way through the crowd before he had to deal with more gestures of affection. Jurian followed close behind. Once they were clear, he put a hand on Beast's shoulder and turned him around.

"You are sin now, Beast. We work together."

"I get it. I get it. Let's not make a whole thing about it."

Jurian laughed and clapped him once on the shoulder before removing his hand. "Fine by me. Also, I meant to tell you, there was a reason I sent a messenger to summon you in the first place. I have orders. Yuki wants to see you. In the tower when the sun sets."

Beast ground his teeth, his good mood evaporating like a puddle on a blazing summer day. Loyalty was one thing. Being summoned like a dog was another. "Another meeting?"

"Yes, and a new assignment. I think you'll like this one, though."

Beast raised an eyebrow at the big man.

All Jurian would say was, "You'll probably want one of those big axes you favor so much."

3

Sato sat in silence across from Yuki and Shin. The girl's hatred of him had faded from a rolling boil to a low simmer, but Sato still felt it. At least now he knew the reason. He'd asked her friend, Corin, about it a few days ago. Her parents had been sentenced to death, and subsequently killed, by sentinels. They had been hiding food and, based on the strict letter of the Path, had received their just punishment.

But Sato now understood that the Path required interpretation. The words of the Path were important, but their spirit was even more so.

The magistrate in Dahl had squeezed the farmers to the point that they had to steal just to survive. They couldn't walk the Path because their betters had strayed too far themselves. A year ago, Sato would have argued that it was still the peasant's responsibility to remain on the Path despite their suffering, but no more.

A peasant had no role but to labor from sunrise to sunset to feed and support all of Samas. That was right and good.

But for their labor, the peasants deserved a fair share of the food they raised and the protection of the local magistrate.

That was the true Path.

He hadn't bothered trying to broach the subject with Shin. Words would never mend the hatred she harbored. But it also wasn't her place to understand. She was, after all, still a peasant. A powerful one, if Yuki was to be believed, but still a farmer at heart. It fell to those like Sato to fix the system, to make it so that no one in the future would feel like Shin did today.

He sighed loudly. His time was wasted here.

"Will he be much longer?" Sato asked.

"I told him to meet at sundown, same as you," Yuki replied.

Sato nodded and tamped down the growing resentment in his chest. He hated wasted time.

After a few more minutes of silence, the door to Yuki's chamber, located high within the former magistrate's tower, burst open.

"Let's make this quick," Beast growled. "There's ale to drink and it won't wait all night for me."

"I'm sure you'll manage," Sato replied.

"Not if someone gets to it first!"

"I don't think anyone is foolish enough to drink all the ale in Dahl before the legendary Beast gets his share," Sato said. He couldn't quite keep the bitterness out of his voice.

Beast, of course, was oblivious. He roared in laughter and clapped Sato on the shoulder. Sato tried not to, but couldn't help wincing. There would be a bruise in the morning. "Too true! You're not so bad, for a sentinel."

Sato shook his head. He considered cutting the criminal down where he stood, but he wasn't sure there was a blade sharp enough in Samas to cut through the man's thick neck.

And though he hated to admit it, he had a measure of respect for Beast. The man was a fool, but an honest one, and straightforward. He cared for the people of Samas in his own way. When Sato became Firstborn, he'd grant Beast a quick death in honor of the good he'd done.

"Don't worry, Beast," Yuki said, breaking up their conversation, "we won't keep you long. I've handed the relief efforts here in Dahl over to another commander. You'll be pleased to know I have something more suited to your unique skills."

The giant man was nodding. "Jurian said you needed some killing done?"

Yuki said, "Perhaps. A farmstead was burned to the ground on the east end of the island. The family raised cows. Our report states that the animals are missing and the family is dead."

"Tomi, Jin and their kids. Sari and Nori," Shin whispered. "They're the only cattle farm on that side of Dahl. Most are on the west side of the island, where the land isn't as suitable for crops. Sari was only a few years younger than me. We used to play whenever our families exchanged food."

"Exchanged food?" Sato interjected. The magistrates were supposed to supervise all such matters.

"Well, we preferred not to starve, so we tended to take matters into our own hands," Shin snapped, vitriol dripping from each word.

Sato held his tongue. In time, she would see reason.

"Don't worry, Shin, I'll find who did this and pull their spines out through their assholes. While they're still alive, if you prefer," Beast suggested.

Shin flashed him a warm smile. "I'd like that."

A shiver ran up Sato's spine. There was something about the girl that unsettled him. Something in her had changed since the battle of Dahl. She was colder now, more vicious than before. It wasn't just her hatred of the sentinels, but something more.

"I'll head out first thing tomorrow. I've got a few mugon in mind that should join me. Can I bring Raya too?" Beast asked with a grin.

"Raya is busy here, but I'd like you to take the twins. I'm worried this may be a larger issue than one farm burned. The missing cattle, in particular, concern me. There aren't many places to hide cows on this island."

"I'd rather have Raya accompany me. She's a warrior I trust in battle."

Yuki shook her head. "I don't believe for a moment it's battle that's motivating your request."

"It's just that I feel more safe when she's around." Apparently Beast's overwhelming thirst didn't prevent him from arguing the point.

Yuki shut down the argument. "You're taking the twins. We can't spare many fighters, and I want to send out as much strength as I can."

Beast relented. "Fine. What are these two going to be doing while I'm out doing all the work?" Beast asked, gesturing to Shin and Sato.

"Do you really care?" Yuki asked.

Beast, though, was already out the door. "Nope," he called from the hallway.

Sato just shook his head at the giant's retreating footsteps.

"I know he's a force on the battlefield, but can you count

on him for operations like this? What if he runs into a problem he can't punch?" Shin asked.

Sato answered, even though the question had been directed at Yuki. "He's capable of far more than he seems. Though he had Benji's help, it's still a rare leader who could unite the bandits of Samas. Only a foolish warrior doubts the intelligence of their foe based on appearance alone."

Shin glared at him but said nothing. After a moment, she gave him the briefest of nods, acknowledging his point.

The gesture almost made him laugh. It reminded him of Crispin, who by his very nature seemed to hate all of Sato's ideas, but was sometimes forced to acknowledge Sato had the right of it.

And Crispin was one of his lieutenants.

Yuki directed her next question at him. "Sato, ours is a partnership. I have no right to command anything of you, but I feel that our goals align. Would you allow me to make a request?"

Sato smiled at the idea that she would actually give him a choice. Despite his sun stalkers being camped outside Dahl, she possessed the overwhelming advantage here. But for either of them to get what they wanted, they needed to cooperate, at least for now. "Please."

"The Maraman threat is dealt with for now, but the war is far from over. I believe Dahl should remain our central hub for operations in Samas. Unfortunately, there is much work to be done to make it a defensible position."

"Which means you're stuck here," Sato finished her thought.

"For the moment, yes. We'll continue to guard the rifts, but I'm afraid I don't know how useful we'll be otherwise. I'd hear of your plans to prepare Samas for the dangers ahead."

"My plan is to move on Versun. My lieutenants assure me the city is rife with corruption and is ill-prepared to face the Maraman threat. I intend to fix that."

Yuki stroked her chin. If his sun stalkers controlled Versun, then he would have his own defensible hub of operations. Under his command, the sin would have no welcome in the city. Sato had no illusions that she didn't understand all of this, but his movement north was the only logical next step. She'd have to let him go, or they'd make no progress. The Maramans forced their hand. "Very well, when will you leave?"

"Tomorrow morning."

Yuki nodded. "You will keep me updated?"

"I will." He paused, waiting to see if there was anything else she would add. "If there is nothing else, I'd like to prepare my forces for the journey."

"Of course. Thank you, Sato. Your help in this is invaluable."

Sato stood and gave a small bow to Shin. "I know why you feel the way you do about me, and I'm not asking you to change that. Just know that I want to create a world in which sentinels live up to the tenets of the Path, instead of using the Path for their own gain."

Sato didn't wait for a response. He turned on his heels and left the room.

He'd just fought on a battlefield and survived.

He wasn't sure if Yuki was being honest about not wanting to rule Samas, but instinctively, he believed her. She was focused on the Maramans, and truly thought that the sin and sentinels could work together to defend the nation. Perhaps, when it came to the Maraman threat, that was true. Once they had defeated those barbarians, however, the sin would have served their purpose.

There was no room for those who strayed from the Path in Samas. When Sato became the Firstborn, he would make sure of it.

4

Shin blocked Corin's strikes while giving ground. Fooled into thinking he was pressing an advantage, Corin pushed harder. Sensing an opening, Shin followed up a parry with a quick step forward and swept his legs from under him. A second later, Harmony's blade was at his throat.

"Damn," Corin said.

"Don't be fooled by what you think you see," Yuki said, "especially if what you think you see is what you want to see. The best time to doubt your senses is when you think your dreams are coming true."

Corin grinned. "With an attitude like that, it's a wonder anyone listens to you."

Shin gasped at the disrespect, but Yuki cackled. "Ha! If your sword was half as fast as your wit, we'd have a warrior of legend on our hands."

Corin stood up. "Then I suppose I should keep practicing."

Shin was impressed by Corin's ability to remain upbeat while getting his ass handed to him. His skill was improving, slowly, but he matched even the strongest of the sin when it came to resilience.

"Your good humor serves you well, Corin," Yuki said, as if reading Shin's thoughts. "If you continue to work this hard, you will soon be formidable."

"Well, maybe not formidable," Shin quipped, unable to resist taking one last dig at her friend. "What's just below formidable?"

"Sub-formidable?" Corin said.

"Hmm, maybe lower than that. How about barely competent?"

"It's a step in the right direction! Thank you for believing in me, Shin," Corin said, laughing as he took his stance. "Jokes aside, you're really amazing with that weapon. Mateo would be proud."

"Who?" Shin asked.

Corin rolled his eyes and smiled for a moment before reading the look of genuine confusion on her face. "Are you serious?"

"Are you? Am I supposed to know someone named Mateo?"

Corin's face dropped and Shin saw a rare sight—Corin gripped with rage. "What the fuck do you mean, 'Am I supposed to know someone named Mateo?' Of course you are! He saved your life. He saved all of our lives!"

Shin stepped back under the force of his tirade. This was a side of Corin she hadn't seen.

He continued, "He gave you that sharpened stick you're waving around!" He looked like he was about to launch another verbal assault when Yuki stepped between them and laid a hand on Corin's shoulder.

"Why don't you get some water, Corin? Shin and I need to begin her training with sacrifice," Yuki said, her tone firm.

Corin looked like he was going to argue, but after glaring at Shin, followed Yuki's instructions. Not even he was so much a fool as to pick a fight with the leader of the sin.

"Why is he so upset? Who's Mateo?" Shin asked after Corin was out of earshot.

"He was the one who gifted you that weapon. He did so right before giving his life so that you, Corin, and the rest of the luan could survive."

"That's not true." Shin would remember something like that. She felt panic rising in her chest. Her body knew that somehow, something was wrong. She searched her memories. Of the luan there were plenty, but none of this man named Mateo. She sensed the gaps, though, the holes that should have been filled with her experiences. She couldn't even remember how she first came upon the weapon she now held in her hand and called her own.

"I now understand what you gave when you bound that weapon to you. I'm sorry, my child," Yuki said.

"The realm took memories of this Mateo from me?"

"The shadow realm takes what it chooses. As I've explained, adepts invoking a sacrifice don't know what the cost will be until the realm reveals it. Then they decide if it's a price they're willing to pay. In your case, it appears to have taken a memory of a loved one. You and Mateo were close, I understand."

"But if that was the cost, wouldn't the realm have shown me?"

"I assume that once it took the memory of Mateo, you forgot him completely, so you wouldn't remember what the realm was taking."

Shin considered Yuki's words for a long moment. Benji had lost his arm, and then his life, for the sacrifices that he invoked during the battle for Dahl. She had lost the memory of a friend. It was hard for her not to feel like she'd gotten the better end of the deal.

Then she watched Corin, glaring at her as he worked, his expression reminding her of a gathering storm. "He was important to me, wasn't he? To me and Corin."

"He was. He was one of the reasons you found the courage to fight. Perhaps *the* reason."

Again, Shin thought about what it would cost her to wield power as Yuki did. Whatever the cost, she would pay it. If it could save others, she would.

"If Mateo helped me find my will to fight, then he'd understand me giving up my memory of him so that I could defend those who need it, right?" Shin asked hopefully.

Yuki smiled her placid smile. "Come, Shin, we have work to do."

It wasn't an answer, but she supposed the question had been an impossible one. She nodded and sat down beside Yuki. She hoped she was right about Mateo, but it didn't really matter. Her regret was more an impulse—a thing she knew she was supposed to feel. But how could you regret what you didn't remember?

"The first step in controlling sacrifice is sensing the shadow realm. We don't know enough about it, but it's clear that it sits on top of our realm. Or beside it, however you prefer to picture it in your mind. In any case, it is always present and ready to be called upon. The rifts are an example of great power that was used to put a permanent tear in our world that allows the realm in. Not many can wield power like that."

"Is that why you don't just permanently close the rifts in Samas to prevent the demons from coming through?" Shin asked.

"Power is a fickle thing, Shin. Just because I have the

power to do something doesn't mean I have the power to deal with the consequences. So, instead, we guard the rifts. The portal that the Maramans tried to create outside Dahl was a frightening level of sacrifice, even divided amongst their summoners. But, to my point: people need to be exposed to the rifts in order to find out how attuned they are to the shadow realm. Most who are exposed will gain the abilities you see in the sin. Improved speed and reflexes. A lighter step and an innate knowledge of how to bend light so walking in the shadows becomes easier."

Shin nodded. She'd seen the abilities often enough.

Yuki continued. "Novices are those who can use the most basic levels of sacrifice. They can seal the rifts, based on the spell created long ago. They are limited, however, in their capacity. They can use techniques given to them, but cannot create their own. Beyond novice, there are adepts such as Benji and Raya, who can weave their own sacrifices."

"But we're something different, aren't we?"

Yuki smiled at Shin's intuition. "We are elites, rare individuals who are capable of hearing the demands of the realm and finding another way."

"You're sure I have that kind of power?" Shin asked.

"You are so attuned to the shadow realm that the mere act of someone else using sacrifice awakened your gift. Once that happened, you were able to instinctively reach out and find the realm. Today, I am going to teach you how to do that more deliberately. Finding a connection to the shadow realm is your first step in being able to call sacrifice when you need it."

Shin nodded at Yuki and tried to remain calm, but her mind was reeling. It was a lot to take in.

Shin closed her eyes and did her best to sense the realm. But all she heard was the wind in the trees and the birds calling to one another. She waited, then waited some more. When nothing came, she became frustrated. She had found it so easily when the demon was upon her. As her frustration grew, she lost focus. Soon she was struggling to keep her eyes closed.

Sparring with Corin was a far better use of her time.

"Focus on me, child. Focus on me like you would an enemy before you with a sword."

Shin took a deep breath and settled herself. She focused her thoughts on Yuki. First, it was just the physical presence she knew was beside her, but soon, she felt the threads of Yuki's will just like she had outside of Dahl. From there, the process became easier. She followed Yuki's will until she sensed the shadow realm lying parallel to their own world.

It was like an invisible blanket, or a layer of air, laid over everything she knew. As she sensed more, it revealed more of itself to her examination.

And it was more than she had ever thought possible.

5

The sun cast long shadows in front of them as they traveled east. Despite the late hour, he felt better than he had in days. Maybe even weeks. He was out in the open, away from the suffocating walls of Dahl and all the memories they held.

He was Beast, and he belonged in no cage. Even a city-sized one.

Hanz and Jurian walked beside him, and a group of five singun followed behind. The five, until recently, had been a part of his mugon. Even though they had been absorbed into the sin, Beast had a hard time thinking of his warriors as anything but mugon. It was something he'd have to get used to.

"Another?" Hanz offered the basket of rice balls to Beast.

He took one, and then after a moment's consideration, picked out a second. He liked traveling with the twins. They always made sure to have plenty of food for the road, and freely shared of the bounty that could always be found in their packs.

"Thanks. Shouldn't be long to the farm now," Beast reported.

The twins nodded in unison and smiled identical smiles. Beast wasn't sure they were bothered by anything. They could have walked another four hours and been just as content.

A bend in the road took him them close to a fence that marked one of the many fields of crops they'd passed by. Two kids, neither older than ten, stopped their work to watch Beast and his retinue pass.

Beast smiled and waved. After a moment's hesitation, due no doubt to his imposing visage, they waved back.

"Hold on," Beast said, taking the basket of rice balls from Hanz.

"Hey there," he called, "are you kids hungry?"

The skinny children exchanged a look before nodding.

Beast grinned wider and brought the basket over to them. They tentatively reached in and each grabbed a rice ball. The food disappeared into their mouths so quick Beast almost wasn't sure they'd taken anything.

"Why don't you take the rest back to your folks? I'm sure they could use a meal, too."

The bigger of the two children took the basket and grinned. "Thanks, Beast! My father says you're a hero!"

"And don't you forget it!" Beast roared and then flexed his massive arms.

The children laughed before running off to share their good fortune with their parents.

Beast returned to the twins and shrugged. "They were too skinny. Can't ask anyone to fight on an empty stomach."

Hanz and Jurian nodded, but then Beast saw the rest of the singun faces. He had seen those looks before. Eyes bright, and there was a hint of a smile on every one.

Variations of the same expression were on every mugon's face as they looked at him.

Not quite worship. Respect, though, and pride.

This was why they had joined. To live free, and to help others do the same. That was all that mattered. Beast couldn't lose sight of that.

They continued down the road.

The scents of destruction reached him first. The smell of an old fire wafted into his nostrils. He tensed and glanced back. The others had hands on their weapons. They'd smelled it, too.

The road ran down into a small dip before rising up again on the other side. When they crested the next hill, they were met with carnage.

The entire farm had been burned to the ground. Even the fields the animals grazed had been torched. In the distance, the skeletal remains of a modest home still smoldered. The blackened timbers jutted out of the landscape like the dark bones of some giant creature.

"This wasn't just a raid. They wanted to make sure no one could use the land anytime soon," Jurian observed.

Beast motioned his force forward. They moved cautiously, but Beast didn't expect any resistance to remain. This had happened a day or two ago. The raiders had gotten what they wanted and moved on.

When they got to the gates that led into the field, Jurian stopped them. He crouched down and examined the dirt road where some mud still existed from the last rain. "Hoof prints. A lot of them. They led the animals out this way and continued east with them."

Beast frowned. "There's nothing to the east. Through those woods is the coast." He could smell the salt on the air even through the smoke.

Beast continued into the ruined home. He looked around, but as expected, found nothing of interest. The destruction of the farm had been thorough. The ground was a mess of tracks, but Beast thought he saw a few large prints that were distinct. Prints as large as the ones he left behind. "Let's follow the trail the livestock left."

Jurian nodded and led the way, eyes focused on the ground.

Beast's mind was elsewhere. His thoughts kept returning to the skinny kids just up the road. Was their farm next? Who would protect them?

Thoughts of the children opened the floodgates for other thoughts, ones he hadn't had proper time to consider in months.

The children were hardly unique. The farmers of Ilos had suffered for years under sentinel rule.

They continued to suffer now, even though the sentinels were gone.

The sentinels had starved them, then beaten them when they tried to feed themselves. Beast had always intended for his mugon to change the country, to fight back and feed the people. But as soon as he'd united the bandits, the sin had appeared and he was faced with bigger problems.

Hopefully, now that the sin controlled Dahl, and by extension Ilos, the levies put on the farmers would lessen. But that would take time. This year's harvest was done and already the food in Dahl was hard to come by. The sin were supplementing from their own supplies but they wouldn't last long.

And now someone was razing farms to the ground, destroying their capacity to recover.

Whatever he found here, Beast knew one thing: when he returned to Yuki it would be to tell her he was committing a force to protect these people. His mugon, at the least, could help with this, and if she saw things differently, maybe his oath of loyalty would be short-lived.

Jurian led them off the road and through the trees. The trail through the woods became easier to follow as the giant animals bulled their way through the flora. After a short walk they came to the edge of the tree line. Beyond that, Beast saw a small beach.

The smell of rot hit their noses, and a cloud of flies flew into the air as Beast and his interloping force disturbed their feast.

The hastily butchered remains of the livestock sat in a pile on the sand. The flies, seeing the new arrivals as no threat, resumed their meal. A few chunks of flesh clung to the white bones of the animals, but most of the meat had been taken. White salt stood out against the darker sand.

"Looks like they took everything out to sea," Beast said.

He had a sinking feeling in his stomach.

He hated the water, but it looked like that was where the food had been taken.

"We're going to need a boat," he grumbled.

6

Sato's sun stalkers had made good time to Versun, which pleased him. He had the feeling there wasn't a moment to waste when it came to cleansing the city of corruption and preparing it for the battles to come.

His first order had been to set up a camp outside the walls. There'd been no end of complaints from that order, but he'd held firm. He didn't know enough about the current disposition of the city, and while his sentinels would have been more comfortable inside the walls, they'd also be more susceptible to corruption and bribery. For now, the separation was important.

As most of the sentinels finished setting up camp under the supervision of Captain Roko, he walked to the gates of Versun, accompanied by Crispin and Alonzo. They hadn't made it more than a few feet through the gate when they were met by a magisterial envoy.

"Greetings, General Sato," the well-dressed man said with a bow, "Magistrate Izuki has sent me to welcome you to Versun. I have been instructed to offer you any amenities you wish before your meeting."

Sato took in the man's opulent clothing and, though he couldn't place why, got the same feeling he did when he needed to correct an obvious mistake that his forces were making. "Thank you, but we are eager to meet with the magistrate first thing."

The envoy bowed again. Somehow, he made the gesture of respect look almost condescending. "Of course, general. Would you like to bring your men inside the city? The magistrate has arranged for the finest accommodations within the palace district."

Sato raised an eyebrow. He had made a point of not sending ravens ahead to Versun so that his arrival would be a surprise. Izuki was well informed if she had time to prepare accommodations for his entire force.

"That is very kind," Sato said, "but I'm afraid the nature of our mission requires us to remain outside the walls for the moment."

The envoy bowed once more, his expression unreadable, and gestured for Sato to follow him. Sato allowed the man to get a fair distance ahead before following along.

They walked through the city in silence. It had been years since he'd been to Versun and he was eager to assess the condition of its defenses more closely. For now, though, he focused on his meeting with Magistrate Izuki.

The palace in Versun was, like the rest of the city, a shining monument to the wealth that accumulated here. As the main hub for trade within Samas there was no shortage of funds coming into the city. Only Bulas surpassed it in grandeur.

Sato turned to his lieutenants. "You two, I need information. Find out what's happening in this city. The real story. We'll meet back at gates to the port district at noon."

The men nodded and gave brisk salutes before they

headed off. Sato steeled himself and navigated the palace hallways to the receiving hall. The envoy announced him as they entered.

"Lord Sato, we are honored by your presence. I only wish you would have sent word ahead so we could have given you a more appropriate reception," Magistrate Izuki said, gesturing around the grand receiving hall as if its ostentatious decor was somehow lacking.

Sato took a brief look around the room and resisted the urge to shake his head in disgust. He realized now why the envoy's clothing had bothered him. All the trappings of ceremony that he once thought necessary, the tables full of food that would mostly be thrown out, the honor guard that lined every wall, seemed so wasteful in the face of the crisis that Samas faced. He wanted to berate the magistrate for her foolish adherence to empty traditions.

Instead, he smiled diplomatically.

"Not at all, magistrate, you honor me as always. I would have sent word, but my decision was made at the last possible moment, and thus there was little time to send a raven." Sato was about to continue to the matter at hand but Izuki interrupted him.

"Ah yes, your special unit designed to hunt the mugon. How is that endeavor faring?"

The question brought Sato up short. As chief magistrate of Versun, Izuki knew everything of importance throughout Samas. She knew what had happened in Dahl. The question itself was pointless. But its meaning was clear. She wanted him to have to announce his failure publicly.

Izuki was a ladder climber who had succeeded in securing a prize portion as the chief magistrate of Versun. In his past life, Sato would have praised the woman for her ambition, but knowing now just what depths some magistrates were willing to sink to in pursuit of their goals, Sato could barely hide his disgust with her.

Fortunately, he had never been known for his warm countenance. Still, he tried his best to remain diplomatic. "Your interest in my endeavors is, as always, much appreciated. The sun stalkers are one of the most unique and impressive units in Samas—"

"But they could not stop Dahl from falling?" the magistrate interrupted again. "I understand sentinels no longer control the city. That instead, it is run by a collection of these mugon and sin. To hear the news from Ilos is to wonder if you're stuck in some nightmare."

It took all of Sato's control not to draw his sword. That the magistrate spoke so brazenly to him was evidence enough of how much favor she thought he'd lost at Dahl. If she had considered him the Firstborn's favorite, she never would have dared.

What really made the comment sting was that Sato wasn't sure if she didn't have the right of the situation.

"Dahl has fallen," Sato admitted. He raised a hand to forestall the magistrate's next interruption. He would only indulge so much. "My sun stalkers acquitted themselves well, but the forces arrayed against the city were too great for us to fight alone. Unfortunately, the magistrates in Dahl were not prepared for any of the calamity that befell them. One of my primary reasons for riding here is to prevent the same fate from befalling your city."

Izuki looked as though she had been slapped. Which, verbally, Sato supposed, wasn't that far from the truth. She responded just as harshly. "Forgive me, Lord Sato, but if you could not defend Dahl, then what good are your sun stalkers here?"

Sato held his tongue, though the effort required was

considerable. She really did believe he had no favor left. That his assignment with the sun stalkers had been a dismissal from the Firstborn's court. And now she saw an opportunity to turn his failures to her advantage. It made him sick. "My sun stalkers were not the ones who failed to hold a fortified position, Magistrate Izuki. That incompetence falls squarely on your fellow magistrates. I am here to ensure that the sentinel order is not embarrassed once more."

Izuki's eyes widened slightly at Sato's tone.

Surprise?

Had she really expected him to be deferential?

She thought for a moment before speaking again. Her tone, now, was less aggressive. He'd forced her to reevaluate the situation. Her response was almost conciliatory. At least, her words were. "Of course, my lord. I did not mean to disparage your military prowess. Any help you could provide would be most appreciated. I do have to say, however, that Versun is no Dahl. Our complement of sentinels is far greater, and the unique design of our city makes it almost more defensible than Bulas."

"I am well aware," Sato said and paused, reminding the insolent magistrate of her place. "What you don't understand is that you face an enemy that you have never seen before. This is like no war the sentinels have ever fought. I am here to make sure that you don't lose Versun in spite of its defensive advantages."

Izuki's expression went dark, but she wisely held her tongue. After a moment she put on a smile Sato could almost believe was genuine. She bowed slightly to him. "Thank you, general. Whatever help you could provide would be much appreciated. Tell me what you need."

"Not much. My sun stalkers will remain camped outside

the walls for the moment. In the next day or two, I will head to Bulas to report to the Firstborn personally. My captain, Roko, along with my lieutenants, Crispin and Alonzo, will spend the days I am away inspecting the defenses of each district. When I return, they will report to me and we will be able to better see what we can do to aid in the defense of Versun."

"Of course. But will they not stay in the city? We made room in the barracks right here in the palace district. It would be far more convenient and comfortable."

"I do not wish to be a burden, magistrate, and my forces are more comfortable in their camp."

"Nonsense," Izuki said, still smiling. "I insist. I would be honored to offer whatever comfort I can to your brave troops."

"Your hospitality is greatly appreciated. But for now, I must insist that my men remain outside." Sato held up a hand once more to forestall the magistrate's coming objections. "This is not a discussion, magistrate. This is the very reason the stalkers were created, and I will not have them indulging in creature comforts while one of the jewels of Samas is at risk."

Again, his reputation as a difficult and dour commander worked in his favor. It at least gave him an excuse for his behavior.

Izuki's hesitation was so brief that a less trained eye would have missed it. He hadn't been involved in court drama for some time, but his skills were still sharp. She would burn with anger for days.

Longer, if he was as successful here as he hoped.

By the sun, he hated court politics.

"Of course, General Sato. Can I offer you a bath and meal before you leave for Bulas?"

"Thank you, but no. I will get my officers situated and oversee the sun stalkers' accommodations, but then I must be on my way. Thank you again for your hospitality. I look forward to working with you." Sato bowed to the magistrate, and the moment she returned the gesture he spun on his heel and left the hall.

As his boots echoed through the opulent chamber, Sato suppressed a sigh. He had scored a victory in keeping his stalkers outside the city, but Izuki would still be able to find plenty of ways to make their lives difficult.

They had their work cut out for them.

7

Yuki and Shin left Dahl and traveled to the woods of Ilos. Corin and Raya accompanied them, supposedly for "protection," although Shin wasn't sure what they would need protecting from.

Shin knew the eastern half of the island well, but this spot wasn't one she had frequented often. If she had, she wondered if she would have been able to sense the shadow realm the way she could now. Here, any struggle she had to feel the realm's presence was long gone.

In fact, it would have been harder *not* to feel it. When they sat and started their training, Shin found the realm with ease.

"Good work," Yuki said. "You made that seem easy."

"Pretty hard to miss."

Yuki chuckled, which sent a bit of a shiver down Shin's spine. The empty sound always reminded Shin more of a habit more than a genuine reaction.

Before Shin's thoughts could linger on the subject, Yuki focused her attention on the problem at hand. "We are close to a rift, which means...?"

"Which means that the realm is closer to us here," Shin responded.

"Not exactly. The realm is always in the same place in relation to our plane. What you feel from the rift is more like a like a door. One that we only open when necessary. Take a moment, and then we'll see if you can find it."

Shin nodded and stood up, stretching her limbs. She looked over and watched Corin training with Raya off in the distance. He continued to improve, but Shin was never sure he would be anything more than an average fighter. Her heart twisted at the sight of him. They hadn't spoken in more than passing since Shin had learned she'd sacrificed her memory of Mateo.

Yuki followed her gaze. "You should talk to him."

Shin sighed. "I know. He just seems so hurt, and I don't feel anything. How am I supposed to regret what I can't remember?"

"You feel sad that he's hurt, right?"

"Of course!"

"I'd lead with that," Yuki said gently.

She was right, of course. It still didn't make Shin eager to initiate the conversation, but the best time to take care of wounds was as soon as possible. They only festered with time.

"Thanks, Yuki," Shin said, and walked towards her friend.

As she approached, Corin committed too hard to a strike and Raya knocked him to the ground. As always, Corin bounced back up. Raya laughed and shook her head before noticing Shin's approach. She waved at Shin.

The lithe sin had quickly become one of Shin's favorite people. She was efficient, competent, and everything from her long braid to her perfectly fitted clothes projected strength. Then, when you least expected it, she would flash her impish grin. It was no wonder Beast was attracted to her.

"Hi Shin, you want a crack at this guy? I'm getting tired of winning all the time," Raya said.

"I *could* use a quick warm-up." Shin risked the joke but was rewarded with a genuine, if reluctant, smile from Corin.

Raya grinned and gave them some space. Corin dusted himself off. He looked at the wooden training sword for a moment before tossing it away.

"Corin, look..." Shin began.

"No, it's fine. I over-reacted."

Shin was surprised that Corin forgave her so quickly. "Well, I still wanted to say I'm sorry. Yuki says he was important to us, and I get that it must be hard that you can't share his memory with me. It's just the sacrifice I needed..."

"I get it!" Corin snapped before taking a calming breath. "Look, Raya explained about sacrifice to me and why you gave up what you did. I understand."

"But?" Shin asked, sensing Corin had more to say.

"But I hate sacrifice."

"If we're going fight the Maramans we need it," Shin said.

"Do we? All it brings is destruction and ruin and then asks good people to give something up for the privilege. Maybe we need it to stop them. Maybe. But what's it going to cost us?"

"Whatever the price, I'm willing to pay it so long as it means people like you, and kids like the luan, aren't under anyone's boot, Maraman or otherwise. But I won't let it change who I am. What I fight for."

Corin looked like he wanted to be convinced but wasn't. "Promise me."

The words seemed childish, like a brother demanding

his sister make time to play with him, but the intensity of Corin's request removed any humor Shin might have found in the moment.

"I promise."

"Good."

Shin decided it was as good a time as any to change the subject. "Now, stop putting all your weight on your lead foot when you throw a strike. Not only does it make you commit too much, but any opponent worth their salt can read that like a book," Shin said.

"But I can't hit as hard without putting weight on that leg."

"It's a sword, Corin, not a club," Shin said. "Let it do the work."

Raya broke in. "Break's over, Corin."

Corin shook his head but picked up his training sword. He never stopped trying. In that way, he inspired Shin to continue with her own training. She returned to Yuki.

"Feel better?" Yuki asked.

"A little," Shin said, sitting down.

"Good. Now you can focus."

Rather than respond, Shin closed her eyes searched for the realm. As before, it came naturally.

"Well done. Now, show me where the rift is."

Shin sought out a difference in the shadow realm she felt all around her. The more effort she put in, the more it seemed to slip away. Instead of forcing the issue, Shin pulled her senses back and focused on a calm center inside herself. As she did, the realm came into greater focus in the periphery of her awareness. She resisted the urge to snap her focus in any one direction. Instead, she let her awareness expand.

Soon the rifts, some distant and some close, revealed

themselves to her. They were small points where the shadow realm seemed to seep slowly into Samas.

Something felt wrong.

The closest rift, the one on Ilos, was *open*.

Her eyes snapped open. Whatever fear she felt was doubled when she saw Yuki's eyes wide. Panic was too strong a word for the look, but on a face that showed next to no emotion, even an expression of mild concern was chilling.

"I thought we only opened the rifts when the moon finished its cycle?"

"We didn't open it. Come, we must go. Now."

Yuki was already up and moving. Corin and Raya looked over at Shin, confused. Yuki gestured for them to approach. She turned to Corin first.

"Corin, Jira and Seb are waiting for us at the road back to Dahl. Go and tell them we need a unit of singun with an adept to meet us at the rift on Ilos. Raya and Shin will come with me to the rift, and we'll contain it as best we can."

"I'll come too," Corin said.

"No, return to Dahl with the others. It's too dangerous," Yuki said, and her tone left no room for argument.

Corin, frustrated, nodded before running off.

Yuki turned to Shin and Raya. "It can't have been open for too long, but we must be ready for anything. Prepare yourselves. There's no telling what hell an unguarded rift will unleash."

8

A s Beast watched the water, he made out a small speck far away.

"We need to know where the raiders are coming from," Beast said as he kept his eyes on the water. "We need to know where that juggernaut is."

Hanz shook his head. "If they're coming from the deep water, there's not much we can do. Our boats are only designed to travel in the shallows between the islands. We'd capsize long before we had an answer."

"No sin connections in the guilds?"

Jurian laughed. "Oh, plenty of connections. But even we can't have a deep-water boat designed. The laws are too strict and the project too big, and before there was no need."

Beast nodded absently. Access to shipping lanes had always been strictly controlled. In the past, he'd assumed it was just another overreach of sentinel power. Now he wondered if there wasn't more to it. Fortunately, there was another answer. He pointed out to the ocean. "Maybe we can borrow one of theirs."

While he and his singun rested on the beach, the speck

grew larger, taking on the outline of a ship. It was shaped differently than any Samasian ship he'd ever seen. Combined with the enormous prints around the destroyed farmstead, Beast was certain of their enemy.

It looked like they hadn't killed all the Maramans after all. Some had remained on the juggernaut during the battle for Dahl.

If his estimation was correct, the ship would hit Ilos about a mile north of them.

"Are there any more significant farms north of here, near the coast?" Beast asked.

Hanz and Jurian shrugged.

"There's one, crops mostly. One of the larger ones in the area," one of the singun said.

Beast raised an eyebrow at the man.

"Before I joined the mugon, I used to run with bandits on Ilos. The farm was visited by sentinels too often to be worth the risk, but there was a girl that lived there I sometimes tried to visit."

"Can you lead us there? How far is it?"

"We can be there in twenty minutes or so. I know the way."

"Then lead on...?"

"Everyone calls me Flea, sir."

"I won't ask why. Lead on, Flea."

Flea nodded, and they ran. It was a pace that Benji and Beast had drilled with the mugon. One that ate up the miles quickly but wouldn't exhaust well-trained warriors before battle.

At the memory of his lost friend, Beast felt a pang of sorrow and rested a hand on the hilt of Benji's broken sword. He had picked it up after the battle of Dahl, and now it was always tucked in his belt. It made him feel better to have a piece of Benji close to him.

Beast hoped they would make it in time. Flea's path took them away from the water, so they had no way of knowing who would win the race between them and the Maramans.

When the farm came into view, Beast shouted in anger. The farmhouse was surrounded by ten hulking figures, one of whom was lighting a torch. Then he tossed it at the house. The flame sputtered as the torch arced lazily through the air. The moment it hit the thatch, though, the roof started to smoke, then burn.

Beast and his forces drew their weapons and their measured pace turned into a sprint. The deep gash in Beast's arm, a gift from his first battle with the Maramans, protested as he unlimbered the battle axe strapped to his back, but the pain faded as his rage took over.

"You two, see what you can do about getting those farmers out," Beast ordered two of the singun as they closed the distance on their foes.

They nodded and veered toward the house, swords in hand.

The Maramans saw them coming and readied their own weapons. The closest leveled one of the giant spears they seemed to prefer to bows and threw it at Beast. The missile flew with surprising speed, and Beast felt the air rush past his face as he leaned to the side to avoid it.

Flea wasn't so lucky.

The sharpened point of the giant spear burst through Flea's chest. The force of the sudden impact caused the man's lifeless body to fly backwards.

Then Beast was among the Maramans, swinging his axe.

Blood pounded in his ears as he brought his axe to bear on the first of the Maramans. The large man parried two of

Beast's blows before Jurian's sword appeared in his neck and he fell. Another Maraman looked to capitalize on Jurian's exposed flank, but Beast stepped inside the swing of his blade and knocked him to the ground. Hanz ran a sword through his chest before he could stand.

Beast saw the two remaining singun take down one of the Maramans before being cut down themselves. Beast cursed. Skilled as his warriors had become, they would need more training to keep up with these monsters.

The remaining Maramans advanced on Beast and the twins and all his other thoughts fled. They were outnumbered, but the Maramans had no idea that they faced three of the finest warriors in all of Samas.

Beast, Hanz and Jurian fought together like a three-headed dragon. Their movements were tied together through hours of training. They knew each other's tendencies and strengths. What weaknesses existed in the three men individually were mitigated by their collective presence.

Beast parried a blow intended for Hanz while Jurian cut down a Maraman before he could kill Beast.

Hanz used the time Beast's parry gave him to remove the head of another invader.

Beast stepped into the space created by the man Jurian killed to bury his axe in a Maraman who rushed to help his comrades.

The Maramans, still believing they had an advantage, rushed into the churn that the three men created and died for their confidence.

Then it was done.

Beast looked around, breathing heavily, but not nearly as winded as he normally was after a battle. Having the twins by his side was certainly easier than having to cut down everyone on his own.

Hanz and Jurian were smiling, and Beast wondered what exactly it would take to wipe the grins off their faces. "Looks like all that training paid off," they said in unison.

"Ugh, you know it creeps me out when you two do that." He groaned, then matched their smiles. "But I agree, all that time spent fighting with me has certainly made you two better."

The twins laughed.

The two surviving singun had dragged the farmer and his family out of the house, which was now a raging inferno. The father was comforting the mother as she cried and a girl who looked to be in her twenties was holding a small boy in her arms. Beast approached the family.

"Did everyone escape?" he asked.

The man gave Beast a look of terror, but his wife laid a hand on his arm. She whispered in the man's ear, and Beast heard his name mentioned. The man looked at him for a moment, then nodded. "We did, thanks to you saving us from those...people."

"They're Maramans," Beast explained, "and I fear you haven't seen the last of them. The sin will offer protection against them."

"The sin?" The farmer had found his courage. He laughed bitterly. "The sentinels protect us. The sin are a myth. Bedtime stories for children." The farmer's words were a mix of anger, fear, and confusion. Beast couldn't blame him.

"I assure you that I am very real. Dahl has fallen to the sin and we intend to protect this island better than the sentinels ever did."

"At what cost? The sentinels already bled us dry. We

can't afford to give away more food," the young girl said. She still held the boy in her arms, but her eyes blazed with fury.

"We'll take nothing without paying. The days of sentinel corruption are over," Beast said, and smiled as magnanimously as he could.

The farmer scoffed, and Beast fixed him with a glare. He quickly held up his hands. "I'm sorry. I don't want you to think that we aren't grateful for your help, but the sentinels claimed they walked the Path while stealing the food from our mouths. It's hard to believe you'll be any different."

Beast was impressed with the man's courage. It took a lot to stand in the face of a force like Beast and speak the truth. He considered for a moment. "I will have supplies provided for you to rebuild your home. It will take a few days, but they will come. In the meantime, I will leave these two here to help clean up the mess left by the Maramans, and to offer some protection."

The singun that had helped the family escape the burning home looked surprised at the orders but nodded to Beast.

"We'll start with the bodies. That's something a child shouldn't have to see," one of the singun said.

The farmer continued to look at Beast skeptically. "Clear the bodies, fine, but please leave after that. My family and I will rebuild. I'll believe in your supplies when I see them."

Beast was about to insist his singun remain, but he saw the look of fear in the wife's and daughter's eyes and understanding dawned on him. Strange men hanging around their farm weren't likely to make them feel any safer. "Fair enough. But my offer of aid stands, should you request it."

"Sure," the farmer said and motioned for his family to head over to the barn that had survived the attack.

Beast and his men dragged the corpses down the path before piling them up and lighting them ablaze. If the farmer was so keen for him to leave, he could tend to the fire.

Once they had left the farm behind, Beast stopped and turned to the twins. "We need to hurry back to Yuki. The supplies need to be sent here, but more importantly, we need regular patrols of Ilos. We can't let the Maramans continue to terrorize these people or they'll never support our cause."

"We'll make haste back to Yuki, but one problem remains," Hanz said.

"Where are the Maramans coming from?" Beast guessed.

The twins nodded and Beast sighed as he looked out over the water.

He had a feeling he was going to need to find his sea legs after all.

9

———

Before Sato left the city, there was other business for him to attend to.

While he'd been busy with the magistrate, Crispin and Alonzo had been making their own, more important rounds. He'd been shown what the magistrates wanted him to see. His trusted lieutenants were responsible for finding out how the situation actually stood.

When he returned to the camp after his meeting, he was greeted by two officers with surprisingly glum looks on their faces.

"Did all the brothels close?" he asked.

Alonzo looked horrified at the thought, but Crispin just shook his head. "You've been a bad influence on me, sir."

"Why's that?"

"Before I met you, I always loved visiting Versun, and it still holds much that would appeal to a man of my particular proclivities. The gambling halls are doing brisk business, and it looks like there are plenty of merchants around practically begging me to take their coin."

Sato looked between the two men. "You can't possibly

expect me to believe you two have reformed so greatly in so short a time."

Crispin cracked a smile at that. "Not at all, sir. It's just that, for all the fun that Versun promises, I'm not sure there's going to be enough time to get in any trouble at all."

"That bad?"

"I'm not saying that the walls will collapse if a guard jumps too hard," Crispin said, "but it also wouldn't surprise me all that much."

"Show me," Sato ordered.

Crispin nodded, expecting the order. "Where do you want to begin?"

"You mentioned the wall, so let's start there."

Without a word, the three men set off. Sato realized he hadn't even thought to change out of his formal dress. It made no difference, though. He had every right to inspect Versun, no matter what the local magistrates might believe.

Crispin brought him to the wall that surrounded the port, the first line of defense against a naval invasion, as unlikely as such an event would ever be. Sato didn't need anyone to point out the problems. The wall was made of stone and mortar, and neither were in the condition Sato would expect. The mortar was cracked throughout, and in places, stones had even fallen from the wall. No matter how far they walked, he couldn't see any sign that repairs had even been attempted.

They passed through one of the gates in the wall, and Crispin led him to the top. Regulations demanded that the wall be ready to repel an invasion at any time, but none of the standards were met. Arrows looked like they had been exposed to the elements for months, and the catapults looked like they were as likely to break as the wall.

They passed a pair of guards, and Sato stopped them.

They took in the rank on his formal dress and bowed deeply, clearly surprised to see a general here.

"Tell me about the wall," Sato ordered them.

They looked to one another. "Sir?"

Sato swept his hand out, encompassing the whole wall. "This is my first visit to Versun in years, and the lack of repair along this wall is inexcusable. I want to know why."

The two guards looked to one another again, but neither rushed to answer Sato's question.

Sato was about to demand answers more forcefully when Crispin sighed. "May I?"

Sato nodded for him to go ahead. Crispin took the two guards aside, and they huddled tightly together, whispering back and forth. Finally, they nodded, and returned to attention in front of Sato.

"Sir," the woman said, "from what our commander tells us, there's no money or support for the repair of the wall. He claims to keep demanding more, but the magistrates are too stingy."

There was something more they weren't saying. Sato could tell that easily enough. "And?"

The two guards glanced at Crispin, who nodded. The woman spoke again. "It's just that quite a few of us have noticed that our commander wears some really nice clothes, sir."

The other guard chimed in, "And has a taste for expensive wine."

Sato nodded. "I see." He thought for a moment. "And if someone else were put in charge?"

The woman shrugged. "Not much difference, I'd imagine. Our commanders seem to change with the seasons. The wall stays the same."

Sato thought, after all he'd been through, that he lacked

the ability to be surprised. But he had been wrong. To think that so many sentinels would be so easily corrupted.

The task he'd set for himself was no easy one.

Then he noticed the guard's sword. "Show me your weapon, sentinel."

The woman grimaced, but drew her sword. It was notched in several places.

"You don't even have a functioning weapon," Sato exclaimed.

"One of the best I could find, sir," she said. "Blacksmith is too busy working on other projects to repair our weapons."

Sato was about to sputter that she was responsible for the safety of a city, but realized it would do no good.

He bowed to her, offering her recognition for the burdens she bore. "Thank you for your candor. I will do what I can to help."

Her look had shifted to one of resignation, and he wondered how many other high ranks had promised something similar.

Probably more than he cared to admit.

They left the guards, and Crispin continued their tour. As they were still in the poorer parts of the city, Sato didn't expect much, but he was still surprised by the complete lack of concern everywhere he looked.

At one point, he stopped in the middle of the street, just to take it all in. The buildings were in disrepair everywhere he looked, but more disturbing was the fact that there wasn't a sentinel to be found anywhere.

As near as he could tell, these people were on their own.

He wondered if he even would have noticed on one of his previous visits. Before, he'd always spent the majority of his time in the richer districts, where they didn't have these problems.

Crispin led him to an enormous warehouse, guarded by a handful of sentinels. They bowed to Sato when they saw his rank. He couldn't help but notice that they looked afraid to have him here.

He knew what this place was, and before they even stepped foot inside, he had a guess of what he would see.

Crispin opened the door and led him in. They ascended the stairs and stood on a platform that ran along the wall of the building. From their vantage point, Sato could see the whole warehouse.

It was mostly empty.

Sato clenched his fists. "There's no way they should have so little. Even with the mugon attacks, our supply wasn't that disrupted."

Crispin shrugged. "I checked their ledgers when I came here. What's here is honestly accounted for. They haven't been receiving much of anything."

"But I've seen the reports being sent to the Firstborn. Everything is reported as normal."

Crispin just shrugged again. "You can see it for yourself," he said.

And he could. Sato struggled to believe it, but the evidence was right in front of him. "If something were to happen here, Versun would crumble."

Alonzo nodded, then made a series of gestures Sato could understand. *At least the outer districts.*

Sato turned to Crispin. "Is it as bad further in?"

Crispin shook his head. "It wouldn't meet your standards. All the walls have been neglected, but not as much as the outer one. Sentinels are better equipped further in, but not as well as we are. And the warehouses have stores, but not as many as they're supposed to."

Sato almost cursed. Corruption was one thing, but when it endangered the lives of so many, it became treason.

"We've got our work cut out for us," he said.

Crispin groaned. "I was afraid you were going to say that."

10

———

Yuki led Raya and Shin through a thick clump of forest that Shin, in all her years on Ilos, had never explored. They were several miles out of Dahl and the three of them had ridden hard to the edge of the woods before dismounting and heading into the thick brush on foot.

Yuki said little as she moved unerringly through the forest, but she stopped abruptly at the massive, rotting stump of a great oak tree.

"Prepare yourselves. I do not know what we will find when we reach the rift, but we may face many foes. Raya, focus on sending the demons back. Shin, you and I will remove their heads. Once that's done, we will see if we can repair the rift." Yuki adjusted the chained weapon that was wrapped around her body and took the handle of the wickedly curved blade in her hand.

Raya and Shin nodded, and Yuki turned and stepped into the giant stump.

Shin blinked as she saw the woman's body disappear as if she were heading down a set of dark stairs. Raya followed, and the effect was the same. Shin stepped into the large crack with her hand out. Instead of pressing against the rotted wood, her hand disappeared, and Shin stumbled slightly as her foot landed lower than expected. Moments later she was descending a set of rough stairs that led not into a hole, but down a steep incline.

"What kind of sacrifice is required for something like this?" Shin asked as she took in the scope of the illusion that was hiding the rift.

"A large one, from a great person," Yuki replied, and her tone implied that the subject was now closed.

As they descended the stairs, the sense of wrongness that had led them here grew exponentially. There was no need for Shin to open herself up to the realm for her to sense it. The rift was like an open sore, pulsing with infection.

When they got to the bottom, Shin saw that they were in a large cave. The opening was large enough to allow some light in. Down here, there was plenty of space, but the stone narrowed almost to a point the higher Shin's eyes traveled. The appearance of the cave was like a conical tent with a hole at the top. And right now the entire space was bathed in crimson light.

Shin's eyes widened once they adjusted to the light. There were several demons milling about. Mostly, they were enormous rat-shaped things. They averaged the size of a small dog, with disproportionate limbs and noses that sniffed the air. Jagged teeth jutted well past their elongated muzzles. Shin shivered when she saw a huge, dark form uncoil itself from a corner and slither into the light. The giant snake's tongue flicked out so far that it dragged on the ground before returning to its mouth. The fangs were as long and curved as a sword, and every bit as deadly.

"Raya, once we thin out their numbers, start sending them back," Yuki said.

Without waiting for a reply, Yuki spun the end of the chain that had the stake on it, letting out more length with every revolution. Once the momentum built, she wrapped the chain back around her body and used the tension to fire the stake forward and into the body of a surprised rat-demon.

Being impaled only drew its attention to Yuki, but the sin leader wasn't done. She yanked on the chain and the demon flew towards her. She met it, midair, with the curved blade on the other end of the chain and sliced its head clean off.

Then chaos broke out.

Yuki moved on to the next demon. Her chain was a blur of destruction that even the demons couldn't penetrate. Before Shin had taken a step, Yuki claimed another demon head. Shin had never seen such speed but didn't have time to enjoy the show. The demons came for her, too. She turned to the demon advancing on her and met its claws with Harmony's steel.

She used Harmony's reach to keep the thing at bay until she could close in and strike at the neck. Unfortunately, the head didn't sever cleanly in one blow and Shin was forced to leap away from the demon's back claws, Harmony still embedded in the rat.

Neither the blade in its spine nor the fact that its head was flopping at all angles seemed to bother the demon as it pressed its advance. Shin backed up a few steps before having to scramble sideways to avoid the slash of another demon's claws. As she dashed away, she raised her hand and called Harmony back to her. The embedded blade stuck for a moment before slicing through the rest of the rat's neck and returning to her hand. She stopped abruptly, her lead foot skidding out as she did so, and attacked the demon chasing her. It couldn't get its claws up in time, and Shin's blow was clean.

Shin looked around the cave and saw that Yuki still battled demons but was now surrounded by clouds of mist. Shin couldn't believe what she was seeing, but Yuki had her eyes squeezed shut as she fought, flawlessly, against their enemies. Behind them, Raya sent the misty forms back through the realm as fast as she could before they could re-form. Shin realized she would have to help Raya before the demons overwhelmed Yuki. She couldn't keep her eyes closed forever.

Shin calmed herself and sought the realm. In this place, it was easy. She felt what Raya was doing and copied it as best as she could.

Then the realm showed her a different way. The path she was sure she needed.

Quickly she formed the necessary weaves and felt the realm prepare to take its toll from her.

Then she couldn't breathe.

Her eyes snapped open, and she was engulfed in the massive snake's body. The pressure drove the air from her lungs so quickly that the edges of her vision were already turning black. What she could see was something out of her nightmares. In addition to the giant fangs, the snake-thing had a mouthful of smaller sharp teeth, giving it a toothy smile that made her wish she *was* trapped in a nightmare.

A blade flashed in front of her face and the grip loosened. A shallow breath of oxygen made it into her lungs, and her eyes focused a little more. The blade flashed again, and she saw the snake's head fall to the side, flapping slightly as it struggled to unwrap itself from Shin and defend against this new attacker.

The blade struck a final time and the snake's head toppled before the whole body turned into mist. Shin fell to the ground and gulped air into her burning lungs. Each breath was agony on her ribs, but she drank the air in anyway. She looked up and saw Corin standing with his sword held loosely in one hand.

"Corin! Thank the sun you came. I—" Shin stopped when she realized Corin was staring into the formless black mist that had just been wrapped around Shin.

He didn't know not to look.

Quickly, Shin closed her eyes and found the weave she had prepared. It was there, waiting for her. She readied herself, and the realm came to collect.

An instant later, the demons were gone. Shin felt Raya and Yuki react in surprise but Shin's sacrifice wasn't done. The rift was sealing. Once it was closed, the last threads of Shin's weaving snapped into place and the rift disappeared completely.

Corin collapsed on the ground, stunned, and Shin knelt so she could wrap her arms around him. "Corin!"

The others seemed far less concerned about Corin's fate. "How did you do that?" Raya asked, her face pale. "The rift isn't just sealed it's—gone."

Before Shin could answer, Yuki stepped beside her. "More importantly, what did it cost you?"

Shin looked up, confused. "I don't know."

11

—————

Night had fallen, but before they left the farmhouse, Beast and the others went to check to see what evidence the Maramans might have left behind. What they found was a simple longboat. Beast stared at it for a moment, then out to the raiding vessel he'd seen from the previous farm.

"Oh, fuck," Beast sighed.

"What is it?" Jurian asked.

"I've got an idea."

"That's never good," Hanz said.

"How stupid is it this time?" Jurian asked.

"Stupid enough to work," Beast said and turned to the sin behind him. "You five, stay with us. The rest of you, head back to Dahl and report to Yuki. Let them know the Maramans are raiding Ilos from the juggernaut, but more importantly, tell her about the supplies and laborers needed to help those farmers."

The remaining sin nodded and took off without hesitation.

"We're going for a boat ride, aren't we?" Hanz asked.

"By the sun, I hate the ocean," Beast growled in response.

"We know," Jurian said.

"You've made your position very clear," Hanz followed up.

Beast glared at the twins and their mocking smiles but kept his mouth shut. He was more nervous than angry about being on the water, but the fact that he was nervous made him angry all the same.

Beast sighed again.

Raiding made sense. Yuki had told him about the juggernaut. If a floating island was responsible for bringing the Maramans here, it would need an incredible amount of supplies. They had to be almost out of food after the eight-month voyage.

It would be a perfect location to launch raids from. If they knew the Samasians were limited in their seafaring capability, they could strike with impunity.

Now Beast was going to go looking for it. Because if they found it, they might be able to destroy it. No longer would the people of Ilos have to live under anyone's thumb. He gestured to the others and issued his orders.

"You five will be prisoners and the three of us will be the Maramans who've captured you. It's getting dark enough that we should be able to get close without raising an alarm, but we need to hurry. If those clouds clear, there might be enough moonlight to blow this whole plan to shit. Hide your weapons at your feet and keep your hands together like they're shackled. I want our two best archers in the stern with me. Any questions?"

"What's the plan once we get there?" one of the sin asked.

Beast grinned wolfishly. "Kill some more Maramans."

The sin seemed satisfied with that answer and headed towards the boat. Beast tucked his long hair underneath his tunic. The twins already had shaved heads and so would pass more easily as Maramans. Beast's stomach twisted as he thought of his two friends being more Maraman than he was. But that was a bit of self-reflection better left alone.

"I'll row the boat and keep my head down," Beast said.

Before long, they were out on the water rowing towards the Maraman raiding vessel.

"Are you expecting the Maramans to tell us where to find the juggernaut once we board their ship?" Hanz asked.

"No, I think they'll be a little less friendly. Since we can't understand them, it seems easiest to just kill them and take their ship."

The sin in the boat kept their heads low, but Beast heard them chuckling.

"Then we just go looking?"

"From the reports, it's as big as a city. Can't be that hard to find," Beast replied.

"Well, you're right about that," Jurian said, and when Beast looked over his shoulder, he saw him pointing out past the Maraman raiding ship.

The men peered across the water and tried to make sense of what they were seeing. Rising from the horizon were more masts than there were ships in Samas. The closer they got, the larger the monstrosity became. As it took form, Beasts was reminded of the walls of a city, except these walls were floating on water.

"That was easy," Beast said.

"Sure, but what do we do about it?" Hanz replied.

"One thing at a time. For now, our job is to get a hold of this raiding vessel. After that, we can decide how to tackle the juggernaut."

Beast continued to row, but any good humor on the boat disappeared under the looming shadow of the giant vessel on the horizon. Beast knew that as small as they were, there was no way the juggernaut could see them. The ship they were approaching was the far greater threat. Still, the sheer scale of the enemy vessel was hard to fathom, and Beast's mind kept wandering to it.

The constant waves didn't make it any easier to focus. Though they'd only been on the water for a few minutes, he already felt sick. He needed to get off this damn boat. The world wasn't supposed to rock constantly back and forth.

Finally, the ship grew close, and the cloud cover kept the night dark. When the silhouettes of the Maramans on board appeared on the deck, Hanz and Jurian raised their hands in greeting. The Maramans waved back, and Beast allowed himself a small sigh of relief. He had feared the Maramans would call out to one another.

They were close enough now it wouldn't matter if they were found out or not.

Beast navigated the boat alongside the ship, and the moment the lines were tossed down, Beast whispered, "Now."

The two sin in the stern raised their bows and fired in one smooth motion. Both arrows struck true and two dark shapes tumbled towards the water.

Beast was moving before they hit.

He leaped onto the ropes and climbed. Jurian was on the rope beside him, with Hanz right below. Beast didn't have to look down to know that the rest of the sin were following behind.

Beast heard the twang of bowstrings again, and this time the dull thuds of arrows striking flesh followed by bodies splashing in the water was impossibly loud in his ears. Beast was normally all for charging headlong into battle, but he had no idea what was waiting aboard the Maraman ship. Better to be quiet for as long as possible.

When he pulled himself over the gunwale, he crouched low and made his way behind a stack of barrels that lined the deck. Hanz and Jurian were the first sin to hit the deck behind him and they both drew their daggers with identical vicious grins.

Beast was finding his battle rage hard to tamp down as he watched the twins disappear into the shadows of the ship but managed to hold himself in check. Soon enough he would unleash himself on these animals.

And every drop of blood he spilled would be repayment for the farmers of Ilos.

12

———

The trip to Bulas would take several days, and as much as Sato wanted to get to work in Versun, he felt the time was necessary.

To say the least, he had some thoughts to share with the Firstborn.

He'd spent the first day of travel organizing those thoughts, but when he left the ferry this morning, he decided it was best to calm his mind before his meeting. Crispin had assured him that the time he was gone wouldn't be wasted and that, in fact, was necessary for them to put plans into motion. Sato had been a little nervous that his duplicitous lieutenant wouldn't go into more details, but Roko had promised to keep an eye on both Crispin and Alonzo.

Now, as he neared the capital, he felt a little more centered.

Returning to Bulas was an interesting experience. For as long as he could remember, the capital of Samas had been the place he called home. It was the city he knew best, and the place where the few people closest to him lived.

He'd only been gone for a few months, but today the city felt different, though he couldn't put his finger on any detail that made it so. The same taverns were open, the same guards were on duty, and the walls were as firm and imposing as they'd ever been.

Yet it felt as though he were visiting it for the first time.

After leaving Nightmane at the stables, Sato wandered around the streets for a bit. It was already well past noon, and Sato suspected the Firstborn wouldn't want to see him until the day's scheduled work was done. He'd always enjoyed Sato's visits near the end of the day.

Bulas didn't anger him the way Versun did. In Versun, the wealthy seemed to demand recognition. Shops and buildings were far more elaborate than any function required, and even the dress was gaudy.

There was even more wealth in Bulas. But when one lived so close to the light of the Firstborn, there seemed less need to flaunt it. Sato traveled through one of the richest districts of the city, prepared to be offended, but he wasn't.

People's clothing was fine, but the styles were subdued. Houses were sturdy, large, and well maintained, but the display of wealth ended there.

As always, Sato felt that Bulas represented what the Path could create. This was still a place where he would be happy to make a more permanent home, when his labors were over.

His first stop upon arriving was one of the bathhouses, where he briskly cleaned off the dirt and grime of the road. He imagined the Firstborn would have no complaints if Sato rested for a few hours, but Sato needed to put this meeting behind him, and he wouldn't make the same mistake as he had last time, appearing dusty and disheveled.

No. If the Path required him to stand against the

Firstborn, he would look the role. Although he ascribed little importance to appearance, he understood its importance in leadership.

From the bathhouse he went to his rooms in the castle. He still lived in the same room he'd had when he was young. It was a small room, barely large enough for a bed, a desk, and a washbasin. But it was all he'd ever needed. The Firstborn had offered him larger quarters twice—once when Sato's father had passed away, and once again when Sato had earned his first commission. Both times, Sato had politely declined. He'd never had need for more, and he was rarely home.

His walls were bare, and apart from a few clothes in the trunk at the foot of the bed, there was almost nothing to identify the room as Sato's. The only decoration was a sheathed sword leaned against the corner of the room, as though its owner had only put it down for a moment.

His father's sword.

He picked the sword up and ran his hand along the lacquered sheath. It was of the highest quality, although plain. Like Sato, his father had always detested ornamentation, particularly of weapons. Though Sato didn't draw the sword, he knew he'd find the same ethos at work on the blade itself.

What would his father make of all this?

Sato didn't know.

Truth was, he'd never known his father all that well. He'd been a commoner, raised to the highest ranks of the nobility due to his skills with a sword and an otherworldly grasp of leadership.

Sato almost knew more legends about the man than he had memories. Father was always out campaigning, always returning with glory glinting in his eyes. Sato had treasured their brief times together, often spent in training. Father hadn't been Sato's primary instructor, but he'd been the teacher who transformed Sato from a competent swordsman to a great one.

But they'd rarely talked with one another. Sato's father tended to speak more in commands than in dialogue.

His father had been close to the Firstborn, though. Perhaps as close as it was possible for anyone to be to the ruler. They'd been friends. Would his father frown now on the direction Sato's thoughts traveled?

Sato put the sword back in the corner. He didn't know, and what did it matter? His father was dead, no longer able to influence the course of the world. What mattered now was Sato. Sato, the Firstborn, and the Path.

He took a deep breath and left the room, walking through the castle until he reached the receiving chambers. It was near the end of the day, and the Firstborn's advisor asked if Sato might not wait for a few minutes while the Firstborn finished one last audience. Sato agreed without hesitation and waited.

While he waited, he meditated. All the way from Versun, he'd thought about this meeting and how it might unfold. But the truth was, even after all these years, he found the Firstborn frustratingly difficult to predict.

Sato trusted in the Path, and that it would show him the way as soon as he entered the receiving hall.

Now that he was this close, he was surprised by how difficult he found his anger to control. The Firstborn bore the ultimate responsibility for the people of Samas. It was his duty to protect them, and thanks to his magistrates, he'd failed. Even worse was the possibility he'd known. Sato clenched his fists, glad that swords were not allowed in the presence of the Firstborn.

He took several deep breaths, finally mastering his frustration.

The Firstborn owed him answers. More than that, the Firstborn owed the people of Samas change.

In time, a group of advisors left the receiving room. They gave Sato inquisitive looks as they passed, but he ignored them. No doubt, his arrival had already been noted by dozens of nobles, each one wondering what role Sato would play now that he'd returned.

Let them guess.

This...this was between Sato and the Firstborn.

The Firstborn's chief advisor gestured for Sato to enter. He stood smoothly and straightened out his attire, ensuring he was prepared for an audience. Then he stepped toward the door.

The Firstborn would bring Samas back to the true tenets of the Path.

If he wouldn't, then Sato would do it for him.

13

———

"You're sure you don't know what was taken from you?" Yuki asked again.

Shin considered the question as she looked back at the sin arrayed behind them. Twenty warriors, including four adepts, road at brisk pace towards one of the beaches the sin used to travel back to the village.

Shin would have felt better if it was an army.

"I'm sure," she answered.

Yuki nodded but said nothing. Her impossible-to-read face didn't add any comfort to the gesture. "Once we secure the next rift, we'll figure it out. I don't want you using any sacrifice while we're there. We still don't know what effect your actions on Ilos will have. Not to mention we don't know what's happening to you. Until we can figure out a way for you to control what the realm takes, I don't want you losing any more memories."

Shin was about to protest, but Yuki held up a hand to forestall her. Shin nodded. It was frustrating, but for now she had to trust that in matters of sacrifice and the realm, Yuki knew best.

As usual, Yuki guessed her thoughts.

"I understand. You've tasted what you are capable of and now you want to gorge yourself on the power. Restraint in the face of such temptation is difficult, but I promise you this: if you feast too soon, the consequences will be dire. You may have already upset a balance that has existed for generations."

Shin stewed in the boat. Though Yuki was as expressionless as ever, Shin knew the sin leader was furious about the events on Ilos. Shin didn't fully understand why. She'd solved a problem. If Yuki would just trust her, she'd solve more. She tried convincing Yuki again.

"But it doesn't seem like I'm losing anything. How much could a memory matter? You said yourself that I was different. Maybe the realm takes less from me?"

Yuki raised an eyebrow and smiled. The expression seemed calculated rather than a genuine reaction. "The barrier that surrounds our home is a spell of infinite complexity and magnitude. Hiding an entire island in plain sight is a feat I don't think could be repeated. Do you know what toll the realm exacted in order to allow it?"

Shin shook her head.

"Neither do I. The sin who cast it lost herself completely in the days that followed. She retreated into herself for a while before finally attempting to wrest control of the sin away from its founder. Many lives were lost that day, including her own. I may not know what it cost her, but the cost to the sin was far too high. And she had even more promise than you. Remember this when you begin to feel like you are special."

"I would never—" Shin began.

"No. *You* wouldn't. Buy whatever that realm takes from

you, slowly over time, may just turn you into someone who would."

"Is that what happened to the sin who cast that spell?" Corin asked. He hadn't spoken much since he had stared into the demon mist, and Shin was relieved to see him participating in the conversation.

"I believe so. At our level of power, the cost is higher than we even know, usually until it's too late."

There was something there, a tone as close to regret as Shin had ever heard spill from Yuki's lips.

"Can I use—I mean, I stared into that thing..." Corin started to ask before drifting off and staring at Yuki with a concerned look on his face.

"No, Corin. You can't use sacrifice now," Yuki responded to the half-posed question.

Corin sagged with relief.

"Mere exposure to the realm will not result in the ability to use sacrifice if the subject doesn't have the aptitude to begin with. I am curious, though, what result your exposure will have."

"Really?" Corin asked.

"Yes. Why else do you think I allowed you to come with us? I want to keep as close an eye on you as I can. We've had enough surprises for one month."

Corin nodded, and Shin wished she knew how her friend was feeling. His face was surprisingly difficult to read. It was as if he'd been taking lessons from Yuki. She leaned toward him. "How are you? Getting sucked into one of those things is horrible."

Corin's face dropped a little and the mask finally slipped. "I'm fine. It was scary, of course, and I know if you weren't there I would have been killed. Probably by a demon version of me." He looked down at his hands. "But I feel strong now. I *know* how to fight. Like I never did before. Now I can get a little payback for Mateo."

Shin bristled slightly at the mention of Mateo but contained it. Mateo's memory, and the obligation Corin felt towards it, was like an oath he invoked to ward away his fears. The image of her parents' heads on spikes in front of her family home flashed in her mind.

Shin could relate.

"I'm sure you'll make him proud," Shin said, and Corin grinned once more.

As worried as she was, Shin was glad to have a friend by her side as they rode towards the sin island. The rift there had expanded, but the question was: how bad was it? They'd hurried to the island to find out.

The rest of the journey passed mostly in silence. They had managed to get most of the sin onto the boats at the beach, but a few would need to return to pick up the remaining sin. Yuki had been sure to get all the adepts on the first boats.

Before Shin could ask if they were nearing the island, they hit the edge of the spell and it came into view. An eerie crimson glow emanated from the woods above the village.

"The rift..." Shin began.

"We're too late," Raya finished.

"We don't know that yet. The sin will fight the demons until their last breath, and I refuse to accept there are no sin left on the island," Yuki said.

No one responded to Yuki's words, but the rising fear in the group stopped just short of panic. Once they hit the beach they started running.

They moved along the forest trail as quickly as they

could, but could only run so fast along the twisted, narrow trail. The switchback that led them down into the valley where the village was concealed slowed them even more. The natural defenses of the village worked against them.

When they finally made it down the steep incline, the village was in a state of organized chaos. The sin weren't evacuating yet, but preparations were being made. The youngest among them, including most of the luan that had come here with Shin, were huddled near the edge of the village. Adults organized their small belongings and prepared packs with food and water. Shin saw no warriors and guessed that they were all at the rift.

"They're following protocol," Raya said. "Someone must have noticed the disturbance in the rift before it was too late."

Yuki nodded but said nothing. They continued running through town, towards the rift.

When they got to the center of town, the screams began. Shin looked ahead to see a sin warrior running at full speed towards them. At first, Shin assumed they were running from one of the demons.

Almost too late, she realized it *was* a demon.

Yuki's curved blade shot out and tangled in the sin-demon's feet, felling it. When she pulled the weapon back, it severed one of the demon's legs. As it staggered towards them, Raya's sword cleaved its head off and it turned into mist. Raya closed her eyes, and a crimson glow surrounded her and the mist. Before she could send it back, another sin-demon charged her.

Raya remained perfectly still as the sin behind her surged forward.

The sin engaged the demons, always in groups of at least

three, and the adepts took up positions behind the line to send them back.

At first, it seemed as though the battle would go smoothly. They were dispatching demons without taking losses and Shin dared to hope. Then they advanced past the center of the village and Shin saw what they were truly up against.

The sin villagers valiantly held back the demons so that the youth could escape. Here, there was a mix of both sin-demons as well as wildlife demons from the surrounding forest. She looked at Yuki.

"Prepare yourself, Shin. I think none of the sin who went to defend the rift survived."

The demons' uncontrolled rage was all that worked in the sin's favor. Had the demons fought as a unit they would have overwhelmed the sin in moments. Instead, they piled onto villagers, wasting precious moments and allowing the sin to gain the slimmest of footholds against their advance.

She waded into the fray with Harmony spinning. She parried blows and struck only when she was certain that she could remove a limb. Flesh wounds meant nothing to these enemies. She kept Yuki close so she didn't have to face any demon alone.

The villagers were no helpless victims, either. While not all sin served as warriors, all possessed the training of one, and they fought bravely. Unfortunately, they were no match for the insidious mixture of demon strength and sin skill that so many demons possessed. The sin warriors who had returned from Dahl did their best to help but refused to break their disciplined formation. It took them too long to advance

"The villagers are dying! We have to help them," Shin screamed to Yuki.

"If we rush forward, we'll die. Only our discipline gives us a chance in this battle," Yuki shouted back calmly.

"How many people will die for our victory?"

"As many as it takes."

Shin couldn't believe what she was hearing. They could save so many more. "Let me close it!"

"No! We can save our home without taking that risk."

Shin could hardly stand the insufferable calm with which Yuki condemned her own people to death. She wrestled with the idea of closing the rift anyway but held off. Instead, she took her anger out on the demon she and Yuki were fighting. When the head was removed and one of the adepts sent it back, Shin looked around the battlefield.

Ten paces ahead of her, an older woman fought a demon that stood nearly a head taller than her. The woman fought it off with a digging fork, but was losing ground quickly. With a glare at Yuki Shin broke ranks and moved to help the woman. The demon knocked the fork out of woman's hand, and Shin sent Harmony spinning through the air. The sacrificial bonds that connected her to the weapon allowed her to throw it with more accuracy than she could have on her own. The spinning blade caught the demon's neck and its head tumbled to the ground. The weapon's momentum carried it into the wooden door behind the demon.

The woman looked around briefly in astonishment before turning and running towards the evacuation on the other end of the village. Shin opened her hand to call back her weapon, but before she could, she was knocked to the ground.

She tried to roll her attacker off of her, but the long limbs and unnatural strength gave it leverage she could never hope to budge. She ended up on her back, staring into the nightmare eyes of a sin-demon.

The rictus grin opened wide and warm drool spilled onto her face. The hot breath filled her nose as she struggled to free her pinned arms, but the grip was like iron.

She couldn't move.

14

Blood pounding in his ears, Beast forced himself to take even breaths and assess the battlefield before him. The ship stretched out impossibly large in front of him. It was hard to tell in the dark, but he guessed it was no less than sixty feet long and thirty feet across. Even the largest skiffs used to transport goods between the islands of Samas were tiny by comparison.

Beast couldn't help but appreciate a vessel that could accommodate his size a little better.

When he looked onto the deck, he couldn't see the twins anywhere, but there were two crumpled forms lying in the shadows as evidence of their handiwork. They had moved quickly to prevent anyone from noticing the disappearance of the Maramans who were tasked with bringing up the longboat, but their absence could only be masked for so long.

Beast counted about ten remaining Maramans, including one manning the large steering wheel towards the back of the ship. If anyone was going to see the twins, it was him, but he seemed focused on keeping the vessel steady as they picked up speed. There were another two lookouts mid-ship, but their focus was out on the water.

Beast saw one of them disappear.

A moment later, the second one fell.

Beast still couldn't see the twins and was once again shocked by just how invisible the sin could be. Finally, he saw a shadow moving towards the bodies of the Maramans the twins had killed first. This was about to turn into a fight.

The twins were doing well, but Beast thought it would be best to move into a position where he could help. He set about picking a target.

Before he could move, one of the Maramans called out in their language to the man steering. The helmsman acknowledged what was said and spun the wheel. The sails caught the wind, and the ship turned toward the enormous fortress.

Beast decided he should definitely kill him.

He had a better idea.

As silently as he could manage, Beast crept toward the Maraman. The hardest part was creeping alongside the elevated platform where the Maraman was steering. Beast's bulk, normally his greatest asset, was difficult to keep hidden.

He lay on his belly and crawled behind a stack of barrels. From that point there was only one small open space where he would risk being seen. He watched the Maraman for a few minutes and tried to see a pattern. The man studied the ocean in front of him before checking on his heading. Beast just had to wait until his head was turned away.

There.

The moment the Maraman checked the opposite side, Beast moved, quickly and quietly, to the cover of the elevated platform. Now, sneaking up on his target would be child's play.

He may not have been as silent as the twins, but he was still quiet enough to get within arm's reach of the Maraman. As he drew his dagger a cry went up. Beast guessed the dead Maramans had been found. The helmsman turned at the sound and saw Beast just in time to catch Beast's wrist as he struck out with the dagger.

The moment the Maraman let go of the wheel, the ship turned sharply and they were both thrown to the deck. The two men rolled together briefly before they were tossed apart. Beast's dagger skittered across the deck.

Beast heard the battle as the mugon who had been waiting for the twins to thin the ranks charged onto the deck. The helmsman regained his feet first and moved to get the ship under control. Beast, itching to join the fray, weighed the danger of an out-of-control ship against leaving an enemy alive and promptly buried his axe in the back of the Maraman helmsman.

The ship bucked again, but Beast kept his feet. He grabbed the wheel to steady them and then bellowed for his mugon to join him. He strained to keep the ship straight as he watched mugon engage Maramans coming up from below the deck.

Finally, one of his mugon reached the platform.

"Steer!" Beast bellowed and pulled the man towards the wheel.

"How?" the mugon asked.

"Figure it out!"

Beast leaped down the stairs to help one of his mugon who was being overwhelmed. Suddenly, the planks shifted beneath him as his mugon lost control of the ship. Beast hit the deck hard but bounced up quickly.

He moved towards the Maramans who, after regaining their balance, looked around to see what was happening. Beast cut them down before they had time to react.

The mugon and Maramans continued their battle midship, but Beast was looking for the twins. Finally, he saw them battling against a knot of Maramans towards the bow. Their sneaking had gotten them deep into the Maramans but now they were cut off from the rest of the mugon.

Beast barreled towards them.

The Maramans converged on the twins. Hanz and Jurian tossed their daggers, more to buy time than to kill, and picked up swords from the fallen Maramans.

Beast sprinted into the battle to help. He hopped up onto the platform where the mast rose from the deck, shimmied around the wooden pillar, and leaped off, intending his full weight to land on one of the Maramans.

Instead, the man steering lost control once more while Beast was in the air, and he landed in a crumpled heap beside his intended target. The Maraman, a seasoned sailor, navigated the quick turn easily and closed in on Beast with his dagger drawn.

Beast had time to spin onto his back and catch the dagger, as well as the full weight of the man holding it, before it plunged into his skull. Beast's arms burned, but he only had to hold out long enough to get his feet on the man's hips.

The dagger inched closer while Beast pushed with his knees against the man's body. Slowly, space began to form, and he was able to get one foot under his assailant. Then another. Finally, he pushed with all his considerable strength and sent the man flying off the boat and into the ocean.

Beast sprang up and moved to help once more. Only two

Maramans remained, each engaged with one of the twins. Beast joined them and the matter was quickly decided.

"I think that's all of them," Jurian said as he surveyed the mugon celebrating their victory.

The ship bucked again, and the three men grabbed onto the gunwale to stay themselves.

"Sorry!" the mugon at the helm called.

"I found us someone to steer," Beast said, smiling.

"Is that why we were being thrown all over the place?" Jurian asked.

"I'm not sure what you're talking about," Beast responded. "He's doing great. Do you know how to get to the port from here? I think we should show Yuki our new toy."

"I do, but what if they follow?" Hanz said, pointing at the giant Maraman ship in the distance.

"By the time they realize that someone else is in control of their ship, we'll be long gone. Besides, these are raiders. Pirates. They won't hit a fortified position like Dahl. They'll keep terrorizing the poor farmers unless we get back and organize a proper defense of the island."

"Agreed. We must reach Yuki at once. Good work, Beast. You were pretty quiet," Jurian said.

Beast was about to thank him when Hanz interrupted. "For a mugon."

Beast shook his head.

15

—————

Sato wasn't sure exactly what he'd expected when he entered the Firstborn's receiving room. Though he'd imagined the situation a hundred times on the journey to Bulas, he'd never settled on one outcome as being most likely.

The Firstborn was too unpredictable.

But as Sato stepped into the familiar room, he saw the Firstborn, who beamed at him as though he were a child just returned from distant shores. "Sato! As always, it is a pleasure to see you."

And just for a moment, Sato was a child again, kneeling before the Firstborn, accepting his instruction and wisdom. His home wasn't the palace, nor even Bulas. It was here, before this man.

His anger burned too bright, though, its flames devouring the momentary peace he felt.

He bowed stiffly and formally.

When he rose, he studied the man who had raised him as a son.

No doubt, the Firstborn's sharp eyes had caught every nuance of Sato's movement. But the smile on his face never faltered. He studied Sato for a moment, then said, "This hall is too formal for our reunion after so long. Will you join me in my study for tea?"

Sato bowed, agreeing to the request. No doubt, the Firstborn saw his anger and sought to placate him in some way. But no amount of tea would douse the fire burning in his chest.

The Firstborn led the way, exiting through one door, passing through a short hallway, and opening another. This door led to a small room, the walls filled with books. The Firstborn's study, one of his two favorite rooms in the palace. There was a desk there, where the Firstborn often caught up on the reports his advisers prepared for him. Today, he ignored the desk and took one of the seats near a small table in the corner.

A teapot was already sitting there, steaming.

Sato sat down next to the Firstborn. "You never intended to remain in the receiving hall."

The smile never left the Firstborn's face. He shook his head softly as he poured the tea. "I suspected the matters you and I have to discuss are better shared here."

"I came to give you my report on the events in Dahl."

"No, you didn't."

The Firstborn's voice was calm and even, but it still surprised Sato. His tongue tied itself in knots as he searched for a response.

The Firstborn sipped at his tea, the look of contentment on his face one that could never be faked. He set his cup down, then spoke. "I would hear of the events in Dahl, but there is a matter even more important that we must address."

"More important?" Sato felt as though he were stuttering. What could be more important than the fall of Samas' breadbasket? And the corruption that had led to it?

"You," the Firstborn said. "And the reason you have come here today. Would you like to talk about it?"

If it was possible, Sato's tongue tied itself even tighter.

The Firstborn sipped at his tea again. When Sato remained unable to reply, he spoke again. "You are here because you have met the sin. Most likely, you've even met Yuki by now. You've seen and experienced the power of the sin firsthand. But more important than all of that, and the problem that truly consumes you, is that you've finally understood the corruption that eats at Samas from the inside. All of this causes you to doubt. You doubt your fellow sentinels. You doubt much of what you've been told. Perhaps you even doubt me. Am I close?"

Every sentence had been stated calmly, and though the Firstborn no longer smiled, that same sense of peace still radiated from him.

"Yes," Sato managed to say.

"Tell me about it," the Firstborn said. "Tell me everything and leave out nothing."

"Nothing?"

"Not even the smallest part."

Sato knew it for a test. As much as he loved the Firstborn, everything was always a test.

Today, though, the tables were turned. It wasn't just his test, but one for the Firstborn as well. He wanted to know everything? Sato would give him everything. Then, based on the Firstborn's reaction, perhaps Sato would know how to proceed.

So Sato spoke, the words pouring out of him faster than the contents of the teapot. He spoke of his own struggles with leading the sun stalkers, and how he'd come close to losing them before the mission had even started. He spoke of his efforts to fight the mugon, and the encounter with the sin and the demons. And he recounted his capture in Dahl, the disgraceful behavior of the magistrate, and the battle for the city.

The Firstborn listened well, asking questions whenever he wanted a point of clarification. His face fell when Sato spoke of the magistrate and the corruption in Dahl. But he neither interrupted nor protested, which made Sato think the information was less newsworthy than Sato had thought.

By the time Sato finished, the sun had fallen, and the Firstborn had lit lanterns to keep the darkness at bay.

Sato took a deep breath, waiting for the result of his monologue. When the Firstborn made no reply, Sato blurted out the question that had tormented him for so long. "I know you know about this corruption, this disease that eats at Samas. Why have you not done anything to stop it?"

The Firstborn raised an eyebrow. "What makes you think I've done nothing?"

When Sato had no answer, the smile returned to the Firstborn's face. "Is it because you believe I would succeed? Do I still sit so high in your estimation?"

"You're the Firstborn!" Sato said, as though that explained everything.

"And I sit upon a base of power made of dozens of magistrates and nobles. If you had told Crispin, 'follow the Path, or else,' how would that have gone?"

Sato laughed at the thought. Crispin couldn't find the Path unless it was lined with gold pieces.

"Do you think the magistrates and nobles are so different?"

The question froze Sato's thoughts. He'd never thought to compare the magistrates to Crispin. His lieutenant had always seemed like something of a special case. With one question, the Firstborn had cracked open Sato's narrow vision of the world.

Again.

How much wider would his vision have to stretch?

"You've guessed, by now, why I put you in command of the sun stalkers."

"You wanted me to experience commanding officers not as committed to the Path as I am."

The Firstborn nodded. "And not just because I believed it would make you a better commander."

The implication felt like a punch to the stomach. Sato saw now that it would make him a better Firstborn, too.

But at the same time he was basking in pride, his anger flared up again. There was a flaw in the Firstborn's logic. "I understand now that the Path must sometimes be bent for the good of Samas. But it has been bent out of shape under your rule, and the people suffer because of it."

The Firstborn still smiled, but it seemed to Sato there was no joy in it anymore. "Do you believe this corruption began during my rule?"

Sato frowned.

"When I became Firstborn, I inherited all the systems of my predecessor, just as she did those before her. You're right to be angry at the corruption, but you also must realize it is a part of the system."

He held up a hand to stall Sato's outburst.

"That is no justification. And yes, perhaps I have been

too lenient. I have always made the choices I thought best for Samas when I made them, but I am not always right." The Firstborn paused. "Sometimes, I think that is why I feel such great hope when I look at you."

The confession caught Sato by surprise. "What do you mean?"

"Have you ever asked yourself why you? Why I've groomed you so closely, even as other nobles and magistrates have begged for more consideration?"

Sato hadn't. It had just been a part of his life for so long he'd never really thought much about it. And, if he was being honest, he'd always assumed it was because he was the best choice there was.

"I chose you, not because you're a strong soldier or an inspired strategist. I've plenty of those. I chose you because of who you are. Your character and commitment to the Path. You needed the sun stalkers to teach you the world isn't as black as white as you thought, but I also knew you wouldn't accept the world as it was. You would fight to change it. Seeing you here, as angry as you are, makes me more certain than ever I was right in my decision."

Sato stopped, uncertain how to respond. In the end, he went with how he felt. "Thank you, sir."

The Firstborn looked out the window of his study. "It is getting late, and there is much yet to be done. Come to me again when you are ready."

"Ready?"

"There's no reason to wait," the Firstborn said with a smile. "If you have solutions to the problems plaguing Samas, I would hear them. Perhaps together we can achieve what I alone have failed to do."

Sato couldn't believe what he was hearing. He'd prepared himself to do whatever it took to bring Samas back to the Path. Even if that meant usurping the Firstborn, his closest friend and mentor. He hadn't realized just how much he dreaded that prospect until he felt the relief of avoiding it.

He left the study that night with a smile on his face.

16

Shin desperately sought the offerings of the realm. Dead, black eyes glared down at her as a mouth full of razor-sharp teeth neared her face. She tried to form a tangible desire that could save her, but her thoughts couldn't escape those jaws, ready to devour her like prey. The realm was there. All she needed to do was ask and her desires would be met.

But she couldn't form the question.

Panic welled up inside of her as the hot breath of the demon caressed her exposed neck. She struggled with all her might to get free. She tried to call her weapon to her, but she couldn't focus on the task. In her final moments, despite how far she had come and all she had learned, all she could do was close her eyes and hold her breath like a child diving underwater.

Then the weight on top of her was gone.

Shin stood up, careful to avert her gaze from the shadowy mist that would try to steal her form. She locked eyes with Corin instead.

"Are you hurt?" he asked.

"No, thanks to you," Shin replied.

Before she could say anything else, another demon was upon them.

Shin called Harmony back to her hand while Corin engaged their attacker. His forms were crisp and clean. He parried the fused sword arm of the attacking sin-demon competently and Shin could see in him a confidence that wasn't there a day ago.

The demon, unfortunately, was more than competent. As Corin gave ground, Shin moved to help him. The moment that Corin was about to be forced back, Shin stepped in and pushed the demon back instead. Once it focused on her, Corin leaped in. After a brutal minute of attrition, the demon was overwhelmed, and its head severed. It lost its form, and the mist was wrapped in a crimson light that Shin traced back to Raya.

Raya sent three demons to the rift while Yuki danced around her, engaged with a final demon. Corin and Shin joined Yuki, finally hacking the demon's head off.

"Are we winning?" Shin asked as she looked around the village turned battlefield.

Everywhere she looked, trios of sin were methodically pushing back demons. Their lines held, but their progress through the village was painfully slow.

"There is no winning if we don't push towards the rift. This fight will last forever if we don't seal them away."

As if to prove her point, a pair of demon-wolves emerged from the path heading toward the rift and charged the village.

"The bulk of the sin warriors assigned to defend the rift are unaccounted for here. If we head to the rift, we'll need most of our forces to seal it," Raya said.

Yuki watched the approach of the wolves for a moment

before coming to a decision. "You three, help the villagers hold off the animals and send any of them you kill to the rift. The rest of us will go seal it."

The three sin nodded and ran to engage the wolves. Raya sprinted off, shouting orders to the remaining sin. Shin stared wide-eyed at Yuki, who returned her gaze.

"The villagers can't hold off this onslaught with only three sin to help them," Shin said. "Let me close it. I can save us right now!" Shin demanded.

"Likely, but what if we lose you in the process? A few lives saved here could cost us everything later."

Shin swore. What was the point of having her abilities if she couldn't use them?

She hated this feeling. Her mentor was a coward, unwilling to use the weapons at hand. But Yuki was her senior, both in power and experience.

"Fine, but I'm staying here to help fight," Shin said through gritted teeth.

Yuki considered her calmly for a moment. "Allowed, but Corin stays with you."

Corin nodded. Shin, for her part, didn't bother answering. She whirled away and ran back towards the demons assaulting the village.

The small bubble of calm that had been created by the sin's meticulous advance through the village collapsed as Yuki led her force towards the rift. The sounds of battle grew louder in her ears as Shin sprinted to help.

When she reached the closest demons, the sight of the remaining villagers almost brought Shin to tears. They fought valiantly against the grotesque enemies, but they were losing.

One woman's stomach was ripped open by sharp claws. Intestines spilled to the ground as she tried to make one last killing blow against a demon that didn't know death. Shin and Corin cut the demon down and moved on, trusting the adept to do her job.

Around another corner, an old man was thrust through a wall.

Here, a child lay still.

Shin fought furiously, but all the while she knew that every minute lost was a minute more sin died.

"The luan!" Corin said after they dispatched a wolf.

One of the sin warriors with them had died, his throat torn out by oversized fangs. The adept sent the mist forms back to the rift and then staggered to one knee, exhausted. After a moment, she and the remaining warrior with her moved on to the next demon. Corin moved to follow, but Shin held him back.

"I'm closing it," Shin said.

Corin looked like he was about to protest, but instead nodded grimly. "I'll watch your back."

Shin shut her eyes and opened herself up to the realm. This time, her focus was razor sharp. She formed her request and the scaffolding of the sacrifice she'd used to close the rift on Ilos laid itself out before her. She began to form the sacrifice in her mind and felt the weaves of the rift before her.

"Shin!" she heard Corin call out, and the sacrifice faltered.

Shin felt a strange pressure in her mind. Too late, she opened her eyes to see a crimson-robed Maraman sprinting toward them. Before she could move, the stumps where his arms should have been extended into flickering red blades. He leaped through the air and struck out with a blow that was barely blocked by Corin.

The blow knocked Corin to the ground, but, with a skill

he hadn't had a day ago, he bounced back to his feet and engaged the Maraman. The crimson blades were a blur, but Corin parried the blows in time. The deadly exchange took the two men away from Shin and she looked for a moment to engage. Finally, Corin sidestepped a cut and put the summoner between himself and Shin.

Shin threw Harmony. She directed the whirling blade towards the Maraman's exposed back, but at the last moment, he seemed to sense something and brought his own sacrificial weapons up to deflect her attack. Corin tried to capitalize on the opening, but the Maraman turned in time to block Corin's strike. Then the summoner headbutted the smaller man in the nose, crumpling him to the ground.

Harmony had bounced away, but Shin brought it back to her hand. It slapped into her palm just as she reached the Maraman. Her attack was furious, but he survived it. Each time she blocked one of his blows, a small blast of light emanated from the point of contact that pushed Shin back. It was enough to keep her from getting her own offense going.

Finally, instead of blocking a strike, Shin sidestepped a looping swing and brought Harmony up and into the summoner's chest. The crimson blades winked out of existence, and he fell to the ground with a wet gurgle.

"Corin?" she shouted.

"Go! I'm fine!" Corin interrupted her question.

Shin sprinted towards the edge of the village where the luan had been huddled with the other children. The place in the village farthest removed from the rift. As she ran, she felt the rift seal shut and was flooded with relief. Finally, Yuki had done something.

When she reached the luan, that feeling was gone.

The last remaining sin warrior was staking a demon wolf to the ground. The elongated jaws snapped futility at the sin. The adept saw her round the corner and smiled grimly.

"We couldn't send this one back before the rift sealed. We'll have to coordinate with another adept to open the rift and send it back."

Shin barely heard her. Her eyes swept across the crowd of children cowering together. Within the crowd, she could see her luan clutching each other.

All but four of them.

The four oldest luan were lying on the ground in front of the other children. Their bodies were ripped and broken, and weapons lay scattered around them. They died buying the younger children time so that the rift could be sealed.

Time they wouldn't have needed if Shin had been allowed to close the rift.

Shin dropped to her knees and looked to the sky. She let out a scream of grief and rage that echoed across the village.

She hoped Yuki heard it.

17

"Slow us down!" Beast bellowed as he clung to the gunwale for dear life.

"How do you suggest we do that?" Jurian said back, infuriatingly calm.

"I'm trying, but I've never sailed anything this big!" the mugon who was manning the helm shouted.

"Just drop whatever sails you can!" Beast ordered to the mugon. Unfortunately, most of them had never been on the water before today.

The mugon scattered, doing their best to drop sails wherever they could. But the sheets were filled, and it wasn't going well. The helmsmen cried out and spun the wheel as he realized he was going to charge right into an outcropping of rocks. He managed to change course, but the sudden sharp turn threw Beast to the deck. By the time Beast stood up, the sails were down, but the momentum of the ship carried it forward. They weren't going to stop in time.

"Better hold on to something," Jurian said.

Beast grabbed the gunwale once more and heard a

sickening crunch as the ship ran aground in the shallows and finally came to a stop.

"Well, that could have been worse," Hanz said, smiling.

Beast rolled his eyes and stalked up to the helm. "Well, at least we know this ship's not going anywhere," he said. He looked out at the port, still being repaired after the Maraman assault. "Do you think any of our sailors could handle a boat like this? I mean actually handle it, not crash it into the shallows."

The mugon who was steering turned red and beat a hasty retreat to his comrades. Beast couldn't be too hard on the man. He'd done more to get them home than almost anyone else.

"Perhaps," Jurian said. "I know very little about sailing, but this ship is far more complex than the skiffs used to ferry people and supplies between islands."

"I think this ship is going to be the key to fighting back against the Maraman pirates, if we can figure out how to sail it. Maybe Yuki will have an idea."

"She usually does," Hanz said, his tone dry.

As he did almost every day, Beast thought of Benji. Perhaps he was being overly sentimental, but he just had this feeling Benji would know what to do here. He'd always known.

The loss of Benji still hit as hard as a falling building, but Yuki and the twins were able to fill at least some of the void left by his friend. He touched the hilt of Benji's broken sword, still tucked in his belt, before nodding and climbing off the grounded vessel.

The trip to Dahl was short and the three men spoke little. Beast noticed a fair amount of food being transported in carts and wagons towards the port. He made a note to ask Yuki about it. When they reached the gates of Dahl, Beast was impressed with the progress that had been made in repairing the city. The gates themselves had been the priority and were almost as good as new. The rest of the city was coming along nicely.

Despite all the work, there was an air of despair that was palpable. Eyes were downcast, people weren't talking much, and when they were, they seemed to be huddled together as if comforting each other.

"What's going on here?" Beast asked the twins, who simply shrugged.

They made their way to the magistrate's tower, but were informed that Yuki, Shin and Corin were currently in the sin village attending to urgent matters.

"What matters?" Beast asked.

"I'm afraid I don't know for certain," the young sin woman who met them at the tower explained. "All I know is that Sheyric is handling the affairs in Dahl while Yuki is away."

Beast raised an eyebrow at the familiar name. During Beast's ascension to Bandit King, Sheyric had been a member of his honor guard and fought beside him often. After joining the sin, and complicating his life immeasurably, Beast had lost track of the quiet swordsman. "Lead the way."

The sin nodded and led them through the tower. When they entered the receiving chambers, Beast broke into a grin at the sight of Sheyric sitting behind Yuki's large desk shuffling papers.

"Yuki must not have the eye for talent she claims she's got if she's relying on you to run a whole city. I've never seen you solve a problem without cutting it in half."

When Sheyric looked up and saw Beast's giant form filling the doorway, he gave a tight-lipped smile, which was the equivalent of jumping up and down in joy for Sheyric. "Well, she had me take over your bumbling efforts, so she has some sense, at least."

Beast laughed and rounded the desk to wrap the unwilling man in a giant hug. When he put him back down, Sheyric's face had become serious once more.

"Yuki left word for you before she left. The Maramans somehow tore open the rifts around Samas. Yuki, Corin and Shin dealt with the one here on Ilos and then headed to the sin village to fix that one."

Hanz spoke up. "How is that possible?"

"Yuki believes the summoners were involved, but that was only a guess. I'm sorry Hanz, Jurian, I know that's your home."

"Don't worry," Hanz said calmly.

"Yuki can handle it," Jurian finished. He echoed his brother's tone, but they were both straining to maintain the facade.

"She wants us to help?" Beast asked.

"No, she said she wants the three of you to continue defending against the raids on the farms in Ilos. My instructions are to support you however you need."

"Perfect. It's the Maramans raiding the farms. They're using their ships to hit Ilos fast and get out even faster. If we allow it to continue, most of the farmers here are going to be slaughtered within the month," Beast said.

"Similar to how we were striking at the sentinels," Sheyric noted.

"Exactly. The first thing we need to do is establish regular patrols of the island. The twins and I have already discussed the moving parts involved and think we have enough forces to do a passable job. We can implement that immediately."

Sheyric nodded.

Beast smiled at their reversal of roles. It wasn't so long ago that he was giving the orders to Sheyric. Not for the first time, Beast noted how much he preferred being in the action rather than overseeing it. "I think we need to address the bigger issue, though. We followed one of their ships out to sea and found a giant floating fortress. Until we destroy it, we're constantly going to be on our back foot."

"Sounds like you have a plan," Sheyric said.

"The beginnings of one. We stole one of their ocean-faring ships. And if we can steal one, we can steal more. Steal enough, and then we head out and sink that monster."

"But?"

"But the Maraman ships are difficult to sail, and we don't have time to learn. We need to find people that can handle a ship like that."

Sheyric leaned back in his chair and considered the problem. After a moment, he nodded. "I may know someone who can help."

"Of course you do," Beast said. Sheyric had always been well-connected. That, plus his sword skills, had made him a valuable part of the mugon in the early days.

"It may require you to head to a less-than-reputable part of the port. Do you think you can handle a place like that?" Sheyric's tone was as dry as a tavern after Beast had visited.

"It may surprise you to know this, but I've got a bit of experience in less-than-reputable establishments."

This time, Sheyric did smile. "Of course you do."

18

The next time Sato went to see the Firstborn, he had a scheduled appointment and notes. As he walked through the hallways, he couldn't help but draw comparisons to when he'd been a younger man.

He'd walked through the same hallways then, just as confident, papers filled with answers to the questions the firstborn had given him. They'd go over the work together, the Firstborn examining Sato's solutions.

It was never about being right or wrong, though Sato tended to believe he'd gotten most of the answers right. But governance was rarely so simple. It was about finding the best answer.

Or, in Sato's opinion, the answer that kept Samas closest to the Path.

Was it really that different now?

He arrived early and waited for his audience. At the appointed time, he was shown into the Firstborn's study.

The Firstborn already had tea prepared, and they immediately went to work. To honor the Firstborn's other commitments, Sato would take up no more than his allotted time.

"Our first problem is Ilos," Sato began. "Between the mugon's raids, the fall of Dahl, and the Maraman invasion, we have little in the way of sentinel strength on the island. What we do have is disorganized and probably in hiding."

"In this, I can ease your mind," the Firstborn said. "For now, we must abandon Ilos."

Sato wasn't sure he'd heard right. "Sir? If we abandon Ilos, we won't have the food to last the winter."

"Yuki has already sent a raven. She will send food in line with the amounts the magistrates agreed to."

"At what cost?"

"None."

Sato frowned. "That makes no sense."

The Firstborn studied Sato, and once again, he felt like a child before the master. "Why not?"

"That food represents one of her most valuable assets. At the very least, I would expect her to demand concessions."

"You speak of her as though she's our enemy."

"Isn't she?"

The Firstborn took a sip of his tea. "I don't believe so."

Sato almost spit out his tea at the words. "How so?"

"I believe her aims to be the same as ours. To protect Samas, both from the corruption within and from the Maraman threat. She could, in fact, be one of our most valuable allies."

"I'm sorry, sir, but I don't believe that."

The Firstborn considered for a moment, then answered. "I don't believe you have to. We can hold both ideas in our heads. Whether enemy or ally, her immediate priorities are the same, correct?"

Sato nodded. "She needs to defend Ilos and rebuild Dahl. The sin are weaker now than they've been in ages. Which is exactly why we should attack her before she can consolidate power."

"You would launch an assault?"

Sato glanced down at his notes. "If we strip units from guarding our supply lines, and weaken the units guarding the cities, we can create a force large enough to overrun Ilos quickly. Even with the sin's unnatural abilities, we could defeat them before winter."

"You would weaken our own defenses when we know an enemy has just assaulted our lands?"

"We defeated the Maramans."

"At Dahl, yes. But you've seen the reports of raids along the coasts?"

Sato grimaced. He'd seen the reports but not paid them much mind. He assumed they were mugon, returning to their ways.

"I believe the risk from the Maramans is greater than the risk from the sin," the Firstborn said. "As such, I've already issued orders for all sentinels remaining on Ilos to retreat to Versun."

"You're surrendering it to the sin?"

"For now, yes. It costs us nothing and allows us to prepare for whatever comes next."

"Yuki could be saying the same thing right now."

"She very well might be, but for now, consider the issue of Ilos closed." The Firstborn made it clear there would be no more discussion. "What else do you have?"

"Versun," Sato said. "From what I have learned, its position as the center of trade in Samas has also made it the heart of the corruption eating the sentinels from the inside. If Ilos is no longer a concern, I would ask that you allow my sun stalkers to root out the corruption in the city. As it stands now, it is in no condition to repel an assault, nor does it have the necessary supplies to withstand a siege."

"That is not what the reports say," the Firstborn said.

"I've seen it with my own eyes, sir."

The Firstborn nodded, troubled. "The problem is deeper than I expected. I always expected officials to skim a bit off the top, but never expected them to fail in their duties." He noted Sato's expression. "Say it, Sato."

"Sir, if you tolerate people skimming off the top, it is nearly as good as condoning all other criminal activity."

The ruler of Samas accepted his chastisement. "Perhaps you are right." He thought for a moment. "I assume you've thought about your plan?"

"I've given it considerable thought, but I'm afraid it's still light on details. I simply haven't spent enough time in the city to know which magistrates and sentinels uphold the Path and which don't. My mission, with your permission, would be to purge the city of those who have sucked it dry, and replace them with sentinels and magistrates loyal to you and to the Path."

The Firstborn tapped his finger against the side of his teacup. "It's a dangerous game you play. The magistrates you accuse are also the ones who best know how the system works. If the corruption is as deep as you say, we may be harming the people best able to coordinate moving supplies from one island to the other."

Sato shrugged. "The sentinels have logistics officers. It is a solvable problem."

"And those you find? What will you do with them?"

"Interrogate them. Learn all that they know. Then execute them publicly for their crimes."

The Firstborn grimaced.

"You don't agree?" Sato asked. The men and women had betrayed the trust of the Firstborn and of Samas. What else did they deserve?

"Even you will need allies, Sato. Though the Path demands a life for the crimes many of them have committed, think through what that might mean for you. You will be killing people's mothers, fathers, and friends. All in the name of the Path."

"I do, so that no one else will stray from the Path."

The Firstborn took a long sip of his tea. "Two days ago, you told me about the young woman, Shin. About the hatred she holds in her heart, not just for you, but for all sentinels. Her parents were punished according to the tenets of the Path, were they not?"

Sato immediately saw the Firstborn's point. The Firstborn feared a land full of those like Shin.

But in his fear, he missed the point.

"Shin's parents only stole because those supposed to protect them failed in their duty. Yes, the medicine I bring will be difficult for the land to swallow. But it's necessary all the same. Once we have returned to the Path, there will be no more like her. Because we will do our duty."

The Firstborn nodded. "I hope to someday see such a world, Sato. You have my blessing, and the orders will be delivered to your sun stalkers. But if I might leave you with one word of caution: there is a place on the path for mercy. Sometimes, it is the most powerful weapon we can wield. Don't let yours rust."

19

An unfavorable wind carried the smell of smoke and death up the switchback behind them. Shin did her best not to wonder at how many sin had been lost to the demons. The dead had been piled high and set ablaze, the necessity of safely disposing with the bodies outweighing any kind of ceremony honoring individual deaths. Shin took some solace in the number of people they had been able to save, but even that line of thinking ended in darkness. How could she be pleased with how many survived if even one person was lost because she didn't act?

Because she wasn't *allowed* to act.

She glared at the back of Yuki's head as she followed her up the trail. The woman had lost her power, and now she was a coward. Afraid of what Shin could do. Afraid Shin could do things even she couldn't.

Shin shook her head, suddenly bewildered. Yuki had done nothing but cultivate her strength. Why, suddenly, would she try to hold Shin back? The more she thought about it, the more she realized her theory didn't make sense.

Shin disagreed with Yuki's caution, but her intentions certainly shouldn't have come into question.

She was just tired. And worried.

She sped slightly so she could match pace with Yuki. "I'm sorry if I was short with you back there. I just wanted to help."

"I will never demand blind obedience. I am pleased you were willing to question orders and even more satisfied that you accepted my explanation. Both are marks of a good leader," Yuki said, then fixed her with a hard stare. "Just be sure you understand your own intentions. Desperate situations often appear as though they require desperate measures. In truth, they are often the time where your response should be the most measured."

Shin said nothing. The fire of anger she had felt towards Yuki only moments ago may have been tamped down, but she could still feel it smoldering despite her best efforts.

"Shin!" A tiny voice in the darkness interrupted her brooding.

"Tomas! What are you doing back here? You should be with the rest of the luan."

"We wanted to make sure you were safe," the young luan said before jumping into Shin's arms. "We don't want you to leave again."

Shin's heart broke with both pride and sadness when she saw the resilience on the young boy's face. With Corin's help they had buried the four luan who had died protecting their younger friends. The group had wept and held each other for a long time before Yuki gently insisted they had to return to Dhal.

"I know, Tomas, but the sin are your family now. You like all your new friends in the village, don't you?" The little boy nodded. "Good! And I'll come back and visit soon, I promise. Now, you run back to the village. It's late and you need sleep."

Tomas nodded and wrapped his arms tightly around her neck before hopping back to the ground. "We love you!"

Shin grinned through tears at the earnest, unconditional love of one so young.

"Keep them in your mind, Shin," Yuki said, nodding towards the tiny form running back down the trail. "They are as good a compass as any you can find in this world."

Their grim procession made their way up the switchback and through the woods to the beaches. By the time Shin arrived, the first of the skiffs returning to Dahl were already heading across the water. Shin noticed that the adept who had remained in the village, she had never gotten the woman's name, had remained on the island. Presumably to guard the rift, now repaired.

She didn't waste the opportunity to ask Yuki the questions troubling her mind. "Yuki, what happened? First the rift on Ilos, and now here? Was it the Maraman summoner?"

"I believe so. I expect he was the one who tore open the rift," Yuki said.

"Are the Maramans that powerful? To be able to manipulate the rifts at will?" Raya asked.

"They are. Their knowledge of sacrifice, or calling the realm, as they say, certainly surpasses our own. At a guess, I would assume the emperor sent summoners to each rift in case their main assault failed. Once it did, the summoners tore the rifts in an effort to sow chaos within Samas."

"How could he find the island, though?" Raya pressed.

"He wouldn't need to see through the sacrifice that kept the island hidden, only follow the presence of the rift. Which might have been easier if he was the same summoner who ripped open the rift on Ilos. Even so, it would take one keenly attuned to the realm to accomplish such a feat. The summoners are not to be trifled with."

Shin thought about the scaffolding of sacrifice she'd felt around the rift on the sin island when she had been trying to close it. Before the summoner's attack had interrupted her, she felt that scaffolding extend out to the other rifts in Samas. She could understand how the summoner had followed it like a map.

She was beginning to think she could do more than just follow it, but she kept the thought to herself.

"He didn't seem to be controlling the demons, though. How did he intend to survive?" Shin asked.

"He didn't," Raya said grimly.

Yuki nodded. "It was not a mission from which he intended to return. It seems our enemy, the emperor, inspires great loyalty in his subjects."

"Loyalty, or fear?" Raya asked.

"What could be worse than being torn apart by demons?" Yuki asked in turn.

"I don't know, but I worry we may find out whenever the emperor arrives. While we wait, it seems we have some work to do."

"Sealing rifts," Shin said, conviction in her voice. Having a task to complete was far better than waiting around for some unknown enemy to arrive.

"To begin with, yes. You and Raya will take some of the adepts and deal with the demons at the rifts. Along the way, she will mentor you in the ways of sacrifice. Show you how to be selective in what you allow the realm to take. Right now, you are acting purely on instinct. This is what the realm wants. It allows the realm to dictate all the terms of the toll. You need to take some control."

"You aren't going to teach me anymore?" Shin asked.

"For now, I will be needed in Dahl. There is already much to navigate in our uneasy alliance with Sato, and I fear that Beast's scouting trip will bring more problems than solutions. Raya is one of our best. She can guide you almost as well as I."

Shin couldn't believe that her mentor would abandon her so soon, but slowly that frustration gave way to another thought. A thought that seeped up from the same place in her mind where her anger with Yuki and her caution burned. There was an opportunity here. "Of course. I understand."

"Don't worry, Shin," Raya said with an exhausted smile. "I'm sure you'll surpass me in no time."

Shin smiled back. Raya had no idea how right she was.

20

———

Beast looked around the crowded tavern and wondered how such a glorious dive could have existed without his knowledge. Tankards clinked, and the collective murmur of dozens of conversations settled over the room like a warm blanket. Beast smiled and quaffed his ale.

This was his kind of place.

"Sheyric said his contact has been seen around here the last few days. We just have to hope they stop in today," Jurian said, sipping his own ale.

"Today, tomorrow," Beast replied. "Whenever they show up is fine. I'm willing to spend as much time as needed here. You know, for the cause."

"Your commitment is impressive," Hanz said. The wineglass he held looked comically small in his large hand.

"Never pegged you for a wine man, Hanz. Would have thought you'd stick to ale like your brother."

"Nope. It's one of the many things that makes us so different from each other." Hanz didn't so much as smile as he and his brother took sips from their respective drinks in perfect unison.

Beast watched and shook his head. Then movement near the bar caught his eye. The bartender was directing a new patron in their direction. He knew who Beast and the brothers sought.

The woman who strode towards them was tall for a Samasian and had the sturdy build of an individual who was no stranger to physical labor. Her hair hung well below her shoulders and was done in a tight braid on one side while the other side hung loose. Her ears were decorated with gold and silver rings, one of which attached with a fine chain to a ring in her nose.

"She moves like she can handle herself," Jurian said.

Beast nodded and leaned back in his chair. As she sauntered over, he took another long pull of his ale and smiled.

"You must be Colas."

"And you, the legendary Beast." She smiled, but her tone was all iron.

"Sheyric said you might be able to aid me with a little project."

"Did he? Sounds like that silent fuck overstepped, as usual. Why don't you head on back with your tail between your legs, and tell him I have no interest in any more jobs for Yuki or any of you damned sin?"

Beast bristled but kept his peace. He couldn't help it. He liked her. "Perhaps, then, you would consider taking on a contract for *me*?"

Colas looked him up and down, demonstratively assessing him, and then smirked. "No."

She turned and started to walk away. Beast braced his hands on the table and shot out of his seat to pursue her, but before he could even call out, a thick-handled dagger embedded itself into the table between his hands.

He didn't get the sense that she had missed.

"Sit back down, bore, or the next one finds a home in your chest," Colas said icily.

The room had quieted in order to better watch the show. Beast, hands still on the table, regarded Colas for a moment.

Then he burst out laughing.

As his deep peals of laughter filled the room, a few of the other patrons joined him and the rest turned back to their own business.

"There aren't too many that would risk insulting me. Not too many I'd let live to tell the tale, either. Please, sit down and let me buy you a drink. We clearly got off on the wrong foot." Beast sat back down and motioned the bartender over.

Colas hesitated, then lowered herself into the remaining chair. Beast pulled the dagger from the table, flipped it in his hand, and offered it back to her.

"Thanks for the support, you two," Beast said to the twins, who had remained seated the whole time.

"You seemed to have things under control," Hanz said.

Beast shook his head as the bartender arrived with a tankard of ale for Colas, who took it with a nod of thanks.

"If you don't want to do a job for Yuki, I understand, but you wouldn't be working for her. You'd be working for me," Beast said, smiling.

"Forgive me if I don't see the difference. I had heard you were the Bandit King, leader of the mugon and scourge of the sentinels. Now, you're nothing more than one of Yuki's lackeys." Colas' tone was still hard, but Beast thought he was making progress.

She wasn't trying to kill him, at the least.

"There are greater threats in the water than the sentinels. You must have at least seen the destruction the

Maramans brought?" Beast realized he'd hit a sore sport when he saw her eyes darken, so he kept pressing. "Well, they're not done. They're still a threat and we need your help to stop them."

"Appealing to my idealistic side is a mistake, bore."

"I'm not. I'm appealing to your vengeful side. This port was torched during their attack. I'm willing to bet that cost you."

Colas stared at him. Her eyes once again assessed him, though this time it wasn't for show. "I'll hear you out."

"That Maraman ship grounded in the port? We stole that from Maraman raiders that have been murdering and then stealing from the farmers on Ilos. We need someone who can sail it."

Colas couldn't help her smile. "What for?"

"So we can steal more ships, train more sin to sail those and then stop the raids at their source."

"Their monstrous floating castle," Colas said softly.

"You've seen it?" Beast asked.

"We did when they first arrived. We ran. Made it to port just in time for those bastards to torch everything. Including our ship." Colas drained her tankard and motioned for another.

"So, we need a crew, and you need a ship. Seems like we could help each other?"

"I don't like being under anyone's thumb. Least of all someone as clever as Yuki."

"Then you really don't need to fear. You'll be under my command, and no one has ever called me clever."

She snorted, but Beast hadn't sold the deal yet. Ideals, even vengeance, weren't enough. But what could he offer?

"The first ship we steal is yours. So long as you teach our

people how to crew a vessel like that," Hanz said, surprising Beast.

"You can promise that?" Colas asked.

"We can," Jurian said.

"Yuki has other matters to attend to," Hanz finished for his brother.

"You guys know how creepy that is, right?" Colas asked.

"They do, and they don't care," Beast answered. "What do you say?"

She studied him one last time. "I can't promise anything alone. I may be the captain, but my crew is like family and this is a decision that will require some discussion."

"Okay, so, what next?"

"So, you'll buy me a few more drinks, since we're here anyway, and then you can come back to our home and convince the rest of my crew that your crazy plan isn't suicide," Colas said and finished her drink in one gulp.

Beast joined her and then called for another. "Deal!"

This was a partnership he was going to enjoy.

21

———

Sato returned to Versun with a war waging in his heart. He'd expected to confront the Firstborn and to leave Bulas with answers. But, of course, it hadn't been so simple. It never was with the Firstborn.

Today he returned to Versun with even more questions than when he'd left.

He wasn't any too pleased about the direction that his questions pulled him, either.

The Firstborn wanted to treat Yuki as an ally?

Sato followed the logic easily enough, but it rested on an unspoken assumption, an assumption that the sin were not a blasphemy that ultimately deserved to be wiped off the face of Samas. He looked down at his gloved hand, focusing on the pinkie that was missing.

The sin weren't allies.

They were tools to be used. Fodder for the demons that came from the rifts. Once the rifts were closed and the Maramans repelled, the sin could all die, too.

The Firstborn frustrated him. Sato could not tell, even after their conversations, where the Firstborn sat on the

Path. The man had a way with words, of slipping around questions that had no easy answers.

So for now, Sato would continue as he had planned. He and the Firstborn agreed that Versun needed to be cleansed from the taint of corruption. It needed to be made ready for invasion. The Firstborn had urged mercy, but had also stopped short of ordering it. He left the method to Sato's judgment.

As the walls of Versun came into view, Sato shook his head. Why mercy? The corrupted sentinels didn't just dishonor themselves. They risked the lives of thousands of citizens. Yes, their loss would be inconvenient, but why mercy? It was a weakness, a fear of making the hard changes that were necessary.

Sato carefully considered his next steps. Versun was a political nightmare, with dozens of competing interests. He would need to speak with Crispin and Alonzo to get the lay of the land. Then he'd need to complement his lieutenants' information with research of his own. He'd want to speak with more sentinels and magistrates. Only then would he be able to chart a course through the troubled waters of Versun.

The ship docked just before the sun set, and as Sato disembarked, he saw that both Crispin and Alonzo were waiting for him. He'd sent word ahead but was still surprised to see them here. He would have expected Alonzo to be asleep at a brothel and Crispin fleecing money from unsuspecting card players. Instead, they both offered him bows.

Something was very definitely wrong.

"What?" he said, dreading the answer.

Crispin grinned, that grin that made Sato immediately distrust whatever came next out of his mouth. "We've arranged a meeting for you, sir. Tonight. I'm sorry that we weren't able to give you any more warning, but there was no way of reaching you while you were on the ship."

"What kind of meeting?"

"We're meeting with Tando, sir. He's a sentinel here."

The name was familiar to Sato from the research he'd already done. "The sentinel in charge of the dock area?"

"Yes, sir."

Sato thought of the dilapidated condition of the defenses he'd seen around the docks. Whatever Tando had to say, it had better be good. There was no excuse for the state of affairs. The man was already near the top of the list of sentinels Sato expected to have to either replace or execute. "Why do you have me meeting with him? We've already explored the dock area, and there's little he could say to defend himself."

"Alonzo and I have been studying the docks more carefully since you departed, sir, and the situation is even worse than we thought. Supplies are definitely being rerouted to other parts of the city, and most likely to magistrates. They aren't even being recorded in the books. Tando's most trusted lieutenants have overseen the process, and then reported to him directly after. There's absolutely no doubt he's guilty of treason."

"Then why are we meeting with him? Do you expect him to give us more information?"

Alonzo and Crispin shared a devious look that Sato didn't like at all.

"No, sir. I think he's been too well-rewarded by those he serves to turn on them. We set up the meeting to dupe him. Everyone knows about your return, but we led him to believe that you're looking for sentinels who might be loyal to you."

"Why would he take you up on that?"

Alonzo made the sign for gold. Crispin elaborated. "We've let it be known that the Firstborn has given you unlimited access to his coffers."

Sato looked between the two of them. "That's not true."

Alonzo rolled his eyes, and then Sato understood. "By presenting him a better offer, you think he'll turn over the people he collaborates with."

"Yes, sir," Crispin said.

"My promises will only go so far. Eventually he's going to want to see money."

"I'm working on that, too, sir. For today, all you need to do is meet with him and promise him a lot of money. We'll see what happens after that."

Sato was dubious, but allowed himself to be directed through the docks by his two sentinels. By the time they arrived at a tall, nondescript warehouse, it was already dark. "What is this place?" Sato asked.

"A warehouse owned by Tando."

"His own territory?"

"Makes him feel safer. It's only going to be you and me meeting with Tando and his lieutenant. Alonzo will have to stay here."

Sato really didn't like the idea of walking into the warehouse without a stronger guard, but he supposed he and Crispin could probably fight their way clear of most dangers.

They hiked up several flights of stairs before reaching a third story balcony that overlooked the warehouse. They walked around it, coming to an opening that led them outside. A platform had been built, a waist-high railing around it. It was a beautiful location, looking out on the port and the calm waters of the harbor beyond.

Two sentinels were there. One was a big, tough brute, and the other was likely Tando. His clothes were too nice, and his belly was starting to grow too large. Too much money and not enough discipline. Tando didn't even bow. He just grinned. "The legendary Sato, here to bargain. I'm surprised that you even know what money is."

Sato was at a loss for words. He'd expected to have to play a role, but what did he say to that? Was he supposed to be offended? Or did Tando have some perceived advantage here? Sato's mind twisted upon itself as he tried to remember all the political connections Tando had, all the ways he was woven into the tapestry that was Versun's ruling elite.

Coming here had been a mistake. A corrupt sentinel was one role Sato couldn't play.

Then Crispin solved Sato's problems.

He stepped forward, and without a word, pushed Tando over the edge of the railing.

22

"Mind if I join you?" Corin asked sheepishly.

"You know you never have to ask."

"Well, I wasn't sure after yesterday," Corin said as he lowered himself into the waters of the hot spring. "You've been so busy with all the preparations for Egzuki. I wasn't sure if you'd have time for me."

Shin realized she hadn't even spoken to Corin since they'd arrived back in Dahl. Yuki had led them to the magistrate's tower where Sheyric had filled them in on Beast's information about raiding Maramans. After that, Yuki had launched preparations for sealing the remaining rifts in Samas. This was the first moment she'd had to just sit since Yuki had handed her training over to Raya.

Training that had nothing at all to do with sacrifice.

"I'm sorry, Corin. Once Yuki told me she wanted me to be Raya's lieutenant I lost track of everything else. I've never led soldiers before. I barely know what I'm doing with sacrifice, let alone ordering people about!"

"You don't need to apologize to me, Shin. Sacrifice alone is more than I can wrap my head around. I was barely touched by the realm and it still fills my mind sometimes. I can't imagine what it must be like to manipulate it the way you do."

Shin stared dumbly for a moment before she grasped what he was saying. "I completely forgot! You were almost taken by one of those things. I'm so selfish, I didn't even ask if you were hurt."

Corin laughed. "Not even close. In fact, I feel better than ever. Don't get me wrong, it wasn't something I want to do again, but it showed me things, Shin. It unlocked the training that I'd been doing in a way I never thought possible. I feel like I've surpassed anything I could have hoped to achieve on my own, and there's still room to improve."

Shin grinned at his enthusiasm. All he wanted was the power to make a difference, just like her. In a way, he was even stronger than she was. It wasn't until Yuki showed her the kind of power she could wield that Shin had found the courage to commit to the fight. Corin had been committed even when he was more dangerous to himself than others with a sword in hand.

She needed to commit to leadership the same way.

Corin, as he often did, knew her mind was elsewhere. "What's going on?"

The truth was dangerous to reveal, but if she couldn't trust Corin, who could she trust? She spoke low. "I think I can close all of the rifts at once. I just need to be close enough to one."

Silence hung between them.

"What will it cost you?" Corin finally asked.

"More memories, I think."

"Like Mateo?"

"Yes." She chewed on her lower lip. "Did I ever tell you about growing up on a farm?"

Corin frowned. "Of course you did. It was your whole childhood."

"I met a farmer yesterday in Dahl. I recognized him and we talked a little. He mentioned my family's farm and I had no memory of it. I don't remember what it looked like, how it smelled, or anything."

"So, the realm took the memory of your farm? Did it take any other memories?" Corin asked.

"I mean, I didn't even realize I'd forgotten growing up on a farm until it came up. How am I supposed to know what else I've lost?" Shin stopped short of shouting, but it was an effort.

"You're right," Corin said. "Sorry."

"No, I'm sorry. You're trying to help. I remember my mom and dad. I remember them teaching me how to work a field and how to cook and clean. I still know how to farm. I just can't remember the farm itself."

"That's very specific. Just like Mateo."

Shin nodded. Mateo had been the first thing that Corin had wanted to go over after the revelation of her lost memories. The pattern was the same. She could remember the luan and their hideout in Dahl. She remembered Davin and his betrayal. But there was nothing about Mateo. Corin had filled her in at length. It was a memory she was sorry to lose.

"So what happens if you just keep using sacrifice like this? You'll forget everything?"

Even me? It was left unsaid, but Shin knew the thought was on Corin's mind.

"I'm not sure. I think it depends on the level of sacrifice."

"Did you tell Yuki you could close all the rifts at once?"

"I will. Just not yet."

"Don't you trust her?"

"It's not that. Well, maybe I don't. I think she's holding me back. Maybe not intentionally." Shin shook her head in frustration. "No, it's not that. It's..." She couldn't articulate what she felt.

"She's worried you'll burn out too quickly, and then Samas will have one fewer power left to defend it," Corin said quietly.

Shin was about to be angry at Corin for taking Yuki's side, but he continued before she could yell at him. "But the demons, the Maramans, hell, even the sentinels. If now isn't the time for you to go all out, then when is?"

Shin looked up at Corin's earnest expression and felt tears prickling her eyes. He had the courage to speak the thoughts she couldn't give voice to. "Yes!"

"Will you tell Raya?" Corin asked.

"Maybe. I'll see what I can learn from her first. Her power may not match mine, but the things she was doing back on the island, the way she was dividing her focus between so many targets, was impressive. She's a master in her own right."

"Then we keep it between us. But you have to promise me you'll be completely honest with me."

Shin thought for a moment and realized that she couldn't imagine lying to Corin. "Deal. Now, let's get a bite to eat and then we have to meet with Raya."

Bellies full, Corin and Shin made their way to the port where they were supposed to meet Raya and the sin unit that they would be leading. Along the way she ran into Tia, a sin adept that would be coming with them. Shin had tried to introduce herself once she'd learned she would be in command of the woman, but Tia had replied curtly before turning back to her friends.

Shin's first impulse was to avoid the awkward situation, but then she recalled the game she had overheard Tia and her friends playing before she'd walked away.

"Tia," she called out, "what kind of room has no windows and no doors?"

Tia looked like she was going to continue to give Shin the cold shoulder, but the riddle pulled her in. She fell into step beside Corin and Shin. Her face was screwed up in concentration.

"A mushroom!" she said finally.

Shin laughed. "Thought I had you there."

Tia appraised her for a moment before smiling. "You'll have to do better than that. I've got one you'll never guess."

Before Tia could ask the riddle, Raya approached the trio and gave Tia a pointed look. "I need to borrow the lieutenant."

"Of course," Tia said with a nod to Raya. "I'll ask you on the boat."

"Looking forward to it," Shin responded.

"Tia seems to have taken a shine to you." Raya observed.

"Have to start somewhere."

"You've got good instincts when it comes to leadership. Hopefully those same instincts will help with your sacrifice training."

Shin gave Raya a small bow. "I'm eager to learn from you. The level of control you showed in the village was incredible."

"It took a long time to learn. I was never going to be as strong as you are even now, so control was key for me. I had to be able to wield what I could as accurately as possible. Make every sacrifice count. Can you accept slowing down in order to learn more?"

"What do you mean?" Something in Raya's tone nagged at Shin.

"I mean, Yuki told you to stop using sacrifice as often as you do. It was clear to anyone with eyes that you had to bite your tongue pretty hard at that. Then, she told you that I would be replacing her as your mentor. You acted as though you were eager to learn from me, but again you swallowed your anger."

"So, you don't want to train me? I was just disappointed that Yuki was pushing me away. I really do want to learn from you!"

Raya didn't look convinced. "Yuki isn't the only one that thinks you're pushing too hard and too fast. The things you're doing are incredible, but they are taking a toll. Because the toll seems small, a memory you can't even remember, you either don't think it's dangerous or you don't care. I'm not sure which is more terrifying, but I do know that I'm not teaching you anything unless you agree to only use sacrifice when I give you permission. Can you handle that?"

Shin shared a look with Corin, who quickly found something out on the water that demanded his attention.

"Of course, Raya," Shin lied.

23

———

Beast had enough ale in his belly to float the ship he'd just stolen, and as consequence, was in a better mood than he'd been in for quite some time.

It turned out that he and Colas got along quite well once the initial specter of Yuki was exorcised from the situation. They both hated taking orders and were both leaders of bandits, cutthroats, and thieves. That Colas tormented the sentinels on the sea and Beast on land made little difference. They both championed the same people the sentinels crushed underfoot.

They proclaimed it loudly to anyone who would listen. Though at the moment, that was only the twins and one exhausted barkeep.

Beast finished the story he'd been telling. "I kicked dirt right into his sun-blessed sentinel face and knocked him on his ass."

Colas roared with laughter. "Serves the bastard right! Who needs honor when you can beat the snot out of everyone who looks at you funny?"

"I've always found honor to be about as useful as a

broken leg." Beast's laughter joined with Colas' and he finished his tankard of ale.

"So, what happened with the Red Aces?" Colas asked.

"They caused his join," Hanz slurred.

"Joined his cause," Jurian corrected him.

"Right, they joined his cause."

"That's when the sin decided he was join to worthy us," Jurian said, his eyes half closed.

"Worthy to join us," Hanz corrected him.

"Right, worthy to join us."

The four of them looked at each other for a moment and broke out laughing once more.

"Closing time, Colas," the gruff bartender called from behind the bar, for maybe the third or fourth time.

Beast looked around and was surprised to find that the sconces had burned low and all the stools in the tavern were up on the tables. The bartender came around from behind the bar with a broom in his hand.

"Sweep-up time!" Beast shouted, causing their group to laugh again.

"Yes, yes, sweep-up time. Off you go now," the bartender said, shaking his head.

"Thank you, Gavin, your service was as bitter as your ale," Colas said with an exaggerated bow.

"That's not my name, but you're welcome."

"It's not? Well, that's fine. I would have forgotten your real name anyway," Colas muttered as she headed for the door.

Beast stood up, swayed slightly, found his balance, and began to consider if he was going to throw up or not. After a moment, he decided he would not be throwing up just yet and staggered to the door with Hanz and Jurian in tow.

"Let's go convince your crew to join our cause!" Beast bellowed.

"Yes! And drink more ale!" Colas bellowed right back.

"Lead the way," Beast said.

The night air was cool and the breeze coming off the ocean was salty and fresh. Beast's head cleared a little. As they walked through the port, Beast noticed that the repairs here were happening almost as quickly as the ones in Dahl. Clearly the sin intended to see the port repaired as quickly as possible.

"Where's your place?" Beast asked when he noticed that Colas was leading them beyond the port and along the beach away from Dahl. He'd expected her lair to be closer.

"Not far, just down along the beach, maybe a twenty-minute walk."

Beast nodded amicably. His mind was covered in the kind of warm fog that made every idea seem like a good one. A walk sounded perfect.

They proceeded along the shoreline with the ocean on their right. The sand gave way to rocks and soon a natural rise in the land on their left grew steeper until it turned into the rocky cliff walls that made up most of the shorelines of Ilos.

The fog in Beast's head traveled down to settle over his eyes, and his vision blurred. He focused his attention on the narrow rocky beach so that he didn't fall, but a shadow along the top of the cliff kept catching his attention. His hazy vision made it seem like it was moving, following them as they walked.

"Is it much farther?" Beast asked. "I'm beginning to think I need a soft bed more than I do ale."

The shadows following them took on more distinct shapes.

"It's not far," Colas snapped over her shoulder, stumbling slightly as her head turned toward them. "Quit your whining."

Beast struggled to think of a witty comeback, but the fog in his brain thickened at an alarming rate. He grumbled nonsensically and kept walking.

When they rounded the next bend, the beach opened up as the shoreline dipped inward. The cliffs climbed higher, cutting them off from the rest of the island. Beast saw two torches burning in the distance. Through the darkness, Beast made out what appeared to be a wide cave mouth.

"Home sweet home!" Colas slurred cheerily.

"You live in a cave?" Beast asked.

"It's cozier than it looks. Come on."

Beast nodded and glanced back up at the cliffs. The shadows had returned to normal and no longer appeared to be following him. They made it about ten paces before they heard a voice calling across the beach.

"Colas! Colas, wait!" The voice echoed through the darkness.

"I'm coming, Gib, relax," Colas laughed.

"No! Stay there! Something is hunting us!" Gib shouted.

Colas seemed unfazed by the information and Beast, too drunk to do otherwise, followed her lead. Hanz and Jurian sang in low, identical voices. Something nagged at Beast, and he glanced at the cliff tops once more, but any real concern was incapable of penetrating his thoughts.

"Colas!" Gib called out again, but the captain continued to ignore him.

They were halfway to the cave entrance when Beast noticed a figure, presumably Gib, sprinting across the beach towards them and gesturing madly. Beast finally began to understand something was amiss.

"Colas, your man seems concerned about something," Beast said and put a hand on her shoulder to halt her movement.

"He's always concerned," Colas said, her words slurred. "He's a big, concerned type of guy, you know?"

Beast was tempted to smile along with the woman's drunken grin, but worry broke through his drunken stupor. He looked over her shoulder at the man running towards them and then moved his gaze to follow Gib's wild gestures.

The giant, crimson spear flying towards them sobered Beast up significantly.

"Look out!" he called and dragged Colas to the ground.

"What—" she managed to get out before the spear passed through the space they had been moments before.

"Run back to the caves. It's here!" Gib said, while pulling Colas to her feet.

Hanz helped Beast up and the three men joined the sailors in their mad dash across the beach. The cave, though not far, seemed an impossible goal.

"Gib, what is that thing?" Colas asked. She was finally taking her crew member seriously.

"We don't know," he said without turning back. "It started—"

The words cut off as the spear slammed into Gib's chest and sent him flying backwards. The spear cut through Gib's rib cage and out the other side. His body went flying in one direction as the spear curved around and reoriented on Beast and his friends.

"Keep running," Colas said, but Beast grabbed her.

"No, that's what it wants. To pick us off as we flee. We have to fight."

"Fight what? A flying, sentient spear?"

"No, we fight the person controlling it," Beast said and pointed to the shadow that had, indeed, been following them from the clifftops.

"Are you mad? We don't even know what that is, and we're all drunk. How would we even get up there?" Colas protested.

Beast licked his lips and grinned as the spear shot toward him again. "Let's find out," he said.

24

———

For only being three stories up, it seemed to take Tando an awfully long time to hit the ground. Sato feared that he would peer over the railing and find the magistrate dangling by some handhold, about to scream for help. Finally, he heard the sickening thud of a body hitting the street below.

Despite his surprise, Sato recovered quickly. There was still a threat on the balcony, and he wouldn't let his shock be the last mistake he made. His sword cleared its sheath in an instant, and he turned toward the brute who served as Tando's bodyguard.

The man made no move. The assassination had caught him by such surprise he hadn't even begun to react. Sato advanced, prepared to cut the giant down if he so much as twitched in a threatening manner.

"Easy, sir," Crispin said.

His lieutenant's calm voice froze Sato in place.

The enormous man looked over the balcony railing, completely unconcerned one of the greatest swords in the land had come a heartbeat away from killing him. He grunted, a deep guttural sound. "Not as big a mess as I thought it would be."

Crispin positioned himself so he stood between the bodyguard and Sato. "General, I'd like you to meet Dion. He's been Tando's chief of staff for several months now, and knows the magistrate's operations better than anyone else."

Dion looked over, and though his eyes were gentle, there was a quick intelligence lurking beneath the surface. Sato had misjudged the man. Dion might appear a brute, but there was more to him than he let on. Sato was reminded uncomfortably of Beast. This land was becoming too crowded with enormous and far-too-clever warriors.

Sato offered the smallest of bows, then looked between Crispin and Dion. "I imagine you two arranged this?"

"You imagine correctly, sir. Dion felt like his talents weren't being recognized or rewarded, especially considering the profits he was raking in on Tando's behalf."

"So, you paid him?"

Crispin shook his head. "I'd never be so crude, sir. I believe that the Path frowns on bribery, as you yourself have tried to remind me several times."

Sato raised an eyebrow, daring Crispin to explain.

With a flourish, Crispin bowed again. "As of this evening, I'd like to present to you magistrate Dion."

"What?"

"We put all the pieces in place while you were gone, sir. Dion has negotiated with the council in private, and they all know and trust him. Tando had been growing greedy, even by the council's standards, so no one will complain about the change of leadership. The council believes Dion will uphold the status quo and cause less headaches for them than Tando. What they don't know, and won't know until it is too late, is that Dion is actually loyal to you, sir."

Sato turned his skepticism over to the giant. "Why?"

Crispin was about to speak, but Sato held up his hand. He was terribly close to pushing Crispin off the balcony to join the former magistrate. He didn't want to hear his lieutenant's convoluted explanations.

Dion's voice was surprisingly soft, closer to a whisper than a shout. "My sister lives in Dahl, sir. I know what's coming, and I know what you've done to keep everyone safe. Better you than that selfish bitch, Izuki."

The words kindled a fresh hope in Sato's chest. After all the corruption and all the dishonor, this was finally a reason he understood. For the first time in days, he felt like he was standing on solid ground and that the world made sense.

He bowed again, this time more deeply. "Welcome to the ranks of the sun stalkers, Dion. It's a pleasure to have you with us."

The giant offered a respectful bow. "The honor is mine, sir. But if you would, there will be much to do tonight to ensure a peaceful transition of power. I must move quickly."

"Is there any aid we can offer?" Sato asked.

"No, sir. I'll have a list of requests drawn up within the next day or two, so that we can begin repairing what's been destroyed. But for now, the work is mine alone."

Sato took note of the giant man. There was no uncertainty in his gaze. Every movement the man made reeked of quiet confidence. And he understood what Sato fought for.

Crispin couldn't have found a better ally.

If not for the murdered magistrate on the ground below, Sato would have considered Dion's sudden promotion an auspicious start to their endeavors in Versun.

Unneeded, Sato and Crispin took their leave. They met

Alonzo once they exited the warehouse, after they passed two men cleaning Tando's remains off the street.

The sight rekindled Sato's anger. As soon as they were out of the district, Sato turned on Crispin. "Just what in the name of the sun did you think you were doing?"

Sato's anger did nothing to wipe the grin off Crispin's face. "Helping you take over Versun, sir."

"You just assassinated a magistrate!"

Crispin scratched at his chin. "I suppose that's true enough. But he was rotten to the core and we both know it. If you were given the chance, wouldn't you execute him?"

"After he'd been tried and found guilty!"

Alonzo rolled his eyes, earning a burning glare from his commander.

"What Alonzo is trying to say, sir," Crispin explained, "is that you're still not understanding how this is going to work. Let's say that you managed to gather an enormous amount of evidence, and you presented it at council. Do you think they'd find him guilty? Or would they bog down the process with demands for more witnesses, or for more evidence? Or maybe Tando would simply disappear one day. What do you think are the odds your justice would ever come to pass?"

"The other magistrates would have no choice but to condemn him!"

"Really, sir? If they were to sacrifice one of their own, the others would have to reevaluate their own positions. The system works because it protects itself. Damning one of them leaves the rest of them open to prosecution. So no, you'd never have a chance to execute Tando. You'd be subverted every step of the way. All you would do is openly reveal exactly what you intend, and the magistrates would be able to counter your efforts without a problem."

Sato shook his head. It wasn't that he disbelieved Crispin and Alonzo. It was that he couldn't believe how far the magistrates had fallen.

Crispin continued. "This way, we can start fixing the docks, which is going to be vital if those giant fuckers ever show their ugly faces here. And though you didn't know it, you earned Dion's loyalty in Dahl. He'll fight for you, and he'll follow the Path. All while being our inside mole on the council."

Sato shuddered. "It's disgraceful."

Alonzo just shrugged, but Crispin sympathized. "That it is, sir. But if you want Samas to return to the Path, truly, this is the only way it comes about. We need to beat them at their own game."

Sato looked up at the sky, but the sun was already well down. There were no answers there for him. There was only the moon, reminding him once again of his disfigured hand.

He didn't have to like it.

He just had to make sure that he won.

For all of Samas' sake.

25

The trek inland from the clandestine beach on the east end of Egzuki had been fairly pleasant, all things considered. Shin hadn't spoken to Raya since the more experienced sin had delivered her ultimatum, but that didn't bother Shin much. Now that she knew where Raya stood, she was confident she could continue to progress her training rather than slow down.

All she had to do was convince Raya she had fully accepted Yuki's decisions.

Shin spoke little with Corin on the walk, and any time Raya looked in her direction, she did her best to look chagrined. Finally, Corin had enough.

"What's wrong?" he asked softly.

"I'm fine," Shin snapped. She slowed so that there was more distance between the two of them and Raya. Then she whispered, "I need her to think that her lecture hit home."

Corin's look of concern required no acting on his part. "Does that mean it didn't?"

"She's right that I need to learn better control."

"But?"

"But I don't think that means I need to start doing less. If anything, I should be pushing harder so that I can learn what I need to know."

Corin stared at his feet. "Please be careful, Shin. I get that memories don't feel like they mean much if you can't remember them." He paused, then gulped and set his shoulders. "But I see how their loss changes you. Maybe most don't see, but you're changing. You're harder now than you were when we met you."

"Because I have to be! Everything I've given up, I've given up to save myself and others."

"I know! And I can't tell you that you were wrong, but you don't remember how important Mateo was to you. You don't even know how much you're losing, and it makes me worry."

Shin snorted. "From what you've told me about Mateo, he'd think it was the right choice."

Corin looked like he'd eaten something bitter, but he retreated. He had to understand that she was right; it would just take him a little longer to accept it.

Their party came to an abrupt halt. She looked ahead to see why they had stopped and saw that the dry forest floor was turning spongy and rank.

Raya addressed the two of them. "The Egzuki rift is located in the center of a bog. If it's been open as long as the other rifts have, we'll have some difficult fights on our hands."

Shin hated the tone in Raya's voice, as though Raya knew so much more than she did, but she swallowed her instinctive response. Raya still had necessary information, so she needed to be the dutiful sin for a while longer yet. "I understand. Whatever comes, Corin and I will be ready for it. We'll make sure you have the time you need to send them back." Shin emphasized the last "you" to make it clear she had no intent to use sacrifice today.

Raya seemed satisfied. "Good. You two stick with me. Each adept has sin assigned to protect them while they send back the demons. The farther the distance and the more demons there are, the harder it is to send them back. We need to be methodical in our approach. But once we are closer to the rift, we can focus on sealing it."

Their boots sank deep into the muck and Shin constantly smacked small biting insects. Behind her, one of the sin used their sword to remove the head from a venomous snake. Even without the demons, there were plenty of dangers in the swamp that slowed their progress.

Raya held up a hand and the sin stopped, readying their weapons. There was a stillness in the air. The continuous drone of swamp life faded to silence.

Then violence erupted all around them.

Vicious frogs burst forth from the swampy waters. Behind them, a deformed snapping turtle emerged, headfirst, from the water. The neck stretched for an unnaturally long distance.

To Shin's mind, it was a miracle the sin didn't break as soon as the nightmares approached. They fought with the discipline that could only be built through exposure to the horrors they now faced.

The monsters' fury crashed upon calm steel.

Every time a demon head was severed, an adept would send it back to the rift. Some adepts were able to send two back at a time, others just one.

Raya alone was able to handle three or four at once, allowing the sin warriors to take down the demons as quickly as possible without worrying about being possessed by their mist forms.

Shin and Corin held their own. They battled a grotesque frog until Corin removed the top half of its body. The creature writhed on the ground for a moment before Corin struck again, closer to the beast's mouth. It faded into mist and Raya sent the demon back.

"Couldn't get its head the first time?" Shin teased.

"It's a frog, Shin. Kind of hard to tell where its neck is."

Shin laughed and was reminded of Beast's odd levity in the heat of battle.

"Focus, you two," Raya snapped, as she sent multiple demons back to the realm.

Shin surveyed the battlefield and felt good about their chances. The sin were well practiced against demon animals. Thus far, no demon versions of sin warriors had appeared. They were winning.

The water in front of one of the adepts bubbled briefly and then a monstrous maw of teeth clamped down on his leg. Shin moved to help, but he disappeared beneath the water well before she could reach him. The shadowy figures that he had been sending back broke free, and one of them caught a surprised sin in its gaze. The thing started to take on the shape of the sin.

But Raya was faster.

She contained the demon and it returned to its mist form. The sin it was trying to emulate shook her head and then steadied herself. Sweat broke out on Raya's forehead with the effort of splitting her attention in so many directions. She couldn't issue orders when they were so desperately needed.

Shin took charge. "All of you, surround the adepts. We can't afford to lose them while they're sending back the demons. Move away from the deeper water."

The sin responded instantly. The adepts moved away

from the deceptively deep waters that the huge demon had emerged from. Then the sin formed a wall around them. She and Corin took up places side by side with the others.

For a few moments, nothing happened. Then the demon that was stalking them broke the surface and tried to snap up another sin. But the wall responded well. The closest sin danced backwards as those on either side struck out with swords, driving the beast back.

Once it broke the surface, Shin saw that it was a giant demon alligator. It was over twenty feet long with claws like sword blades. The snout possessed a mouth full of more razor-sharp teeth than should have been possible to fit in one jaw. The giant tail, adorned with pitch-black spikes, whipped around lightning quick and caught one of the sin on the side of her head. Her skull collapsed with a dull thud, and she was left twitching in the boggy water.

Shin threw Harmony as the demon swung again. The blade didn't penetrate the flesh of the tail, but the force of her throw saved a sin and knocked the demon off balance.

Corin picked up the sword of the fallen sin, then dashed forward and pressed the attack as the alligator retreated a step. He used both hands, his flurry of strikes pushing the beast back farther.

Corin was so intent on his attack that he didn't watch his footing. The demon, able to swim better than it walked, had backed away so smoothly that Corin didn't notice the steep drop-off into deeper water. He staggered forward as his foot sank into the water.

Shin reached out and grabbed his shirt. She pulled so hard they both fell backwards. The demon's jaw snapped in the empty space where Corin had been. Then the wall closed around them, the other sin keeping them safe from the terrible demon.

"The other demons have been returned. We should head to drier ground," Raya said. "This one will require something more."

Shin and Corin scrambled to their feet. As one, they retreated, fending off attacks from the alligator. The demon pressed for a while but then it stopped, seemed to consider the sin for a moment, and slid back under the deep water.

"It's retreating?" one of the sin asked warily.

"Never saw that before," one of the adepts added.

Raya seemed content with what they'd accomplished. She cut the conversation off with her orders. "Come, we'll need to find a place to camp."

"Camp? But there are still hours of daylight." Shin was surprised that Raya wouldn't want to press for the rift.

"Yes, and we'll need every one of them if we're going to be able to build defenses," Raya said. "Otherwise, that thing is going to hunt us down one at a time."

26

Beast wasted no time with a plan. Whoever controlled that spear wasn't going to patiently wait for them to form up and make it a fair fight. By the time their alcohol-addled minds came up with anything, they'd all be dead.

"Get ready," Beast said as he broke into a sprint in the direction of the magical weapon.

"Get ready for what?" Colas asked.

He'd already forgotten, but it didn't matter. The spear gave him no time to answer. It hurtled toward his heart like a merchant leaping toward spilled coin.

The moment before the spear met flesh, Beast dropped to his knees and slid beneath it. He reached up and grabbed the haft of the spear and, with a satisfied grin, pulled down with all his strength.

His grin vanished when the spear pulled him straight up instead.

Beast heaved himself up and hooked his elbows around the spear, latching on tight to the weapon.

The sudden change in altitude, combined with the speed of the spear and the cold night air, cleared Beast's head better than any hangover remedy he'd ever tried. His thoughts regained their typical sharpness, and he took in the scene below.

The height of the spear gave him a unique vantage point, and Beast saw a ship speeding towards the small beach that hid the pirates. He recognized it as a Maraman ship. "Colas! Out on the water!"

Colas broke her gaze from Beast's impromptu flight and saw the ship. She broke into a run towards the cave. The twins followed, leaving Beast alone to handle the problem of dealing with the spear and its owner.

Unfortunately, the owner was more concerned about Colas and the twins than they were with Beast. The spear ceased trying to shake Beast loose. It tilted down and launched itself straight for Colas.

The crimson missile flew towards Colas' exposed back. The twins, who had kept a wary eye on Beast's flight, moved to protect her.

"Out of the way, idiots!" Beast hollered.

Hanz and Jurian, to Beast's relief, obeyed instantly. They stopped and spread apart, trusting Beast to save the captain. As the spear came parallel to the ground, Beast slammed his feet into the sand of the beach and heaved with all his might.

The spear fought and struggled like a human opponent, but Beast rarely lost a contest of strength, and he wasn't about to make an exception for sacrificial weapons. Even as it pulled him across the beach, he yanked at the point until it wasn't aimed straight at Colas.

Finally, it passed by Colas harmlessly as Beast pulled himself back on. This time, he looped his legs around the shaft as well as his arms, spreading his weight across the entire weapon.

Colas reached the cave, and after a few seconds of indecipherable shouting, took full command of the battlefield. Her crew poured out onto the beach. The bulk of her pirates moved towards the approaching vessel, but two sprinted toward the cliff with short bows drawn. The pirates fired but their arrows fell short. Their bows were designed for repelling boarders. Beast cursed himself for wishing Sato and a few of his sentinel longbows were here right now.

He must still be more drunk than he thought, if he wanted that prick anywhere nearby.

The Maraman summoner directed the spear towards the two archer pirates, ignoring Beast's presence as though it was nothing more than an inconvenience. Once again, Beast readied himself to throw the spear off course. As it lined up with one of the bowmen, Beast kicked his foot out, connecting with the opposite pirate's shoulder, and then used his weight to pull the spear down, point first, into the ground.

"Go help your captain!" Beast shouted at the men as he held the head of the spear in the sand with all his strength.

Hanz and Jurian they weren't. Instead, the two men did the opposite and added their weight to the spear as well, jamming it deeper into the sand.

"We'll hold it. You climb up there and kill him!" one of the pirates said.

Beast swore at their disobedience, but then realized it was the better plan. He gave the spear one more shove before running for the cliff.

Fortunately, the wall presented plenty of holds for him to grab onto.

Unfortunately, he was still very drunk.

The wall rippled like a wave in his vision as he searched for hand and foot holds. A few times he had to hug himself close to the cliff face as the world decided to spin on its axis. All the while, he could hear the men below him struggling to keep the spear buried in the ground. Considering how hard the effort had been for him, he didn't expect them to last long.

Problem was, they didn't last at all.

"It's out!" one of the men called.

Beast swore at their lack of strength. He'd been drinking, dammit, and having a wonderful night. And then these Maraman assholes had to come and ruin everything. Beast's body filled with his familiar battle rage. His mind cleared.

He looked down and saw the spear curving up and away from him. He pulled himself higher up the cliff, dividing his attention between the climbing and the spear. The weapon completed its arc and paused in the air, taking aim. Beast saw the next hold and braced himself.

The spear sped toward him, faster than he'd seen it move yet. Beast bunched the muscles in his legs and dropped into as much of a squat as the length of his arms would allow. The spear devoured the distance between them.

Beast pushed off with his legs and leaped up the wall. The spear stabbed into the cliff where he'd been a moment ago. He grabbed the hold he'd scouted out and let his feet land on the spear. Before the Maraman could retract the weapon, Beast jumped once more, pulling with his arms as well, and scrambled the remaining few feet to the top of the cliff.

"Hi," he said to the Maraman as he gained his feet and dusted his hands on his trousers.

The Maraman, adorned in crimson robes, backed away. A red glow surrounded him as he tried to bring his weapon back in time to defend himself.

Beast's wolfish grin spread across his face, and from the look on the summoner's face, it was just as terrifying as Beast expected it to be.

Futilely, the summoner raised his hands to defend himself, but Beast knocked them away as he closed the distance and rammed the broken blade of Benji's sword through the man's throat. He heard a clatter behind him and turned to see the spear, now devoid of its glow, on the ground a few feet from him.

Beast looked out onto the water and saw the Maraman boat was almost to the beach. A few of the Maramans on the bow were readying themselves to hop out and pull the vessel the rest of the way in. Beast looked around for a faster way down the cliff but short of jumping there was no way he was going to make it down before the battle started.

Colas called out an order, and a group of pirate archers facing the water lit their arrows on fire. Another order was shouted and a pirate a ways down the beach cut a taut line that led into the ocean. Barrels floated to the surface of the water, surrounding the ship.

Before the Maramans could react, the pirates loosed their arrows. The wet barrels took a moment to catch fire, but whatever the rags on the arrows were soaked in burned through the damp wood quickly.

The barrels exploded.

The Maraman ship disappeared in a flash of fire and a haze of black smoke. The pirates waded into the water and put any survivors out of their misery. Beast laughed, the sound echoing off the cliff. He grinned like a madman.

Colas looked up at Beast on the cliff and the expression on her face mirrored his own. A cheer went up from the victorious pirates, and no small part of it was directed toward Beast. He soaked in the glory and decided that he had likely won Colas' crew to his cause.

The twins looked around and demonstrably folded their arms across their chests. He wondered what it would take to impress them. Tonight, though, he didn't care. Even they couldn't spoil his good mood.

Beast gave them the finger.

27

———

Sato cut the air with his sword, imagining Crispin's smug grin as he did. He sliced his lieutenant into small pieces, but no matter how vividly his imagination painted the scene, he couldn't seem to wipe the grin from the liar's face.

He shouted as he made one last cut, then gave up his efforts. His sword returned to its sheath, and he walked to the far wall of the practice space. He sat on a stool, toweled himself off, and stared at nothing in particular.

There was a knock at the door.

"Come in," Sato said.

Only one man would be brave enough to face him right now. A handful might be foolish enough to try, but Sato had a good guess who it was.

He was right.

Roko entered. His sharp eyes took in the puddles of sweat on the mats and his commander's disheveled appearance. His old friend raised an eyebrow. "That last shout caused a few of the new recruits to soil their pants," he reported.

"They should have been wearing darker pants," Sato replied.

Roko barked a laugh, then frowned. "Since when did you develop any sense of humor?"

Sato opened his arms out wide, unable to keep the bitterness from his voice. "It's a new age."

Roko looked around the small practice room one more time. "At least there aren't any bodies here. Some of us were worried." He took a seat next to Sato. "Crispin, I assume?"

"Who else?"

"He told me the story. He hadn't warned me that was his plan, though. I might have stopped him. Even though it sounds like it worked out well for us."

It wasn't quite an apology, but Roko didn't bear any more shame for Crispin's actions than Sato himself did.

Sato pressed his palms into his eyes. "But that's the problem, isn't it? I'm not sure he was wrong. Now, a loyalist controls the ports. Repairs are being made to the walls. New equipment is being ordered. No one misses Tando. As far as I know, there hasn't even been a whisper of complaint, not even from the other magistrates. By any objective measure, Crispin's plan was genius. I keep trying to imagine what an alternative looks like, but nothing I create is as clean or effective."

"Your reason says one thing, but your heart argues something else."

Sato nodded.

The two men sat in silence for a bit before Roko found something worth saying. "Perhaps all is not as bad as you believe."

"I watched one of my lieutenants throw a magistrate off a balcony and I've done nothing to punish him. How is it that I haven't lost the Path?"

"Your own heart tells the truth, Sato. You acknowledge that, on some level, what Crispin did was best. Yet, you rage against yourself and him for the bending of the tenets. To me, that says that not only do you hope to return this country to the Path, you wish to do so in a way that honors the tenets. You haven't lost your way until the day you accept Crispin's methods in your heart." Roko paused to meet Sato's gaze. "I propose to you that what you're enduring right now is the sacrifice that must be made so that your vision of the future becomes a reality."

Sato frowned.

Roko continued. "You said it yourself. Nothing you came up with worked as well as Crispin's plan. This isn't the type of battlefield you're used to, but it is one that both Crispin and Alonzo excel at. Promoting them was a wise choice."

"It was your idea," Sato reminded Roko.

Roko's grin told Sato that he hadn't forgotten. "You know you'll need to make hard choices to bring the corruption within the ranks of sentinels and magistrates under control. Your lieutenants will help you. But don't forget your purpose. You will do what must be done, but if your heart ever grows callous, then you become no better than those you seek to replace."

Sato stared up at the ceiling. "I don't like it."

"And if you ever do, I'll be the first to stop what's happening here."

Sato nodded. "Thanks."

"You're welcome." His grin grew wider. "But I also came for another reason. Crispin asked me to invite you to join him."

"He's summoning me, now?"

"Not like that. He approached earlier, but when he heard the enthusiasm you were displaying for your practice this morning, he thought it wise to retreat and send in reinforcements."

Sato grunted. "Smarter than he looks."

"He's in the mess hall." Roko stood up. "But please take my words to heart. I believe in what you're doing here, and if that belief ever begins to wane, you'll be the first to know." He reached out a hand and Sato took it, gratefully.

"Thank you, truly. That means more than you know," Sato replied.

As he left the small practice hall, he was pleased to see there was a line of sun stalkers waiting for their chance at daily training. While Crispin and Alonzo plied their trade within the city, Roko had this camp running as smooth as any army had ever been. His sentinels were already competent swords, but under Roko's constant guidance, they'd grown truly dangerous.

Sato longed for the day when he could unleash them upon a prepared enemy. An honorable battle.

As he headed toward the mess hall, he had the feeling it would be some time before that particular dream became a reality.

Crispin sat among a small group of sun stalkers, the group he'd personally selected for the work within Versun. They had their heads together when Sato entered, but as soon as they spotted the commander, they all sat up straight, as though they were simply enjoying breaking their fast together.

All of them except Crispin seemed to finish their meal just as Sato reached the table. They stood up in unison, bowed, and retreated.

Sato sat down. "Where's Alonzo?"

Crispin looked chagrined. "Well, you see, there's a woman he knows here..."

Sato held up a hand. "Never mind. You wanted to see me?"

"I know how to take care of Azazel."

"Did you find a balcony that he likes?" Azazel was the magistrate in charge of the neighboring district of Versun. It bordered the ports on one side and the nicer residential areas on the other. Most of the area was filled with small shops, the family merchants who formed the backbone of Versun's economy.

"Unfortunately, I don't think removing Azazel will be that easy," Crispin said. "He's well liked among the council. He's made a lot of people very wealthy, and that's a great way to make friends. If he dies, people are going to start asking questions."

"So, what are you thinking?" Sato wasn't sure he wanted to hear the answer to the question, but Roko's words kept echoing in his ears. The sin believed they understood sacrifice. His pinkie was evidence enough of that. It was time to teach the world that sentinels did, too.

"I think you should kill him," Crispin said.

Sato blinked. "Didn't you just say—"

"I did, but there's one very convenient aspect of the Path I think you're forgetting."

Sato never thought he would live in a world where he was going to be lectured on the Path by Crispin.

But here they were.

"Go on."

"Well," Crispin said, leaning in conspiratorially, "Azazel is a man prone to angry outbursts."

"And?"

"And so all we need to do is make him angry enough to challenge you to a duel. He served as a sentinel for years before becoming a magistrate, and is by all accounts a strong swordsman. So, we get him to challenge you to a duel, and then you kill him. Preferably, in front of a lot of other magistrates, so there won't be any rumors about what happened."

Sato considered the idea. "And the replacement?"

"Someone you choose. You are the highest-ranking sentinel in Versun. Your will supersedes that of the council. The council will know you're on the move then. No doubt, they'll take steps to undermine you, but if we act quickly, they won't have enough time. And we still have the advantage. They don't know what we've already done."

"How would we get him mad enough at me that he'd challenge me to a duel?"

Crispin's grin sent a chill down Sato's spine. "Don't worry, sir. Alonzo and I have that part taken care of."

Something about that moment twisted Sato's insides. Maybe it was Crispin's quiet confidence. Maybe it was the regret and anger he still felt from Tando's murder. Whatever the reason, Sato knew that if he kept walking down this road, he'd lose the Path completely.

He shook his head. "You'll need to do better than that," he said.

"Sir?"

Sato took a deep breath. He imagined how Roko would handle the situation. "Crispin, I'm grateful for what you've accomplished here, but we need to find ways to win that don't take us so far from the Path."

"But the duel will literally be demanded by the Path!" Crispin was almost sputtering in his attempt to get the words out as fast as they could escape his lips.

"And this method Alonzo is using? Does it follow the Path?"

Crispin's flinch was answer enough. He tried to protest,

but Sato held up a hand. Crispin wisely held his tongue. "Find a better way," Sato said. "I trust your imagination."

For a second, they glared at each other, wills competing. Then Crispin bowed his head. "Understood, sir."

"Good." Sato stood.

He left the mess feeling better than he had all day. Crispin had one of the most devious minds he'd ever come across. If Sato could get him to follow the Path, there was nothing they couldn't accomplish together.

28

The work of creating a defensible camp took too long. Though they had only lost two sin, their remaining forces still needed to be divided between setting up the camp and defending against the demons that pressed the assault. Fortunately, the few demons foolish enough to approach were killed easily enough, but it still wore them down.

The demon alligator they all feared had yet to make another appearance.

They made camp in a slightly elevated clearing. The land was dry, which gave them solid footing and allowed them to set up their tents. More importantly, it prevented the demon from using water as cover. Shin stood in the center of the clearing, watching the tree line and the deeper waters they had left behind.

Soft footsteps sounded behind her. "Still quiet?" Raya asked.

"No sign of our alligator friend yet. Have you ever seen a demon behave like this?"

"No. Usually their rage overwhelms whatever form they

take. Even when they take on the form of a human, with all our supposed rationality, they lack this type of cunning. It's worrying."

"Maybe alligators are incapable of rage."

Raya snorted.

"Well, at least it gave us time to prepare," Shin said and looked over the camp.

The sin had cut down the biggest trees they could and then sharpened them into enormous stakes. So far, they had created a circle around about three quarters of the camp that would hopefully slow the demon. At the very least, it would prevent a surprise attack.

Raya changed the subject. "You showed impressive self-control back there. I expected you would use sacrifice to fight that thing."

"I've had some time to think about what you said. Decided you were right." Shin sighed deeply. "When I see how much control you have, I realize how little I know." She kept her eyes downcast, hoping Raya would accept her change of heart.

"I'm glad you've come to understand," Raya said.

Shin breathed a long sigh of relief as Raya continued. "Control, I can teach you. The easiest way to begin is to teach you the first sacrifice that most sin learn. How to seal the rifts."

"But I can close them completely. Why seal what I could just close for good?"

Raya fixed her with a hard look. "We don't know enough about the rifts. Sealing is a process we understand. But if we close a rift, does it cause another one to tear wide open? Or does it cause a new rift to open someplace we don't know? We open the rifts to control the pressure, but what happens if there's no place for that pressure to go?"

Shin kept her face down, but her thoughts were churning. Perhaps some doubt was justified. But if she could close them all at once, it had to solve the problem once and for all.

"This is a good place to start, trust me," Raya said.

Shin waited to answer, as though she was considering, but her answer was easy enough. She needed to learn what Raya had to teach, even if this sacrifice seemed useless. "Very well, show me."

"Close your eyes and open yourself to the realm. Follow what I'm doing."

Shin quickly found the threads of Raya's connection to the realm. As soon as she did, she felt Raya weave the patterns that she used when sending the demons back. The realm flowed through the ethereal finger shared by all the sin who used sacrifice.

All except for her.

"Keep your connection with me. I'm going to send one of the demons back now. The action doesn't require a new sacrifice thanks to the generational spell, but the process is still the same. The request is made, but the realm has already collected its toll."

Shin felt the call and response of Raya and the realm and was reminded of the first time she attempted to use sacrifice. The spell flowed freely, but the transactional moment was clear in Shin's mind. It was so similar, and yet so different from her own experiences with sacrifice.

"Did you feel it?" Raya asked.

"Clear as day. I think I can recreate it without a problem," Shin said. She knew she could, but didn't want to seem too confident in front of Raya.

"Let's wait for now," Raya said. "Perhaps when we get to the rift, we can—"

A geyser of water erupted on the far side of the camp as the demon alligator burst forth, teeth and claws glinting in the fading sunlight.

Shin swore and pulled Harmony out.

"It planned this," Raya said as she pointed.

From the opposite side of the camp, a small but disparate group of swamp creatures emerged from the trees to flank the sin. Shin counted three oversized snakes, two toads that had grown claws, and one particularly disgusting centipede.

There was still a small break in the rows of thick spikes, but it was better than nothing. The barrier prevented the sin from being overwhelmed all at once. Knives and arrows were hurled at the alligator to slow its progress. Shin threw Harmony as soon as the demon recovered from the first volley of projectiles. It retreated a step or two but was still a threat.

"We can't fight them from both sides," Raya said.

"What do you suggest?" Corin asked in a tone that made it clear he didn't really want to know the answer. Shin caught Harmony in her hand as it returned and waited for Raya's plan.

"We get that thing's attention and draw it away from the camp. If we can draw it closer to the rift, we can finish this there. All we need to do is kill it and seal the rift."

Shin thought for a moment and then agreed. The idea of being chased through a swamp by a giant demon alligator wasn't terribly appealing, but if she could get closer to the rift, it would give her an opportunity to close it once and for all.

"Tia!" Raya shouted. "We'll draw the big one away, but you and the others will need to handle the rest. We're going to try to seal the rift."

"You're sure?" Tia asked.

"Nope, but we're doing it anyway. Shin, Corin, let's go!" Raya shouted.

The trio leaped over the makeshift barricades right in front of the alligator and pressed an attack that momentarily drove it backward. Before the demon had time to recover, they sprinted in the direction of the rift. For a terrifying moment it looked as though the demon would ignore them, but its rage took control, and it chased after its attackers.

Shin spared a quick glance over her shoulder at the sin as they met the attacking demons. She hoped it wasn't the last she saw of them.

Her distraction almost cost her an arm as the demon swung its spiked tail at her.

But Corin was by her side, hacking at the appendage. The steel of his swords rang as they struck the hardened spikes. The moment the alligator pulled the tail back, Corin pulled her forward, and they were running.

Towards the rift that only she could close.

Whether Yuki and Raya liked it or not.

29

B east took another long drink from the steaming mug of bitter liquid that one of Colas' crew had given to him. He didn't know what it was, but it was performing wonders.

"What did you call this stuff again?" Beast asked as the warmth spread from his chest into his head, clearing the haze of booze. But no one was there to answer, and he didn't much care. He was just happy to be alive.

He glanced over at Hanz and Jurian snoring softly in the corner of the small room. Big as they were, the two sin didn't handle their liquor all that well. Beast wasn't sure when they were going to wake up.

Colas walked into the room with her own cup and eyed the sleeping giants. "They've earned their rest, I suppose." Her sharp eyes turned to Beast, and it made him think she was doing better than him.

He swore to himself. It was just because she hadn't battled a spear that sent her flying all across her precious beach. If they went drink for drink again, he'd show her.

Colas' mind appeared to be on other matters, though. "I

need some answers from you, Beast. When you asked me to do this job, you never mentioned anything about whatever that was."

"Just a man, and now a dead one at that," Beast replied.

"*Just* a man?" Colas was incredulous.

"Well, flesh and blood, anyway. He's what the Maramans call a summoner. He can call upon another realm to do extraordinary things."

"Like make flying spears that even a giant like you has trouble stopping?"

Beast nodded.

"Makes for a dangerous enemy."

"True, but we have the sin," Beast replied reassuringly.

Colas' snort told him what she thought of that. Then she hesitated. "Can they stand against summoners?"

"That's actually not the worst I've seen. The sin have dealt with worse already outside of Dahl."

"So, you're still keen to work with Yuki on this?"

"Honestly, you're starting to see the reason why. I can't say I like Yuki all that much, but I don't see another way of fighting against what's coming. If nobody stands against the Maramans, they'll wipe out Samas, or take it over and make our lives even worse. I didn't fight for all those years just to lose it all now."

Colas digested Beast's rant slowly. "I suppose. Seems to me that whoever wins, there will still be room in the margins for people like us. Freedom can always be had if one looks hard enough for it."

"I get what you're implying, but you're wrong. The way the Maramans use those demons—I'm not sure life under their rule would be as similar to the Firstborn's as you think."

Colas shrugged, and Beast worried they were at an

impasse. It caused some of the anger he kept buried to crawl toward the surface. "I thought you said you'd help. And now what? One little magic man and you get cold feet? I didn't take you for a coward."

Colas had the good sense not to pick a fight with a hungover Beast. "I still want to help you. I want that ship. But I'm not the one you need to convince, especially not now. You'll need to talk to my crew, and they're scared after what happened last night."

Beast supposed that was reasonable enough. "It's the only way to protect Samas."

Colas shook her head. "You're not going to win them over with some talk of noble sacrifice. These aren't sentinels."

Beast growled. "Listen, I've done the solo act and as appealing as it is, we need the sin to stand against the Maramans and their demons. We even need the sentinels if we want to survive. The Maramans are a threat like no other."

"To who? To Samas?" Colas scoffed. "So what? What has this great, sun-blessed nation ever done for you? You hated this place so much that you rallied every bandit that plagued its shores into a force that makes even the Firstborn have nightmares. Now you want to risk everything to save it?"

"You've got me wrong, Colas. I created the mugon to protect people who couldn't protect themselves. The way the sentinels are supposed to. This was always about helping the people like you and me."

"Bullshit. You wanted to kill sentinels." Colas rubbed at her eyes, revealing the same exhaustion Beast was battling that the twins had already surrendered to. "But I suppose it doesn't matter. With one of their ships we'll be able to sail places we've never been before, and that's good enough for me. For now, let's get some sleep."

"Sounds good to me," Beast said, trying not to let the captain's words get to him. But Colas made him doubt. Had he been lying to himself?

He did like killing sentinels. Always had.

But his tired mind couldn't come to a conclusion.

Everything he'd done had seemed like the right decision at the time. But had his decisions been his own? Benji had been more than instrumental in helping Beast organize the mugon, and although Beast still called him a friend, Benji had also been working for the sin.

Had he been nothing but Yuki's plaything this whole time?

Tired as he was, the question itched at him and prevented him from falling asleep. He took his cup of Colas' mysterious beverage and wandered around the cave system. The pirates had already looked after their wounded and burned their dead. There was no ceremony in death. They simply disposed of bodies the quickest way possible. No doubt, if they'd been at sea they'd be dumped overboard.

The caves were far nicer on the inside than Beast had originally imagined. The pirates had reinforced weak parts with wooden beams, installed doors, and made the place seem surprisingly like a home.

In a way, it reminded him of wandering among the various mugon encampments over the years. Comfortable as the caves were, they were still caves, a cage of a different sort. Colas might not answer to the Firstborn, but if this was her idea of freedom, Beast found it lacking.

There was something to that, a seed of a thought that hadn't yet bloomed.

Of course Colas and the pirates were self-interested. Ultimately, wasn't everyone?

Beast couldn't fault them for that. Now all he had to do was find a way to take that self-interest and turn it into a reason to fight.

Because he knew one thing for certain.

If they didn't stop the Maramans now, there'd be no freedom for anyone.

30

Sato was meditating inside his personal tent when he heard the commotion of someone demanding to get past the guards. The very sound of Crispin's voice made Sato grind his teeth together. The guards stopped the visitor, but not for long. One of the guards poked his head inside the tent, looking chagrined. "Lieutenant Crispin is here to see you, sir. Sorry."

Sato took a deep breath. Any thoughts of peace fled his mind. Better to get it over with. "It's fine. Let him in."

The order had barely left his lips when Crispin strode into the tent as though it were already his. Sato managed to ignore the deliberate provocation, but just barely. He waited for Crispin to speak.

With a flourish, a piece of paper appeared in Crispin's hand. "I've managed to secure an invitation to a dinner and dance tonight."

"Congratulations?" Sato wasn't sure what Crispin was expecting.

Crispin rolled his eyes. "It's for you, sir. Or, more accurately, for you, me, and Alonzo."

"If you haven't noticed, I'm trying to take control of this city. I don't have time for dinners."

"Sir, if you attend this party, you'll be taking a step towards that very goal. Azazel is the host." Crispin spoke as though he were offended Sato hadn't realized it yet.

Sato blinked, his mind not quite catching up to Crispin's devious ways. Then he frowned. "Just what are you up to?"

Crispin grimaced. "Originally, I had hoped the duel would take place tonight, but we followed your orders, sir. After I spoke with you last, I found Alonzo and had him halt his activities."

"Then why go?"

"Because every magistrate in this city is going to be there. It's important you be there, too."

Sato growled, but he had to acknowledge that Crispin had a point.

Crispin set the paper down on one of Sato's writing desks. "It's a formal affair. You'll want your nicest uniform, and don't forget to polish your sword."

Before Sato could object, Crispin was gone, off to cause chaos somewhere else.

Sato looked at the paper. Though he was too far away to make out the words, he could see the fine calligraphy inked by a skilled hand.

He sighed and went searching for a clean uniform.

The sun had already set by the time he, Crispin, and Alonzo reached the dinner. It wasn't being held in the lower merchant district, but in the next district, where the houses grew in size beyond all need. Sato pulled at the collar of his uniform, but it did nothing to ease his real discomfort.

Beside him, his two lieutenants looked like proper soldiers. Both had bathed, trimmed their hair and nails, and found uniforms that still had creases.

Would miracles never cease?

If either of them felt any of his unease, they didn't show a hint of it. They kept their backs stiff and their eyes straight ahead. A stranger seeing them would think nothing of it, but knowing Crispin and Alonzo as he did, the act was almost comical.

They reached their destination, and Sato fought the urge to swear under his breath. Ever since they'd passed through the wall that formed the boundary of the lower merchant district, they'd seen nothing but nice houses, too large for the families that lived within.

This one was something else. It was larger than its neighbors. A full three stories tall, it was an edifice of brick and lumber that must have cost an exorbitant amount. A small wall protected it from the street and from nearby houses, and two guards stood watch at the main gate. They weren't wearing the uniforms of sentinels, which meant they'd been hired privately.

Sato's invitation got them through the gate without problem. When the main doors of the home opened, Sato almost froze. How many years had it been since he'd had to attend one of these? Two, maybe? It felt like a lifetime since he'd taken his leave from Bulas to focus his efforts on patrolling Samas.

The cost of the clothing here would pay for the repairs of the outer walls. There was enough food served just as appetizers to feed the whole island of Ilos for a week.

Two years ago, he'd found these types of gatherings an annoyance, something that distracted him from his focus on the Path. Now, the gluttony and selfishness within this home horrified him.

Did they have no idea what the world was like for the people outside Versun? By the sun, did they even know what life was like for the people down in the ports?

He was grateful he was wearing gloves, because he knew his knuckles were turning white from how tight he gripped the hilt of his sword.

His feelings didn't improve when he saw Izuki making her way toward him. He met her with a bow. "Chief Magistrate, it is an honor."

She bowed, matching his depth. "General Sato. I heard that you secured an invitation, but I'm surprised to see you here. You seem like a commander more content among his own troops."

Sato forced a smile to his face, his body remembering what it had been like to endure these interactions. "You're right, ma'am. But in the course of my inspections, I realized it would be important for me to know more of the merchants and magistrates in the city. Their support will be vital in preparing Versun."

Her patronizing smile brought hints of red to the edges of his vision. She thought him such a fool.

And maybe, before he'd met Crispin and Alonzo, he had been. His willful blindness had been a weakness. But no longer.

Still, it was better to be underestimated, and he didn't have to pretend to be judgmental. Let them think he was unchanged.

The red faded as she spoke. "Of course, of course. How have your inspections gone?"

He grimaced. "Not as well as I'd hoped. Your outer walls

are in a state of disrepair, and the magistrate who was trying to aid me died several days ago."

"We all mourn his loss. Is his replacement not up to your standards?"

Sato saw the trap and avoided it smoothly. "I haven't had the chance to meet with him yet. He's claimed to be busy learning everything for his new position."

"Well," Izuki said, her smile never fading, "if you believe he needs to be replaced, please let me know. I would be willing to put in a more amenable magistrate, if you insisted."

"Your cooperation, as always, is appreciated," Sato said, bowing again.

Izuki, content that he was still a fool, left him after making the proper farewells.

Sato turned to Crispin, then narrowed his eyes. "Where's Alonzo?"

Crispin grimaced. "Something came up, sir. He's handling it."

Sato decided he didn't want to know. His two lieutenants couldn't turn around without falling into some new plot. He didn't have time for them tonight.

Sato decided not to waste the opportunity he had here. Trying as the gathering might be, he would need allies as they took over Versun. He introduced himself to magistrates both familiar and new. He tried to remember what he'd been like, before the sun stalkers, and be that man once again.

Based on the reactions, he thought he did well. The magistrates he met were pleasant enough, and said all the right things, but they all seemed relieved when he finally said his farewells.

He didn't like them, and they didn't like him.

Truth be told, though, he didn't care. By the time he was done, the life of these magistrates would be upended. They just didn't know it yet.

Crispin nudged him after he finished speaking with another one of the magistrates. "Sir, we might have a problem here."

Sato turned in the direction that Crispin was looking. A man, built like a sentinel, charged toward them, his face red. The man stopped twenty paces away from Sato and pointed an angry finger. For a moment, Sato worried the man was going to fall over, his heart exploding in rage.

"You!" he shouted. "I challenge you to a duel!"

He didn't even wait for an answer. The man grabbed the sword at his hip, drew it, and charged Sato where he stood.

31

The sounds of the demon alligator crashing through the swamp behind them drove Shin to run faster than she ever had before. Her legs pumped as the muddy bog sucked at every step.

"Good," Raya said between breaths. "It's following us."

"Are we sure we wanted it to work?" Corin asked, panting himself.

"Shut up, Corin," Shin snapped.

Then her legs were knocked from under her, and Harmony went flying.

"Shin!" Corin yelled a moment before she was face-first in the ankle-deep muck.

She spun around, thrashing in the mud, just in time to see the demon alligator about to land on her. She called Harmony to her hand, but even as she felt it respond, she knew it would arrive too late.

"Move!" Corin shouted.

Then he was there, driving the demon back. His two blades were a blur of steel that parried claws and took chunks out of the alligator's toothy maw. The demon made no sound, nor did it react as though it felt any pain, but the sheer ferocity of Corin's attack pushed it back.

"Let's go," Raya said as she hauled Shin to her feet.

The demon gained ground when it brought its massive tail into the fight. Each time Corin had to dodge the tail, the enormous monster advanced into the space he'd vacated. Shin dashed forward and blocked the next tail strike with Harmony, giving Corin a safe moment to disengage.

The force of the blow made her hands go numb, but she held onto her weapon.

"Thanks," Corin said, but he was already running.

Shin tossed Harmony behind her, hitting the beast on the snout as it snapped at their legs, then caught the weapon without looking back.

"Almost there," Raya said.

Shin felt the rift up ahead. They pushed through a screen of trees reaching feebly out of the mud and saw the land begin to rise. In the center, the rift hung open.

It was surrounded by black shadows waiting for hosts.

"I'll send these back. You kill the alligator, then I'll seal the rift," Raya said, and stopped running. Despite the demon on their heels, she closed her eyes. All around them, misty forms were surrounded by a crimson glow as Raya wove the sacrifice.

Corin and Shin had no choice but to prove Raya's trust in them wasn't foolish. Thankfully, they now had better footing. They turned and charged the demon together. Corin, twin blades whirling, led the attack. He parried the claws and landed blows on the snout. Shin covered Corin, protecting him from the enormous tail.

They fought the demon to a stalemate. The creature's hide was too tough, and its weapons too many. Beast might have been able to hack through it with one of the massive weapons he always found, but neither she nor Corin had that kind of strength.

And the demon wouldn't tire like they did.

"What's the plan here?" Corin asked through ragged breaths.

"Raya?" Shin asked hopefully. There was no response. When Shin risked a glance back, she saw that Raya was completely absorbed in the sacrifice she was weaving.

"Perfect," Shin said. "Corin, you're going to need to handle that tail for a moment."

Corin could only manage an affirmative grunt in response.

For a moment she heard Raya saying something, but there was no time. She blocked her voice out.

Shin closed her eyes and connected with the realm. This time, she waited for the moment of offering, curious what the realm would demand of her. She thought back to what Raya had shown her with the pinky and sought the pattern that was in place for all sin to use.

She saw the moment.

Then changed the nature of the spell.

She wanted to drag all the demons nearby into the rift and then close it forever. She kept that thought in her mind. She felt the framework of the rift and its connection to the two remaining rifts in Samas. She saw how she could tear it down and close all three. How she could rid Samas of these feral demons for good.

The realm came.

It showed her the toll it wanted to take.

Her eyes opened momentarily and welled up with tears. It was nothing compared to the benefit. Benji should have been so fortunate. Quickly, she shut them again and agreed to the terms.

A smiling face faded.

The feeling of strong arms around her became unfamiliar.

The smell of earth and sweat mixed with soap disappeared on the wind.

Then the rift flared and crimson tendrils shot forth. All the shadows that Raya was holding were pulled into the rift immediately. The alligator was suddenly bound in crimson ties, and instead of attacking Corin, now fought to remain on this plane. As the monster was dragged into the rift, tendrils shot far and wide, pulling back any demons that had escaped. Finally, the alligator was pulled into the rift, and it slammed shut.

Corin collapsed to his knees in exhaustion. The tips of his swords sank into the mud, and he looked at her from under lank, sweat-drenched hair.

"What did you do?" he asked.

There was no sound as the rift winked out of existence, but the silence that followed seemed to roar in Shin's ears. For a moment, elation welled up inside her. She'd done it! Let Yuki chew on that.

Then she felt it.

Far to the north, so far it could only be the rift on Iru, she felt the realm tear into their world like pus bursting from an infected sore.

Iru, where the Firstborn ruled, where over half the population of Samas lived. Shin collapsed to her knees, the weight of what she'd done stealing her breath.

She felt Raya crawling across her mind. Then she fell forward as Raya's boot slammed her into the muck.

"Something very foolish," Raya said, answering Corin's question. She spoke softly, but there was an edge to her voice that reminded Shin that Raya was one of the most dangerous sin alive.

"I thought I could—" Shin began.

"I don't care what you thought!"

Raya let Shin return to her knees, but her sword hovered close to Shin's neck.

"I was going to close them all at once. I saw the framework of the rifts. I knew how to do it!"

"Did you? Or did you see what the realm wanted you to see? We told you how dangerous it was to deal with sacrifice at an elite level. Damn it, Shin, we trusted you!"

"I'm not a child. Don't speak to me—" Shin was cut off by a backhanded slap from Raya that made her ears ring. She tasted blood on her tongue.

"Feel it, Shin. Open yourself up to the realm and really feel what you did," Raya said quietly.

Shin tamped her anger down momentarily and opened herself to the realm. She felt the open sore that was the rift on Iru. It pulsed with malevolent power and malicious intent. The realm wasn't just open to her world, it was pouring through, eager to lay claim to the other side.

The enormity of her error froze her thoughts in place. What had gone wrong?

"I'm sorry," Shin said. It wasn't enough. Not nearly enough. But what else could she say? What else could she do?

"Enough!" Raya snapped. "What's done is done. We have to collect the others and get out of here. Give Harmony to Corin. I will spare you the embarrassment of binding your hands, but understand that as of this moment, you are my prisoner." Shin started to protest but Raya fixed her with a cutting stare. "You disobeyed a direct order from Yuki and have possibly doomed us all. If not for your possible use to the sin, I'd cut you down where you kneel."

Shin nodded and handed her weapon to Corin, who took it with wide eyes. He looked as though he would rather be anywhere in the world than caught between Shin and Raya.

"Where are we going?" Shin asked.

"To Iru. We don't have time to take you back and let Yuki deal with you. You will be under armed supervision the whole time. And if you so much as reach for the realm, either I or another adept will kill you without hesitation. Don't make me regret sparing your life." Raya didn't wait for a response before walking purposefully ahead of them.

Shin looked at Corin and tears welled up in her eyes. "I didn't know. I thought—"

Corin snarled and turned sharply away from her, leaving her speechless. He followed after Raya, Harmony at his back.

Shin stood there, more alone than even the night her mother had died.

32

———

By the time the pirates were assembled in the cavern that served as their mess hall, the sun was high in the sky and Beast's head only felt one size too large. Which was a considerable improvement over the five sizes it had felt like after he'd woken from what little sleep he'd managed to find.

He took another long sip from his steaming mug. Colas sat next to him, nursing her own.

"This is everyone," Colas said. "Be convincing. I want my boat."

Beast smiled. "I'm always convincing."

Hanz and Jurian sat near the back of the room and gave Beast their nods of approval. They seemed no worse for wear after the previous night's activities. The longer Beast spent with them, the less convinced he became that they were actually human. They'd easily consumed as much drink as him, if not more.

"OY!" Colas bellowed, and every head in the room swiveled towards them. Beast's head almost exploded at the volume. "My friend Beast has the floor. Pay him mind."

The pirates banged their cups on the tables briefly before quieting down again.

Beast stood, not quite sure how to proceed. But he'd fought much harder battles than this. He'd figure it out. "Thanks. I know I haven't met all of you, but some of us had the pleasure of fighting together last night."

Again, the pirates banged their cups, but this time it was accompanied by raucous cheers and whistles. His deeds the night before, as usual, were already halfway into becoming legends. Beast raised his hand in the air at the cheers. "I was happy to rid your beach of that scum, but it wasn't the reason I came."

"Who were they?" a pirate called from the crowd.

"They are called Maramans. They are the ones that attacked Dahl and burned your ship. Those we killed last night are the remains of a much larger raiding party."

"What about that flying spear?" another asked. "Never seen anything like that before, and I've seen some damned strange things."

A third chimed in, and Beast feared he was about to be overwhelmed by questions. "Can all Maramans make their spears fly like that?"

Beast shook his head. "Those are Maramans called summoners. They're capable of terrible deeds, but there aren't many of them."

The crowd shouted even more questions, and Beast feared that the entire exercise was getting away from him. He looked to Hanz and Jurian, who smiled identical smiles and acted like he was doing great.

"OY!" Beast bellowed, mimicking Colas. The crowd quieted. "Look, I'm sure you have questions about the Maramans. Hell, I have a bunch of questions, too. We can get you answers eventually. But for now, I want to talk to you about the threat they pose."

"Seems like we just dealt with the threat they pose," one of the crew said, eliciting laughter from her colleagues.

Beast slammed his fist on the table. "I took out the summoner. Your cute little trap dealt with the rest. Tell me, how many more times can you blow up a bay and catch them by surprise?"

Silence answered his question.

"You can't just wait here for the threat to return. We need to stop them at the source."

"Bah!" the woman shot back. "Ain't you sin? Sounds like a problem for them, or for the sentinels. We're not the damned defenders of Samas, in case you haven't noticed."

"And I'm not asking you to be. My warriors and I stole one of the Maraman ships. We need you to train my mugon to sail it. Once we steal a couple more, you can take one to replace yours. They run deeper and faster than anything in Samas. Your captain has already expressed interest in obtaining one."

The crew murmured amongst themselves, and Beast knew better than to interrupt. He'd dangled the carrot and needed to let them salivate a little. He turned and smiled at Colas instead. Rather than return the smile, she shook her head. Beast's heart sank. She knew her crew well.

The woman in the front spoke again, acting as the unofficial spokesperson for the group. "Seems like a lot of risk. We can find another boat, captain."

Colas fielded the objection. "That might be true, Mina, but not one like this. This is no island hopper. She'll take us into the deep."

"All due respect, captain, but so what?"

"Think, Mina! Since we were kids, the Path has taught us

that Samas is the world. *The entire world.* That there is nothing out there to explore. The Maramans' arrival proves that was just another Firstborn lie. Imagine what we could find beyond the coast of Samas!"

Again, the crew whispered amongst themselves. Beast couldn't be sure, but they seemed more amenable.

The room quieted and Mina spoke up again. "That all sounds good enough, cap, but so does a backdoor deal with the Firstborn. Chances are, no matter the terms, you're still getting it in the arse."

Beast laughed so hard that the crew couldn't help but join in. He looked around the room and once everyone recovered, motioned for Hanz and Jurian to leave. Perceptive as always, the two sin complied. Beast made an exaggerated show of waiting for them to exit before he spoke again.

"I understand where you're coming from. You don't want to be indebted to the sin any more than you do the sentinels. I promise you that won't happen. You will be working for me, and only me. Beast, the Bandit King. Once my mugon are trained and we've taken enough ships to take over that damned juggernaut, then we'll be on our way. I'll let you talk. You can discuss amongst yourselves what you want to do," Beast said, and moved to leave.

"Wait!" Mina called. "You're going to take over the juggernaut?"

Beast hid the smile that threatened to form on his lips. "Damn right I am. I've always wanted an enormous piece of floating land, free from the sentinels and the sin. Figured it was kind of the Maramans to bring me one."

Beast wasn't sure taking over the juggernaut was actually possible, or even wise. But hell, most of the time he didn't know what was a boast and what was a plan. But what did it matter? When Beast boasted, the world trembled.

He saw it here, too.

The pirates had wanted to hide from the juggernaut. Wanted to believe that the storm that was coming would pass them by.

Beast didn't offer them shelter. Instead, he offered them a way to tame the storm itself. From anyone else, it would be nothing but a dream and empty words.

But Beast, Beast they believed.

The crew began murmuring again, and some shouted follow-up questions, but Beast, true to his word, gave them the room to think about what they wanted to do next. Colas gave him an approving nod as he walked out into the hall.

"Did it work?" Hanz asked.

"Not sure. They don't trust the sin, but they might trust me."

"Is that what you're betting all of our hopes on? That complete strangers will love you as much as you love yourself?" Jurian followed up.

"Of course," Beast said. "Worked on you two, didn't it?"

33

Sato's quick reactions kept him just outside the man's first strike. His sharp gaze tracked everything, from the expression on his opponent's face to the balance with which he cut. Livid as his enemy was, the quality of his training was apparent.

Against a lesser opponent, Sato would have stepped in and drawn, trusting his opponent would be too off-balance to respond in time. Underestimating this man would be a fatal mistake, though.

Sato assumed this was Azazel, and assumed this sudden desire to kill Sato was not due to any particular action Sato had taken. Crispin and Alonzo would be cleaning latrines for a month after this. And that was if Sato felt merciful.

Sato drew his own sword. There would be no reasoning with Azazel, not in front of so many witnesses. Besides, everything Sato knew about this man told him that Azazel was near the heart of the corruption in this city. Perhaps the means were detestable, but the action was nevertheless necessary.

Azazel attacked again, the tip of his blade moving so fast

it was invisible to Sato's sight. Sato gave up ground again. He judged himself the better swordsman, but only by the width of a hair. A shame such skill was possessed by a man with a heart so black. The magistrate would be a powerful ally if his heart was less corrupted.

Azazel snarled and added several flourishes to his next attack. The onlookers gasped as the steel flashed between the combatants. Impressive as the cuts looked, they gave Sato an opening. He thrust into the space, careful not to make the same mistake he'd initially expected of Azazel.

Azazel closed the opening in an instant, parrying with the quickness and confidence of a man who had planned the move ahead. Azazel's sword sliced clean through the collar of Sato's uniform.

Sato's eyes narrowed. If he'd been just a bit more aggressive in pursuing that opening, his dreams of becoming Firstborn would have ended here, in front of the glittering masses of the spoiled. His heart beat faster at the thought. He wouldn't die like this.

Sato's world contracted until he and Azazel were the only two who still existed. As they passed again, he felt himself slip into a different state of mind. They weren't two individuals fighting over whatever silly argument Crispin had started. They were two opposing forces, light and dark, battling for supremacy of this land.

For now, they remained balanced, each advance negated by the response of the other. Sato swore he could hear Azazel's heart, could predict where the man would strike before his muscles even began to move. Sato's sword became a part of him, a longer, sharper limb that severed life from his enemies.

They passed again, and again neither gained that moment of advantage that would decide the duel.

Azazel faltered first. It was a small mistake, too small to be anything but true. He was slow responding to a parry, and Sato pressed the advantage. The final cut sliced across the side of Azazel's neck. It wasn't deep, but it was deep enough to open the artery that ran there. Sato stepped away so as not to get any of the blood on his uniform. Azazel clutched at his neck and moved as though he planned to fight with one hand. But then he faltered and stumbled to a knee.

He was dead a few moments later.

Gradually, the sights and sounds of the world returned to Sato, and all he could hear was the excited whispering of the crowd. A few of the more drunk revelers even had the audacity to clap at the display.

Sato had killed before. He was a sentinel, tasked with carrying that burden so that others might not need to. He was not squeamish about blood or bodies. They were nothing but flesh, and because he followed the Path, he could kill without staining his hands.

But when he looked around the room at the revelers, who had treated this like a spectacle, he felt sick inside. He had killed their host, and they applauded. His knees felt weak, and he feared he might fall. To distract himself he snapped the blood off his blade, then grabbed a cloth from a pocket to wipe the remainder off. He sheathed the blade in one smooth motion, and now several others were clapping.

Sato felt dizzy. The room spun around him.

The crowd began to close in on him. Sato almost drew his sword again, but they were only congratulating him on a well-fought duel. He nodded, using every bit of his training and experience to maintain a neutral expression. They were all around him now, ignoring the body on the floor as though it were nothing more than a spilled plate that would soon be cleaned up.

He needed to escape. He needed fresh air and the warmth of the sun. Crispin emerged from the crowd of onlookers. He said something in an official tone that Sato didn't catch, but the crowd parted, and Crispin led him from the site of the duel.

Several young ladies bowed deeply and blushed when Sato caught their eye, and he could do nothing more than give a tight smile and return a short bow of the head. He followed Crispin as though he was drowning and Crispin sailed the only ship for miles.

Before they reached the door, Crispin stopped. His lieutenant turned on his heels and gave a smart bow. Sato let his gaze follow Crispin's bow and he saw Izuki. More out of instinct than any sense of propriety, he offered a short bow of his head to her as well. He focused enough to hear her speak. "An impressive display, general. That was some of the best swordsmanship many of us have ever witnessed."

He couldn't think of what to say, didn't know what angle she was playing. Nor did it matter. He needed to be out of here. "Thank you," he said.

She regarded him with a cold eye. "Indeed, it will be a night that we'll be talking about for some time. I think your name will be on every lip soon enough."

Sato had a sudden and overwhelming urge to step back in time, to fight the duel with Azazel once again. At least there, with a sword in hand, the world made sense to him. Life was black and white, without the shades of gray that was the rest of reality. He wasn't armed or trained for the type of fight Izuki engaged him in.

The chief magistrate didn't wait for Sato to respond. She bowed again and left, and Crispin resumed their march to the streets of Versun. Thankfully, they made it without interruption. The cool air returned some normality to Sato's thoughts, and he looked back at the house they'd just left. "What just happened?"

Crispin gave Sato a worried look. "For now, let's just say that you killed a man who needed killing. We can figure out the rest later." Sato nodded, unwilling to press his subordinate for details. He would sleep, and with any luck, the world would make far more sense in the morning.

34

Shin sat in the boat and stewed. They were on their way to Iru to deal with the last rift. Well, so that *Raya* could deal with the rift. Shin was stuck with Corin and Tia in the last boat that left Egzuki. Yes, she'd made a mistake, but Shin had felt that rift clear as day. It didn't matter how much control Raya had. They needed Shin. Not as a prisoner, but as an ally. And now Tia was here, ensuring she didn't so much as reach toward the realm.

Making it worse, Tia kept asking her these damn foolish riddles. "Okay, here's one," Tia said. "I'm tall when I'm young and I'm short when I'm old. What am I?"

Shin glared at the sin. Tia refused to wither under Shin's look. Then she sighed heavily. "Fine. I tried."

Shin growled. "You were left here to guard me. Me! It's like nothing I've done to help the sin has earned me even a modicum of trust."

Tia's friendly face grew hard. "Of course we can't trust you. You were told, Shin. And the moment you had a chance, what did you do? Closed those rifts. *Closed* them. I don't have your aptitude for sacrifice, but even I know you can't just go around and do whatever you want. Hell, sin children know that."

Shin glared at Tia. She knew most of her frustration lay with Yuki and Raya, but having this *nothing*, this future subordinate of hers, lecture her about sacrifice made her furious. "That's enough. When we land, stand aside and let me join the fight," Shin said with all the authority she could muster.

Tia laughed derisively. "First of all, Raya's orders are for you to stay behind. Second, you're not an asset to anyone right now. You're staying with me." Tia dropped her hand meaningfully to the hilt of her sword.

Shin's anger flared even brighter. "You all followed my orders in the swamp when the demons attacked. Now that I'm not saving your life, you won't listen?"

Shin expected an angry reaction, so she was confused when Tia didn't fight back. Instead, the adept looked genuinely concerned. "What happened to you? When we first met, you seemed like someone I would willingly follow into battle."

"She's right, Shin," Corin said, inserting his nosey self into the conversation. "You aren't acting like yourself."

"You mean I'm not acting like the scared little girl you used to know? What's the matter? Don't like that I can fight on my own now? Don't feel needed?" There was acid in Shin's tone.

"Scared little girl? I never saw you like that. You were one of the bravest people I ever met. You also cared about what happened to others. Now—"

"What? Now what?"

"Now you're just selfish," Corin said.

From anyone else, she could have shrugged the

comment off. But from Corin, the words cut deep. "Selfish? I'm trying to save Samas!"

"At what cost? Do you even know? The two people in this world who know the most about sacrifice are telling you to slow down. And you ignore them!"

"All I'm doing is trying to get stronger to help others."

"Bullshit. It's all about you. It always has been," Tia said.

"I don't answer to foot soldiers," Shin snapped back.

"Shin!" Corin shouted, finally raising his voice. "Tia's your ally. How can you call yourself a leader after you attack her when she tries to show you the error of your choices? What would your father think of that?"

Shin opened her mouth to respond, but hesitated for a moment. "My father?"

"Yes, you've always talked about how well he dealt with others. How much you've learned from him."

"I don't remember."

Corin scoffed. "Don't be an ass. Of course you do."

"No, I mean, I don't remember my father."

That broke up the argument, at least for a moment.

In the silence that grew between the three sin, Shin found that any sadness at the idea that there were lost memories of a father she now didn't know were far outweighed by a hot anger. Anger at the judgment she felt from Tia and Corin. She had given up something to save Samas. To save everyone. If he'd been important enough to her, she wouldn't have given away his memories. If they were too weak to understand that, they had no right to judge her choices.

"Shin, I'm so sorry," Corin said. "I know—"

"Shove your sorry. I did what needed to be done. Something neither of you understands."

"Shin, Corin is only trying to help," Tia said.

Each kind word infuriated her more than the backhanded slap Raya had delivered. At least that rebuke had been delivered with strength and conviction. "I don't recall asking for your thoughts on the matter, adept. If I require your input, I'll demand it from you."

Shin barely saw the blow that rocked her head backwards. She looked at Tia but realized it was Corin's fist that had lashed out.

"I don't know who you think you are, Shin, but it's not anyone Mateo would recognize. It's not someone I recognize. I don't know what needs to happen for you to understand that you can't use your power without understanding it first, but until you do, you don't need to worry about Tia. You don't even need to worry about Raya. If I think you're trying to use sacrifice, I'll kill you myself."

Shin's mouth dropped open at the vitriolic steel in Corin's voice. He fixed her with a hard stare before turning around and facing away from her. Shin looked at Tia and tried to summon some of the rage that had filled her only moments ago but came up empty. Tia shook her head and leaned back in the boat, cold eyes on Shin and a hand resting on her sword hilt.

The rhythmic pull of the sin rowing their boat through the water was the only sound that accompanied the beating of Shin's empty heart.

35

Beast swayed along with the rocking of the ship beneath him. The ocean sent wave after wave to pummel their vessel, intent on throwing him to the deck, but Beast refused to give it the satisfaction. Beside him, Colas grinned as the salt water sprayed them. She stood with ease, making him feel like a child learning to walk in comparison.

She leaned toward him. "You're getting better. Before long I'll almost be ready to believe you won't hurt yourself just trying to stand."

Beast snorted. "Of course I am. If I can tame every bandit on Samas, I can tame an ocean!"

Colas shook her head. "You can't tame the ocean, Beast. It's not about breaking it like a stallion, it's about learning to feel where the ocean wants to go and using its power to your advantage."

"I prefer things I can break," Beast grunted.

But he couldn't maintain the grumpy facade for long. The past few days of ocean faring had changed his mind on what sailing was all about. The ocean wasn't his home yet, but he started to see why one might call it such.

The repairs to the Maraman ship had taken less time than Beast had feared. True, his access to sin engineers had helped, but Colas' crew were no strangers to ship repairs either. While Colas and the pirates focused on repairing the ship, Beast and the twins selected a crew to learn from Colas. Hanz had noted that almost all the recruits were former mugon, but made no other comment on the subject.

Soon, they had started sailing.

True sailing. Not the slow, wobbly ferrying that facilitated travel between the islands of Samas, but fast, smooth ocean travel that wasn't restricted to shallow water and shipping lanes. Colas and her crew adjusted quickly to the larger, deeper-hulled Maraman vessel, and by the end of the first day were operating it as if they'd been sailing Maraman raiding ships their whole lives. Colas named the ship that day.

Cutter.

Today marked the third day of training for Beast and his mugon. The ship's deck was crowded, as each position was manned by two sailors. One learning and one teaching. Colas stepped away from the wheel and gestured for Beast to take her place. He did so willingly.

"You know, until now I've hated boats."

"That's no surprise. The skiffs most Samasians travel on can barely be considered boats. What do you think now that you've got a taste for the real thing?"

Beast smiled wide. "I see why you love it."

"I thought we'd had it good before. We'd learned how to sail our little ship beyond the safe shipping lanes, and that had felt like freedom enough. But this..." Colas trailed off and looked out at the ocean. "This ship is real freedom."

The comment sparked a question in Beast. "Do you think you could have built something like this?"

Colas considered. "I doubt it. We're not engineers. We can patch a hull, sure, but building a ship like this? That's beyond us. The engineers' guild might be able to pull it off given enough time and money, but why would they?"

Beast nodded. "They never thought there was anything else worth sailing to." He stood beside Colas, filled with thoughts and questions that had no easy answer. This ship would never have existed here because the damned Firstborn and his Path constrained all of Samas in ways few could even conceive. But instead of overthrowing the Firstborn or creating a haven for those the Path stepped on, Beast was practically acting as an unpaid sentinel.

Most days, he was certain it was the right thing, but his life had grown too complex since the sun-cursed sin had stepped into his life.

The open horizon seemed so much simpler. To simply sail and explore, with no one and nothing to care about but that day's survival.

In that moment, he longed for the same freedom Colas desired.

Colas nudged him and pointed. "Looks like what we've been waiting for."

Beast looked to where she was pointing, off the left—no, the port—side of the ship. One of the Maraman vessels was anchored off the coast of Ilos. The longboat the Maramans used to make landfall was almost to shore.

"Time to recruit another ship into our fleet," Beast said and smiled wickedly.

Colas stepped in and took back the helm. "My crew to all positions. You sin bastards leave the sailing to us and get ready to bloody those swords of yours!"

A raucous cheer went up from both groups as the sin did their best to stay out of the way of *Cutter*'s suddenly very active crew. The ship tacked smoothly and soon Colas was giving the order for sails to be dropped. She tacked once more and brought the ship alongside their target with less than a foot between the vessels.

Beast didn't have time to appreciate the feat of sailing as he led his mugon onto the Maraman vessel. Most of the crew had boarded the longboat leaving only a few sentries aboard. Beast's first step was almost his undoing before, at the last moment, he adjusted to the new ship's different pattern of rocking caused by the waves in the ocean. He still stumbled, but caught himself and brought his axe to bear.

His first duel lasted longer than it would have on land, as the Maraman had seasoned sea legs and fought more fluidly on the moving deck than Beast. In the end, though, Beast was still Beast, and he overpowered the other Maraman. With his contest over, he surveyed the battle. Despite an overwhelming numerical advantage, the mugon were still struggling to kill the last of the sentries. Maramans were hard enough to kill on dry land, but out on the ocean, where the footing was more treacherous for the inexperienced mugon, they were a real problem.

Still, the Maramans had no chance. Eventually, the last of the sentries fell, and a final cheer went up among the mugon.

"We'll need more training to fight well out on the ocean," Hanz observed, mirroring Beast's thoughts.

"A lot of it. I thought a few days out here would be all we'd need, but I guess not."

"Even for the legendary Beast?" Jurian, appearing on the other side of Beast, asked sweetly.

"I didn't see either of you join in," Beast snapped back.

"Too busy laughing at you as you tripped," Hanz said.

"I caught myself!" Beast growled. He had more important things to do than argue with the twins. He pointed toward the longboat which had made landfall and was disgorging the raiders. "What do we do about that?"

"Sheyric has organized patrols on Ilos. Farmers have been set up with special flares so that if they see the Maramans, they can call for help," Hanz answered.

"We could stop them," Beast argued.

"Our first responsibility is to get this ship someplace safe. You can't go chasing after every raiding party. Nor do you have to. You can rely on us," Hanz said.

Beast watched the raiding party as they disappeared deeper into Ilos. His stomach twisted at the thought of what might happen to whomever the Maramans encountered. "We're right here!"

"And you can't be everywhere. Your role in the sin is to destroy the juggernaut," Hanz said. "Let other sin protect against the raiding parties. You won't accomplish anything if you try to do everything."

Beast shook his head but gave the order to prepare the newly captured ship for launch. He watched, though, as the last of the Maramans disappeared.

He wasn't reassured.

36

When the sun rose the next morning, Sato didn't feel any better about the events of the night before. He lay in bed even after waking, staring at the ceiling of his tent, allowing his mind to wander.

He knew he should meditate and practice his forms, as he did every morning. A sharp mind was even more important than a sharp blade, and his was dulled by the repeated blows it had endured over the last year.

Whenever he closed his eyes, it wasn't the scenes from the battle he relived, but the moments right after. The duel itself had been honorable enough, according to the dictates of the Path. Azazel had proposed the duel verbally, and Sato had implicitly agreed by drawing his sword in response.

But after.

After haunted him.

The decadence of the guests contrasted with the disrepair of the city. They'd treated the duel as spectacle, even though one of city leaders had lost their lives. The dictates of the Path had been obeyed, and yet the whole affair made him feel unclean.

He pressed his palms against his eyes.

He could debate with himself for days and come no closer to an answer. Azazel was dead, and the city moved one step closer to safety. He would have to take solace in that. Too much remained to do for him to lie around.

Sato rose and went through the routine that had carried him through so many years of his life. As his body moved, his mind eased. As always, the practice of his forms allowed him to find his center.

After bathing and changing into his uniform, he went searching for Crispin. His lieutenant wasn't hard to find, but Sato didn't expect him to be in the camp's training grounds. Crispin stood in the center, taking on all challengers. Sato briefly considered taking out his frustration on Crispin but decided against it. He'd learned his lessons about fighting his subordinates.

Sato waited for Crispin to finish. With a sword in hand, Crispin became a different person. The easy smile vanished. His eyes narrowed. And he won clean victories. Crispin was a skilled swordsman, a fact Sato kept forgetting every time his lieutenant angered him. When Crispin fought at his best, he looked a lot like a man who Sato would respect.

Crispin knocked down his last challenger, then called it quits. He stepped off the training grounds and offered Sato a quick bow. "I assume you want to speak, sir?"

"What happened last night?"

When Crispin didn't immediately answer, Sato began to suspect he was about to lie. But Crispin surprised him for the second time that day. "Would you mind walking with me while we speak about it?"

Sato motioned for him to proceed. Crispin took them outside the camp and into the heart of Versun.

As they walked, Crispin answered Sato's question. "I just

want you to know, and I'll swear this on anything you ask me to, that Alonzo and I followed your orders. Do you want to know the details?"

In the past, Sato might have been annoyed by such a question, but today he found Crispin's concern considerate. He didn't want to know the details, but he needed them, nonetheless. He nodded.

"Our original plan was to make it seem that Alonzo was having an affair with Azazel's wife."

The words came out fast, as though Crispin hoped Sato wouldn't be able to keep up. But Sato held up a hand to stop him. "Seem?"

Crispin grimaced, which told Sato all he needed to know. He needed to speak with Alonzo, too. Sato, not for the first time, wondered if his life would just be easier if he killed his lieutenants.

No doubt, Crispin sensed the danger. "We called it off as soon as you ordered, sir. Honestly."

To Sato's amazement, he believed Crispin. But it didn't answer his questions. "If it was called off, why did Azazel challenge me to a duel? Why not Alonzo?" It was within the bounds of the Path to challenge a superior. After all, commanders were responsible for the behavior of their sentinels. But it was unusual all the same.

Crispin stared down at his boots. "We might have also spread rumors that you were aware of the affair and did nothing to punish Alonzo. We think that Azazel caught word of everything even after it had ended. What happened last night was our original plan, sir."

After all this time, Sato shouldn't have been surprised at Crispin's ideas. But he was. He stopped mid-stride and shouted, "Crispin!"

Crispin didn't break stride. He waved at Sato. "You're furious. I know. It's why I brought you out here."

"So you would have witnesses when I challenge you to a duel?"

Crispin looked hurt by the suggestion but shrugged it off. "Just follow me. If you still want to duel once we leave our destination, I'll accept it." His lieutenant kept walking, not giving Sato a chance to answer. Sato growled but followed.

They came to the lower commercial district, and Crispin wound his way through the tight streets with a familiar ease. Sato followed but noticed that his uniform was attracting no small amount of attention. Every eye seemed to be on him. Whispers followed in his wake. Had word of his deed spread so fast? How would the people here react, knowing that he had killed their representative on the council? He fought the urge to reach for the hilt of his sword.

Crispin stopped outside a small forge. The building was in a state of disrepair, the walls so dilapidated they looked like they might collapse in a strong breeze. The sounds of a smith at work clanged against Sato's frayed nerves. Crispin led the way inside. Sato followed, shaking his head.

As soon as the smith saw Sato, his eyes went wide, and his hammer dropped weakly on the red-hot iron he worked on. He quickly set aside his work and hurried over to Sato. He bowed deeply, then yelled for the rest of his family. One after the other they emerged: four children, the smith, and his wife. "This is General Sato," the smith said. As one, they dropped to their knees and bowed their heads to the floor.

Sato took an involuntary step back. "That's not necessary." When they didn't move, he was firmer. "Please, rise."

They did, although slowly.

Sato studied the family and the forge. He wasn't an expert in metalwork, but the pieces he saw on display seemed to be of excellent quality. The steel in the shop looked like it had received more attention than the humans who made it. Everyone was too thin, with one of the children looking particularly sickly.

Sato had seen enough. He understood now why Crispin had brought him here. He bowed to the family, wished them well, then stepped out.

The street was more crowded when he emerged. Everyone appeared to have somewhere to go, but Sato noticed the looks. He stood tall, letting himself be seen.

Crispin emerged a moment later. "Azazel was taking their work and selling it for far less than it was worth. Despite his skill, that man could barely support his family. You're the first sentinel that has ever stood up for him."

"I understand."

"Do you?" Crispin challenged him. "Because I saw how you reacted last night."

"My disgust was at the people of Versun, standing around like a magistrate's death was no more than dramatic show. I do not mourn Azazel's death. It is easier, seeing this, though. Thank you."

"Good," Crispin said. "Because after last night, Izuki is going to suspect you're up to something in her city. It's only going to get more difficult from here on."

Shin shook her head as she watched Raya lead the group of sin away from the beach and towards the open rift on Iru. They had arrived as the sun was coming up and, despite the urgency of the situation, Raya had insisted they take an hour to rest and eat.

After, Raya had ordered Tia and Corin to stay behind and watch her. Her orders were to stay on the beach, no matter what. According to Raya, her role in the fight was over.

Shin was offended Raya would think so little of her strength. As soon as the other sin were gone, she turned on Tia. "Does she believe you're strong enough to stop me alone if I try to use sacrifice?"

Tia shrugged off the attack. "Ideally, she would have left another adept, but Raya needs all the strength she can muster to close that rift. If you knew how to listen, we could both be there to help her."

Shin ignored the jab and pushed at her own point. "So, she does believe you're strong enough?"

"I know I'm strong enough." Tia snapped back. "You're not as invincible as you think you are."

"Maybe you're not as useful as you think you are."

Tia was right about a few things. Shin didn't want to have to waste a sacrifice against her, nor did she want to have Tia waste her own sacrifice. Their enemy was the demons, if only the others would open their eyes and see that. And Tia had studied sacrifice a lot longer. She might know techniques that would defeat Shin.

No, the key to escaping this situation wasn't sacrifice. All her talk was just bluster. Bluster that was having the desired effect.

She wanted Tia mad.

Shin wasn't sure if she could beat Tia in a fight, even if Harmony was in her hand instead of strapped tightly across Corin's back. But she certainly wasn't going to test the sin adept without a weapon.

Also, whatever happened needed to be quick. Any prolonged conflict might give Tia time to use sacrifice. Added to all that was the young man she'd once called a friend. Corin kept a solemn, watchful eye on her always.

She kept pushing. "You can't be too strong if Raya left you behind. There's a rift torn open like the sin have never seen before and she still thinks she can spare you? That can't feel good."

Corin finally came to Tia's defense. "Shin. What's gotten into you?"

Tia, already angered by Shin's change in attitude towards her, didn't back down. She waved for Corin to retreat. "There is strength in following orders, Shin. Maybe if you grow up a little, you'll learn that."

Shin watched Tia's body language. Saw how she took a

step towards Shin's seated position and leaned her body over her.

Almost.

Shin mumbled unintelligibly but made sure her tone remained combative.

"What was that?" Tia said and bent a little closer to Shin.

Shin swung her hand up and connected solidly with Tia's temple. The large rock she had palmed in her hand made a dull thud, and the adept crumpled to the ground.

Corin was on her before she could fully get to her feet. The edge of his sword poked into her neck. "Sit. Back. Down."

Frozen mid-crouch, Shin smiled. "No."

Before he could react to her answer, Shin reached out with her sacrifice and called Harmony. Instead of bringing it to her, however, she pulled it back across the beach, taking Corin with it.

Shin stood and stretched as Corin was dragged around the beach. He bounced on his ass as Shin pulled him straight back. For a few moments he tried to fight the blade, but quickly realized how futile it was. He grabbed a knife and worked at the leather strap across his chest. Finally, he cut the strap and freed himself. He fell to the ground in a heap and Harmony spun around in a wide arc, landing in Shin's waiting hand.

"Stay down, Corin. I don't want to hurt you, but I'm going to deal with that rift."

Corin stood up and dusted the sand from himself. He looked at Shin for a moment before drawing his swords. "How?"

"I'm going to close it. And you're going to get out of my way."

"By the sun, Shin, are you that bullheaded? Do you refuse to learn? I'm not going to let you make things worse."

Shin threw Harmony at Corin and sprinted behind it. Corin deflected the blow and moved to close the distance across the beach. Shin caught the returning weapon and slid forward on her knees, slicing low at Corin's legs. Rather than block the blow, Corin jumped over the blade and pivoted to face Shin when his feet hit the ground.

"I won't make things worse, Corin. I'll close the rift and we'll be done with the demons."

"Yuki knows more about sacrifice and those rifts than you ever will. Why can't you just accept that she's right?"

"She said the rifts release pressure. Close one and the pressure builds on all three. Close all three and there are no more rifts. No more rifts, no more pressure."

Corin looked away from her in frustration, then focused and charged forward. Shin barely had time to block his first blow and the second would have cut her had she not scrambled backwards. Once she'd created space, even his two blades weren't fast enough to get inside her guard as she danced backwards.

"How do you know? Maybe closing the third rift will tear whatever keeps our worlds apart and overrun us? Why can't you just accept that they know better?"

"I've seen the rifts within the realm, Corin. You haven't. I can see how they work. The realm has shown me every intricacy. I'm the only one who knows how to close them!"

"Can you hear yourself? The realm isn't there to help you. Even I know that. It's hungry. It wants your sacrifices. You don't think it would do whatever it could to get them?"

Shin dismissed Corin's words even as they battled for a foothold in her mind. When had she stopped accepting that others might know more than her? When had she started to trust the realm so completely?

Before the thoughts could grow, she let out a primal scream and pushed forward against Corin. She mixed up her strikes with throws and made Harmony attack him at odd angles. He couldn't keep up, and she scored several cuts. Finally, she drove him to his knees, and she knocked the swords to the ground.

"I'm leaving," she said evenly.

Corin moved to pick up a sword, and she slapped his hand with the flat of her blade.

"Stop it," she said.

Corin stared in defiance and moved to pick up the other sword. She brought the blade down again, but this time left a gash across his arm. One that would scar.

"Do that again and you'll lose your hand. It'll be an example to anyone else that tries to stand in my way."

Corin's eyes widened and for a moment she thought he would relent. Instead, his eyes grew hard. "The same way the sentinels made an example of your parents?"

Corin's words hit her like a blow to the stomach. She didn't remember her father, but she remembered mother, dying on that terrible night, her body left as an example.

Shin looked at her friend, on his knees in the sand, blood pouring from the wound she'd given him, and something that had been hard in her cracked.

She wasn't wrong. She needed to save Samas and close the rift.

But how had it come to this? Her own weapon pointed at her closest friend in the world.

She shook her head and backed up a step, unable to reconcile the two certainties in her life. She was the only one who could close the rift, and Corin was the person she trusted most.

The battle waged for a moment before one side finally claimed victory.

Harmony fell from her hands and she fell to her knees, and tears trickled down her cheek.

38

———

"Did you stop those Maramans?" Beast shouted.

They'd returned the newly stolen Maraman ship to the port in Dahl and Beast had left training a new batch of sin up to Colas' second, Mina, so that they could come and see Yuki. Her lack of concern over the Maraman raiders he'd allowed to slip away was eroding his patience.

What patience he had, anyway. "Well?"

Yuki regarded him, cloaked in her insufferable calm. She sat in the receiving chambers of the magistrate's tower. Beast thought she'd taken to the new chambers awfully quick. They hadn't even cleaned all the blood from the streets of Dahl yet.

"I haven't received any reports that could give me that information, Beast. We've increased patrols on Ilos, just as you suggested, but we can only patrol so much of the island at once. Even if I had received a raven today, there wouldn't be mention of Maramans if our patrols didn't engage them," Yuki said.

"So for all we know, those men could be burning farms to the ground as we speak? All so you can have a little ship?"

"We are at war, Beast. If you are looking for me to promise you that no civilians of Samas are hurt in that process, I can't do that for you. Not unless you want me to lie to you as if you were a child. And as I recall, it was your suggestion that we start stealing Maraman ships. I don't remember you being so uptight about casualties when you were the Bandit King."

Beast ground his teeth together to avoid screaming in rage. He knew that everything she was saying, strictly speaking, was correct. That didn't change how wrong it felt.

Colas, silent up to this point, came to his aid.

"I think what my big friend is trying to say is that if we are truly waging a war to liberate Samas, we need to be careful about how reckless we are with the lives of the people we claim to be fighting to liberate. Right, Beast?"

Beast grunted the affirmative.

"Thank you, Colas, but at this point I am quite adept at reading between the lines of Beast's shouting and teeth gnashing," Yuki said, her tone almost imperceptibly hardening before returning to its more neutral tenor, "and I don't wish bloodshed on the people of Samas any more than you do. Unfortunately, we will have to make sacrifices. We are trying to protect the people of Ilos, but our resources are limited."

Now Beast allowed his simmering anger to boil over. "Yet we have enough to send food to the sentinels on Egzuki?"

"We've already been over this. Not only do we need the sentinels as allies, but we need the people of Samas, too. If we didn't send food, they'd attack Ilos and we'd be fighting a war on two fronts. Besides, it's not food that's our problem. It's warriors. If I could defeat the Maraman raiders by throwing bread at them, I'd have already done it."

Beast glared at her, but she wasn't cowed.

"You need to trust me, Beast. I know you did once. I do have the interests of all of Samas in mind."

Before Beast could respond, Colas laid a hand on his arm.

"I'm sorry to interrupt, Yuki, but most of this talk is above my poor sea-addled mind. I just wanted to report that you have your ship and I've trained Beast and his crew as well as I can," Colas said, deftly changing the subject.

"Yes, my apologies, Colas. My understanding is that you're keeping the other Maraman ship as payment?"

"That's right. I would be happy to stay on and help Beast build up your fleet, though. I'll charge my normal rate, per ship we steal."

"Done. I'm sure Beast is learning quickly, but your expertise on open water is indispensable. Thank you."

Colas nodded to Yuki and then turned to leave, pulling Beast along with her.

"I—" Beast began.

"We have a lot of work to do, Beast. Let's leave Yuki to run the sin," Colas said.

Yuki nodded to Beast, and he allowed himself to be dragged from the room. He wanted to ask Colas why she pulled him out of there, but she gave him a look that suggested he keep his mouth shut. They left the magistrate's tower and Colas started for the city gates.

Beast looked around Dahl and was pleased to note that the repairs to the city were coming along nicely. They walked through the market where Beast had first met Shin and he noted that the shops were open again and business was bustling. Yuki may not be perfect, but the sin were clearly better than the sentinels when it came to the interests of the people.

So why was he so conflicted?

When they exited town, Colas finally spoke.

"All of that? The politicking. The planning. Deciding whose lives are worth what like they're pieces on a chess board. Is that really something you want to be part of?"

"What other choice you think I have, Colas?" Beast grabbed her arm and pulled her to face him. "The mugon and the Bandit King are done. Whether I like it or not, this is what I've committed to."

"But you admit it feels wrong? That being a servant of the sin isn't much better than being a servant of the sentinels?" Colas asked.

Beast wasn't sure. When he had been the Bandit King, he had a clear and simple goal: unite the bandits and give people a place where they could be free. Once he realized the danger the Maramans and the demons posed, it had seemed clear and simple to let Yuki lead them. It was hard to serve someone else. He hadn't killed Yuki yet, which was more than he could say for most people who gave him orders. Still, it wasn't the dream he'd envisioned. "It's more complicated than I'd like," Beast said.

"Of course it is. You're still fighting someone else's war."

"I want to help people!" Beast shouted.

"That's the trap, Beast. You can't. Not on the scale that Yuki has deluded herself into thinking she can. But you can help yourself, and those closest to you," Colas said, pulling her arm out of Beast's grip.

Something about her logic nagged at Beast, but he couldn't place it. It sounded good, though, so much like the old Beast.

"Even if that were true, what can I do now? My mugon have become sin. I'm committed."

Colas smiled. "Tell me more about this juggernaut.

Because I think it might be the solution to all our problems."

39

Sato's trip to the smithy with Crispin had unlocked several doors in his thoughts. As small a moment as it was, it had shifted Sato's perspective and given him an insight that just might win him Versun.

His mistake was the same one far too many sentinels made. He'd forgotten, again, that when sentinels strayed from the Path, it was the citizens they were honor-bound to protect who suffered most.

As they returned to camp that day an idea had occurred to Sato, one he wasn't sure would have occurred to him prior to his time with the sun stalkers.

His problem was straightforward. He needed to control Versun. He possessed a small group of skilled soldiers who would fight to the death for him, but not nearly enough to either take or control the city after. In a more perfect world, he would simply command the sentinels within Versun's walls to obey him, and they would. He was the highest-ranking sentinel on the island.

But his command was the sun stalkers, putting him outside the normal chains of command. With the lines of command as blurred as they were, if he were to give such an order, he didn't know who the soldiers would follow. He feared that most of the sentinels would choose the path of greatest familiarity, leaving him the laughingstock of the whole city.

He'd also considered returning to the Firstborn, to demand the orders that would put him in control of the city.

But that approach also presented problems. To begin, Sato wasn't sure the Firstborn would dare wrest control of the city away from the entrenched magistrates. Perhaps more important, one of the lessons he'd learned from the sun stalkers was that there was a difference between leading and being obeyed. If Versun was going to have a chance against the threats that gathered on the horizon, he needed to lead it. Simply giving commands to unwilling subjects wouldn't be enough.

Fortunately, some of Crispin's talent for scheming seemed to have rubbed off on him. Although he still preferred a head-on attack, he'd learned the value of an oblique approach. Since visiting the smithy, he knew what his attack on the city would look like. The magistrates would never see it coming, because up until recently, he wouldn't have seen it either. The citizens were his path to rule. They had numbers, but no strength of arms to express their displeasure with the current magistrates. All he had to do was convince them that their desires and his coincided.

Starting the very next day, he and the sun stalkers began a campaign unlike any he'd run before. Instead of seeking to win territory, he sought to win hearts. Instead of standing upon the highest hill of the battlefield as the sole victor of a bloody contest, he walked the streets and the alleys, the places too long hidden from the sun and its everlasting gaze.

He listened and he helped. Thanks to his connections at

the docks, he rerouted food shipments to the districts that needed them most. He hired smiths, craftsmen, and tailors to equip his sun stalkers. Alonzo designed special patches for the unit, who wore them whenever they travelled the streets of Versun.

Progress was slow. Land was easier to conquer than hearts and minds. Daily, Sato doubted his strategy.

Crispin and Alonzo seemed to think it was a brilliant plan, though, and they threw themselves wholeheartedly into its execution. Sato couldn't decide if their approval meant he was a genius or the worst kind of fool.

The response from the wealthy inner districts of Versun was silence.

Crispin argued the magistrates had no idea what Sato was hoping to accomplish. Sato didn't hold his opponents in such low regard. Even if they didn't understand the full breadth of his strategy, they could guess at the important parts well enough. The only question was, how would they respond? Their silence unnerved him.

Today, Sato walked towards the lower district to supervise the establishment of a small kitchen that would offer free food to residents. They were about three blocks away from their destination when an older man hobbling on a cane approached. Sato's guards stopped him before he could get too close, but when they were sure he wasn't carrying any hidden weapons, they let him past.

"You're Sato, aren't you?" the man asked.

"I am."

The man glared at him. "Everywhere I walk, all I hear is people saying, 'Sato this, and Sato that.' All I hear is the things that you've done and all the things you promise to do. If half of what they say is true, you'd be the greatest ruler Samas has ever seen." The old man almost spat the words, and Sato's guards tensed at their weapons. Sato stretched out his hand and urged them to remain calm.

"While I am grateful for their kind words, I can tell you that I've made no great promises. I wish only to follow the Path."

At the mention of the Path, the man spit on the ground. "Fuck the Path! The Path is no more than a crooked justification for all the crimes sentinels commit day in and day out. Where was your precious Path when I was injured, when I needed the mercy of the sentinels the most?"

A crowd had gathered, keeping their distance from his guards' swords, but close enough to hear every word. They'd assembled quickly, faster than Sato would've expected. His eyes narrowed. Perhaps the man was a plant, sent by the magistrates, but Sato didn't think so. The anger this man bore was all too real. Sato believed he was exactly what he appeared, although it seemed this meeting had been preordained.

It was a test, then.

Though his hands itched to draw his sword and punish the man for his disrespect, he knew now such an action would only cause more harm. So he kept his posture open and forced himself to do what he'd done so much of the past two weeks. "Tell me your story," he said. And then he listened.

The man launched into his history. "I was a horse trainer, one of the best on the island. When one of your commanders needed a new horse broken in, when they knew they needed an animal that would never quake in fear at the advance of an enemy, they knew where to turn."

People nearby were nodding. Sato took note. He suspected many in the crowd had known him before his fall.

The man continued, "But when I was thrown from a

horse and my leg broken, the sentinels provided no aid. I was hobbled, unable to work while my leg healed." He looked like he was about to spit on the ground again. "The horses I'd trained saved the lives of their riders. I know it to be true because they've said as much. But when I was injured and couldn't work, where were the sentinels? They just went to the next trainer, and when my leg didn't heal properly, because I hurried it in my haste to return to work, did they still come to me?"

Sato could guess the answer to that. Training horses properly was demanding work. Chances were, an injured man would fail, and as the man himself had said, training warhorses was no small responsibility. He, too, would have gone on to the next trainer.

The trainer lifted his chin high. "So, if all you're promising is the Path, then you might as well kill me now, because I don't want to see the future you bring."

Sato couldn't deny a part of him wanted to. No sentinel deserved such disrespect. And if this scene was planned, as Sato suspected, the man's actions were even more detestable. He'd asked to be killed, which absolved Sato of all blame. The Path justified it. Respect was sacred.

But the Path also demanded he protect the people. Cutting this man down protected only the sentinels.

Sato took a quick step forward, and the whole crowd seemed to inhale at the same time. He didn't draw his sword. He spoke loudly enough for the crowd to hear. "You say that you were the best horse trainer on this island?"

The man lowered his chin and gave Sato a small nod.

"My sun stalkers have recently acquired several new horses. You will train them."

"I don't want your mercy, sentinel."

"It is not mercy. It is an order. I expect you to report to

my camp by noon." It wouldn't give the man much time, but he could make it if he hurried. "And I want you to know one thing."

"What's that?"

"My sun stalkers are more precious to me than any gold. The mounts they ride must be prepared for battle and terror greater than any normal warhorse. I accept only the best horses for my warriors. If you can meet my high standards, you will be rewarded richly. But if you fail me—if your poor training puts my warriors at risk, I will kill you."

It was a gamble, but Sato believed he understood this man.

He was right. The man straightened. He met Sato's eye, judging Sato's sincerity. When he was satisfied, he offered Sato a small bow. The crowd relaxed.

After a few more moments, Sato was on his way to the kitchen.

One heart at a time, he would win this city.

40

"I'm so sorry," Shin said, feeling how inadequate the words were but unable to come up with anything else to say.

Corin was tearing up, too. "You didn't kill me, so we can figure it out." He paused. "We will figure it out."

The war in her head wasn't over yet. Anger still seethed and bubbled below the surface, and her desire to smash something was almost irresistible. But she held it off. A memory of her mother floated before her, as her mother told her to wipe her tears and be brave.

They'd been right. In taking her memories, the realm had taken something more from her. Something that had made her *her*. Now she'd have to find a way to recover it. The process started with repairing what she'd broken with Corin. "How can you ever forgive me?"

Corin chuckled and got to his feet. "It's what friends do. I just hope you never forget again."

Shin moved to hug him but saw the blood flowing freely from between his fingers. She ran to the supplies the sin had left with them and pulled out some clean bandages.

"How bad is it?" Shin asked as she bound the wound.

"Looks worse than it is. I can still hold a sword."

Shin nodded and then hugged Corin tightly. He gave a surprised gasp and then hugged her back. He was the one constant that she had. The one person who was as close as family. Only now, when she realized how much she had lost with her memories, did she understand how much he meant.

And she'd given them away so willingly. It was almost childishly foolish when she considered it now.

Tears filled her eyes as she pulled away from Corin and stared at him. "Whatever happens, I will never sacrifice your memory. I promise."

Once again relief filled Corin's eyes, followed quickly by tears, and the two friends held each other once more.

Shin pulled away and looked around.

"What is it?" Corin asked.

"I don't know. It feels like Raya or one of the other adepts is flaring their power."

"What does it mean?"

"I'm not sure, but I'd guess it means they're in trouble. Flaring her power like that is a distress signal to other adepts," a voice said from behind them.

Shin jumped and spun around to see Tia smiling at her coldly. "Tia! Listen—"

Tia's fist connecting with Shin's nose stopped her mid-sentence.

Pain exploded in her face, and she fell to the ground, but bounced back up again. She pressed her hand to her nose, but it wasn't even bleeding. Tia had pulled the punch. "I deserved that."

"You did."

"And more."

"Certainly."

"I'm sorry?"

"That's a start, but we have more pressing concerns. I'm going to assume since Corin was just hugging you that you're done being a complete ass?"

"Yes! What's going on, though? Is it the demons or the rift?"

"No way to know," Tia said. She focused on Shin. "How much can I trust you?"

Shin chose honesty. "I'm still struggling, but I'll try."

Tia looked uncertain, but she had no good options. She nodded. "Then let's go see if we can help."

Shin's heart pounded in her ears as they ran through the woods. Corin was close behind her and she noted how much quieter he was, despite keeping up with her pace. He really had grown as a warrior.

"How much farther?" Corin whispered.

"Not far, but let's slow down and focus on being quiet. They've been moving at a steady pace, and we've closed a lot of the distance," Tia said.

Shin nodded. "I think it's sentinels. We're headed back towards to the capital and away from the rift. I doubt Maramans would be headed there. Even moving quietly, we should be able to get around the sentinels and wait for them to pass us by."

"I agree. Looks like the woman I wanted to follow into battle is making an appearance again," Tia said.

Shin smiled at the kind words, but inside, her mind reeled. Half her attention was on the battle ahead and the other half was on what she'd lost. She scoured her brain for memories of her father but found none. So far as she could remember, she grew up with her mother somewhere on Ilos.

The farm that Corin insisted she had told him about was gone.

And apparently, so were the lessons he had taught her.

In the cold light of that realization, she reexamined her earlier argument with Tia. She was right that Shin had treated her differently when they first met. She had worked hard to get to know all the sin and earn their respect. Her sudden dismissal of that respect and its value coincided with her closing the rifts.

And the way she was becoming more and more reckless coincided with her sacrifice of Mateo's memory at Dahl.

As they continued to move, she risked speaking quietly to Corin. "What did Mateo teach us?"

Corin was silent for a moment before answering. Probably wondering why she suddenly wanted to broach a subject that she'd always avoided before. "How to steal, how to sneak through crowds, you and Mateo trained with quarterstaffs a lot, but he never got around to showing me any of that."

Strange. Shin still retained the ability to do those things. She was even better at them, in fact. Perhaps skills she had built on or practiced remained. "Anything else?"

"Lots of things, I guess. He just taught us how to survive. How to take the right risks and when not to take them at all. He wouldn't even show Davin and I how to fight because he was worried we'd do something stupid with it."

"Fuck," Shin muttered.

"What?" Corin asked, surprised at the word.

"I owe Raya the biggest apology," Shin replied, glancing sidelong at her friend.

Corin grinned in what looked like relief. Shin couldn't blame him. She'd been an ass. Now she had to figure just how much of herself she'd lost.

"Shhh!" Tia hissed and grabbed her arm.

They had circled around and come to the road. The distress signal was growing closer. They settled into places where they wouldn't be found. Eventually, they found what they had been pursuing.

"Oh no," Corin said almost soundlessly.

Shin's heart sank in agreement with her friend. A battalion of sentinels were riding smartly down the road in formation. In the center of the horses were a dozen sin, hands bound, jogging along with their captors. Shin scanned the faces until she found Raya. A dark bruise was forming under one of her eyes, but she seemed otherwise unharmed.

"If they go into the capital there's no way they come back out. The Firstborn would never let sin leave alive," Tia whispered.

Shin nodded, but she was, very carefully, reaching to the realm to access her sacrifice. The moment Raya was passing the spot where they were hiding, Shin sent a small pulse through her sacrifice. As if she was about to call the realm, but stopped. Raya's head remained forward, but her eyes snapped to the side and met Shin's.

"Did she just look at you?" Corin asked.

"Yes. I used her trick. Just to get her attention. If we can somehow find a way to ambush the sentinels, the sin will be ready. I hope."

"You hope?"

"All I could do is let her know I was here. Hopefully that's enough for her to be ready."

"Oh, I just thought you could..." Corin trailed off.

"Talk to her with my mind?"

"Well, I mean, you can do a lot of things!"

Shin chuckled and leaned her head onto Corin's shoulder. "Thank you."

"For what?"

"For not losing faith in me. For being here for me even after I was so terrible with everyone."

"We've been through too much, Shin. You're like family to me. Family fights, but they always support each other."

Shin leaned her head on Corin for another moment, enjoying the calm that fell over her amidst the chaos of the moment.

"Well, that's adorable, but if we're going to catch up to our friends, we'd better get going," Tia said.

"I should thank you too, Tia," Shin said.

"Thank me later. Any idea how three sin are supposed to chase down a battalion of sentinels and rescue their friends?"

"I vote we let Shin do some crazy sacrifice magic," Corin said, only half-joking.

"I don't like it," Tia said cautiously, "but we are desperate."

"No," Shin said, the word was barely a whisper.

Corin and Tia looked at her in surprise.

"I know it's not the best time for me to have learned my lesson, but until I understand just how much of myself I gave to the realm, I don't think it's safe for me to use sacrifice."

The three would-be rescuers stared at each other for a moment in defeated silence before battle cries and the sounds of weapons being readied broke the silence.

The sentinels were under attack.

41

Beast gripped the wheel of his ship and pretended that it felt natural. Colas said that *Warhammer* should feel like an extension of his own body, the way a weapon did when Beast went into battle. Unfortunately, the helm of the ship felt about as natural as it would if he woke up to find he'd sprouted a pair of breasts.

Beast sighed.

"Prepare to come about," Colas said quietly in his ear.

"Prepare to come about!" Beast bellowed before spinning the wheel.

He watched as Colas' crew, who had volunteered to run *Warhammer* while Beast's crew sparred on the deck, moved as one unit to accomplish his orders.

He then watched every member of his crew stumble or fall as the ship moved under them.

"They're getting better," Colas assured him.

"Doesn't seem like it. Let me go down there and show them," Beast said and removed his hands from the helm.

"No! You need to learn this. You already know how to

fight, and they don't need you to show them how good you are. *They* need to get used to the movement of the deck."

Beast sighed heavily and put his hands back on the wheel. His stumble the last time he fought on a ship kept replaying in his mind. Mistakes like that could easily become fatal, and Beast had yet to find any time to shore up the weakness.

"I'm better suited to lead from the front of the assault than from back here," Beast said.

"If you're going to captain a ship, it is far more important that you are here at the helm. You can't be leading every charge."

"Other people can learn to steer a floating chunk of wood! No one fights like me."

"You need to be able to oversee your crew. This is where you can do that. More importantly, your crew needs to see you with a steady hand on the wheel. Out on the open water, the ocean itself is far more dangerous than any fool with a piece of sharpened metal. It's between your crew and that foe that you need to stand."

"I thought you said the helmsman steers," Beast replied.

"Aye, but you need to know how your ship moves like it's second nature. Eventually, you'll find a helmsman that can steer while you oversee the ship. Then your steady hand on the wheel will be metaphorical. For now, though, you need practice!"

Beast could see the wisdom in Colas' words, no matter how he chafed at them, so he remained silent.

"I'm still waiting for you to tell me about this juggernaut, and exactly what you plan to do about it," Colas said.

"I don't really have a good plan; I just know we need to figure out a way to sink it."

"And you said that ships like *Cutter* and *Warhammer* attach to it somehow?" Colas asked.

Beast frowned, not quite following the path of Colas' thoughts. "It seemed like it. We were far off when we saw it, but the ship that pursued us seemed to separate from the hull of the juggernaut."

"The Maramans must come from very far off if they need a ship that size to safely traverse the ocean," Colas said thoughtfully.

"Even if we steal every ship the Maramans have, I'm not sure how we destroy that thing. I've seen the sin use a black powder that can destroy walls when lit. Maybe if we had enough of that? Or maybe one of them could use sacrifice to blow a hole in it? I've seen that once before." Beast reached around to touch the hilt of Benji's broken sword that was tucked into his belt.

"Tack to port," Colas said, her mind still elsewhere.

"Tack to port!" Beast bellowed. This time, a few of his crew managed to stay on their feet.

"Just out of curiosity, what if we *didn't* destroy it?" Colas asked.

Beast thought for a moment. "I suppose once we steal enough of the smaller ships, we could isolate it. Cut it off from food and water long enough and the Maramans would starve. We couldn't steal all their ships, though, so we'd end up just running around trying to prevent the raids before they got to Ilos. It's little better than patrolling on the island itself." He looked to his crew, still trying to find their feet. "But they'll be the better sailors. It's better if we can take the fight to them."

"I agree. All I'm saying is why destroy a prize like that? Wouldn't having a juggernaut of our own be the bigger advantage?" Colas asked.

"Sure, but destroying it is hard enough. Why make it harder?"

Beast thought about his own question. "More of the Maramans are on their way. A juggernaut of our own might turn the battle before they even made landfall," Beast said, his excitement growing.

"I think—" Colas started, but Beast interrupted her.

"How do we do it? Something like that, we'd need far more soldiers."

"Well, we did tell Yuki we'd build her a fleet. I'm assuming that means she'll part with her sin."

"How many ships will we need? With all the refugees from the sin island, space is becoming an issue in Dahl, anyway." Beast's mind was churning with possibilities.

"Are there enough of your former mugon to crew half a dozen ships?" Colas asked.

"And then some. Good plan. They already know how to work together as a unit. That's half the battle out here."

"And they're loyal to you," Colas said softly.

It was her tone that finally got Beast's attention. "Of course they are. Why do you say that?"

"Beast, with a juggernaut at our disposal, we can do what we please. We'd answer to no one."

Not even Yuki. Colas left the words unsaid, but they reverberated in the air as if they'd been shouted inside a cave.

"What would we do with that kind of freedom?" Beast asked warily.

Colas looked at him and gestured out to the empty expanse of ocean that stretched beyond site. "Whatever we want."

"We would be taking hundreds of good swords away

from the defense of Samas. Not to mention stripping them of any kind of naval defense."

"I told you before that you're fighting someone else's war. Is that really who you are? Is that *what* you are, a sheep led around by Yuki?"

Beast looked out over the horizon and felt something tug at his heart. Was it freedom?

Fuck if he knew.

Beast sighed. "One thing at a time. First, let's figure out if we can even steal a juggernaut. Then we can decide what we want to do with one."

42

"You're sure this is a good idea?" Crispin asked for the third time in as many minutes.

"I'm sure," Sato responded.

Alonzo tugged at his sleeve.

"You don't have to ask again, Alonzo. No, I don't think we can trust him, but he won't kill us outright," Sato said.

He understood their concerns. The game, such as it was, had gotten dangerous. He made no claim to being a master of political maneuvering, but he'd fought in enough battles to recognize when lines were being drawn in the sand.

"How do you know this magistrate?" Crispin asked.

"Magistrate Helios served under my father when he was a general to the Firstborn. Helios was one of my father's most trusted men. After he died, Helios took over as general for a short time, but he lacked the skills the Firstborn demanded. Eventually he became a magistrate. I lost track of him after that. Until I found him here."

"Where he's worked his way into Izuki's good graces."

"Indeed," Sato said grimly, but didn't elaborate on his dark thoughts.

The man that he had known was an honorable sentinel, but if Sato had learned anything, it was that those two words didn't go together as often as he had once believed.

Still, Sato felt he knew Helios well enough that he could risk a meeting in person. At the very least, it would allow him to take the measure of the man he once knew.

"I still think we should be trying to remove him, not ally with him," Crispin prodded.

"It's worth the risk." Sato thought back on the Firstborn's words back in Bulas, that he needed some experienced hands helping him once Versun was on the Path once again. He hoped Helios could be one of those hands. If the man was anything like he once was, this meeting could be the start of exactly the alliance they needed. "Don't you think?"

"Not quite sure what to think, sir. I just get a bad feeling about this one."

"It's tea, Crispin. Don't you like tea?"

Crispin sighed heavily and fell into step behind Sato.

They passed through the gate that separated the merchant district, now firmly under sun stalker control, and the residential district. The citizens of the port and the merchant districts lived near where they worked, some right above the very shops they ran. The residential district was filled with those merchants who had done well for themselves, as well as the most talented artisans in Versun. Here they were closer to the center of the city and farther away from the noise of the shops.

"Just one of these homes could go a long way to solve the housing issues down by the port," Crispin muttered.

Sato looked over his shoulder at his lieutenant and raised an eyebrow. "That's surprising, coming from you. I'd have expected you to buy one of these places up after you leave the sentinels."

"Leave the sentinels? Sir, you've changed me. Now I'm definitely completely on the Path. Probably die on it, too, the way things are going."

Sato shook his head. "You're Path-adjacent at best."

Helios' home was modest, at least for the area he lived in. The two-story structure was designed with clean lines and subtle adornments. Despite being far larger than a man and his family could possibly need, Sato still sensed a modicum of sentinel restraint in its presentation.

Maybe there was some hope for Helios yet.

"Sato, welcome. It's been years, and by the sun, those years have been kind."

Standing in the courtyard of the home was an aged sentinel. His short hair was completely white, a color matched by his eyebrows and a neat moustache under his nose. His skin, while wrinkled, was still tanned from the sun, giving the effect of three white lines drawn across a brown canvas.

"Magistrate Helios, you honor me. You're looking well," Sato responded with a bow, and he wasn't lying. Helios stood rod-straight and his broad shoulders still appeared muscular.

"Thank you. Please, come sit. It's a lovely day. I thought we could take tea in the courtyard. Your men are welcome to join, of course."

Sato nodded and then introduced his lieutenants. Before long, the four men were sitting in the warm sun and sipping tea. Only the large number of sentinels surrounding them and the house broke the spell of old friends having afternoon tea.

"This is the Firstborn's favorite blend," Sato said, raising the tea to his mouth.

"It was actually a gift from him." Helios changed the

subject quickly, surprising Sato. "You don't look much like your father."

"Indeed?" Sato said over his raised cup.

"No, you have his bearing, but you take after your mother far more."

"I've not heard that before. Most people say I resemble him."

"Well, most people have good reason to lick your boots, wouldn't you say?"

Sato laughed. "Up until a year ago, I would have said you were correct. Lately, I've been keeping different company."

"So I've heard," Helios responded, sparing a glance at each of his lieutenants, "and I think your father would be proud. I say that with no reason to sample the soles of your footwear, of course."

"Thank you for the kind words. Father always was the dutiful sentinel. I think he'd approve of my high rank," Sato responded.

"I don't mean that. Of course, he would have been proud of your rank, but he never had any doubt that you would earn plenty of promotions. None of us did. You used to run around and quote the Path to your father and I all day long!"

Crispin and Alonzo both laughed at that. Sato smiled to himself.

"I don't recall you straying much, Helios, but I'm glad you thought me entertaining."

"I thought you a self-righteous little shit! But an honest one and, even at a young age, worthy of respect." Helios looked at him meaningfully. "I'm impressed to see that hasn't changed."

"I walk the Path, Helios. It's not so hard."

"Ah, there's that self-righteousness I was once so familiar

with." Helios raised his hands. "I meant no offense, Sato. If anything, I'm envious. Perhaps even a little jealous."

"Of the sentinel I've become?" Sato asked wryly.

"Of the sentinel you remain. And that's what I meant when I said your father would be proud."

The two men stared at each other for a moment and Sato shifted slightly in his seat. He kept his hands on the table in front of him, but the movement put his sword hilt in a better position should he need it.

"I've heard that since your arrival, the walls in the port and merchant districts have finally received some much-needed repairs," Helios said.

Sato shifted a little more. "Indeed. Given the fall of Dahl, Magistrate Izuki was happy to have me inspect Versun's defenses. I suppose my presence has resulted in cleaning up some of that which has become derelict over the years."

"Indeed. I approve, of course. I could just never seem to free up the appropriate time, or coin, to do so. Being magistrate tends to pull your attention in a lot of directions. I'm sure you can understand what I mean."

Sato spared a quick look at Crispin, who was doing a remarkable job of calmly sipping his tea. He did manage a slight nod to indicate he was reading between the same lines as Sato.

"As you are an old friend, and in fact a former mentor to me, I would be more than happy to share any expertise I have in that area. Were you to come to the port district, I'd be happy to show you what I've accomplished. And what I have in mind for the future. You could join me right now, if you'd like."

Helios smiled at Sato, but it never reached his eyes. The old sentinel glanced briefly, too briefly for most to notice, at the guards surrounding the house. "Oh, I'm afraid I could only make time for this meeting today, Sato. As much as I'd love to join you and see firsthand all that you've done, my schedule won't permit it. You understand?"

"Of course, old friend. Perhaps someday soon?"

"I'd like to think so, but my duty will likely keep me here. I'm sorry. It was good to see you, though," Helios said, and stood.

"You too," Sato responded, taking the hint and standing himself. "I know you think those that walk the Path are impervious to change, but I've come to understand there *is* interpretation required. Finding one's way to the Path is a great accomplishment."

Helios surprised Sato by embracing him and even more so when he whispered in Sato's ear. "Make haste."

When Helios broke the embrace, he was still smiling, but Sato could see tears prickling the old man's eyes.

43

———

As one, Shin, Tia, and Corin hurried toward the sound of battle. They stayed in the trees but prioritized speed over stealth. Whatever was happening, they didn't need to worry about the sentinels. From the sound of it, all their attention was occupied. Shin held up her hand for the group to stop and poked her head out around a tree.

They were behind the battalion of sentinels, but that didn't stop her from seeing the horror they faced. The sentinels were engaged with a pair of demonically perverted bears. The animals must have been huge in life, because their elongated heads sat well above the sentinels on their war horses. Each bear was already a pincushion of arrows, but, of course, that hadn't slowed them down one bit. Several sentinels lay in crumpled heaps along the road.

"Should we help?" Corin asked.

"We need to stop the demons, but our priority should be freeing our friends," Shin said and then after a moment looked at Tia. "Right?"

Tia nodded.

Having realized that the arrows were useless, the

sentinels were now trying to keep the demon animals contained with long spears.

Shin squinted. These didn't look like any sentinels she'd seen before. Their splint mail, while still standard-issue sentinel craftsmanship, was colored a deep maroon. Embossed on the front was the image of a sunburst rising above an inky black landscape. Their discipline, even while facing off against otherworldly monsters, was unshakeable.

"Some kind of special unit?" Shin asked Tia.

"Yes, but they still don't know how to handle those demons. They can only hold them off for so long."

"What do we do?"

"What the sin do best; kill some demons," Tia said.

Shin and Corin nodded and the three of them moved through the foliage that lined the road and into position behind the bears. As the demons pushed forward, absorbing spear and sword wounds to cut into the sentinels, Shin threw Harmony. The blade spun through the air and embedded itself in the thick neck of the closest demon.

The monstrosity turned toward its attacker, causing its head to flop around a little, but Harmony remained lodged inside. Corin dashed forward and landed deep cuts on the bear, causing it to bring its claws up to defend. Tia moved in behind him but didn't draw her weapon. Instead, she darted into an opening caused by Corin's attack and leapt into the air, grabbing Harmony and wrenching it down with all her might.

The sharp blade cut the rest of the way through the thick neck of the bear and its body melted into black mist.

Tia tossed Harmony into the air before closing her eyes and sending the demon-mist back in the direction of the rift.

Shin drew her weapon back into her waiting palm and

sprinted towards the second bear. The sentinels adjusted their tactics, hacking at the limbs of the demon. One of its back legs was gone, and the second was just barely holding the weight of the beast as it pushed itself forwards.

"Remove the head!" Shin shouted above the sounds of battle.

The sentinels who were not engaged with the demon had closed ranks around the captured sin in order to assess the three strange additions to the battlefield. The commander, a wizened-looking man who was still built for combat, considered Shin for a moment before relaying her orders to the sentinels attacking the bear.

With a discipline that Shin couldn't help but admire, the sentinels changed tactics once more and removed the bear's head without losing another life. Once the demon turned to black mist, Tia sent it back to the rift as well.

Before Shin had a chance to speak, two dozen spears pointed at her and Corin, and the tip of a sword was pressed against Tia's throat.

"Tell her to stop what she's doing," the commanding officer ordered Shin.

"You don't want her to do that," Shin said as she dropped Harmony to the ground.

"Why?" the commander asked.

"Those monsters you just fought aren't done for yet. If you don't let her complete what she's doing, they will return, quite possibly more dangerous than before."

The commander considered her words for a moment before nodding slightly. The tiny motion was enough to drop the blade from Tia's neck and give the three sin a little more space.

But not much.

"How long until she's done?"

"Not long," Shin replied.

The commander nodded again, and they waited in silence. It was clear he had questions for her, but he wanted to make sure the immediate threat was dealt with first. Shin felt a grudging respect for the man.

He reminded her of Sato. A pain in the ass, but very useful to have on your side in a pinch.

The minutes seemed to last for hours as Shin stared at the ring of steel around her. She caught Raya's eye at one point, but the adept's expression was unreadable. Dried blood painted the side of her face, and her hair was matted in blood. Shin wondered how foggy her mind was.

Finally, Tia opened her eyes and looked around. "It's done."

"Good. My name is Commander Harris. What are you doing here?"

Shin looked at Tia for a moment and they both shrugged. The time for secrecy had passed. "We're here to seal that rift and prevent any more of those demons from getting out."

"How do we know that you didn't cause these demons in order to justify your presence here?" Harris asked.

"Did it look like they were at our command when you came upon us?" Raya asked from behind Harris.

"No, I don't suppose it did," Harris said without looking over his shoulder. "But we have never seen anything like these demons before, and now, here they are, along with a unit of trained warriors we've never seen before either."

"Normally we handle this kind of thing without being interrupted by sentinels," Tia said.

Harris raised an eyebrow.

"My point is, we usually do this kind of work without

you knowing. It would be easier for us if that continued to be the case," Tia said.

"I'm not sure I can allow that," Harris responded, but again he appeared to be considering all options.

"And I'm not sure that's true this time, Tia," Raya said.

Harris turned to look at her.

"Normally, we can send the demons back and seal the rift. But not this time. I can't seal it. Something happened," Raya looked pointedly at Shin, "and now the pressure on this rift is too high. I don't know what to do other than contain it. We were pushing towards the rift to do just that when you came upon us. We need to get to there and set up a perimeter, or this island will be overrun."

"You're asking us to let you go?" Harris asked.

"No, I'm asking for your help."

"Raya—" Shin began, but the adept fixed her with a hard stare.

"Help you? A group of armed soldiers who aren't sentinels? Under the Path, you should be put to death."

"Commander Harris, let's not play games. This is an elite unit of sentinels, and you were dispatched to the very area where we found the demons. I don't believe that to be a coincidence. The Firstborn sent you to deal with these demons, which means he briefed you on what to expect. I'd be surprised if he left the sin out of that briefing."

The sentinel commander regarded Raya with a small smile before finally nodding his head. "You're correct."

"Am I also correct in assuming that his orders were to keep us alive?"

Harris nodded, the smile never leaving his face.

"Good. Then you know we are the only ones that can stop these demons. To that end, we will need your fighting strength. Do you need to run back to the Firstborn to get permission to help us, or does he trust you to use your judgment in the field?"

"Careful, sin. I'm a patient man, but your tone comes dangerously close to insolence. I am captain of the Firstborn's personal guard. He dispatched me with Rosa's unit to be an extension of his voice. The threat these demons pose is clear. My duty is the safety of Samas. You'll have our help."

"And your discretion?"

"These men and women are the best the sentinels have to offer. I would pick any one of them over any warrior in this land. They are loyal to the Firstborn and no one else. Until this issue with the rift is solved, we will be the only ones that know of your presence on Iru." As if to punctuate his point, Harris ordered the sin held prisoner set free.

The sentinels parted, and the sin joined Tia, Corin and Shin. Raya continued to fix Shin with a hard stare.

"Raya, I—" Shin began.

"Not now," Raya snapped.

"Right."

"Definitely later, though," Raya said. Her voice was iron.

"Right," Shin replied nervously.

"Now, what do you need from us?" Harris asked. "Because I don't want to have to fight any more of those demons than necessary."

44

"Coming about!" Beast called out.

His crew moved as one and *Warhammer* turned along with the rest of the fleet, their sharp bows cutting through the choppy ocean. Beast grinned as he thought of the progress his crew had made.

And at the freedom of sailing the open ocean.

They weren't nearly as good as Colas and her crew yet, but he and his mugon could operate *Warhammer* well enough. Perhaps most surprising, though, was how much he enjoyed it. He still remembered how he had yelled every time Benji had ordered him onto the tiny skiffs that ferried the people of Samas from one island to another. Of course, those boats were as similar to *Warhammer* as Beast was to Sato, so how could he have known what true sailing was like?

"The new crews are doing well. Not perfect but mostly keeping formation," Gorou, his second in command, said.

Beast took another look around at the ships sharing the ocean with him. Up ahead was Colas in *Cutter*, followed by

Warhammer, and behind him was *Dusk*, the latest addition to their family of warships.

Maybe their last, too. They'd trained dozens of former mugon, but there weren't as many ships raiding Ilos as there had been before. Speculation abounded as to the reasons, and Beast personally suspected a few factors were involved.

For one, Yuki had been true to her word, and the increased patrols on Ilos were doing an adequate job of protecting the farms. But the Maramans also had to be hurting. There couldn't have been that many left after the failed attempt on Dahl, and between their latest losses and the lack of resources returning to the juggernaut, Beast couldn't imagine the Maramans had much fight left in them.

What worried him, though, was how the juggernaut would react. The most dangerous enemy was the one backed into a corner, and this cornered enemy had the most powerful sea weapon Samas had ever seen at its disposal.

So the training continued as they debated ways to end the Maraman threat for good.

"Colas has been a good teacher. Given enough time, we'll have ourselves some real sailors here," Beast said to Gorou.

"Let's hope so. Stealing these raiding ships is one thing, but that juggernaut is something else entirely. I finally got a look at it the other day. It really is a floating city."

"Come now. Cities aren't so hard to take. Look what we did to Dahl," Beast said with a confidence he didn't feel. Gorou, though, looked cheered by the bravado.

Beast watched the crew as they went through a few more exercises, then decided they'd done enough for the day. He gave the order for the ships to return to Dahl, where they docked at the port.

After making sure the ship was secure, Beast started

toward Dahl, Colas at his side. The two of them had plans to drain one of their favorite taverns of ale in celebration of all they'd accomplished.

They didn't make it far. They were barely halfway up the road to the city when a messenger intercepted them, out of breath. "Yuki needs to see you," she said.

Beast glanced up at the magistrate's tower, visible even from outside the city. He could well imagine Yuki there, looking down on the port and seeing their hard-won ships as nothing more than chess pieces to be used in her game. "Tell her I'll come after I've slaked my thirst."

The sin messenger snorted. "She also said that if you showed any signs of resistance, that I had permission to assemble a team of adepts to bring you to her. She insists that it's urgent." The messenger glanced toward Colas. "You were included in the order as well."

The messenger was lucky Colas didn't take her head for that. Beast saw the storm clouds building on Colas' expression and stepped in. "Thank you. We'll be there right away," he said.

The messenger looked like she might press the issue and demand to escort them, but then saw the look on Colas' face and chose a more reasonable approach. "Yes, sir. I'll let her know." Then she scampered off as fast as she could.

Colas growled. "You can't tell me you don't tire of being at that woman's beck and call."

Beast watched the departing messenger and felt himself torn between two futures. He knew well enough what Colas wanted from him. She wanted the juggernaut for herself, with all the freedom that entailed.

The problem was, he wanted that too.

But he also wanted to help the people of Samas, trampled for too long under the feet of the sentinels.

A better person than him wouldn't have such an issue. Obviously the needs of a whole nation were supposed to come before his own desires. His own mugon, by and large, were people who had tried to live on the Path but had been denied the opportunity. Banditry had been their only reasonable option, and Beast had made it even more lucrative.

He'd given them a new Path.

The only problem was, he didn't know where it led.

For now, he pushed the problems aside. He had to deal with Yuki first.

She was waiting for them up in the tower. Immediately, Beast knew something big was afoot. Yuki and Sheyric were there, as was Gorou, Hanz, Jurian, and a handful of other sin commanders. None of them looked to be in a particularly happy mood.

Yuki opened without even a greeting. "We need to destroy the juggernaut."

Beast blinked twice, not sure he'd heard correctly. Colas was quicker on her feet. "Why?"

"The situation in Samas is deteriorating rapidly," Yuki said. "Shin tore open the rift on Iru, and we're not sure we can contain it. I plan on sending what reinforcements I can, but we're fighting too many battles. I've been tempted to just forget about the juggernaut and focus on the demons, but the surviving Maramans have shown a remarkable tendency to make themselves a pain in my ass. The only way to move on is to destroy the juggernaut."

"How?" Beast asked. "We've been trying to answer that question for weeks and still don't have an answer."

Yuki shook her head. "Because you still haven't learned to ask for help. We'll solve the problem the same way we've saved Samas for generations. Through sacrifice."

Colas stepped in. "We don't have to destroy it. We can capture it."

Every eye in the room turned to her.

"Convince me," Yuki said.

"It'll be harder," Colas admitted, "but if you're willing to spare sin adepts, we have options we haven't considered yet. And there's no denying having a juggernaut under our control would be useful. Beast has told me you expect more Maramans to arrive before long. They will bring at least one more juggernaut with them. Wouldn't it be better to meet them at sea, with equal strength?"

Yuki gave Colas a hard stare.

Beast understood the game Colas was playing, and he admired her courage.

But it was foolish. Yuki was clever enough to know that Colas had her own plans for the juggernaut. The sin leader would never fall for such an obvious ploy, especially if she risked sin adepts.

Yuki turned to Beast. "What do you think? Are your singun able to take and control the juggernaut?"

Even Beast caught the hidden meaning of the question. If they took the juggernaut, would *he* be able to control it? Would he keep it in sin hands?

He looked over at Colas and saw the same question in her gaze.

Beast returned his gaze to Yuki.

"Absolutely."

Yuki stared at him for a minute longer, and Beast wondered how well she could see into his heart. Would she trust him, if she knew the competing desires that tore at him?

Yuki gave them a brief nod. "Very well, then. Let's figure out how we're going to steal a juggernaut from the Maramans."

45

———

Crispin and Alonzo followed Sato as they walked briskly away from Helios' home. Sato's mind was racing. "Crispin, I need you to find out whatever you can, however you can. Something is binding him to Izuki, but I don't think it's greed. There's more happening that I don't know about."

Before Crispin could answer, Alonzo flashed a series of gestures.

"Alonzo has some contacts that might be helpful," Crispin translated.

Sato nodded, and Alonzo melted into the afternoon crowds.

"You think you can win him over to our cause?" Crispin asked.

"I don't think I have to. Despite how far he's strayed, I believe he's still an honorable sentinel at heart. But Izuki has something. And those guards weren't just for his protection. They were keeping him prisoner, as well. If we can see what power she holds over him, we may be able to wield it to our own advantage."

Crispin scratched at his chin. "Just how do you see this working?"

"Find the leverage Izuki has over Helios. Remove it. He might not have the rank he once did, but his word will carry significant weight. Between him and the citizens of Versun, it might just be enough to flip control of this city peacefully."

They made their way toward the port district, Crispin chewing on Sato's ideas. But Sato knew his lieutenant well enough to know that something bothered him. "Spit it out, Crispin."

Crispin shook his head. "It isn't something I can put my finger on, but this city's been bothering me for a few days now. Izuki can't be a fool, not if she's chief magistrate. And since Azazel, most of your moves have been in the open. She must know, at least in broad strokes, what you're trying to do. Why hasn't she moved against us?"

"The same reason I wouldn't have. She doesn't understand how powerful the will of the people can be. If they aren't sentinels, she doesn't think about them."

"Sorry, sir, but I don't accept that. All due respect, she understands running a city a lot better than you do. I'd like to bring Roko and the others in. It's time for the sun stalkers to enter Dahl in force."

Sato hesitated for a moment. They'd talked this over a few times. The sun stalkers had a place set up for them in the port district, where they didn't have to fear ambush. But Sato had been reticent to bring them in. Given how the situation stood with Izuki, it might bring the very escalation Sato hoped to avoid. He didn't share Crispin's unease, but he understood it. He had the feeling that things would start to happen quickly now. "Do it."

When they left the residential district, Sato felt a wave of relief. This, at least, was territory he knew he controlled. He took the time to speak with the various merchants and craftsmen that approached him. Some came with thanks, others with questions or concerns. Sato helped them all as he was able. It felt good, to lead like this.

But of course it would. This is what walking the Path meant. If not for his time with the sun stalkers, he might not have realized as much.

Crispin didn't seem to share Sato's joy. He was looking everywhere at once, expecting an ambush, but Sato didn't believe Izuki would be so stupid as to attack them outright in his own territory.

He was wrong.

They had only made it a few blocks into the merchant district when Sato heard the familiar sound of marching footsteps. Ahead of him, at least two units of sentinels, their armor shining in the sun, rounded the corner. As soon as the sentinel in the lead saw Sato, he pointed.

Sato's stomach sank.

"Sir, maybe we go this way?" Crispin pointed to a side alley.

Sato nodded and followed Crispin into the alley. They emerged on the next street over.

"Best we hurry, sir," Crispin said.

Sato agreed. He was grateful to have Crispin beside him. If anyone could escape a slowly closing trap of sentinels, it was him.

More sentinels appeared, on both ends of the street. Behind them, the alley filled with sentinels as the first group they'd spotted pursued them.

"Might be time to run," Crispin said.

Before Sato could agree, more sentinels appeared, cutting off their last avenue of escape. One of the commanders held up his hand. "Halt, by order of Magistrate Izuki, you're under arrest!"

Angry murmurs rippled across the crowded streets. All commerce stopped as every eye turned toward the unfolding drama.

"For what crime?" Sato demanded.

"Treason against the city of Versun and the nation of Samas," the commander replied. "We have evidence that despite all your claims to be fairly distributing food among the people, you've been claiming an exorbitant amount of supplies for your sun stalkers."

At that, the murmurs grew louder in the crowd. They were confused, but anger wasn't far behind.

Sato glared at Crispin, who looked wounded by his commander's doubt. But he shook his head, and Sato believed him. Crispin hadn't been taking from the city. Sato gave a sharp nod, and Crispin sagged with relief.

Sato turned his glare on the commander. "That's an outright lie, and you know it. If not for us, hundreds, if not thousands of citizens would continue to starve while you all feasted in the inner districts."

That raised a few shouts from the crowd. He might not be as good at running a city as Izuki, but he was no fool. This was as much a performance for the people as it was an arrest. The crowd might not have been completely on his side, but they believed him over the other sentinels. His work hadn't been for nothing.

The commander seemed to recognize the same. "You can plead your case to the honorable magistrates of Versun." He paused, taking in the crowd. "Now, will you come peacefully?"

Sato weighed his choices. He didn't see anything good coming of following the sentinels. If Izuki was bold enough to take this step, there was no telling how far she would go. He'd be cut off from his sun stalkers.

But if he didn't, the streets of this district would be filled with blood. The crowd outnumbered the sentinels, but there were a lot of sentinels, and every one was worth several citizens in a battle. In the end, there was only one decision to make. "I'll go willingly."

The angry murmurs continued, but the crowd stayed where they were. Sato bit down on his anger as sentinels disarmed him and put him in shackles. As they took Crispin's sword, the lieutenant surprised one of the sentinels with a solid punch to the nose. The other sentinel returned the favor in kind, and Crispin flew back into the crowd, who caught him before he could fall to the ground.

"Thanks," Crispin said and patted the man who caught him on the chest.

"Any more of that and you lose that hand, understood?" the sentinel shackling Crispin's hands said.

"Got it," Crispin said and winked at Sato.

As they led them away, Sato could hear the crowd shouting in anger.

"You could have let them help us," Crispin said.

"Too many would have died. We'll just have to figure a way out."

"Assuming Izuki doesn't kill us on sight," Crispin said.

"Enough chatting," the sentinel mounted beside Sato said, and kicked him in the ear.

Sato turned and studied the sentinel's face.

He didn't want to forget the first person he would visit the moment he got his sword back.

46

———

"We can't keep this up indefinitely. There are just too many demons, and sacrifice isn't as easy as you think it is. Even our generational spells take an incredible level of focus and will," Raya explained to the young woman before her.

"So get your leader to send you more adepts." The sentinel lieutenant, Rosa, practically spat the words. "When Captain Harris asked what you needed you told him you needed sentinels to kill demons so you could send them back. We've been holding up our end of the deal. Now hold up yours."

A few days ago, Shin had been impressed by how open Captain Harris, a sentinel so close to the Firstborn, had been to working with the sin. It didn't appear, however, that all the sentinels shared the same openness.

Big fucking surprise, there.

Raya drew on what seemed to Shin to be a bottomless well of patience. "Lieutenant Rosa, you have to understand. The sin don't have unlimited adepts any more than you have unlimited sentinels. Every adept we can spare is here, dealing with this."

When the first wave of sin reinforcements had arrived, Shin had half-expected, and half-dreaded, Yuki to show up herself. Fortunately, that hadn't been the case. Yuki didn't want to leave Dahl undefended, and Beast also required support for some crazy plan to steal the juggernaut from the Maramans. Yuki's orders had been to do their best to contain the rift until she could work out a way to close it.

And if they couldn't, well, they were fucked. Yuki had suggested that Versun, where Sato was apparently fighting for control, might be an option, but Shin didn't see how. Iru was just too big with too many people. They had to fight here.

Rosa jerked Shin out of her macabre thoughts. "The Firstborn said we need to contain this thing, so that's what we'll do. I don't want to hear any more talk about falling back."

"You're a fool if you don't start getting people behind walls," Raya argued. "We're holding for now, but all it will take is one mistake for this line to break. If we screw up, the mists start taking the shape of sentinels, and that's not something any of us want. Have you ever had to fight a demon version of yourself? I assure you it's not fun," Raya snapped. It appeared the well may finally be running dry.

"Every sentinel here will stand against any enemy. No matter their appearance," Rosa retorted.

"I'm not questioning your bravery, lieutenant," Raya said, "but you aren't fighting something that just *looks* like you. You're fighting something that's another version of you. Only stronger, faster and angrier. It's not a fate I wish upon any of you. Please, you need to start getting people behind the walls."

"The entire island? You can't be serious. No, we won't slink away like cowards. We'll fight and die if we have to."

"Very honorable," Shin said dryly.

"I strive to walk the Path," Rosa replied.

Shin couldn't help but scoff at her earnest response. "Well then, as usual, your obedience to the Path will be the death of the very people you seek to defend."

"Watch your tongue," Rosa replied, and her hand dropped to her sword.

"She's right," Raya said, but raised her hands placatingly. "If you die here, killed by a demon that possesses every skill you've ever learned, along with some of their own, then who on Samas can stand against it? I know you aren't boastful, Rosa, but tell me, one on one, how many people in Samas can best you?"

Rosa considered for a moment. "Only a handful."

"And I'm willing to wager the same is true of many sentinels here. If you were to be possessed, it would be a disaster. I'm telling you now, we can't continue to prevent that from happening. Not for much longer. We need to get the citizens somewhere safe so that when the demons do break through, all they have are chipmunks and squirrels at their disposal."

Lieutenant Rosa looked at Raya. "Then we'd better not fail here."

"Rosa!" Raya called but the lieutenant was already striding away.

"What do we do?" Shin asked.

"What else can we do? We keep containing this rift. Unless we can find a way to seal it or convince Rosa to remove the shit from her brains, that's all we can do."

Shin felt her rage simmering and took a deep breath. She thought about Corin and how he would want her to handle this situation. All she wanted to do, despite knowing better, was flex her power and close the rift so she could get away from these sun-cursed sentinels.

But the thought of Corin caused her rage to subside a little.

"I really thought we could figure it out," Shin said, defeated. "We're working together for once, and it shouldn't be that hard to seal a rift."

Raya fixed her with a glare that made Shin want to shrink into a corner. The two of them could fight side by side, but things between them weren't fixed yet. And maybe they never would be.

But Raya's bottomless patience wasn't just for sentinels. She sighed. "Me, too. We use the sealing spell so often I took for granted how complicated it really is. Trying to create a new spell for a rift under this much pressure...I'm just not good enough."

Shin's rage bubbled up again. Rage at Raya and Yuki continuing to hold her back and then acting like they had no way to solve this issue. Once again, she thought of Corin and focused her frustration elsewhere. It wasn't a perfect solution to her anger, but it worked well enough. "Why didn't Yuki come? I understand she can't use sacrifice, but if anyone has the practical knowledge to figure this out, it's her."

Raya scoffed. "Not use sacrifice? You really are dense. I thought you'd understand better than most why she couldn't risk coming here."

"What do you mean?"

"She's still capable of unleashing power that almost no one else could match." Raya gave Shin a pointed looked before continuing. "She has to make the choice, every day, not to use sacrifice lest she *become* something terrible and unstoppable. If she were here, this close to the realm, the temptation would be too great. Sound familiar?"

It was true. Shin had been fighting the urge to throw her power at the rift in a desperate attempt to close it. The temptation was indeed great.

"Hopefully she can figure something out from Dahl, then," Shin said.

"I have no doubt she's working on it. Until then, we keep this up and hope that Rosa changes her tune when things start to get worse."

"She's too pig-headed for that."

Raya smiled grimly. "Maybe. It's amazing what happens when a fight with a demon goes bad, though. It was what brought Beast to our side. If it can work on someone as thick as him, it should work on Rosa, too."

Shin nodded her head in agreement. She knew all too well how a harsh a lesson the realm was capable of teaching.

"Now, Shin!" Tia called out.

Shin brought the blade of Harmony down on the nightmare squirrel and took its head off.

The body turned to mist, which was immediately surrounded by a crimson glow. The demon was sent back through the rift, though it wouldn't be long before they saw it again.

The cycle was never-ending. They would continue doing this forever if they couldn't figure out how to fix the tear in this rift that Shin had created. Or more likely, collapse from exhaustion.

"Corin. Now!" Tia's voice called out once more.

Chop.

Mist.

Glow.

Back to the rift.

"I think that's it for now," Tia said. She was breathing heavily and barely able to stand straight.

"For now," Shin sighed. "I'm starting to hate those words. Almost as much as I hate looking at this rift."

"We all do, but considering the amount of wildlife we've gone through holding this perimeter, pretty soon all that's going to be left for them to possess are ants and crickets," Tia said with a wink.

"That's so much worse," Corin groaned.

Raya's arrival saved her from any more of Corin's humor. "Your shift is done. The relief team is on the way. Go get some rest before we resume this pointless exercise."

"We all hate this, Raya," Tia said.

Raya nodded acknowledgment, but didn't say anything for a moment. The four sin looked at one another, then back to the rift.

"I don't know about you, but I think we can hold out for a long time. Maybe long enough to figure out how to fix the rift." Corin's tone was full of optimism and made Shin smile despite her exhaustion and cynicism.

"Do you ever give up hope, kid?" Raya asked.

"Not if I can help it."

The sin broke apart, and Corin and Shin rotated into their break as another set of sin took up their sentry duty around the rift. Shin closed her eyes, but sleep wouldn't come. She wasn't a very good napper anyway. After another half hour, she began to hear the shouts of warning. Another wave of demons was emerging.

Shin didn't bother opening her eyes. The systematic

routine of dispatching the demons had become so familiar it had faded into background noise. Somewhere in her mind, Shin knew that was almost more terrifying than the demons. It was incredible what horrors a person could become numb to.

A cry of surprise cut off abruptly and Shin sat bolt upright.

"Help! One got Sarin!" another voice called out.

Shin charged back to the rift, calling Harmony to her hand as she ran. When she broke into the clearing, three sin had positioned themselves around Sarin and the demon taking her form, ready to strike. The other adepts were trying to keep up with the flood of demons coming out of the gate.

The dam had finally burst.

The demon-sin finally took form and was cut down at once. As soon as it was mist, Sarin recovered and started sending it back.

Shin stopped watching and moved to engage a deer with a mouth full of dagger-like teeth. The thing spun and kicked like a horse trying to buck a rider, and Shin leaped back and threw Harmony, severing a few limbs before she could rush forward and cut through its neck.

Then she felt Sarin's spell slip again.

The girl was exhausted and couldn't hold the demon. The misty form floated back towards Sarin, but a sentinel got between them instead.

Shin tried to get to the sentinel before she was put in a trance, but a giant squirrel knocked her aside. She managed to keep her feet, but was on the defensive as the demon's claws struck out at her. The moment before the mist took the sentinel, Tia leaped in front of her. Shin fought off the squirrel for a moment, just in time to see Tia's body stiffen.

Shit.

In moments there would be a demon version of her friend to contend with.

Shin took a risk and timed a strike so that Harmony's blade met the squirrel's arm instead of the claws. Had she been an instant slower she would have suffered a deep wound, but her timing was perfect, and the creature's claws went flying. Shin pressed the advantage so she could help Tia, but the squirrel whipped its tail around. She leaped over the spiked tail and was forced back on the defensive.

Shin looked on in horror as the demon-Tia took form and struck out with its strange, sword-fused arm. The blow was true, but Tia recovered and parried. The two launched into a mirror image battle.

Shin was aware of just how hard a fight Tia had ahead of her and tried desperately to kill the squirrel that was stopping her from helping her friend. She was so tired; everything she attempted put her farther back on the defensive. The sentinel that Tia had saved moved to help but was overwhelmed by the demon's skill and strength.

Then Corin came to the rescue.

Blades whirling, Corin drove the squirrel backward. Shin summoned whatever strength she could and joined the charge. It still took them longer than expected but they finally took the creature down and cut its head off. One of the other adepts caught it in a spell and sent it back.

Shin looked around for Tia. Most of the sin were falling back, but Shin saw Tia across the clearing. Her fight had cut her off from the retreat. She ran to help her friend, Corin right behind her.

Before they'd taken more than a few steps, it was too late. The demon ran Tia through. Her body jerked as the sword-arm came out of her belly and a spurt of blood flew out from her open mouth.

Shin screamed. She charged toward the fight that was already over, even as another demon joined the Tia-demon.

Corin laid a hand on her shoulder and stopped her in her tracks.

"We have to go!" Corin called out and began pulling on her arm.

Shin struggled for a moment before coming back to herself. She ran her eyes over the battlefield and realized that Corin was right. The sin were retreating. For now, it was coordinated, but it was on the verge of becoming a rout. The sentinels fought valiantly and kept the demons at bay. Raya directed the forces as they fell back. When Shin and Corin reached her, Shin realized that she had prepared a spell and was just waiting for the others to clear out. The weave around her was as complicated as anything Shin had ever sensed.

"What are you going to do?" Shin asked.

"You'll see. There's no time, though. Just be ready to give the orders, okay? I'm not going to be able to," Raya said. "And Shin?"

"What?"

"I do believe in you. I hope that someday, you'll believe in us."

Before Shin could inquire further, Raya released the weave. A loud clap echoed through the woods and Shin looked up to see a crimson dome falling over the entire clearing. It crashed down between the sentinels and demons.

The first demons to reach the dome smashed into it and fell to the ground. Those that came behind leaped at the dome with more purpose, but had no greater effect. The sentinels that had moments earlier been fighting the demons looked in astonishment at the crimson wall before them.

"How long will that hold them?" Shin asked.

Raya shook her head.

"Not long?" Corin offered.

Raya pointed affirmatively at him.

"Raya," Shin said quietly, "what's wrong?"

Raya opened her mouth. Her tongue was gone. Then she collapsed.

47

Even the wind in his hair and the sight of the open ocean before him didn't settle Beast's restless thoughts.

He'd fought more battles in his life than he could count, but this one was different. It wasn't just all the unknowns, although there were more of those than he could count. Were there any summoners left on the juggernaut? It seemed unlikely, but what did they know? What other defenses did the massive ship possess?

Those weren't the questions that bothered him.

He would fight, and he would win. There was no question of that.

But what would he do after?

Would he give the juggernaut to Yuki, continuing to obey her every wish? Or would he use it to gain the freedom Colas tempted him with?

He and Benji had always talked about creating a place where people could live without the sentinels. But figuring out how to do that on Samas had always been beyond them. A ship, though, especially one like the juggernaut, could be the place the two of them had once dreamed about. He held onto the hilt of Benji's sword, wishing his friend was still around to guide him.

Gorou came up beside him. The man was as calm as a still pond, but Beast saw the doubt in his eyes. "You sure about this, sir?"

Beast grunted, then gestured down to the deck. "Not at all. But we've got the adepts, so hopefully, those Maramans won't know what hit them."

Gorou nodded but didn't seem convinced. The man was implacable, though, and something as trivial as dying in battle wouldn't bother him too much. There was good reason Beast chose him as his second in command.

First mate, Beast reminded himself. If he was at sea, he might as well start talking like a sailor.

"Juggernaut ahead!" a voice cried out from the bow of the ship.

Beast squinted into the distance and thought he could make out something on the horizon, but he wasn't sure. But the lookout had a looking glass, and it was hard to mistake a juggernaut.

There were three adepts at his disposal, one on each of the ships. Their orders were to obey Beast unless the battle looked to be lost. If that was the case, they were to burn the juggernaut down.

Beast gave the signal to the sin on his ship, and they watched as a crimson glow moved skyward.

"This shit always creeps me out," Beast said to Gorou, who nodded.

Beast's skin prickled as the clear sky above suddenly became misty and then foggy. Soon a dense cloud descended upon the ships and expanded toward the juggernaut. The moment they were obscured from the juggernaut's view, an explosion of light shot skyward from *Cutter*.

"Tack!" Beast ordered, and the crew jumped into motion.

The mugon navy tacked starboard, keeping close to one another. They wanted be as far away as possible from the point where the juggernaut had last seen them. The loose trio of ships fell into a single line, with each ship staying in sight of the one ahead of it.

"I know they can't see us, captain, but we won't be able to see them either. How are we supposed to find our target in all of this?" Gorou asked.

"We leave that to Colas. She assured me she could lead us to that monstrosity through any fog."

Gorou nodded, seemingly reassured. Colas had won the respect of no small number of his mugon, something he'd need to consider in his decision.

"Port!" the lookout called back.

Beast spun the wheel, and the crew shifted smoothly as the boat came about. The lookout was crucial now. They didn't want to risk the light signals they'd been using lest they give away their positions to any Maraman ships dispatched to deal with them. Instead, each ship had to stay close enough to the one ahead of it so they could continue to follow Colas and *Cutter*.

Sailing through the fog was nerve-wracking. There was an eerie silence broken only by the waves slapping against *Warhammer's* hull, and Beast was forced to trust the ship in front of him implicitly.

His palms itched.

"Are we almost—" Gorou began, but was interrupted by a sickening crunch. Beast almost flew to the side, but his hands on the wheel kept him locked in place. Most of the crew weren't so fortunate. People went sprawling across the deck, and one poor soul was thrown from the edge of the ship.

Beast turned to see what had happened and was surprised to see the bow of a Maraman ship lodged in the side of *Warhammer*. He snorted as he saw the surprised look on the face of a Maraman who had been thrown from the lookout position on the bow of his own ship onto the deck of *Warhammer*.

The man tried to stand, but one of *Warhammer*'s crew clubbed him over the head with an oar.

"Looks like they found us," Beast said.

Soon, the Maramans were shouting battle orders. But they weren't louder than Beast. "Form up! They hit us by accident! Let's board them before they board us!" Beast bellowed.

Judging by how far the bow of the Maraman ship was lodged into *Warhammer,* Beast guessed they were going to need a new ship.

He'd have to convince the Maramans to give them theirs.

He leaped aboard the Maraman ship, knocking a sailor aside with his shoulder as he did so. His crew were still collecting themselves, but given how narrow the bow of the enemy ship was, Beast was confident he could hold the line until enough of his forces joined him and they could push forward.

The Maraman that he knocked to the deck was quickly replaced by another that Beast hacked at with the short, one-handed sword that he and his crew wielded. The Maraman parried a few of the blows but was soon overwhelmed by Beast's strength. Beast shook his head at the tiny sword in his hands. He'd cut steaks with larger blades.

He would have preferred a battle axe or great sword, but

when fighting in such close quarters he was likely to do as much damage to his allies as his enemies.

The raider that he'd knocked to the deck was getting to his feet, so Beast lunged forward and stabbed him through the chest. He looked at the sword again and decided he could make do.

The Maramans, slower to organize, surrendered the advantage to the *Warhammer*'s crew. Beast led the charge and was immediately met by two Maramans with cudgels. Though not terribly intimidating, when wielded in expert hands, the blunt weapons were deadly. Beast found himself giving up ground to the coordination of the pair. Thankfully, Gorou stepped in and engaged one of the raiders long enough for Beast to feint a strike, dart in, and lift his enemy up in the air.

The Maraman landed a few ineffectual blows on Beast's broad back, but Beast remained unconcerned. He took his time finding the perfect sharp corner on which to slam the Maraman's head.

By the time he was done, Gorou had already dispatched his opponent with his usual detached efficiency.

"They aren't putting up much of a fight, are they?" Beast asked.

Gorou looked around the ship before answering. "They don't look to be in good health."

Beast brought his sword up just in time to parry a few blows from another Maraman's cudgel. On the third parry he knocked the weapon out of the Maraman's hand. The large man grabbed hold of Beast and tried to wrestle him to the ground. Beast easily threw the raider off him, allowing Gorou to run the man through.

"They seem weak," Beast agreed, thinking about his first

fight with the Maramans. He had been beaten within an inch of his life.

Beast nodded and turned back to the fray. He dispatched a few more of the raiders, but soon his crew was throwing bodies overboard and using long oars to push themselves off the wreckage of *Warhammer*. With a loud groan, the two ships separated, and Beast was shocked at the speed with which his old vessel sank into the ocean.

"Alright, looks like we've got a new ship!" Beast bellowed. "Since she's so much like the old ship, we'll just call her *Warhammer!*"

Beast was answered with some laughs and a chorus of cheers as his crew filled their posts.

"Now, how do we find our way to the juggernaut?" Beast asked himself out loud.

"It's that way," Gorou replied and pointed.

"How do you know?" Beast peered into the fog at a loss. If it weren't for the fact that his feet were in their customary place on the deck, he wouldn't know which way was up.

"I made a note of where it was before the fog came in. Just in case."

"But we tacked a few times, got hit by another ship and had a full-out battle since then. How did you keep track?" Beast asked, incredulous.

Gorou shrugged. "I made a note."

Beast laughed at his first mate's matter-of-fact tone. "Seems like you should take the helm, then."

"I thought Colas said the captain should oversee the helm?"

"She did, but you're clearly better at this than me. Besides, I'm the kind of captain that likes to be the first to stab the enemy. I lead from the front. Problem is, the helm is always at the back."

"Is this a promotion, then?" Gorou asked.

"No, I just need you to do the hard stuff while I do the killing."

Gorou chuckled, which for him was the equivalent of collapsing with laughter. Beast headed to the bow. He braced his hands on the railing and tried to look through the fog, but no matter how hard he tried, all he saw was more fog.

Finally, he gave up and closed his eyes. He left all his trust with Gorou and cast out with his other senses. He heard the waves smacking against *Warhammer* as she cut through the ocean and the creaks of the rigging as the wind pushed the full sails along. Then, in the distance, he began to hear something. Suddenly, it sharpened and his mind recognized the song his ears were catching.

Battle.

"Slow!" Beast bellowed to Gorou, who called orders of his own.

The distant sounds grew louder as the ship slowed. Steel on steel. Cries of pain. Roars of rage. Beast felt his heart pound faster and a familiar tingle spread through his hands as he approached his natural state.

They broke through the fog and in front of them, so close Beast could almost reach out and touch it, was the juggernaut. The hull extended upwards like a city wall. Beast looked left and right, and it seemed as though the ship went on forever. This close, Beast could see the mechanisms that allowed the ships to attach to the hull and travel with the juggernaut. Most of the bays stood empty. Beast marveled at the chains that secured the ships beside the floating city.

"By the sun," Beast muttered.

Gorou brought *Warhammer* alongside the juggernaut

and into one of the berths. Above them, the giant chains dangled. They were low enough that they could be reached from the crow's nest of *Warhammer*.

He looked again down the length of the juggernaut and watched as his mugon scrambled up the chains to begin their assault.

"There has to be a better way to get onto ships," Beast said. Then he shook his head and called out his orders. "Up the chains! Let's steal ourselves a juggernaut!"

48

———

Sato's face exploded in pain as his head snapped back. Once he regained his senses, he spit blood onto the dungeon floor. He was surprised to find that no teeth came with it. Izuki might be worse than trash, but she had a powerful kick. Like most magistrates, she had the training of sentinel, even if she'd long forgotten the Path.

Izuki smiled down at him darkly.

"I doubt you'd have the courage to strike me if I had the ability to strike back," Sato said evenly.

Izuki laughed. "You mean I wouldn't be stupid enough to cross swords with someone of your skill? You're absolutely right. Azazel might have been the best sentinel I've ever seen with a blade, and you proved you were better. But it was still a foolish duel."

Sato raised a quizzical eyebrow.

Izuki explained. "I may not have your skill with a blade, but when it comes to politics, I am out of your league. It didn't take much of an investigation to find out one of your most trusted lieutenants had been sleeping with Azazel's wife. It would have been a coincidence, don't you think?"

She laughed and kicked him in the stomach. He couldn't even bend, the chains were so tight. "It didn't take a genius to realize you arranged to have Azazel challenge you to a duel so you could replace him with one of your own."

She retreated and pulled up a stool. "Honestly, it wasn't the worst plan I've seen. Your duel made it an honorable death instead of a murder. But it was too soon after Tando's death. Made it too easy to connect the dots. Too easy to defend against your plan."

Sato glared. But there was no point in talking with Izuki. "So what next? Will you have me killed?"

"You're not a man that one kills lightly."

"For fear of the Firstborn's reprisal, I'd imagine. What makes you think he won't level consequences for your actions now? No matter what happens, you have no future."

Izuki snorted. "Still as foolish as ever, I see. Do you still think you have the Firstborn's favor, even after losing Ilos? After murdering magistrates? He's a patient man, but your loss will hardly be noticed. And if it is, there are dozens of excuses I could invent. You've led a dangerous life, Sato. Any number of accidents could have happened."

"He's no fool. Why would he believe you?"

The chief magistrate shook her head. "You really don't get it, do you? It doesn't matter what he believes. It doesn't even matter if he knows. This is about what he can publicly acknowledge, and what supports Samas. He needs Versun, and I control Versun. It's as simple as that. Besides, before long I don't think it'll matter."

"What do you mean?"

Izuki ignored him. "As amateurish as your attempts were, you did manage to gain something of a following within the city. I blame those lieutenants of yours. Not your kind of sentinels, Sato, but they served you well in this.

They're far cleverer than you've ever been. Not very trustworthy, though. Crispin offered to join my service as soon as you were out of earshot. I'm mulling over his offer, but I fear he's not the sort of man I'd rely on. He will likely share your fate. The other one is still hiding in the city, but he'll be found. Do you see, Sato, what your kind of leadership gets? Your most trusted sentinels turn on you or hide the moment they see your power isn't absolute. I don't know what the Firstborn sees in you. You might think yourself filled with honor, but you can't keep Samas safe. You can't even keep the loyalty of your own little band of sentinels."

Sato grimaced. All those words, and yet no answers. He didn't like her repeated references to the Firstborn. "Why keep me alive?"

Her smile was the most terrifying sight he'd seen in some time. "Because I need you to be." She reached into one of her pockets and pulled out a slip of paper. "The news is all over the streets now. Iru is under assault from demons, just as Dahl was. Your precious sin fucked something up. People are scared and looking for a leader. How do you think they'll react when they find out you're sin?" She cast a meaningful glance at his ethereal pinky.

Sato's world collapsed when he realized the extent of Izuki's ambitions. Outing Sato wouldn't just solidify her power here in Versun. As the Firstborn's favored, the fact that he was sin would cast doubt on the Firstborn, especially if Bulas fell.

"How could you have fallen so far from the Path, Izuki?" He choked out the words, still struggling with the enormity of her plans.

"Path this and Path that. When will you grow up, Sato? Insofar as the Path keeps our society running smoothly, it is a useful tool, but nothing more. Our people need to be kept safe, and it's clear the Firstborn isn't cut out for the job. He's lost one island and is in danger of losing a second. Soon, only Versun will be safe, and I will do everything to make sure it stays that way.

Sato kept his face impassive, but fear gnawed at him. Could she be right?

"That's a pretty good poker face, Sato, but you know I'm right," Izuki said. She stood and gestured for him to follow. "Come on. Let's get this over with."

Two sentinels unlocked his chains from the wall and raised him to his feet, keeping a tight grip on the chains. One shoved him roughly towards the door. Sato turned and recognized the sentinel that had kicked his ear. "I would take care if I were you."

The sentinel grinned and shoved him again.

"Easy, Grayson. You wouldn't be so keen to shove him if he had his hands free," the sentinel's partner said.

"Doesn't, though, does he? And he never will again."

Sato took a deep breath and walked forward to whatever doom awaited him.

Grayson. He wouldn't forget.

When he exited the dungeons, he squinted at the bright morning sun and filled his lungs with fresh air. Grayson took the moment to shove him again, and Sato almost fell to the ground. The night spent on the dungeon floor would have been bad enough, but the guards had made a point of kicking him every hour or so. He was exhausted and bruised.

He staggered to a stop in front of a cart that appeared to have a set of stocks built onto the back of it. The angle was odd, though. It wasn't until Sato realized it would hold his maimed hand high for all to see that he understood.

"Do you like it? It's your chariot, sir. Had it made just for you. It was amazing how quickly the craftsmen down in the merchant's district volunteered to build something specifically designed to humiliate a sin traitor," Izuki said.

Sato was shoved towards the cart again. Then Izuki held up a hand. "Take off all his clothes. The crowds will see him naked, stripped of all his pretense. Let them see what comes to those who defy our order."

Sato centered his breathing as Grayson stripped him of his uniform. He let the waves of shame pass over him as he was locked into the makeshift stocks. Because he walked the Path, his mind was as great a weapon as his body. He would not let it be broken, even in the face of his own death.

But it wasn't his death that worried him. A sentinel was always prepared for that.

It was the failure. The knowledge that everything he'd done had done nothing but destroy the very people he'd sought to protect.

"I almost forgot," Izuki said as she reappeared in his field of vision, "I should return this."

Izuki held his sword in her hands, broken in half. She stabbed the hilt, broken blade down, into one side of the stocks and had a smith hammer the other half of the blade into the opposite side.

Try as he might, Sato couldn't contain his fury at the disrespect.

But there was nothing he could do.

The wagon started to move, and Sato was serenaded by a chorus of insults as he began his parade through Versun. Whatever goodwill he'd built became nothing before the sight of his deformed hand.

They'd never understand how much he'd sacrificed on their behalf.

"Oh, one last thing, Sato," Izuki's voice floated down from somewhere outside his view. "I wouldn't want you to have to suffer alone. We brought you some company."

Crispin was kicked in front of the cart. The lieutenant was battered and filthy. His hair hung in front of his face as he staggered awkwardly to his knees.

Too awkwardly.

"Crispin..." Sato's voice caught in his throat.

Crispin smiled weakly at him, a sickening expression splashed across a pale and gaunt face. But Sato wasn't looking at his face. His eyes were locked lower, staring at the bloody stump wrapped in filthy rags where Crispin's sword hand used to be.

49

———

Shin watched for a moment longer as the demon that had taken on Tia's form grinned with insane fury and smashed its sword-fused arm into the shield. Then she turned to where Raya was reviving, her eyes unfocused.

"You could put a wall up this whole time and you didn't bother?" Rosa screamed at Raya. "Why did you let so many die when you could have contained them?"

Shin stepped between Raya and Rosa and felt a surge of satisfaction when the hardened sentinel lieutenant took a step backwards. "The cost for something like this is enormous and there's no telling how long it will last." She closed her eyes and felt the weave, already starting to unravel. "At a guess, I would say Raya's sacrifice only bought us a few days at most."

"I'm not addressing you. I'm addressing your commanding officer," Rosa said.

"Open your sun-cursed eyes!" Shin shouted.

The shout had the desired effect. Rosa stopped her tirade and truly looked at Raya for the first time. Not only was the woman's tongue missing, her demeanor was completely changed. She had a distant, vacant look in her eyes. Another sin was beside Raya, but the sin commander wasn't responding to any stimulus. Rosa's eyes went wide as she started to understand.

"She sacrificed herself for you!" Shin said, driving the point home. "And we don't have enough time to argue. You need to understand that this barrier is a temporary, and desperate, solution to the issue of the demons. An issue *we told you* was going to happen. Now, are you prepared to get the citizens of Iru behind the walls of Bulas?" Shin was surprised by the command in her own voice.

It only took a moment for Rosa to compose herself to this new reality, and Shin was reminded of just how formidable the sentinels could be. "What you're asking is a giant undertaking. The three largest cities in Samas are on Iru. Moving them all to Bulas and then preparing for a siege—it's weeks of work!"

"If only someone had warned you," Corin muttered.

"What was that, boy?" Rosa snapped.

For a moment it looked like Corin would shrink before the sentinel, but instead he spun on his heel and approached the crimson barrier that separated them from the demons. Without breaking eye contact with Rosa, he waved a hand in front of the barrier and three or four demons all sprung towards the movement, smashing themselves into the wall in the process. "Whatever time we wish we had doesn't matter. Perhaps you should just use what time Raya bought you. She certainly paid a high enough price."

Corin didn't wait for a reply before stalking away to check on the injured sin.

Rosa's face was a thundercloud of rage as she turned to

look at Shin. Before the sentinel could say anything, Shin held up a hand. "He's right."

Rosa looked from the barrier holding back the demons back to the battered and broken sentinels that were standing amongst the equally beaten sin. Something in her finally broke, and she nodded. "I'll see what I can do. Just make sure that shield stays up as long as possible."

"We will," Shin replied, but Rosa was already barking commands to her sentinels, so Shin turned to Raya. For a moment, it felt as though Raya was there. Her eyes focused on Shin, and Shin felt her throat tighten. She embraced the sin commander. "I'll do everything I can to make sure your sacrifice wasn't in vain," she said.

"Shin, we have to go," Corin announced.

Shin wrenched herself away from the demons behind the wall and nodded. The sentinels had long since left to facilitate the preparations for the siege of Bulas. Rosa had returned after a few hours and explained that the retreat to the walls was underway. Hankala was her biggest concern as the citizens would have to pass right by the rift to get to Bulas, and it appeared her concerns were well founded. The mass of humanity was still moving past their position.

Not only that, the wall was weakening. Shin felt it unraveling before her.

Raya's condition hadn't improved, but Shin supposed she'd never expected it to. Sacrifice was permanent. The commander still had moments of lucidity, but for the most part, Shin had taken charge. None of the sin had argued.

Shin had to fight back tears every time she looked at Raya. Shin had treated her poorly, and Raya had done her best. If there was some way she could step back in time, she would have done it all differently.

But the realm just took and took. The power it gave in return hardly seemed a satisfactory trade. She wished she could have made things right with Raya, back when there was still a chance to do so.

Shin took one last look around the site of their failed containment, then ran down the path. Before long she met up with the last of the refugees from Hankala. The remaining sin forces stood nearby, waiting for orders.

Shin gave them. "We'll split our forces, one adept and two sin to the front in case there are demons ahead of us. The rest will stay here with the rear-guard sentinels. We don't know how long that barrier will hold but when it breaks, we need to be ready to buy as much time as possible," Shin said, hoping she sounded more confident than she felt.

Fists went to hearts in unison and the sin dispersed. Shin was about to go searching for transportation for Raya when the sin became lucid again. She started marching toward the rear. Shin ran up to her. "Raya, you can't fight. Let's find you a place to rest."

Raya shook her head and pointed to the rear.

Shin watched helplessly as the woman marched off. After a moment, she chased after her, hoping to apologize while Raya was lucid. But when she got there, Raya was gone, her eyes unfocused. Shin pulled at her, but Raya fought so hard she eventually gave up. If the rear was where Raya wanted to be, she had no right to say otherwise.

Shin and Corin were joined by two adepts, Elissa and Teren. Together, they met up with the sentinels guarding the rear of the evacuation. Shin was impressed to find Lieutenant Rosa commanding the sentinels there.

Rosa looked at them with a grim expression. "You being here can't be good news."

"I'm afraid it's not," Shin replied. "We don't know how much longer it will hold, but it isn't long."

"Any guesses?"

"We think it could fail any time," Shin admitted.

Rosa looked in the direction of the rift. "Well, in that case, I'm glad to see you. We'll get the citizens of Hankala past the trailhead and then let them get ahead a little. If we do end up fighting the demons, I'd prefer to do it where those people can't watch. They're scared enough and the last thing we need is panic."

"Agreed. How long for everyone to reach Bulas?" Shin asked.

"The vast majority should be inside the walls within the next four hours."

"Good. Hopefully, we all make it to the capital before anything terrible happens."

Rosa nodded and called out orders to her sentinels. Before long, they were formed up at the trailhead and the last of the grim parade of citizens was disappearing down the road.

"Let's follow behind," Rosa said. "I don't want them getting too far ahead of us."

They made it two hours down the road before Corin came up to her. "Good job back there," he said.

"Thanks. Did I sound like a commanding officer?"

"That's not what I meant. You sounded like your old self," Corin said.

She knew the comment was meant as a compliment, but it cut her deep. Shin considered telling Corin it was all an act. That she was just doing what she thought he would want her to do, but before she could respond, Shin and the other adepts lurched forward in unison as if blown by a powerful gust of wind.

The shield had broken.

"Ready your sentinels, Rosa," Shin called out.

Rosa wheeled her mount and called out orders. In seconds, the sentinels and sin formed up in their respective units. They didn't have to wait long before the demons were upon them. Shin and Corin moved forward with the sentinels while Elissa and Teren sent back the misty forms that were among the corporeal demons. Shin saw a glimpse of Raya in the middle of the sentinels, but had no time to worry about her.

Shin and Corin fought side by side to take down the demons as quickly as possible. Her intention was to get to the Tia demon and make it pay for her friend's life, but a particularly agile wolf-demon prevented her.

Shin cut down the wolf and moved to help Rosa, who was engaged with the Tia-demon. The two were a blur of steel as they battled back and forth. As always, the unnatural size and strength of the demon proved deadly when combined with skills stolen from a trained fighter.

Rosa mistimed a block that would have led to her death, but Shin threw Harmony and bought the sentinel enough time to fall back. Another sentinel stepped in to land a killing blow on the demon, but it lashed out with one of its long legs and sent the sentinel flying. He landed at an unnatural angle on the ground, and Shin didn't think he'd be getting up again.

Shin risked a look around and saw Corin fighting with a demon that had taken on the form of a sentinel. The demon was strong, but Corin's skills were ever-improving, and he looked to be winning the exchange.

Shin joined Rosa once more, and they pushed the Tia-demon back. Shin finally spotted some openings when one of the misty forms being sent back by an adept suddenly broke free from its binding.

They were all too tired for this fight.

"Rosa, don't look!" Shin called, but it was too late.

Rosa went stiff and stared at the mist in front of her.

Without thinking, Shin moved to kill Rosa before the demon could possess her fully. The woman fought too well to be allowed to spawn a demon form.

Before she could land the blow, the Tia-demon interrupted her with a flurry of strikes that forced her backward. Shin dropped to a crouch and knocked it off its feet with a sweep of her weapon. She used the space to back up and line up a throw that would take Rosa's head, but realized she was too late.

The demon had taken Rosa's form.

Rosa did her best to recover and fight back, but none of her experience in battle could have prepared her for what it felt like to have her body and mind invaded like that.

To her credit, the sentinel died fighting.

"Shin, watch out!" Corin called. The demon sentinel he'd been fighting was disappearing into mist, but he was already engaged with another. Shin followed his pointing finger, though.

A Maraman in a crimson robe was engaged in a pitched battle with Elissa and Teren. Raya was huddled in the fetal position behind them.

Shin moved to help, but Corin chopped down another demon and stopped her. "We have to go. We need to make sure those people get Bulas safely. You have to get to Bulas safely."

"We can't leave them!"

"You know they would tell you to. You're the only one

that can fix this. We can't lose you and we can't let these demons kill all those people."

Indecision warred within Shin. She didn't want to abandon her friend, but they were routed here. The best she could do if she stayed was send these demons back to the rift and buy some time. Was that worth risking losing herself to the realm? "Fine, let's go," she said, her heart heavy.

They ran away from the carnage, but Shin kept looking back at where the two adepts were fighting. What few sentinels remained were either being possessed or cut down by nightmare versions of their friends. Shin watched as Elissa was cut down by the summoner's axe.

Teren fought valiantly, but the summoner was just too strong. The axe took off his head with one clean blow.

Shin screamed and came to a stop. She couldn't leave Raya to die. Not like this.

The summoner took one step toward Raya, and the sin commander stood tall, like the Raya Shin knew would have. Crimson light sprang from her, dozens of tentacles reaching in dozens of different directions. Swords and axes rose from the dead, and then the world exploded in light.

Shin squinted as sharpened steel flew across the battlefield, decapitating demons left and right.

She could barely believe her senses.

The power wasn't much. Shin could summon more from the realm with the blink of an eye. But the control—the control was beyond Shin's wildest dreams. Using Harmony was hard enough for her. This was the same level of control split dozens of times.

Everywhere she looked, demons turned into mist and were locked into the crimson glow of a sacrifice that had to be Raya's last. The summoner brought his axe down, but before it could land his arm went flying from his body. Another sword cut into his leg, and a knife stabbed into his heart as a war hammer crunched down on his skull.

One by one, the demons were returned to the rift.

Shin knew it was another sacrifice that did nothing but buy them time, but it was a sacrifice she swore to herself she would never forget. In those few moments, Raya saved more lives than Shin could count.

The crimson glow faded, leaving nothing but a skeleton standing for one moment in the distance. Then a breeze picked up and the bone turned to ash, blowing away in the wind, taking the last bits of Raya with it.

50

B east forced himself to keep his eyes on the chain he dangled from and not on the choppy ocean waters below him.

Far below him.

If there was one comforting part of this mess, it was that at least he didn't suffer alone. The rest of his mugon also struggled against the impassive, slick metal. But Colas and her sun-cursed crew had climbed the chains as though they were a set of thick and sturdy ladders. Beast knew that a lifetime of ascending and descending their ship's rigging had prepared them for today, but he still cursed them as his grip slipped against the chains.

They didn't have the time to waste. Colas' crew were already engaged with the Maramans above. He squeezed the chain tighter, imagining it was Sato's neck, and hauled himself ever higher. When he reached the top of the juggernaut he allowed himself just a few precious moments to recover.

As he did, he let his eyes drink in the majestic sight of

the enormous vessel. Seeing it from the waterline had been an intimidating sight. Now that he was on board, the size of it was awe-inspiring. The masts were as thick as the oldest trees he'd ever seen and the sails, half raised to move the ship once the fog rolled in, could have covered the magistrate's tower back in Dahl. The deck itself extended out of view in both directions.

Then his break was over. Beast jumped backward to avoid a thrown dagger, then drew his sword in time to parry a blow from a charging Maraman. The massive man struck again, but Beast knocked the short sword out of his hand. In a second fluid motion, Beast ran the man through. He looked for a moment into the gaunt face and sunken eyes of his enemy and realized just how sickly they were. He wondered if they'd just waited another week, if the last remaining Maramans would have died from starvation.

It was too late now. They were here and they had a battle to win. Most of his mugon had completed their climb and were pushing the Maramans back. Beast cut a path through the few who stood in his way and bolstered his forces wherever they needed aid. After tripping one particularly gaunt Maraman he found himself fighting alongside Colas and Gorou.

"This is going well," Gorou said.

"Agreed!" Colas said.

But Beast heard the concern in his first mate's voice. "Too well, you think?"

Gorou gave one sharp nod. He pointed his sword toward a knot of mugon engaged with three Maramans.

"I think we're just winning," Colas said.

At first glance, Colas seemed right. The mugon outnumbered the Maramans, and the Maramans looked thin enough to be threatened by a strong breeze. But when

Beast took a moment to really watch, he realized Gorou was right. The Maramans weren't fighting with the ferocity or skill Beast had come to expect from them. Though his mugon had certainly improved, the Maramans were surrendering ground without even fighting for it. "No, Gorou's right. Even as sickly as they are, this is too easy."

Beast watched the battle for another few moments. His eyes narrowed when he realized all the Maramans were retreating in the same direction, toward the helm. They *were* drawing his mugon forward. "Hold!" Beast shouted. Lieutenants echoed his order down the line.

After a few moments, the mugon halted their advance. If there was any doubt as to the Maraman's purpose, it was dispelled when they continued their retreat. Beast looked over to and saw Hanz and Jurian making their way over to him. The group met to discuss their next moves.

"They look to be headed for the helm," Colas said. "I don't think they have much fight left in them."

Beast was tempted to agree. The battle here was the culmination of the greater war they had waged against the Maraman raiders. Still, he was hesitant. "Best not to underestimate our opponents." He nodded in the direction of the helm. "Is it just me, or is that thing too big, even for a ship of this size?"

"Aye, that, and it appears to have an enormous deckhouse underneath. Far bigger than necessary to house the captain," Colas answered.

Beast rubbed his chin and glanced over at Hanz and Jurian. "Would you two be willing to scout it out? I'm nervous. Feel free to take some of my mugon with you."

Hanz nodded, though he raised an eyebrow at the word mugon. Then he and his brother took off to get a closer look.

Beast sheathed his sword as the last sounds of battle

faded. This fight wasn't over yet. It felt much more like the calm before the final storm. But he would enjoy it while it lasted. He made a slow turn, marvelling once more at the sheer size of the juggernaut. As he took in its size, a realization dawned on him.

"Shit," Beast said.

"What is it?" Colas asked.

Beast ignored her question for the moment. "Gorou, I want scouts checking the perimeter on both sides of the ship. Hanz and Jurian will report on the helm. I know it seems like we drove most of the Maramans back this way, but I'm worried we missed something near the bow." Beast turned back to Colas after doling out the orders. "We've been treating this attack as if we're just taking over another ship."

"Aren't we?"

"This is a floating city, Colas. Not a ship's deck where you can see from one end to the other with a glance. If anything, this is more like a battle on land."

"What does it even matter?"

Beast swept his arms out wide, encompassing the whole juggernaut. "Imagine this more as a forest than as a ship. There are places all over people could hide, and just as trees can disguise the movement of warriors," here he pointed to the deck, "we have no idea what passages are below us. As we speak, they could be surrounding us. It's a different battle than we thought it was."

Colas grunted and looked around, studying the battlefield in a new light. Beast did the same, his attention landing on an odd structure on the port side of the ship.

Hanz and Jurian returned, faces grim. Around them, the mugon fidgeted, knowing there was a battle to fight but not sure exactly where it was or what shape it would take.

"It's a keep," Hanz reported. "Can't think of any other way to describe it."

"If that's the keep, then we're standing in the courtyard," Beast said. "We need to get out of here and rethink our attack."

"Pull back!" Gorou shouted and once again the lieutenants echoed the orders amongst the troops.

Beast kicked himself for not seeing the danger before. Hopefully he hadn't made too great a mistake. He turned and ran, pulling Colas with him.

Not a moment too soon. He heard a loud series of hissing pops. The deck behind him exploded in a shower of wood, the shrapnel sharp enough to cut several deep gashes along his arms.

"What the hell was that?" Colas asked.

Beast risked a look behind him in time to watch a giant arrow, at least four feet long, punch straight through one the mugon running behind him. One second the man was moving and the next he was pinned to the deck, motionless.

"Nothing good, keep running!"

Beast took his own advice and sprinted towards the bow. The scouts, returning with their findings, saw the mugon in full retreat and stuttered to a halt.

Then one of the scouts ran over to report.

"No one on the bow, sir. But we found strange structures up there. Looks like boxes filled with giant arrows. Must be hundreds, all with fuses dangling out the back," the scout said as he ran alongside Beast.

"But no one is up there?" Beast asked.

"No one right now, sir."

"To the bow!" Beast bellowed.

The orders were relayed just as Beast heard another series of hissing pops. He didn't turn around this time, not wanting to see what might emerge from the sin's sacrificial fog.

A moment later, the world exploded around him.

51

The most frustrating aspect of the stocks was how they cut off Sato's awareness. He couldn't look around like he was used to, giving him an incomplete sense of his surroundings. When he tried to look ahead, all he saw was the rears of the horses pulling the cart and brief glimpses of the crowd that had gathered. But looking ahead tired his neck, so he spent most of his time looking down. All he learned from that was that one of the cart wheels had a slight wobble.

Occasionally, he'd catch a glimpse of Crispin, and every time he did, it broke his heart. Izuki's maiming hadn't killed Crispin, but a sentinel's sword was their soul, and she'd murdered that part of him. Judging from his pallor and the way he stumbled with every step, Sato suspected the young man was in shock. If he didn't receive proper medical attention soon, he might lose his entire arm. If he even survived.

Sato grieved, not for himself, but for his lieutenant. A man who had come so far on the Path, only to have everything taken away. Sato had never believed the world a fair place, but this, this was too much to bear.

He forced his thoughts away from Crispin. He wanted nothing more than to comfort his lieutenant, to do something to help, but if he let his thoughts rest on what had happened, he'd never be useful. There had to be something he could do.

A crowd was slowly starting to gather. Here, they were among the wealthy of Versun, those who had benefited every day from the corruption that plagued the city. They fixed him with dark stares as he passed.

What else would he expect? He'd come to return Versun to the Path. And change was always the most frightening for such as these. They would have still been wealthy under Sato's rule, but not to the degree they were now. That was enough for them to hate him.

Besides, he had no idea what lies Izuki had been spreading about him. His ethereal pinky damned him enough as it was.

Eventually the jeers began. Before long, the crowd was shouting for his execution and mocking his nudity. But they were just words. Against a man who had fought demons, they carried little weight.

Despair threatened to overtake him, for he saw no way to escape the situation Izuki had created. His only legacy, if he'd even have one, would be of failure.

Crispin stumbled closer to the cart. He spoke just loudly enough to be heard over the crowd. "Not our best day, sir."

Sato snorted, then, despite everything, smiled. Crispin had broken his dark reverie with nothing more than a few words. After all this, his most difficult sun stalker remained unbroken.

He deserved a commander worthy of such spirit. "I can think of one or two better."

Crispin nodded, but his eyes had a faraway look that Sato recognized. "Any plans?"

"Nothing certain, sir. But I did get a message to Alonzo before we got captured. I'm afraid our fate is probably in his hands now."

"How? I was with you the whole time."

Crispin managed a weak smile. "Sure. But you were so content to be peacefully arrested. You don't think I hit sentinels for fun, do you, sir?"

The memory of the moment came back. Crispin had gotten knocked into the crowd. Sato hadn't thought anything of it, but Crispin must have orchestrated something. He thought back. It had all seemed so random at the time. How would Crispin have delivered a message in the second he was in the crowd? The answer took Sato a moment to find. "You thought something like this might happen, didn't you?"

Crispin looked at his amputated hand. "Not like this, sir. I didn't think she'd go so far. But it did seem like we were heading into enemy territory, so I arranged a bit of back-up."

Sato was stunned. "I don't know what I'd do without you, Crispin."

"We all worry about it, sir. But for now, we have to trust in Alonzo and the others."

Before Sato could respond, the sentinel responsible for Crispin dragged him away from the cart. They hadn't spoken for long, but Crispin had given Sato the hope he needed to keep fighting.

The macabre march through the streets continued. The wheel continued to wobble. The streets were now lined with the citizens of Versun. But the closer the caravan got to the merchants' district, the more dour faces he saw in the crowd. The jeering faded away, replaced by low murmurs and a tense silence.

Sato wasn't the only one who noticed the shift.

"Chief Magistrate, perhaps we should turn back? We are getting close to the merchant district," Grayson said. His eyes darted up and down the street.

Izuki's answer came swift and allowed no debate. "No. The people need to see his humiliation. They need to see he is a traitor. Here, more than anywhere else in the city."

"I understand, but I don't like the feeling of this crowd. I'm seeing a lot of angry faces."

Izuki studied the crowd, then shook her head. "Sato's poison spread deeper here than I thought. But it's no matter. Keep your guards sharp and punish even the slightest transgression. Let them see that there is no one above the dictates of the Path."

To hear Izuki claim the Path as an ally made Sato's blood boil.

Sato's attention suddenly returned to the wobbly wheel. He was no carpenter, but wheels weren't supposed to drift on the axle like that. He thought of the district he was in, and a wild hope occurred to him. Izuki had said some craftsmen had volunteered to build the cart for him. She'd never expect mere citizens to fight against her orders.

He knew that because that's the way he would have thought not so long ago.

A rock meant for Sato sailed wide and struck Grayson on the shoulder. The sentinel growled and drew his sword. "Who threw that?" he asked. Another rock flew from behind Grayson and hit him in the back of the head. He stumbled forward before regaining his balance.

Then the air was filled with stones. Not a one of which came close to Sato. He looked around as best he could and noticed the crowd was closing in. The sentinels drew steel, but Izuki did the math quickly. Blood was streaming from a small cut above her eye, and her gaze was wide. "Turn the cart! There are too many! Call for reinforcements!"

The driver turned the horses around sharply, causing the wheel to finally come off. The cart fell to the side with a crash. Pandemonium erupted as the crowd rushed the sentinels guarding the cart.

With the sentinels' full attention on the crowd, Crispin snuck next to Sato and undid the clasps on the stocks. A moment later, Sato was free. He stood tall, feeling better than he had in some time.

Grayson finally turned to face his former prisoner. When he saw Sato free, he snarled. Before the sentinel could act, Sato stepped in and delivered an elbow to the bridge of the surprised man's nose. The nose crunched and the sentinel was rocked back.

Sato took advantage of the man's disorientation and disarmed Grayson, then cut him down with his own sword. Few kills had ever felt as satisfying.

Unfortunately, the satisfaction didn't last long. Whatever curses Sato might lob at Izuki's sentinels, they were still among the best warriors in Versun. The crowd had caught them by surprise, but as soon as their swords came out, the crowd didn't have a chance. Already Izuki was protected by one squad, and horns called for reinforcements.

It wouldn't be long before the sentinels had control of the situation.

Fortunately, the crowd was wise enough to know better than to fight. As soon as the sentinels tore into the first wave of the mob, the crowd broke.

"This way!" Crispin called. Sato looked up and saw that the mob was now moving towards the gates that led into the merchant district. To safe territory.

Sato let himself be pulled forward by the crowd. Behind him, Izuki called for the sentinels to fall back until reinforcements arrived.

"We don't have much time!" Sato said to Crispin. He pushed himself toward the head of the crowd and urged them forward. The last few citizens that were still engaged with the guards extricated themselves and the crowd hurried towards the gates with Sato, stark naked, leading the way.

The gates closed before the crowd reached safety. A line of sentinels stood guard, swords already drawn.

At their head was the familiar figure of Helios.

The old sentinel waited patiently as the crowd approached. He had nothing to fear. His sentinels were mounted, armed, and prepared. If he decided to charge, dozens of citizens would die. His gaze met Sato's. There was pain in his eyes, but his voice was strong as he shouted above the noise of the crowd.

"General Sato, I'll give you one chance to surrender. You and your lieutenant will be granted a warrior's death, which is more than your traitorous spirit deserves. Everyone else will be allowed to return home to await their punishment from the chief magistrate. It's the best offer you'll get."

Sato stared, almost uncomprehending, at the man he'd once considered a close friend. Helios looked as if he was about to cry, but he sat as tall as ever on his mount. Sato believed he didn't want to be here. But that he would fulfill his duty as ordered by the chief magistrate.

Sato didn't cower. "You know this is wrong, Helios. You know that no matter what has happened to me, I've always sought to serve the Path. To serve Samas." He glanced meaningfully back at the crowd behind him. "All of it."

He felt the crowd pressing behind him. They weren't his sun stalkers, but he commanded them all the same. Unfortunately, the only command he could give them would result in too much death.

Helios ignored Sato's prodding. "Surrender, Sato. At least let me grant you a swift death."

Sato could hear hooves pounding on the cobblestone behind him. Soon, he would be stuck between Izuki's sentinels and those Helios commanded. He looked at Crispin, but the sentinel shook his head. Even his devious mind couldn't get them out of this.

Sato was about to challenge Helios to a duel, one he didn't think he'd win in his exhausted state, when a figure stepped out of the crowd holding a burlap sack. Alonzo, proudly displaying his sun stalker crest, walked calmly into the center of the street and stood before Helios.

Sato had never seen a greater act of courage.

"Stand aside, sentinel. Unless you want to meet the fate of your commander," Helios said.

Alonzo held up the sack. Then he reached in and pulled out a man's head. He presented the grotesque trophy to Helios.

"Is that Heath?" Helios asked, surprising Sato with how calm he was in the face of the grisly display. Sato, for one, was wondering what in the name of the sun Alonzo was doing carrying heads around in a burlap sack.

Alonzo nodded.

"Then I assume the other head in that sack is Faust?"

Alonzo nodded once more.

"And the rest?"

Alonzo drew his hand across his neck.

"Then my family?"

Alonzo pointed beyond the gates into the merchant district.

Helios slumped as if all the wind had been knocked out of him. It took Sato a moment to understand. He'd known Izuki had something on Helios, had some way of guaranteeing Helios didn't defect to Sato's side.

She'd had his family.

And Alonzo had freed them.

Sato took a step forward. "Helios. I am here to prepare this city for the storm that is almost upon us. You have my word that no matter your decision, your family will be safe. But you need to choose, and now."

Though advanced in years, Helios was still a sentinel in his heart. He knew something about making hard decisions quickly, and today was no different. He called out orders. "Raise the gates! Get these people through and then close them again. We're going to seal Izuki's sentinels in this district."

Helios' sentinels obeyed without question.

"How many of this district's sentinels will stay loyal to you?" Sato asked.

"You're looking at them. My personal guard. The rest are Izuki's."

"You think you can hold her back with just this?"

"For a while. These gates, at least, have been well-maintained. We could use some help, though."

The words had barely left Helios' lips when the gates opened, revealing row after row of sun stalkers, lined up in the street on the other side, prepared to do battle.

Roko saw Sato and looked about ready to charge when Sato held up his hand. Sato turned to Helios. "My own sentinels will aid you, I think."

As soon as it was clear there'd be no fighting between Helios' personal guard and the sun stalkers, the citizens made haste to get the gate between them and Izuki's sentinels. Roko rode forward against the crowd to speak with Helios and Sato.

"Roko, take the stalkers and support Magistrate Helios," Sato ordered. "We need to hold the gate."

"On one condition, sir," Roko responded

Sato raised an eyebrow at his old friend.

Roko never broke a smile. "You'll need to put on some pants first."

52

S hin watched from the ramparts of Bulas as the river of humanity poured through the narrow gates of the capital. The gates had been opened wide and the sentinels had given up trying to keep track of the new arrivals. For now, they simply directed the refugees and tried to keep order. Thankfully, thanks to Raya's final sacrifice, they had a bit of time before the demons reached them.

She and Corin hadn't arrived that long ago. They'd bypassed the line. With Raya and Rosa dead, Shin was the only officer remaining among the sin and sentinels. After a discussion with the gate commander, they'd been let through the gates and directed up to the ramparts, for reasons Shin couldn't yet guess at.

For now, she watched the horizon for any sign of the demons and thought about what might come next.

"How much longer before demons arrive?" Corin asked.

"I don't know. But I have a hard time believing it's going to be that long. They're drawn to people, and there's no greater feeding ground for them than here. They'll come. And I'm not sure how long the walls will protect us."

Corin looked at her. "How are you?"

The question was vague, but she guessed his meaning well enough. Raya had died without them ever repairing what was between them.

"I mourn her loss. But I think we understood one another, at the end. She died as a sin adept should die. Fighting for others," Shin said and was relieved to find the sentiment felt like her own.

"As did the sentinels," Corin added.

"It was their duty. They lived to serve the Path," the voice came from behind them, and Shin turned to see an older man approaching them.

It took her a moment to place him. His face was eerily familiar, though Shin was certain they'd never met before. It was only because of the context, though. She'd never expected to meet him in her life, and certainly not on the ramparts of Bulas. Beside her, Corin's eyes went wide, and he dropped to his knees and bowed, head to the floor. She gave the Firstborn of Samas a small bow.

Captain Harris stood behind the Firstborn, looking as stern as ever. When she didn't bow, he almost drew his sword then and there. A slight twitch of the Firstborn's finger halted the motion. "You must be Shin. General Sato has written about you in his letters and spoken to me about you. I'm sorry for what you've endured at the hands of my sentinels."

His voice was as gentle as a summer breeze, but still rocked her back. She studied the Firstborn, as she wasn't sure if she'd ever get another chance. He wasn't at all what she'd expected. She'd always imagined a stern and imposing man, larger than life.

He didn't look like much more than someone's grandfather.

A closer inspection told her more, though. He moved well and looked like he still knew how to use the sword at his hip. And there was an air about him, a quiet sense of command that was as different from Beast's bellicose style as night was to day.

His presence, and his apology, left her on her back foot. "Sir," was all she managed to say. Then she thought about the sentinels, and why she was here. "I'm sorry about Rosa. She died bravely."

"Of that I have no doubt. The more important question is: what do we do next?"

The question again startled Shin. Then her eyes went wide when she realized she was the person in Bulas best equipped to deal with demons. There was no one above her here to turn to. The Firstborn of Samas had asked her a question and expected her to guide him. The weight of that question fell on her harder than Beast dropping a massive hand on her shoulder.

"I...I don't know. We have enough adepts to send the demons back once they're out of their corporeal form, but to do that, heads need to be removed. That'll be tough, being as at least some of them will have the skills of your honor guard. I could try to send them back in their demon forms using sacrifice, but I'm not sure what will happen if I do. Or if I can even do it." Shin realized she was rambling and cut herself off. Her heart felt like it was about to beat right out of her chest.

The Firstborn seemed to understand. He waited while she brought her breath under control. After a minute, he asked an easier, more specific question. "How much danger are we in, here? Before long, we'll have most of the refugees behind the walls."

Shin thought for a moment. Memories of Dahl were still

fresh in her mind. "Walls aren't going to be enough, sir. These are feral demons, so they won't have the same abilities as the ones we faced in Dahl, but I have a hard time imagining the walls will keep us safe for long."

"How do we best defend against them?"

"There's only one way to kill a demon. You need to take its head, and then an adept can send it back. So your archers and catapults won't be of much use. Better instead to give everyone a sword to make their stand on the walls. Our adepts will send them back."

"How long can you sustain such a defense?" the Firstborn asked.

Despite all that he stood for, Shin found herself grateful for the Firstborn. He asked the right questions and accepted her answers. If the sentinels under him had learned from him, they'd be in a much different place right now.

"As long as we have to. I won't let anyone else die at their hands," Shin said, steel in her voice. "But the real danger lies with your former sentinels. If the demons who take their forms are anything like the ones that took on the forms of the Maramans at Dahl, then the walls will mean nothing to them. It will take everything we have to stop them."

The Firstborn shook his head. "I appreciate your bravery, and get your point, but you're not telling me what I need to know. I need your best guess. How long can you hold out?"

Shin considered her remaining adepts, as well as the number of demons they'd already encountered. "A few days at best."

"And there's no way you can think of to defeat the demons?"

Shin searched her memory. Perhaps there was some sacrifice she could weave, but nothing came to mind. She wanted her answer to be yes. But it couldn't be. Even if she thought of some sacrifice, she'd learned her lesson. For now, she needed to be content with what she knew about sacrifice and admit there were some things she couldn't do. Her hubris had already caused enough harm. The thought of what she'd done threatened to crush her, but she held her head up high. "I'm sorry, sir, but not that I know of."

The Firstborn nodded. He turned to Captain Harris. "We'll need to consider evacuation, then."

"Evacuation, sir?" Harris sounded as though he'd just heard a dirty word. "She's just a child! You can't evacuate Bulas based on her word."

The Firstborn raised an eyebrow. "She might be young, but look into her eyes and tell me she's a child."

Harris obeyed, and his expression softened. He turned back to the Firstborn. "I think you're overreacting."

Shin was amazed the captain spoke so frankly with the Firstborn. If most low-ranked sentinels talked to a superior with such familiarity, they'd be regretting their words before long. But the Firstborn took the criticism without comment. "Perhaps, but I'd rather err on the side of caution. This isn't a foe we've faced for a very long time."

Harris looked like he'd swallowed a bitter pill. "We have our port, and the boats are ready. Ravens were sent to Versun and Ilos a week ago when we first became aware of the demons. Preparations are in place, but it'll still take days, if not weeks, to evacuate the city. This will take time."

"Then you best get started," the Firstborn said quietly.

Harris turned on his heel to leave, but Corin stopped him.

"If I might interrupt," Corin said, "the last report we got from Yuki was that Beast and his navy were on an operation to capture the Maraman juggernaut. If he was successful, he might be able to help."

The Firstborn nodded. "A ship that size would certainly speed things up. Shin?"

"If any of his adepts survive the attack, I should be able to signal them."

"Please do," the Firstborn asked. "We're going to need all the help we can get." He thought for a moment. "Shin, would you please wait here? I'll send you my commanders and instruct them to take your orders. Harris, begin the evacuation."

"What about you?" Harris asked.

"I'll do what I can to keep order," the Firstborn answered.

"You should be among the first to evacuate."

In answer, the Firstborn just shook his head, and it was answer enough for Harris. He let the matter drop.

Shin watched as the Firstborn descended the ramparts and, despite her best efforts, was overwhelmed with the feeling that she would gladly follow that man into any battle. He was the best leader she'd come across since leaving home, and it pained her to admit that.

She turned her attention to the matter at hand. It wouldn't be long before the demons arrived, and they needed to be ready.

Beast and his crew huddled at the bow of the juggernaut as the strange Maraman weapons fired volley after volley of arrows at them. Beast had never seen weapons like that before, but he knew enough to recognize that they weren't designed to fire at the juggernaut's deck. They were supposed to be used to repel ships, not invaders already aboard. The Maramans had done their best to swing them around, but their field of fire was still reduced, which was the only reason Beast and the others were still alive.

Beast growled as he poked his head above cover. "They can't hit us here and we can't get to them."

For the moment, they were fine, but Beast feared that if their assault stalled for too long, the Maramans would find a way to win the upper hand. They needed a solution, and quick. If the adepts decided the juggernaut couldn't be captured, their orders were to destroy it.

Hanz spoke, his thoughts paralleling Beast's. "Yuki provided us with adepts. This might be a good time to use them."

"Can we? We've already asked a lot of them, and when

an adept goes too far, you can't use them again." Beast didn't know much about sacrifice, but he knew enough.

"They know their duty. Sacrifice is a gift that must be used to protect Samas," Jurian said quietly.

Hanz nodded in agreement.

Beast still wasn't a fan of the adepts. He preferred cold steel to the crimson glow of sacrifice. But they didn't have a lot of choices. "Fine, someone bring them to me."

A messenger went to find the adepts, still on the stolen ships.

"The twins are right, you know. It's what they signed up for," Colas said.

"Would you risk your crew so willingly?" Beast snapped.

"No, but my crew wouldn't risk my life without thought, either. Can you say the same for the sin?"

The question hung in the air between them. Colas had an annoying way of reminding him of all the weaknesses of the sin. Of reminding him what this juggernaut could represent.

A young girl emerged from the fog and huddled next to Beast. "I'm Vala," she said.

Beast shook his head. She was too young. What monster would order her to sacrifice anything? Benji, at least, had lived a good life. Vala had barely started hers.

"How old are you?" Beast blurted out.

"Old enough to cloak your navy in mist so those weapons didn't chew you up before you even got here," Vala replied coldly.

Colas snickered.

Beast supposed the girl had a point. If she thought herself a warrior, he'd treat her as one. He pointed toward the weapons. "We need to get past these. Any ideas?"

"I do know one technique, but we would need to get closer."

"How close?"

"Throwing distance. We can make an item explosive and then—"

"I'm familiar," Beast said, cutting her off as thoughts of Benji flooded his memories. "I won't ask that of you. Probably wouldn't work, anyway. If we're close enough to throw something at it, we're already dead. Can't you just shoot fire at them or something?"

Vala gave him a look that suggested she didn't appreciate people guessing at what sacrifice could do. "No."

"What about this mist? Can you still control it?" Beast asked.

"Yes, but it's still just fog. It's imperfect cover."

"We only need to get to the first weapon. After that, we should be able to destroy the others," Beast said. He wasn't sure who he was trying to convince, himself or the girl.

"That's a suicide mission," Colas said flatly.

"Does anyone have any better ideas? Specifically ideas that don't cost us limbs from young girls?"

The twins looked like they were about to interject, but Beast cut them off. "I don't want to hear it. This is what we're doing. This is what I'm doing."

Wisely, no one challenged him. He focused on Vala. "Bring in that fog before I stop and think about how foolish this is."

Vala nodded. She closed her eyes, and a crimson glow surrounded her. It took a moment, but then the fog began to move in and soon covered the entirety of the enormous ship's deck. Beast stretched out his hand and could barely see it in front of his face.

It would have to do. He was about to take off running when a massive hand clamped down on his shoulder.

"Wait a moment," Hanz said. He pointed to his ear, and Beast listened.

There, off in the distance, he heard a hissing. The fuses on at least one of the weapons had been lit. A moment later, giant arrows chewed up the deck. Beast couldn't see them, but it sounded like dozens of axes cutting at a tree at once.

"Now go," Hanz said with a wink. "Stay quiet."

Beast decided Hanz's approach was the epitome of wisdom. Without sight, it became a battlefield where sound reigned supreme. Fortunately, one didn't spend so much time around the sin without learning a few things. He moved forward carefully, placing his toe down and testing the boards before putting his full weight on the foot.

Ahead, he listened to Maramans whispering to one another. Sweat beaded down his forehead, and he fought the urge to run as fast as he could. He didn't know his exact location, but he figured he was well within the zone any of the weapons could hit him.

Fortunately, the Maramans couldn't see any better than he did.

He swore when he heard the hissing of fuses being lit somewhere to his right.

He froze for a moment. If he ran, they'd know exactly where he was. But if he didn't move, there was a very good chance one of those arrows would skewer him. He wasn't exactly a small target.

Beast took one more step, then hoped for the best.

The deck exploded beside him as the arrows launched. He used the sound of the impact to mask his own movement. He ran six steps before slowing.

His heart pounded heavier than it had in any other

battle. Give him a straightforward fight any day. This, he wanted nothing of.

Another dozen steps, taken with the utmost caution, revealed the shape of one of the weapons looming in front of him. Maramans swarmed around the placement, reloading the weapon with its deadly ordinance. As soon as they were visible, Beast drew his sword and rushed in.

The first two Maramans fell before they knew he was there. Beast resisted the urge to rush into the fray recklessly. After his approach, all he wanted was to swing, chop, and yell at anything that moved.

Two Maramans advanced to his left and one to his right. On his right, the Maraman wielded a giant two-handed axe. Beast grinned. His enemies, believing he had made a mistake in letting himself get surrounded, pressed their perceived advantage. Beast defended himself as the Maramans attacked. He blocked cuts and gave ground as the three warriors attacked him. Soon enough, the Maraman with the axe overcommitted and buried his axe into the face of one of his allies.

Before he could remove the weapon, Beast threw his sword at the final Maraman, impaling him through the stomach. He rushed the man with the axe. There was a satisfying crunch as Beast's fist and the man's nose briefly united. The Maraman staggered backwards, and Beast wrenched the axe free from the dead man. He took two smooth steps backwards and then split the axe's previous owner from the top of his skull to his chin.

A warning cry went up from the remaining Maraman. Beast charged the culprit, cutting him down before he could draw a weapon.

They knew he was here. He had to find a way to destroy

this thing before reinforcements arrived. He hacked at the base of the weapon with his axe, treating it like a giant tree.

He heard hissing, then dove behind the weapon as his world exploded into sharp splinters. He covered his face as he was showered in pieces of the very weapon he had been trying to destroy.

In the silence that followed, Beast stood up and looked at the shattered weapon. Any relief he felt vanished when he heard more hissing.

Beast ran towards the next weapon, cursing his own foolish bravery.

54

Sato stood on the wall separating the merchant district from the wealthy residential district of Versun. He was dressed in a threadbare tunic and pants. They weren't anywhere near the standards of his usual clothes, but they'd been given freely by one of the citizens, and they at least covered Sato up.

Behind him, the merchant district had largely returned to their day. With the gates closed and the walls guarded by sentinels loyal to Sato, there was little to see.

In front of him, the situation wasn't so calm. The citizens in the upper districts had come to see Sato's humiliation, but now the tables had been turned. The walls that had once protected them now sealed them in. Sato had control of the ports, the most populated residential areas, and the merchant districts. All Izuki had was the wealth, which meant little when there was nothing to buy.

Roko and the other sun stalkers had made it clear to Izuki's sentinels that they'd permit no one to even near the gates. For now, the rogue sentinels had obeyed. But unrest was already growing throughout the inner parts of the city. Before long, there'd be problems.

Sato turned from the scene. Crispin stood beside him, and it was high time they spoke. The situation wouldn't change that rapidly. "You should go find a healer. They'll need to look at that hand."

Crispin, paler than a sheet, shook his head. "Not much for them to look at. I might be filthy, but the cut was clean."

"All the same."

"You're not getting rid of me that easily, sir."

"Crispin..." Sato looked for something he could say that would express even a fraction of what he felt. But nothing seemed adequate.

"It's all right, sir." Crispin looked at him. "Those sin bastards sacrifice themselves all the time. Figured we can't let them show us up."

Despite everything, Sato chuckled. "You know that if there's anything you need, *anything*, all you have to do is ask."

"I know, sir. For now, let's just finish this."

"Any ideas how?"

"Sir?"

"You lost your hand, not your mind. And even though you were getting to be pretty decent with a sword, it's what's up here that makes you most dangerous." Sato tapped the side of his head lightly.

Crispin considered for a moment. "We could poison their water supply."

When Sato glared at him, Crispin held up his good hand. "Nothing lethal, sir. Just something that'll make them all sick. We could walk in and take it over in an afternoon."

"We're not poisoning our own people."

"We could set up a network of spies and have some

rumors circulate. Given enough time, we could probably get the upper districts to turn against Izuki, too. Shouldn't be too hard if we're going to be withholding food. After four or five days, I'd say the people will be just about begging to help you get rid of that bitch."

Crispin leaned against the wall, considering his plan more carefully. Sato could see the young man's thoughts churning. He was sure that if he gave Crispin enough time, he'd come up with something devious and effective. Sato still wasn't sure Crispin had any other kinds of thoughts.

But their conversation solidified something in his mind.

He couldn't have gotten this far in Versun without Crispin's help. But if he wanted to win the rest of the city, he had to do it his way. And they didn't have the time for a devious plan. The longer the situation stayed like this, the more likely it was the citizens rebelled. He'd rather not have their deaths on his hands, if he could help it. "Or I could just challenge her to a duel."

Crispin rolled his eyes. "*Now* you want to duel? Izuki's no fool. There's no way she'll accept your challenge."

"Perhaps. But it's the Path. Besides, right now, it doesn't matter. Versun isn't the keep and the upper district. It's the merchants, the port, and the people. We control those, not Izuki. Get Helios. I want to talk to him. And after that's done, go get that wound looked at." He cut off Crispin's protest. "And get some rest. You'll be needed later."

Crispin couldn't salute properly without a hand, but he gave a quick bow and was off. Sometimes, at least, he listened well enough.

While Crispin was gone, Sato thought the situation over for himself. The more he considered the different angles, the more certain he was of what he planned.

It was time to show this city the power of the Path.

Helios arrived a few minutes later. Sato noticed the dried tears on the older man's cheeks, and Helios gave him a grateful bow. "Sir."

"Your family is safe?"

"They are, thanks to your lieutenant."

Sato took a long breath. He'd been certain about his plan a minute ago, but it was hard following it through, especially now that Helios was here, standing in front of him. He understood, maybe now more than ever before, why it was people strayed from the Path. It would be so easy to take a different route. In many ways, it would feel better.

But follow that route for too long, and everything Samas was would collapse. He exhaled sharply. "You strayed, Helios. Farther than I ever would have expected." He kept any judgment out of his voice, but held up a hand to stop Helios' protests. "You will die for what you did here."

Helios paled, then snarled, "I saved your life!"

"Yes, but because of you, Versun isn't ready to fight off invasion. Because of you, countless people have suffered. And because of you, one of my most promising sentinels lost his sword hand. Not to mention that, if not for Alonzo, you would have charged me down as well as the people beside me. One right act, even for me, does not cleanse your transgressions."

Helios flinched as though he'd been struck but didn't argue. "Will you kill me yourself?"

Sato nodded. "I will grant you a clean death, worthy of the service you've granted Samas. I only have one order for you."

Helios snorted. "Most people have the sense to give the orders before revealing their plan to kill their subordinates."

Sato stood taller. "I'm not here to play games, Helios. It is time to return this nation to the Path, and it starts here, with you and me. You believed in it once, too." He paused to let that sink in. "Your last mission as a sentinel is to carry my challenge of a duel to Izuki. You're the only one she'd see without cutting you down on sight."

"She won't accept."

"Then she'll starve. She doesn't have the sentinels to take the walls back from us. I've already won."

"And if she refuses?"

"Then you return to face your honorable execution."

"Why should I? Why would I do any of this for you?"

"Because it's the right thing. You're no longer a general, and I've given you an order. The Path demands no less, and I'd be well within my rights to cut you down even for the disobedience you've shown in this meeting. But if you need any more encouragement, it is because your family is guilty of treason as well."

Helios' eyes went wide. "You wouldn't!"

"I don't want to. By the sun, Helios, I don't want any of this. But I will, because the Path demands it. Should you complete this mission, no matter Izuki's response, I'll offer a full pardon for your family, as well as positions within the sentinel ranks for your children."

It was the best offer Helios was going to get. A part of Sato felt as though it was too manipulative, but sometimes the line between leadership and manipulation was a gray one. At least here, Sato walked firmly upon the Path.

"You swear?" Helios asked.

"By the sun."

Helios nodded. "Then I'll deliver your challenge."

55

The Firstborn's personal guard pinned the oversized chicken to the ground. The thing writhed around, its elongated beak opening and closing with the unnervingly silent cries so common among the demons. In two hacks, the head was removed. The instant the physical form of the demon dissipated, the adept beside Shin sent it back to the rift.

The distance between Bulas and the rift was wearing them down. Even a simple return like this took a focus and will most adepts rarely had to summon. It was a testament to the sin's strength the walls were still standing. But Shin didn't know how much longer they could last.

The horde of demons silently beating on the gates was crushing their spirit. The subdued murmur of the terrified citizens huddled within the city was breaking Shin's heart.

"Shin?" Corin asked. The former luan had barely left her side since the siege had started. She didn't know what she had done to earn such loyalty, but he amazed her and gave her strength.

"I'm fine," she said. Corin knew it was a lie, though, and she relented under his gaze. "I'm exhausted, but we can keep going."

"Any word from Beast?"

Shin shrugged. She was mimicking the distress call she'd once felt from Raya, pushing it as far as she could. But she didn't know if there was some sort of response the sin normally used, or even how far her call for help was going. All she could do was hope.

"Well, if you want some good news, I have a bit. The evacuation is well underway. Over half the original population of Bulas is on the boats."

The news brought Shin no joy. Yes, they had saved thousands upon thousands of lives. But there were still so many more in danger. Danger that grew with every passing moment.

She caught Corin's grimace. "What?"

"It's just that we could really use Beast right now. Everything that can sail has been used, and now we have to wait for the ships to return from Versun. If the walls were breached right now, there's nothing we'd be able to do. Nowhere for us to go."

Shin rubbed at her eyes. "Great. If only there was a concise way to sum up my feelings about this situation." Shin shared a look with Corin.

"Fuck," they said in unison, echoing Beast's customary reaction.

The two laughed grimly and Shin looked around to make sure there weren't any demons cresting the walls that needed her immediate attention.

"Corin, I know I haven't been myself since…maybe since Dahl? It's hard to say what I lost with every memory I gave away, but I know I'm not the person you first met. I just want to say I'm sorry I let you down."

"Shin, I don't—"

"No, wait. I've been trying to be better, but only because I knew that's what you'd expect of me. But it's all an act. Inside, it feels like there's nothing but anger and resentment left. Every time I need to make a decision, the only way I can make it is by asking what you would do."

"What I would do? That's a terrible way to live!"

Shin grinned at her friend's self-deprecation. "It's been the only way. I have this rage in me and I just want to let it out. I want to let it flow through me into a sacrifice that crushes our enemies and shows the world my power. Until just a few days ago, you were the only idea keeping me sane." Shin paused and forced herself to look Corin in the eye. "Then I saw what happened to Raya."

"Her tongue?" Corin asked.

"It was more than that, Corin. She was a shell of herself. She hardly knew what was going on around her. In the end, though, she found it in herself to fight one last time."

Corin reached out and took her hand, but he didn't speak, allowing her to finish her thoughts.

"How do I move forward? How can I use sacrifice, knowing that the next one might turn me into a monster?" She took a deep breath and shuddered. She didn't feel very articulate, but she thought Corin understood. She looked down at their intertwined hands and took comfort.

Corin didn't speak for some time. "I don't know the answers, Shin. I'm not sure than anyone does. I couldn't tell you what's right because all I'm trying to do is keep you safe. But I think you'll know. You lost some of yourself, in a way that very few people could understand. But guess what? You still want to be better. That, more than anything, is why I care about you. It's been true about you since the first time I met you. So long as you never lose that desire to become a better person, I'll trust that the Shin I know is still there."

Shin wanted to laugh at the simplicity of what Corin said. She wanted to scoff at it. To undercut its meaning by turning it into a joke.

But she couldn't.

"Thanks. What would I do without you?"

"At a guess? Blow a hole in the ocean that sucks all of Samas into oblivion."

This time, Shin did laugh. "That's fair, I suppose. Ready to kill some more demons?"

"Always."

Their reprieve lasted a little longer and then a flurry of activity in their section of the wall drew them towards a few racoons that were being engaged by sentinels.

As always, the sentinels made battle into a beautifully efficient dance. They worked together so seamlessly that five sentinels seemed to fight as one.

By the time Corin and Shin arrived, most of the work was done. The sentinels favored units that combined long spears as well as swords to fight the demons. The spears neutralized the reach of the demon's elongated limbs, while the swords did what they did best.

A few efficient strikes removed the heads of the demons and an adept began sending them back. Shin watched as the misty forms rose over the walls and then stopped. The crimson glow flickered and then disappeared, and the once harmless mist was suddenly full of malevolence.

Corin rushed over and caught the adept as she collapsed. He gently laid her down.

"I think she's just exhausted. I'll call another adept," Corin said.

The sentinels, as quick to pick up their new training as promised, immediately covered their eyes as the mist descended upon them.

Before Corin could look for another adept, a huge, clawed hand gripped the edge of the ramparts. The sight caused the sentinels to look over the wall in alarm. They took a step back as the demon form of a sentinel pulled itself to the top of the walls and grinned grotesquely at them. The sentinels raised their weapons, but Shin could see they were still trying not to get caught by the floating mist.

She reacted without thinking.

For the first time in weeks, she opened herself up to the realm. The feeling of power was intoxicating. Her body hungered to weave spells of infinite complexity, to find a way to rid them of the demons and the Maramans in one fell swoop. The world—no, reality itself—was hers to change as she pleased.

She pushed the temptation aside.

She called Raya's memory into focus and concentrated on the generational spell that her friend had shown her. She followed it to the letter. She let the realm ask for her pinky and she gave it willingly. She gave it with joy. She gave it and finally, truly, joined the ranks of the sin that Yuki was hopeful she could one day lead.

Yes, it hurt. But compared to the sacrifices she'd already made, the pinky was nothing. It was physical pain, which she bore with a smile. She pushed the demons all the way back to the rift and felt them return there.

She opened her eyes and smiled.

"Shin!" Corin screamed, and the smile was gone from her face.

She danced backwards as another sentinel demon just

missed cutting her in half. She brought Harmony to bear and forced the demon backwards. Corin appeared behind it and cleaved its head between his two blades.

The group of sentinels beside her, their numbers halved, had the demon they were fighting pinned. They removed its head as well.

Shin closed her eyes and repeated the spell. Again, she ignored the pull to do more. Again, she relished taking her place among the sin. She opened her eyes again and looked around.

The battle that had happened here was far from the only one being fought.

All along the wall, the sentinels were fighting pitched battles against demon versions of their order. Adepts sent demons back, but too many were falling. Shin was no tactician, but she could see that the walls would need to be abandoned soon. They were slowly but surely being overwhelmed.

It seemed Captain Harris agreed with her. Off in the distance, two long blasts of the horn signalled the retreat. The sentinels reacted immediately, changing formations and giving up ground. They grabbed the adepts and forced them safely behind them.

"We have to go," one of the sentinels in her squad said, and pushed her to the nearest stairs.

"No, I can send some more back," Shin said and struggled against the sentinel.

"You'll get the chance. The walls are the first line of defense. There's plenty more space left for us to kill demons," the sentinel answered.

For the second time that day, Shin allowed herself to surrender to a greater order. The sentinel was right. They were just buying time. As long as she was saving people, she would accept their orders.

As they dropped from the wall she took one last glance toward the sea, Bulas' last hope.

She hoped Beast got their signal. Because they needed him here now.

56

Beast didn't have the option of sneaking to the next weapon. Though the fog was dense as ever, the Maramans knew one of their launchers had been destroyed. They'd act to protect the rest. Fortunately, he'd spent long enough training with the sin that, in this fog, he should be able to descend upon them like a ghost. Killing them before they even knew what was happening.

Beast smiled to himself. He would become death's shadow. He broke from cover and charged toward the next weapon. His footsteps were loud in his ears, but he didn't care.

He cursed as he ran headlong into the back of a Maraman.

The man cried out in alarm and Beast heard weapons being drawn.

"Fucking fog!" Beast swore as he buried his axe in the man who'd had the misfortune of getting in his way.

As chaos made its home in the fog, Beast moved on instinct. More Maramans guarded this weapon than the last, but Beast was in his element. The axe in his hand blocked and parried as smoothly as it landed killing blows. Here, the Maramans fought harder, but they weren't the fearsome enemies Beast had known from their initial invasion. Now they fought no better than sentinels, and if anyone on Samas was good at killing sentinels, it was Beast.

He caught the arm of one Maraman who tried to stab him with a knife, then buried his axe in the neck of another. Beside him, sparks flared as a fuse was lit. Beast ignored it. He could see the weapon wasn't pointing toward him, and the others were safe. He killed the Maraman who'd tried to stab him, and then the weapon launched its deadly payload. From the shouts and sounds of destruction, Beast guessed they'd targeted one of the other weapon placements by accident. Beast laughed at their foolishness.

After another few moments of bloody pandemonium, the last of the Maramans died. Beast began hacking down the launcher. As he did, he braced himself, dreading the hissing would serve as the prelude to his death.

It never came.

Beast, never one to question good luck, finished destroying one weapon and started to sprint in the direction of the next placement. Halfway across the deck, he heard someone cry out. After spending the last few minutes being surrounded by Maramans, it took him a moment to realize that he could recognize the words.

"Weapon down!" Hanz's voice cried out.

Beast ran towards it.

"What are you doing?" Beast demanded as Hanz appeared out of the mist. "You were supposed to stay back."

"And let you have all the fun?" Hanz said with a grin. "Once you had all the attention on you, the others were significantly easier."

"Who took the other one?"

"Jurian," Hanz said.

"Foolish! I had it under control!" Beast calmed himself. Truthfully, he was grateful not to have the other weapons to deal with. "What's the situation?"

"Some of our more quiet sin are smoking the rest of the Maramans out of their deck house now," Hanz said. "The worst of the battle should be over. Vala, would you care to remove this fog?"

Vala nodded and closed her eyes.

The fog covering the deck slowly drifted away and revealed the destruction that Beast and the twins had wrought. The weapon placements were smashed, and Maraman bodies littered the deck. Beast looked to the deckhouse and saw smoke pouring out of the arrow slits. Four sin were already on their way back to the group.

"Nice work," Beast said.

But the giant twin wasn't listening. His pale face stared at the deck with an expression of anguish like Beast had never seen. He followed his large friend's gaze. When he saw the object of Hanz' grief, he dropped to his knees.

Lying beside the broken weapon placement was Jurian's body, riddled with giant arrows.

Arrows that had come from the second weapon that Beast was trying to destroy.

Beast didn't know if he could have stopped the weapon from firing. But he'd been right there.

Guilt hit him almost as hard as grief. Jurian had been one of his closest remaining friends. And he'd always been so competent, so strong. Beast had never expected him to lose a fight.

Beast stared at Hanz, at a loss for words. Beast had lost a friend, but Hanz had lost a brother. More than a brother. The two were like one spirit split into two bodies. What could possibly ease that pain? Before Beast found an answer, Hanz's gaze snapped to the direction of the deck house.

"Hanz..." Beast began, trying to reason with his friend.

Hanz was already moving.

Face like a thundercloud, Hanz raised his sword and strode purposefully towards the Maramans that now streamed out of the deck house. Because they were coughing and gasping for air, they didn't see him at first, and when they did, they involuntarily recoiled a step before charging him.

Beast sprinted forward to join his friend, but Hanz looked back and fixed Beast with a stare that stopped him in his tracks.

Beast didn't agree, but he understood. Some fights had to be fought alone.

He knew Hanz could fight. The man had trained him, after all, but he had never seen him like this. His rage was a controlled fire that burned its way through the Maramans like they were kindling. He blocked and moved before landing precise strikes. He took a few shallow cuts, but accepting the injuries always put Hanz into a better position than he had just left.

"He can't kill them all," Colas said.

"Maybe not, but he doesn't want our help."

"I thought you were the one who didn't want to sacrifice your crew."

Beast nodded. He'd already been thinking the same. The only question was how to save Hanz from his suicidal charge. "Keep everyone here. He won't like my help, but I don't think he'll kill me for giving it. Can't promise anything for the rest of you."

Colas nodded and Beast took off. There were only about

a dozen Maramans left, but Hanz was already slowing down, and the Maramans were pressing hard, seeing an opportunity to have some small revenge for the loss of the juggernaut.

Then Beast joined the fray, and the two giant men together were too much for the remaining fighters. A few moments later, the last Maraman died on Hanz's sword. After the man fell to the deck, Hanz paced like a caged animal, chest heaving, rage far from spent. He threw his sword down and looked around for something else to kill. Beast put himself in the man's path.

"It's done," Beast said.

Hanz punched him in the face. Beast saw stars, but he held his ground. Hanz punched him again, this time in the stomach. Beast fought the urge to double over. But he couldn't take many more.

Hanz lifted his arm to punch Beast a third time, but dropped it a moment later. His body sagged in on itself. Beast closed the distance and wrapped him in a hug. Hanz sobbed while Beast did his best to choke back the sorrow in his own heart.

He wasn't sure how long they stayed like that, but he growled when someone laid a small hand on his arm. He turned around, ready to shout, but it was only Vala.

"I'm sorry, sir, but I'm feeling a really strong distress beacon from somewhere far up north. I can't be sure, but I think it's Bulas."

"Distress beacon?" Beast asked, confused.

"A way for adepts to call for help. We only use it in dire emergencies, and this one is one of the strongest I've ever felt."

Beast looked around at the crews of all the mugon ships assembled before him.

They'd done it. They'd taken the juggernaut. Even though the cost had been far too high, they'd done it.

And now the sin wanted even more from him.

He looked out over the open ocean. A place that could all be his.

Then he looked down at Vala, waiting expectantly for her orders.

"She asked you a question," Colas said with a grim smile. "The juggernaut is yours. So what should we do, admiral?"

57

Sato gave Helios time with his family. He planned on granting more after the sentinel returned, but there was a chance Izuki might go so far as to kill Helios for his betrayal outside the gates. While he waited, he read the report Alonzo had written.

Some of Alonzo's actions were no more than Sato had surmised. He'd sought out the leverage Izuki held over Helios, then dealt with that problem with his sword.

More surprising, and perhaps more useful, was all that Alonzo had done to support Sato during his imprisonment. Because Alonzo didn't flout Sato's orders in the same way that Crispin did, Sato tended to forget that Alonzo had just as devious a mind as his fellow lieutenant. Alonzo figured Izuki would either try to kill Sato or discredit him. Either way, the solution was the same.

For the duration of Sato's imprisonment, the sun stalkers had been everywhere in the parts of the city they controlled, spreading heroic tales of Sato. Including the story of how he'd lost his pinky fighting a demon on Iru. Alonzo had figured the stories would work regardless of Izuki's actions.

If she killed him, he became a martyr. If she tried to smear his reputation, the merchants and lower district citizens wouldn't have any of it.

Sato read the report twice, unable to believe the effort his unit had made in saving him. They'd done everything short of storming Versun's keep to rescue him.

He didn't believe he'd ever think like them, but that had been the point all along, ever since the Firstborn had given him this unit. He gave them purpose, and they made possible feats Sato could never accomplish alone.

As Sato finished his second reading, Helios returned. "I'm ready," he said.

He looked it. Helios still cut a striking figure in his sentinel's uniform, and it looked like he'd gone to the effort of cleaning it since the ordeal at the gates. "Good luck," Sato said, "and remember, whatever happens to you, we'll keep your family as safe as we can."

Helios nodded, and the gates were opened. He rode through on his horse, and Sato watched from the top of the wall as Helios spoke with a few of the sentinels farther up the street. After a brief discussion, the sentinels led Helios toward the keep.

It was odd, knowing that the fate of Versun was being decided somewhere he wasn't. He wanted to be in the thick of battle, earning a clean and decisive victory.

But here, that wasn't how it had played out at all. From the murders of Tando and Azazel to his appeal to the masses, nothing in Versun had gone the way he'd expected.

And yet, it had worked. Sato controlled almost all of Versun that mattered, and the rest would be his soon enough. There were lessons there, but Sato was too tired to learn them today. Once this was over with Izuki, he would reflect and meditate on what he had learned here.

Barely an hour had passed before Sato saw Helios riding back toward the gate. Whatever had happened at the keep had happened quickly. Sato assumed the meeting had gone poorly, until he saw that Helios carried something in his right hand, something he held up as he came in sight of the walls.

Izuki's head.

Sato looked behind Helios, expecting some sort of pursuit, but there was none. If anything, the sentinels seemed apathetic to his passing. Sato ordered the gates opened, then descended from the wall to speak with the older sentinel.

Helios pulled to a stop and dropped Izuki's head at Sato's feet. Sato stared at it for a moment, struggling to believe it could really be her. After all the planning, had Helios ended it so simply? "What happened?"

Helios came down from his horse and disarmed himself, offering his sword to Sato. "When my son comes of age, I'd ask that you give this to him."

"Of course," Sato said.

Helios pointed to Izuki's head. "When I arrived, she was in the keep, staring at a letter and muttering to herself. We never even spoke. I decided then, the simplest solution was to kill her." Before Sato could ask further questions, Helios pulled the letter from a pocket. "You might want to read this first."

The letter was written in the condensed code used frequently by sentinels. Sato read it once, then read it again, not quite believing what it said. He turned it over, verifying the seal of the Firstborn. Izuki had cracked it open, of course, but it was the right seal. He looked up at Helios. "Do you believe this?"

"I don't know what to believe. But there have been strange reports as of late. So, yes, I'm tempted to believe it."

The enormity of the brief message was too much for the moment. Sato put it away. He couldn't even imagine those demons striking at the greatest city in Samas. But it demanded attention. He called Roko to him and told him to prepare the harbor for guests. Then he turned once more to Helios. "You've done well. Go. Spend the rest of today with your family. I'll meet you at the top of the outer walls at dusk."

Helios swallowed hard and bowed. "Of course." He turned on his heels and walked away.

Sato ordered another of his sentinels to put Izuki's head on a spike. Let it serve as a reminder to others what consequences followed when one fell from the Path.

Sato was high on the walls when the first ships started to arrive from Bulas. They confirmed Sato's worst fears. He watched, with a growing pit in his stomach, as more ships appeared on the horizon. There were so many, and yet it wasn't nearly enough. Bulas was too large, filled with too many people.

It felt like everything he believed in was collapsing around him.

But he wouldn't give into despair. It was easy to follow the Path when the way was wide and smooth. True character, true devotion to the Path, was only revealed when the way was narrow and overgrown.

If he could help guide Samas through this period, they would emerge stronger than ever before. He was certain of it.

He heard Crispin before he saw him, and he turned to see his lieutenant climbing the last of the stairs. His bandages had been replaced with new ones, and it looked like he'd gotten that nap that Sato had ordered him to take. Crispin came to stand beside him, and together they stared out at the harbor as it began to fill. Fortunately, they were as prepared as they could be. "So, it's true?" Crispin asked.

"Seems that way. We'll know more once we've had a chance to speak with the first refugees."

"That's a shitty situation, sir, if you don't mind me saying."

"Agreed."

"I heard you've still got the gates closed between the merchant district and the upper district."

Sato nodded. "They'll be fine for now. I need time to decide what to do with all the sentinels that supported Izuki. But they'll need to open their houses for all the refugees, too." He thought of all the work ahead of him, and it almost snapped him in two. But he refused to break. Not now, of all times.

"That's actually what I wanted to talk to you about, sir. Helios."

"What about him?"

"I think you should spare his life."

"Why would I do that?"

"Because he saved us. Because he delivered, almost literally, Izuki's head on a platter. But more than anything, because he's a good man and a good sentinel, and we need every one of those we can get." Crispin gazed meaningfully at the incoming ships.

"If he'd done his part in the first place, you might still have your hand," Sato argued. "He followed the Path this time, but that was only after years of falling off."

"With all due respect, sir, that puts him in the same camp as me. You can see why I might be interested in how you treat him."

Sato swallowed a lump in his throat. After all that Crispin had suffered, he should be the first demanding Helios' head. Perhaps the older sentinel wasn't directly responsible, but he'd been part of the problem. "If I bend now, what hope do I have to return Versun to the Path?"

Crispin rose his right hand to scratch at his chin, realizing too late he had no hand to scratch with. He grinned as he realized his mistake, and in so doing, showed Sato the true depth of his character. Crispin let his arm drop. "Seems to me, sir, that the Path is the ideal we always strive for. It's a destination, more than a road. We're always trying to get closer, and maybe that's good enough."

He turned to leave, then stopped. The sun was dropping closer to the horizon. He left Sato with one last thought. "You were the first commander who demanded more from me. Can't say I always liked it, but here I am, and even without this hand, I'm not sure there are many other places I'd rather be."

He descended the steps, and Sato watched him go. Alonzo was waiting for his friend below, and the two of them walked side by side toward the taverns that dotted the port area. Sato shook his head. He suspected those two would get up to trouble tonight.

To his surprise, he realized he didn't even care if they did. By the sun, if any two sentinels had earned a night off, it was them.

But they left him alone with his decision about Helios.

Ten minutes ago, he'd imagined Helios' execution as a turning point. The events in Versun made him feel unclean. They'd cleansed most of the corruption from the ranks of the sentinels, but not in any way he'd boast of. The Path demanded Helios' death, and it would signify a new start, both for him and for Versun.

But Crispin's words bounced around endlessly in his head, echoing the Firstborn's own pleas for mercy.

The rationalizations were almost too easy. Helios commanded a large force of sentinels within the city, and there were sure to be harsh feelings if Helios died. The man had years of experience in Versun, making him an invaluable ally. And he could serve as a bridge between the old magistrates of Versun and the new ones.

But the Path demanded justice. If Sato bent now, when would he ever return to the ways he knew were best?

When Helios climbed the steps to join him, Sato still had no answer.

The old sentinel had come alone. Sato had halfway expected him to bring his family. He was dressed in his formal uniform. He gave Sato a short bow.

It occurred to Sato that Helios had walked to his own death for no other reason than Sato had commanded it. Sato had never even questioned that Helios would obey. It had just been assumed, because that was what the Path demanded. Had Sato been in Helios' place, he would have done the same.

But how many sentinels would do so?

A year ago, Sato would have claimed almost all of them.

Now he knew better.

Yes, Helios had fallen.

But he was here now, standing beside Sato. And though it went against every instinct Sato had, he knew what he needed to do. He turned to face Helios and bowed deeply to the old man he had once called a friend. Perhaps, someday in the future, he might again. "I've reconsidered. I'd be honored if you continue to serve Versun and the Firstborn."

A mix of emotions played over Helios' face. Sato saw he had a dozen questions he wanted to ask, but he spoke none of them. In the end, Helios just bowed again. But when he straightened, Sato saw the tears trickle down his face. "It would be my honor."

Even though it went against everything he believed, Sato looked at Helios and felt his heart grow lighter. "I assume it goes without saying my standards will be different than the ones you've grown accustomed to?"

The corner of Helios' mouth turned up in a smile. "It does, sir."

"If you fall off the Path like you did before, we'll meet here again, and the next time there will be no mercy shown."

"Understood, sir."

"Go. Spend time with your family tonight." Sato gestured toward the ships. "Because you'll be helping with all of that soon enough."

Helios bowed one last time and practically ran down the stairs. Sato turned back to the view of the harbor. More ships were arriving, and soon the port district would be full. Sentinels stood by, ready to direct the refugees to temporary shelter.

There was still a war to be fought. But for tonight, he basked in the fading light of the sun, feeling victorious.

58

The sentinels guided Shin to the next line of defense in Bulas. The city was designed to funnel anyone passing through the gates into one main thoroughfare. If the gates were breached, the entire road could be used to create defensive choke points. Along the route were various guard houses complete with murder holes.

All of which meant precisely nothing in the face of the demon threat.

The twisted parodies of sentinel soldiers leaped down from the ramparts and into the streets with abandon. Any kind of bulwark or choke point created in the street meant little to the rage-fueled creatures that sought to rend flesh and snap bones. A wave of demonic hatred flowed over the walls and into the city.

And broke against the will of the sentinels.

Seasoned commanders recognized the futility of traditional defensive tactics and abandoned them in favor of fluidity and speed.

Grizzled veterans, born to the Path and raised in its

ways, adapted to tactics they'd only studied in theory and executed them like they'd drilled them their whole lives.

Men and women stood shoulder to shoulder and met an onslaught of nightmares so that the people they had sworn to serve could survive a little longer this day.

They fought, giving their hearts and bodies to the defense of the city.

And they died, in numbers Samas hadn't seen in generations.

But each sentinel made sure the demons paid dearly for every inch they advanced.

Shin and her adepts could hardly keep up. They sent misty forms back to the rift by the dozen, and still there were always more that required attention. Shin split her efforts between returning demons to the rift and fighting them with Harmony.

She opened her eyes just in time to see a sentinel demon leap onto the awning of a building lining the street. The creature used its momentum to run along the vertical face of the stone structure. Its feet, a mind-bending combination of sentinel uniform boots and nightmarish talons, gripped the wall, causing stone to crumble and rain down with each step.

"Get down!" Shin shouted to an adept beside her.

The young man dropped to his knees without hesitating and Shin threw Harmony in a large arc. The weapon spun in the air, and she adjusted its trajectory so that it met the demon as it leaped from the wall. It turned to mist in midair as Harmony's blade removed its head.

"Nice," the adept said from his crouched position.

Before Shin could answer, the adept sent the mist back, along with a few more that appeared during the process.

"They will overwhelm us soon," an eerily calm voice

said from behind Shin. She turned to see Captain Harris surveying the streets with a look of detachment across his face.

"What do we do?" Shin asked.

"I came to ask you that very question. Is there anything you can do to hold them back? Or send them back?"

Shin had known the question would eventually be asked of her, but it still caught her off-guard. *Could* she do anything? Maybe. She had felt Raya create that barrier before. Would that buy them enough time? Would she be willing to make the same level of sacrifice Raya had? Or would the realm take something more?

Harris misunderstood her silence. "If you can't do anything, I understand. These are affairs beyond my scope. I am only an officer exhausting all of my options."

His kindness made her guilt and uncertainty worse. Who was she to question, when all of this was her fault already?

"Maybe," she said. "Give me a minute to see what I might be able to do."

Harris bowed deeply. "Thank you."

Shin nodded and turned to face the hoard of demons. She closed her eyes and felt the realm. It was there, closer than ever, waiting for her to drink from its deep wells of power.

She thought of Yuki and her warnings, of Raya laying down her life, and of all the damage she had done the last time she accessed the realm. How the realm had taken advantage of her desires.

She wanted to drink the power so badly, but she knew in her heart that she just didn't know enough. She couldn't trust the realm. Even if she fought with the best of intentions, there was no telling what may result if she attempted to weave her own sacrifices again.

She opened her eyes and couldn't stop them from watering. "I'm sorry, but there's nothing more I can do. It's beyond my skill," she said without looking the sentinel captain.

"Don't apologize. You did what you could."

"So, what do we do now?" Shin repeated, wanting to quickly change the subject.

"The citizens are mostly gathered at the evacuation grounds. We'll continue to fall back and protect them while we wait for ships to arrive. Our thickest, highest walls remain behind us. The demons might be able to climb them, but they'll still buy us some time. For now, we need to make as orderly a retreat as we can."

"We can help with that," Shin said, glad to be given direction. "Do you know where Corin is?"

"He's helping defend the evacuation grounds from the flying demons. His skill with those blades of his is remarkable."

Shin nodded. She'd seen that skill often enough. How many times had Corin saved her own life? She'd lost count, but she suspected more than she'd saved his. "How long do you think we need to hold out?"

Harris' face turned dark at that. "I don't know, but I fear it's longer than we have. Any ship that can handle the shipping lanes is gone, and it'll be hours before the first of them returns. And that's only if everything goes according to plan. Right now we have nothing but little fishing boats that can't go much beyond the harbor."

"Any sign of the juggernaut?" Shin had continued sending out the distress call, but she'd felt no response.

"Not yet. But right now, it's about the only thing that can save us."

"If Beast can make it, he will."

"I hope you're right. But for now, we have no choice but continue the fight as well as we're able."

"We will, captain."

Harris gave her a sharp nod and started shouting orders. The sentinels reacted quickly, and Shin was once again amazed at how quickly they changed tactics. They fell back without breaking the line. Shin and the other adepts followed suit.

As orderly as the retreat was, it was far from easy. The demons were frightening creatures, and even though the sentinels outnumbered the beasts, the demons were just too strong. Even as the sentinels retreated, they left streets filled with their dead.

Eventually, Shin glanced back and saw the harbor behind them. Thousands of citizens milled about in the marina, hovering on the edge of panic. The harbor was empty, and the demons kept pressing harder, scenting all the food before them. If something didn't change soon, the demons would enjoy a feast like none other.

Shin despaired. Maybe, if there were no other options, she would try sacrifice one last time, hoping she didn't doom people more than she already had.

They retreated through the final interior gate that separated the keep in Bulas from the rest of the city. The moment the last sentinel was through, a giant gate crashed down and crushed a few demons beneath it. Shin wasn't sure how long it would take the demons to scale these walls, but they were at least as high as the ones that surrounded the city.

It was something, at least.

A sentinel messenger ordered her to the walls. She climbed the steep set of stairs, then took a moment to enjoy the breeze from the harbor. Up here she could see for miles.

On any other day, she might have appreciated that. Today it made her miserable. Bulas, the crown jewel of Samas, was on its way to becoming an abandoned ruin. She couldn't look in any direction without seeing the bodies in the streets and the demons converging on the last set of walls.

Because she had thought she could save them all.

A soft pair of footsteps stopped beside her. "There is still hope," a calm voice said. Shin glanced over to see the Firstborn, surveying the same scene.

"I wish I felt that way," Shin admitted. "But we won't be able to hold this wall for too long, and there's no way for the rest of us to escape."

"Your efforts here still saved thousands of lives. Is that not enough?"

Shin shook her head. "Not even close."

Below them, demons gathered at the wall, tearing at the stone. From their experience at the outer walls, Shin figured they didn't have more than a few hours left to live. She could go find Corin. At the very least, they could die together.

A shout sounded from behind them. Shin turned. A sentinel was pointing out to the harbor.

Shin's heart swelled. There, on the horizon, was the largest ship she had ever seen. Even from this distance, it was obvious that it was enormous, and it was moving fast.

She couldn't do anything but shake her head. She didn't know how that lumbering knucklehead had managed to capture something so big, but right now, she didn't care. They had a chance.

"Looks like your friend came through for us," the Firstborn observed.

"Looks like."

Then there was no time. The Firstborn gave the orders. Fishing boats were loaded with people, and as Shin watched, three ships detached from the Juggernaut and raced ahead of it toward the marina. All the while, the juggernaut drew closer.

She turned back to the walls. Now it was a race against time. It would still take a few hours to get people to the safety of the juggernaut, and a few hours was about all the time they had. Shin was beyond exhausted. They all were.

Now they just had to make one last stand. She searched for any last shred of energy but couldn't find any. She stood anyway.

As the Firstborn and the others evacuated, Shin, the sin adepts, and the sentinels held the walls. As before, the initial defense wasn't too demanding. Most of the demons tore at the walls, but only a few figured out they could climb. Those that did were dealt with easily enough and sent back to the rifts. Shin did see several adepts lose their focus, but someone else was always there to catch the mist before it could take shape again.

But as one hour turned to two, and then to three, the situation turned more dire. More demons learned how to crawl up the wall, and the sentinels and sin were at their limit. It wouldn't be long before they made the mistake that broke the line for good.

Before that moment happened, though, Harris gave the order to retreat. Shin glanced back and was surprised to find the marina was almost empty. Where there'd once been thousands, there were now just a hundred or so, and they were boarding ships.

All the warriors retreated, abandoning the last line of defense in Bulas.

Down at the marina, she found a welcome sight. Corin was there, standing as tall as ever. She didn't know how he did it, but he looked as though he'd just woken from a long nap. When he saw her, he beamed. "Shin!"

Then he came forward and wrapped her in a hug.

She practically fell into his arms.

"Let's go!" a sentinel shouted and shoved them towards a waiting ship.

Time blurred and skipped. Shin remembered climbing onto a ship, strong arms helping her board. She remembered looking at the walls as demons crested them and finally claimed all of Bulas as their own. And she remembered watching the flames rising and smoke dancing amongst buildings that had stood since Samas was born.

59

______

Beast's palms itched.

He paced back and forth at the giant helm of the juggernaut, his juggernaut, and imagined swinging his axe through the demons pouring into Bulas.

"You're making me nervous," Colas said.

"I don't like sitting out the action," Beast growled.

"I doubt even you could do much good. Besides, I thought the Bandit King would revel in the sight of the sentinel seat of power burning."

"The city and the sentinels can burn. It's the innocent people dying that bothers me."

Colas grunted, acknowledging Beast's point. There'd been a tension between them ever since they'd succeeded in stealing the enormous ship. She was itching to take it off his hands almost as much as he wanted to charge into Bulas and kill some demons.

She hadn't argued when he'd decided to follow the distress call to Bulas. Nor had she argued about the need to rescue the citizens of Bulas. She'd helped him evacuate the city without complaint.

Their fight would come once the citizens had been deposited at Versun.

They all knew the value of what they had stolen. And now there were hundreds of sentinels upon it, fresh from the defense of Bulas. Not to mention almost two dozen sin adepts. The juggernaut represented not just a breakthrough in ship design, but the only chance Samas had at fighting off the Maramans at sea.

Everyone wanted it, and everyone had a force on board now in case it came to a fight.

It almost made Beast regret his willingness to help.

There wasn't much to be done about it now, though. Beast surveyed all the new arrivals. Most people huddled on the deck were citizens of Bulas, evacuated from their homes with little warning. But among the citizens were plenty of sentinels. At some point, Beast would have to figure out how he was going to deal with them.

But for now, he had other problems that demanded more of his attention. He finished turning the juggernaut around, pointing it in the direction of Versun. He stepped aside to let Colas take the wheel. She looked like a child getting the gift she'd always wanted.

"I'll be back soon. For now, keep us on track."

"Aye, admiral."

Beast shook his head, then made his way to a small group of warriors. They kept themselves separate from the rest of the refugees, and they looked exhausted.

There were also a handful of familiar faces among them.

Beast approached, and a young man stood up to greet him. It took Beast a few seconds to realize who he was looking at. The warrior had an aura about him that hadn't been there the last time they'd met. This, this was a warrior Beast felt like he could respect.

"Corin? Is that really you?" Beast asked, happy to see his young protégé.

"It is." His face grew dark. "I just wish we'd reunited under better circumstances."

Beast shook his head. "Trust me. Celebrate your reunions regardless of circumstances, for you never know if you'll have another opportunity."

Corin nodded, then gestured behind him. "Shin will want to see you."

Beast clapped Corin on the shoulder, then strode into the circle of sin. Shin was near the center of the adepts, but they made room for Beast to come and squat down beside her. She smiled at him, but it was weak and filled with sorrow.

Beast looked around the circle. Raya had gone out with this group, but was nowhere to be found. When he met Shin's gaze again, she confirmed the loss with a nod.

"I'm so sorry, Beast. Her sacrifices saved thousands. Me included."

At this point, there was nothing left in Beast to give. Jurian's death still clawed at his heart. He simply nodded and felt the hole in his chest grow that much deeper. "We lost friends, too."

That pulled Shin from her grief. "Who?"

"Jurian. He died taking the juggernaut."

"How's Hanz?"

Beast shook his head. "Alive, for now, though I don't know how long he'll survive."

"He's wounded, too?"

"No. But I don't think he wants to go on without his brother. He tried his best to kill himself by charging the last of the Maramans. I fear he'll do the same in the next battle."

"I'm sorry. Jurian was great. Did you know he was the

first person to show me around the sin island, back when we arrived?"

"I didn't."

"Maybe it was just a small thing to him, but he made me feel like it was home. I'll never be able to thank him for that now."

Beast sat down beside her, and she curled up against his chest. He draped his arm over her and they sat together in their grief. Eventually, though, she pushed herself away. "Don't you have a juggernaut to sail?"

"I do, but this is more important."

"I'll be fine. Go, do whatever it is you need to do. We can talk more later."

Beast stood. "What I need to do is go straighten out things with the Firstborn. Which is about the last thing I'm actually interested in doing. Sure you can't rustle up a battle somewhere that I can rush to?"

Shin chuckled. "I think you're the one who rustles up battles." She paused. "He's a better man than I expected. Don't underestimate him."

Beast took the words to heart, wished Shin and Corin well, then left the sin adepts. Thanks to their abilities, they might have been the most dangerous group on the ship, but they were a broken and exhausted lot at the moment.

He'd meant to go find the Firstborn, but he didn't have to worry. Almost as soon as he split away from the sin, a sentinel was at his side.

"Admiral Beast, the Firstborn requests the honor of your presence."

Beast thought the sentinel looked like he would have rather eaten a sword blade first than address Beast which such respect. "Does he now? Well, why not. He's a guest on my ship, after all. Might as well be a good host."

The sentinel made a face like he tasted curdled milk but bowed and turned to lead Beast to the Firstborn.

Beast was surprised to find the Firstborn walking among the refugees. His guards followed loosely as the Firstborn stopped and spoke to his broken citizens. As he watched, he got some sense of why Shin might feel the way she did about the ruler of Samas. He wasn't hiding or demanding service.

His sentinel escort didn't give him much time to observe. Soon, they were at the Firstborn's side, and introductions were being made.

Once introductions were complete, the Firstborn spoke first. "The legendary Beast. I've heard so much about you these past years. It's an honor to meet you in person."

Beast scratched his head at that. "Figured you'd probably be more honored to have my head on a pike than meet me in person."

"Once, perhaps. But it's hard to be rude to the man who stole this vessel and then used it to save thousands of my citizens. Not to mention, Sato wrote about your deeds at Dahl. You may be the Bandit King, but you've done as much and more than almost any sentinel I know."

Beast, for once in his life, didn't know what to say. He'd dreamed of confronting the Firstborn since he was little. But never once had he imagined meeting the man and being complimented.

"So, what comes next?" Beast asked.

"That was very much the question I wanted to put to you."

"The first steps are simple. We'll take you to Versun and get you unloaded there. After that, I'll admit I have no idea."

"What would you have done, had you not come to our aid?"

Beast thought about Colas and her insistence that they take to the seas. But he figured that wouldn't go over well with a man who still commanded the largest military force on the juggernaut. "We were planning on training more sin with the ships so that we could fight the Maramans at sea."

The Firstborn nodded. "A wise plan. Once we get to Versun, we'll talk with Yuki about adding some sentinels to the training as well. It's high time we work together to protect Samas."

Beast kept his expression neutral, but it took all his control. If he wasn't locked on a ship with all these sentinels, he'd have punched the Firstborn right then and there.

The sentinels were always supposed to have protected Samas. Instead, they had led the nation to ruin. The Firstborn only wanted to work together because he had no choice.

Somehow, he kept his anger in check. "That sounds good. For now, I have duties to attend to."

"Of course. Thank you once again, for all you've done."

Beast managed a slight bow of his head. He walked away looking calm, but inside, he was looking for something to hit.

They arrived at Versun in the middle of the night and decided to unload the refugees right away. Though the process would have gone easier in the daylight, there were enough wounded and injured that it made sense to get everyone into Versun as quickly as possible.

Beast stood at the helm. In this, there was little for him to do, and he spent most of his time watching the completion of the evacuation. At times, he looked up at

Versun's imposing walls. They'd gotten word that apparently Sato was in charge, a fact that Beast had mixed feelings about.

He could fight, Beast would give him that much. But he also had a stick up his ass that nothing short of death would remove. With Sato in charge of the city, Beast felt like the safest place for him to be was here, on the juggernaut. Odds were, as soon as he stepped on land he'd be arrested.

The Firstborn, of all people, interrupted his thoughts. Beast still forgot, sometimes, that the ruler of Samas was on his ship. He was accompanied, as always, by Captain Harris and the rest of his honor guard. "Thank you again, Beast, for coming to our aid. I've heard that you aren't planning on going into Versun?"

"Not with Sato in charge. He and I haven't always seen eye to eye."

The Firtborn nodded. "I can understand that. Sato has always been a rigid man. But you might be impressed by how much he's changed. You're no small part of that."

"You'll forgive me if I'm not eager to test my luck."

The Firstborn sighed. "We're all allies now. We'll need to learn to put aside our differences. Yuki is there, too, if that makes you feel any better."

It was the first Beast had heard of Yuki leaving Dahl, and it didn't make him feel any better.

Sato, Yuki, and the Firstborn. All in the same city, all thinking they knew what was best for Samas. Each of them born into power tand privilege.

He realized, after a moment, he hadn't responded to the Firstborn. "Maybe in a day or two. The juggernaut took a lot of damage when we fought here, and I want to make sure that it's seaworthy."

The Firstborn looked like he was close to ordering Beast

off the ship, but stopped himself. He changed the subject. "I've decided to leave about twenty of my sentinels on board. If it's not too much to ask, I'd request that you train them on this ship. The more of us capable of fighting at sea, the better."

Beast nodded. It was a good thing Colas was out on *Cutter*, ferrying refugees back and forth. She'd throw a tantrum if she was near. "Of course. We'll be happy to have them."

"Excellent," the Firstborn said. "Captain Harris will be in charge for now. I look forward to working with you, Beast."

With that, the Firstborn was off, toward the ship that was waiting just for him and his sentinels. Harris followed, leaving Beast alone at the helm.

Beast pulled out Benji's broken sword, rotating it slowly in his hands.

A decision was bubbling to the surface, a long frustration finally released. Benji had given his life to save Dahl. Jurian had given his to help take the juggernaut, which had helped saved Bulas. Beast didn't doubt the nobility of their acts. But as he watched the last of the ships filled with refugees depart to Versun, he wondered what, exactly, their sacrifices had accomplished.

They'd saved lives. There was no doubt of that.

But now the sin and the sentinels were all one, big, cozy family. Yuki and the Firstborn would cooperate. Although Beast would have liked to have seen Sato's reaction to that meeting, he took a different view of it. Those who had been in power would stay in power. For all this fighting, for all this sacrifice, nothing would change. If anything, the sentinels would be worse than before with Sato in charge.

He put the sword back, grateful for everything Benji had

taught him. Beast could remain a pawn, or he could seize his own freedom.

He summoned a messenger to keep an eye out for Colas. The next time she joined *Cutter* to the juggernaut, they needed to have a talk.

He watched as the last of the refugees approached Versun. He was glad that he'd saved them. That his mugon had been useful. But now was the time for something new.

He'd done enough.

60

———

Sato woke up the next morning to the sound of someone pounding on his door. He dressed quickly and answered it to find Roko standing there, slightly out of breath. "Something you need to see, sir."

Sato followed Roko up the stairs of Versun's keep. Although the arrivals from Bulas had caused all sorts of problems, the presence of the Firstborn had cleaned up one issue for good. With the Firstborn at his side, Sato had been able to open the gates to the upper district and the keep. The sentinels remaining within didn't dare disobey.

It had been late at night before Sato was able to get to sleep, and he didn't figure he'd rested more than an hour or two before this disturbance. But it had done him a world of good.

Roko and Sato reached the top of the keep, and Sato immediately saw the problem. The juggernaut, which had been near the mouth of the harbor, was sailing away. Roko offered Sato a looking glass, and Sato extended it to see a group of sentinels climbing onto a lifeboat from the water. He couldn't be sure, but he thought he recognized Harris.

"Where's Yuki?" Sato asked.

"Down below, sleeping."

Sato let out a sigh of relief. If that was the case, then what he was seeing was only the decision of one man, not a betrayal by the sin as a whole. It was still a blow, and perhaps a fatal one, but it could have been worse.

"What are your orders, sir?" Roko asked.

Sato handed back the looking glass and shrugged. "There's nothing we can do, at least not now. As I recall, all the deep-water ships in Samas are attached to it. So, I'm going to return downstairs and get some more rest before our meeting this morning."

"As you wish, sir."

Sato went down the stairs alone. He was disappointed in Beast, but not surprised. Strong as the man was, he had no code, no Path to follow. Which meant that when the real storms arrived, he broke against the onslaught like a twig.

When the Firstborn started the meeting much later that morning, Sato almost had to pinch himself to make sure he was awake. The combination of people in this room seemed impossible.

The most surprising of the combinations was the Firstborn and Yuki, sitting side by side at the long table. Though Sato was almost certain the two had never met in person, they whispered to one another as though they were long-lost friends. The sight made his blood boil. But for now, they were allies. Once the threats were taken care of, the sin would be the first to be cleansed from Samas.

But there were other odd pairings, as well. Shin and Corin spoke with Crispin, who was regaling the two with stories from his times before he became a sun stalker. Crispin put on a brave face, but Sato saw the pain hidden on his friend's features. It wasn't just a physical pain, but something deeper. Crispin hadn't just lost his hand. He'd lost his ability to fight. Sato didn't know what came next for his lieutenant, but he didn't plan on letting the rogue out of his sight for some time.

Shin and Corin interested him as well. They had grown considerably since the last time he'd seen them in Dahl. Corin looked like a dangerous warrior, and when he walked, he stalked around the room as though he were a sentinel on patrol. And Shin no longer glared at him quite as furiously as she once had. At times, the way she looked around the room reminded him of Yuki. They were two that would bear watching.

The last group in the room was just as surprising. Alonzo sat beside Helios, Harris, and a sulking giant named Hanz. Harris had indeed taken a swim recently. According to reports, Beast and the pirates had ambushed the sentinels and thrown them overboard as soon as all the refugees were safely ashore at Versun. Then they had sailed off.

The Firstborn led the meeting. "Thank you all for being here. I know that in the past, the factions we represent have often fought against one another. We have different values and different ways of life. But today, I want to focus on what we have in common. All of us here want to see Samas survive the threat of the Maramans and the demons."

There were nods around the table.

"To that end, the first item we need to discuss is Beast and the juggernaut."

Harris interjected, his anger getting the better of his sense of propriety. "We need to pursue him immediately, before he gets too far."

"I'm afraid that's not possible," the Firstborn said. "We don't have any ships that can follow him. I'm afraid that for now, we have to let Beast go."

There were angry murmurs around the table, and even Yuki seemed disgruntled. Sato got some small satisfaction out of that. Beast might have betrayed them, but at least he'd betrayed them all. Still, the loss hurt. The juggernaut had been one of the best possibilities for them to mount a coordinated defense of Samas. Now that it was gone, their only defense was the land itself, and it was already reeling from the blows the last year had delivered.

The Firstborn plowed on. "We're left with two substantial problems. The first is the demons, and the second is the Maramans. Yuki?"

Yuki took over the meeting. "There's not much that we can say for certain about the Maramans. We know that they're going to make another attempt on the islands, but we have no idea when that attack will arrive or what it might look like. All we can do is prepare as best we can. That'll be one of our main goals for this meeting."

She looked around the room, judging the reactions of her audience. "Unfortunately, that's only half our problem, and perhaps not even the most dangerous part. As most of you are aware by now, there have been rifts on Samas for generations that connect us to another dimension. Three of those rifts have been closed, meaning that both Ilos and Egzuki are safe for the time being." Yuki looked at Shin when she said that, and Sato wondered why. "Unfortunately, the closing of those rifts has allowed the rift on Iru to tear wide open. Demons have been pouring through. They've already overrun the island."

"When do we launch an assault to retake it?" Sato asked.

Yuki looked down at the table. "If you're willing to follow my recommendations, never."

"What?" Sato couldn't believe what he was hearing. It was one thing to lose the juggernaut. But they couldn't sacrifice Bulas. It had to be out of the question.

The Firstborn stepped in. "As much as it pains me to admit it, I agree. The demons were too numerous for us a couple of days ago. So long as the rift is open, there's no telling how many have come through. We don't have nearly the warriors to fight them off."

"Nor do we have the adepts," Yuki added. "Our ranks have been thinned considerably over the past year."

Sato shook his head, still in denial. He'd given up so much fighting the corruption in Versun, simply to learn that while he'd been winning one battle, the war had been lost on another island. "What do we do?"

He was as surprised as anyone when it was Corin, of all people, who answered his question. "We fight. The same as we always have. The same as we always will."

The Firstborn nodded. "Exactly. We've taken some hard losses. But we've had victories, too. Despite Beast's untimely departure, I think we can all be certain he doesn't plan on attacking us. The threat from the sea is taken care of, at least for a while. Yuki and her sin have been managing the farms on Ilos well, so for this season we should still have enough food. And thanks to your efforts, Sato, the walls here at Versun are ready to withstand an assault. There's enough food stored here now that we can settle the refugees in an orderly fashion. Separately, we've done just enough to keep Samas alive."

It was true enough, Sato supposed. But it still felt like too little.

The Firstborn continued. "For too long, we've been sin

and sentinel. Peasant and magistrate. The time for those false distinctions has passed. Now we are all nothing more than citizens of Samas, and our greatest challenge lies ahead." He gave the room one last meaningful look.

"Now it's time to fight together and save our world."

THANKS FOR READING!

Thanks again for reading! In this era of unlimited entertainment choices, it means the world to us that you chose to spend your time in Samas, and we hope that you'll join us again soon.

If you'd like to learn more about Ryan or Taylor you can check them out here:

Taylor: www.taylorcrook.ca

Be the first to get your hands on Taylor's solo work, sign up for monthly newsletters or just check out some short stories.

Ryan: www.ryankirkauthor.com

You can purchase all of Ryan's extensive library as well as sign up for monthly newsletters to keep up with everything he is doing. Ryan has also created a membership program with all kinds of incredible benefits.